Praise for Beverly Rae's *I Married a Demon*

"I'm in awe at how Ms Rae manages to toss in pretty much every paranormal trope ever created into her story and still comes up with a coherent *Men In Black*-meets-*Mr. & Mrs. Smith* story. This story is a laugh-a-minute romp and I have a fabulous time reading it..."

~ *Mrs. Giggles, www.mrsgiggles.com*

"I MARRIED A DEMON is a witty, yet intriguing paranormal romance. Ms. Beverly Rae has a wonderful ability to turn what seems like an impossible romance into a tender, loving, compatible couple. ...Filled with tender romance, steamy hot love scenes, witty dialogue, an imaginative plot and interesting characters, this book is a winner. I recommend I MARRIED A DEMON to anyone looking for a truly interesting read."

~ *Dottie, Romance Junkies*

Rating: 5 Angels "I loved this funny, slightly irreverent, and unusual paranormal romance. ...If you are looking to be entertained with a laugh out loud tale of missed signals, miscommunication, and general mayhem, then *I Married A Demon* is the book for you."

~ *Stephanie B., Fallen Angel Reviews*

Look for these titles by
Beverly Rae

Now Available:

Howling for My Baby
Touch Me
To Fat and Back
Wailing for Love

Print Anthology
Magical Mayhem

I Married a Demon

Beverly Rae

A Samhain Publishing, Ltd. publication.

Samhain Publishing, Ltd.
577 Mulberry Street, Suite 1520
Macon, GA 31201
www.samhainpublishing.com

I Married a Demon
Copyright © 2009 by Beverly Rae
Print ISBN: 978-1-60504-416-3
Digital ISBN: 978-1-60504-245-9

Editing by Deborah Nemeth
Cover by Natalie Winters

First Samhain Publishing, Ltd. electronic publication: December 2008
First Samhain Publishing, Ltd. print publication: October 2009

Dedication

Thanks to all the real "supernatural beings" in my life; the brave souls who put up with my strange hours and even stranger ideas. Thank you to my husband and my daughter, the two most important people in my life.

What's a Nice Girl Like You Doing with a Demon Like Me?

I married a demon.

Yeah, I know what you're thinking. Why would any sane woman marry a demon? Shoot, forget the why. *How* does a nice woman even meet a demon? It's not as if demons are hanging out on MySpace or standing in line at Starbucks waiting to get their morning caffeine. No one's ever locked eyes with a demon while pumping gas, right? Of course not—or so everyone thinks.

However, the truth is that the average Jane and Joe would be surprised at how many times they run into a supernatural being in the course of their daily routines. Jane has probably pushed her grocery cart by one and didn't even know it. As for Joe, sometimes that monster of a boss really *is* a monster of a boss.

So go ahead. Scoff away. But keep reading and learn how I met my demon-other-half.

In my defense, a lot of factors played into my failure to recognize my future hubby as a creature of the heat. Heat as in Hell, that is. I didn't know at the time of our wedding that my wonderful and caring husband-to-be was a demon. He didn't bother mentioning this detail to me before the ceremony. But I can't complain too much. I didn't tell him about my alternate identity, either. Don't all marriages have a few secrets?

Yeah, I know. You probably have a lot more questions. Hold your horses and I'll explain right after I give you a little background info. Let me begin where it's always a good place to begin—at the beginning.

My name is Jennifer Randall-Barrington. I picked up the Barrington part of my name when I married Blake. Yup, I'm the independent type and I wanted to keep my last name. These days hyphenating your name is considered almost normal—too bad I can't use the word *normal* to describe the other aspects of my marriage.

To be honest, my life was already unusual before I married Blake. After all, not many people can say they work for a secret society whose primary mission is to protect humans against the evil creatures of the world. I'm not talking about murderers, rapists, drug dealers and other mortal vermin. Let the regular police force handle those scumbags. I'm talking about the undead evildoers like vamps and werewolves who cause the real havoc in this world.

I keep the streets of my hometown safe for unsuspecting citizens. Hey, I'm not asking for any reward or praise—although the occasional free mocha latte would be nice. People say they don't believe in boogie men and monsters—although I know deep down they really do. They're afraid of what goes bump in the night, trying their best to deny the existence of these flesh-eating, soul-sucking slimy things. I can hardly expect them to walk up and say "thank you", can I? Still, a little gratitude every once in awhile would go a long way. Yet, even without any thanks, I'll keep on sticking my neck out for the good of mankind. Why?

Because kickin' evil butt is what I do.

After working my cover job selling fixer-uppers to young couples in Pleasant Hill, a satellite community not twenty miles outside sprawling Tulsa, Oklahoma, I spend my nights slinking through the dark streets, looking for the worst the city has to offer. I'm both a Protector *and* a real estate agent.

Could I interest anyone in a nice little bungalow? I promise it'll be gargoyle-free.

Work aside, I'm also a woman. Being a woman, I have needs and desires like any other romance-loving, I-work-way-too-much kind of gal. Serving mankind while holding down a nine-to-five day job leaves a lady a bit cranky when she doesn't get some hot and heavy fun in the sack to take the edge off. But while holding down two jobs, who has time to find Mr. Right? I'm not even sure I still believed in Mr. Right before Blake came along. Instead, I'd settled for believing in Mr. Scratch My Itch.

What I needed was to get laid. What about love? As the song goes, what's love got to do with it? I told myself I didn't need romance and couldn't care less about love. Love was for normal people with normal lives. There's that word again. *Normal.*

I realize how this sounds. Exactly like the typical thirty-something female bravado, right? The usual crap single women say when they've sat way too long on a barstool hoping to find Mr. Love and ending up with Mr. Buy-Me-A-Drink.

After seven years of a steady stream of ghoul-busting, shifter-smashing and general evildoer-eliminating, I needed a white beach, warm sand and a hot sun. If I got lucky with a sexy sun worshiper, I wouldn't complain. Ah, hell. Who am I kidding? I'd dance in the streets afterward.

The trouble was, at the time, I wasn't aware of my desperate need for R and R. At least, not until I tried to ram a stake through the heart of an elderly priest. Talk about a major oopsie. I tried to whack the sweet-tempered Father Ramsey.

If another Protector hadn't pulled me from the father's prone body and wrestled the stake out of my hand, I'd be in a whole lot of trouble right now. I was so tired and worn-out I'd dismissed certain pertinent facts. Like how the priest hadn't flinched when I'd spilled holy water on him. Or how he'd acted pleased, as though I'd presented him with a gift—albeit rather roughly—when I'd crushed a cross to his chest. Even the fact that I'd found him in the middle of a church on sacred ground didn't seep into my fatigued mind. Nope, I was dead sure the kindly priest was a vampire. This, of course, meant I was hellbent on taking the holy biter out of this world.

Once all the chaos in the church had settled down, I found myself thrown into the rear seat of a state trooper's patrol car, heading toward the nearest lockup. Breaking with his usual forgiving personality, the dear father vowed to see me behind bars with the key buried at the bottom of the ocean in a padlocked safe guarded by fifteen man-eating sharks. Not many people blamed him, either, including me.

Fortunately, the Society for the Protection of Mortals and Control of Supernatural Beings (S.P.M.C.S.B.) has friends on the police force. So instead of spending the night exchanging cellblock stories with drunks and prostitutes, I found myself led into the inner sanctum of the Society. My escort, a huge, unsmiling bouncer type, clutched my arm and escorted me straight into the head honcho's office. I'd been inside the boss's office a few times before to accept assignments, but never to receive a reprimand and possible consequence. Trust me, when I saw the glower on my supervisor's face, I thought seriously about asking Bouncer Boy to haul me off to the Big House without a trial.

My boss, Wilson MacNamara, could have booted me out of the ranks of the Protectors right then and there, but I guess my exemplary record of kicking evildoers' butts bought me a little tolerance and understanding. Still, I'll never forget our conversation if I live to be two hundred.

"Randall, sit down."

Ah, shit. I hate it when he calls me by my last name. I did as he ordered and gripped the chair's arms to keep from clutching the bouncer's hand as I silently implored him to stay by my side. I admit it. I tried everything from the big "I'm gonna cry" eyes to the droopy "I'm scared" frown to the "I'll make it worth your while" batted eyelashes. Yet none of my womanly tactics worked. My escort couldn't get out of there fast enough.

I attempted to keep the apprehension churning inside my stomach from showing on my face, but I'm pretty sure I sucked at it. Up to now, I'd never been on the receiving end of a MacNamara Dressing Down, but I'd heard about them. Tougher Protectors than I had come out of MacNamara's office looking paler than the ghosts they hunted.

"Sir, I can explain." *I can?* My brain whirred with fruitless activity, hoping to dredge up any reasonable explanation for my actions. Yet like the spinning wheel in a hamster's cage, my gray matter was going nowhere fast.

"Don't bother. I know why you acted the way you did." He paced in front of the dozen monitors filling the wall behind his oversized mahogany desk.

"You do?" Did I want him to enlighten me? Because, frankly, I didn't have a clue. But did I want him to tell me? Nope. I'd pass, thank you very much. As long as his ideas about my behavior bought me some leeway, I didn't need to know.

"You need to take some time off."

I waited for the proverbial other shoe to drop, but it didn't. Caught unprepared for his mild manner, I decided my best course of action would be to keep my trap closed.

Mac turned away from the monitors displaying various areas around Tulsa and crossed over to sit on the edge of his desk directly in front of me. "Ease up, Jennifer. I'm not dismissing you or giving you an official reprimand. In fact, we're going to keep the past few, um, indiscretions out of your record."

Jennifer. He'd switched from using my last name to my first. I wasn't sure what the switch meant. I pushed aside the question of why he'd used my Christian name. I mean, why bother trouble? Besides, I'm the suspicious type. In my line of work, having doubts, expecting the unexpected, and letting your intuition take the lead can save your life. I decided to follow my gut instinct and, again, I kept my yap zipped.

Mac sighed, the picture of the distressed yet caring superior. "At least, I hope we can."

I tried to control my nerves, but couldn't help squirming in my seat. "Uh, I appreciate your willingness to, uh, let my mistake slide this time. It won't happen again." *Whoa, Jenn, way too much talking. Shut the fuck up.*

"But we can't let you keep screwing up. You've made more than a couple of mistakes lately."

I felt the heat of the blush rush to my face and hated myself for letting my emotions show. He was right. I'd messed up a couple of times. But how was I supposed to know a group of teens had rigged an abandoned house with ghostly tricks to frighten their friends? The Collins boy hadn't gotten hurt when I'd pinned him in a corner, ready to take his ghostly presence out of this world and over to the Other Side. No harm done, right? And how was I to know the woman gathering herbs was actually the high school's science teacher and not a wicked minion of Hell concocting a deadly potion?

"Look, sir, I realize I've jumped to wrong conclusions once or twice, but—"

"Four times. Five counting Father Ramsey."

I narrowed my eyes at him in an attempt to appear more confident than I felt. "Oh, I don't think I've messed up that many times. Have I?" Could five be correct? I searched my memory.

"You've made five mistakes in less than two weeks."

Five in two weeks? I still couldn't believe I'd gone off the road five times. In fact, I started to question him again when he picked up a slip of paper and thrust it toward me.

"Check it out, Jennifer. It's all there in black and white."

I didn't take the list, preferring not to touch it. Maybe if I didn't touch it, the names written there would fade away as though they'd been written in invisible ink. Instead, I leaned forward and stared at the list.

Collins boy. Check. Science teacher. Unfortunately.

I squinted harder at the other two names.

William Wordsman. A vision of the pudgy man fleeing before me, shouting for help and swearing he didn't have any ghouls hiding in his basement, flashed through my mind. I cringed. I'd called his Friday night poker buddies vile, villainous vultures from the Otherworld. Admittedly, it was not my finest moment. However, the last name on the list, Betsy Salinger, gored a hole in my gut. How I'd ever thought the bedridden octogenarian was a dragon, I'll never know.

Four times. Check. The sweet old priest made number five. No wonder the boss had called me on the carpet.

"Wow." I dropped my gaze to my hands folded in my lap and wondered if I'd lost my mind. And if I had, where could I get help? Did psychiatrists specialize in helping fucked-up Protectors? Would any shrink believe half of my paranormal-based problems?

"Wow is right." He moved and I heard the squish of leather chair meeting ass as he sat behind his desk. "I glanced at your record, Jennifer. You haven't taken a vacation in years. Why not?"

Could I give him the real reason? Would he understand if I told him I didn't have a life outside my existence as a Protector? Would it even matter? "I guess I enjoy my work. I don't want or need time off."

"Obviously, you do need a break and you're going to take one starting immediately."

Alarm slashed through me. "No, I can't." I stood and bent over his desk like the heroes in the old movies did when they went to bat for what they believed in. Hopefully, Mac would respond as the bosses in those old movies had. He'd let me stay on and work.

But life is not a movie.

"Yes, you can and you will."

"But, sir, I can't. Something big's about to happen. I can't lounge around my home and ignore everything happening around me."

Mac handed me an envelope. "I agree."

I let out a sigh of relief. "I'm glad you understand."

"I meant you're right about hanging around the house. I know you, Jennifer. You'd go crazy and end up on the streets against my orders." He nodded at the envelope I'd tried to ignore. "Look inside. You'll find a plane ticket, hotel reservation and a generous allowance to purchase whatever clothes and necessities you need once you arrive. I've also cleared the time off with your boss at Swindle Realty." He paused as most people did when they thought about the name. "Does he realize—"

"Yeah, trust me, he does." I'd heard the same question too many times to let him finish his sentence. "But he doesn't care. Herbert Swindle likes seeing his name on the front door. Even if the name Swindle runs off potential clients. But about this vacation, I don't think—"

"*Humph.* Damned stupid if you ask me." Mac tapped on the envelope. "For the sake of the Society and for the safety of the town, you're taking a two-week, all-expense-paid vacation to St. Thomas. Courtesy of the Society. It's the vacation or else, Randall."

Nevertheless, I opened my mouth to protest again, which he waved off before punching a button on the intercom. "Harris, escort Ms. Randall to the company jet."

"But, sir, please listen." I fumbled for words even though I knew anything I'd say wouldn't change Mac's mind. Bouncer Boy marched over, grabbed me by the arm and led me toward the exit. "Mr. MacNamara, let me speak."

"I've heard all I need to hear. Go. Relax. Enjoy yourself. Get a tan. Don't worry about anything here. Your territory is covered."

"But—"

"Consider this an order, Randall."

A few hours later, I was on the beach of St. Thomas where I met my future husband.

☙

By the time I'd made it to the company plane, I'd convinced myself Mac was right. What other choice did I have? Like my dad had always told me, "When you're stuck in a situation you can't change, change you." So I altered what I could about me— my attitude.

Mac *was* right. I deserved Time Off. Down Time. Serious R and R. I needed a simple vacation with no weird shit, no fights in dark alleys and no monsters lurking around corners ready to rip out my throat. I wanted nothing except mai tai-swilling half-naked humans surrounding me. With my new thinking firmly in place, I jetted off to the tropical paradise of St. Thomas in the Caribbean per my supervisor's order. Ah, yes, I planned to live the company-paid sweet life for two luxurious weeks.

Little did I know Mr. Right was in my imminent future when I spread out my beach towel on sparkling white sand and slipped off my Sex on the Beach T-shirt that doubled as my swimsuit cover. Flopping onto my stomach, I cranked up my favorite tunes on my new iPod—*Thank you, Mac!*—and pretended to concentrate on a book. Instead, I scoped out the hunky beach bums spreading suntan lotion over their hard bodies. I mean, who can read with hot bods around?

At the exact moment I noticed him, he was only a few feet from me. Mr. Ta-DaH—my nickname for Mr. Tall and Dark and Handsome—lay sprawled like the King of the World basking in the sun, surveying his kingdom and the lowly subjects he allowed to share his beach. He held a drink in one hand and scrutinized me through dark sunglasses, his chiseled face a mask of controlled passivity except for the slight lift at the corners of his mouth.

I'm good at playing cool. I have to know how to play it cool in my line of work—*both* my lines of work. But this guy's intense scrutiny was almost more than I could handle. With my sunglasses resting on the bridge of my nose, I nonchalantly spied on him, trying to appear unaware that he studied me. I tried to suck in my ass, hoping to make the dimples disappear, but knew the battle was lost before it began. How do you suck in a bottom, anyway? Is it the same as a butt clench? I sighed and hoped he liked women with junk in their trunks.

The man was perfect. At least physically, but physical was all I had to go on. His wet hair, silky and shiny black, slicked away from his forehead and curled around his earlobes. Just the right amount of matching chest hair glistened with drops of perspiration, drawing my gaze to all the right places. Notice I said perspiration, not sweat. No one this good-looking ever sweats.

I'm talking the perfect model of a man. The kind of man I'd buy if I could call in my order and have him delivered to my doorstep in thirty minutes or less. Remember how moviegoers went gaga over Matthew McConaughey when he started taking off his shirt? Yup, me, too. I was one of the hundreds, probably thousands of women, who sat through his movies, not caring about the plot. Instead we sat glued to our seats and waited for him to strip off his shirt and take the heroine to bed. Take M's sex appeal and multiply it by a zillion times more heat and that's what oozed from this guy.

His shoulders, wider than the beach chair he leaned against, mesmerized me and I couldn't keep from imagining the way they'd feel. I'd have donated my whole stack of traveler's checks to charity just to feather my fingers over them. I could see the strength in his muscular arms and sense the power he could unleash at any moment. He pressed his mouth to the highball glass, moving his square jaw, and I had to fight to keep from dashing over and licking off the tiny drop of whiskey left on his upper lip.

His eight-pack abs called to me. *Come, Jenn. Come and run your hands over me.* I let my gaze glide down his rock-hard abdomen. Can you blame me when my heart started pounding and my mouth went dry? Can you understand why the place between my legs overflowed with wetness?

I pondered what to do. Should I say something? Why didn't *he* say something? How long could we lie here and stare at each other? What would I do if he got up and walked away? Or even more frightening, what would I do if he came over?

Then he smiled at me.

My mouth dropped open. I lifted my head from my beach towel, forgetting to play it nonchalant. Instead I gaped like a schoolgirl with her first crush. He stood and started toward me, making me oh-so-aware of his height and brawn. My examination of this spectacular specimen started at the top and moved slowly downward.

I'd never found men's legs attractive before—I'm an upper torso kind of gal—but the black hairs on his legs, the firm tanned skin stretched over his runner's tendons, converted me to a leg gal right then and there. My membership in the leg lovers fan club was sealed the minute he squatted next to my blanket and gave me a front row seat to the hard bulge in his swimsuit.

Granted, his first words weren't anything particularly clever, but he didn't need clever. He could have read me the directions on how to buckle a seat belt and I'd have thought it wonderful, riveting, mysterious and oh, yes, sexy as hell.

"Hi, there. Why are you watching me?"

Thick as molasses and hotter than the center of the sun, his warm voice traveled over my naked skin and made me shiver in anticipation of steamy nights and luxurious mornings in bed.

"Uh, no. I mean, no, I'm not watching you." I rolled off my stomach and onto my side in what I prayed was a slinky kind of move, and propped my head with my hand.

Sliding his sunglasses to the end of his nose, he arched one thick eyebrow upward and knowing eyes twinkled the word *liar* at me. "Oh, I see. My mistake." His gaze left mine to make a very slow, very deliberate trek down my thong-clad body, and the tips of his mouth tweaked a bit higher.

Thank you, oh tortuous elliptical machine.

I swallowed, trying to force the liar's lump in my throat all the way down to my stomach. Since when had I ever felt guilty about lying? I was proud I could lie with the best of them. In my line of work—both my lines of work—I have to be able to stretch the truth. Otherwise, I might not live very long—or sell a bug-ridden condo. But something irresistible about him drew the truth out of me. "Okay. Maybe I was. But I was simply returning the favor, if you know what I mean."

He reached out to take a wayward strand of my hair off my cheek. Yet instead of putting it behind my ear to join the rest of my ponytail, he played with it, rubbing the strand between his two fingers as if he'd never experienced the texture of hair. I found myself wishing I'd spent the extra bucks for a salon-quality conditioner.

"I do and you're right. I apologize."

Huh? "What for?" I suddenly envisioned those fingers playing with my nipple instead of my hair. Forget the conditioner, think scented body lotion. The image was so intense, I wanted nothing more than to take his hand and bring it to my breast. How I kept from grabbing his hand, I'll never know. "Why are you apologizing?"

"For staring at you. I apologize for my rudeness."

Unnerved by his words, I sat up and tried to position my body as I'd seen countless swimsuit models pose in glossy magazines. Yet instead of stretching my torso and legs in an alluring way, I ended up sitting cross-legged like a big kid. A real turn on—not.

"Oh, were you?" *Argh!* Stupid comeback, especially since I'd already accused him of staring at me.

"Yes, but you can hardly blame me."

"I wasn't blaming you, but I'd be interested in knowing why I can't. I mean, since you're apologizing."

He took off his glasses and, like in all those cliché romance books my mom used to read, our eyes met and a sizzle passed between us. "The answer is very simple. What man could not look at such a tantalizing sight?"

Sure it was a corny line, but I fell for him right then and there. Off the deep end, over the cliff, dived in head first and all those other sayings people use when they fall in love at first sight. As if he could read my thoughts, he leaned closer and placed a feather-light kiss on my lips. Yet, although his touch barely brushed against my mouth, the result rivaled the explosion of a nuclear bomb between my legs. My body's temperature jumped sky high, matching the burn of the sun on my shoulders.

"What are you doing tonight?"

I knew a leading line when I heard it and I heard this one loud and clear. "The same thing I'm going to be doing in about fifteen minutes."

His eyebrows dipped toward his nose and he cocked his head to the side. "And what would that be?"

"Having the best sex of my life."

Scrambling off my blanket—yeah, I know, a bit too eager, huh?—I gathered my things and dumped them into my bag. I shook the sand from my body in a blatant sexy way—yes, I admit it, I brushed my hands over my boobs just for his benefit—and made what I hoped was a come-hither gesture with my head, signaling for him to follow me. Then, in a move more daring than any attack on a ghoul, I took his hand and started walking toward the hotel, letting him trail slightly behind me.

His low chuckle gave me his consent and he repositioned his hand to cover most of mine. I couldn't help but gloat at the scores of women watching me with envious eyes.

Look all you want, ladies, but hands off. This catch is mine and I'm not throwing him back.

I didn't ask his name until we'd made it to my suite and slipped off our swimsuits. In my defense, however, he didn't ask mine, either. Instead, we dropped our suits on the plush carpet and hurried into the oversized shower of my palatial suite. Once inside, we let the warm water run rivulets over our bronzed bodies—his darkened by the sun and mine by the most expensive self-tanning lotion I could find—and learned about each other with our hands and our eyes.

"I'm Jennifer Randall."

"Blake Barrington."

Could a name sound more perfect? No Harold or Wilbur or Ronald for this guy. Hell, no. *Blake.* A hard *B* followed by a quick, no-nonsense, one-syllable ending. *B-lake.* A strong virile name for a virile kind of a man. I suddenly had the overwhelming desire to say my name was actually Angelina, Cassiopeia or even Athena. I needed a beautiful, captivating name to match his dashing masculine one. Unfortunately, my mom had named me after her favorite aunt.

Since I'd gotten a good look at most of his body back on the beach, I went for the prize I'd fantasized about when he'd knelt beside me. In not-so-subtle anticipation, I cast my lecherous look on the reward previously hidden behind Door Number One, aka his swimsuit. His shaft was even better than expected. Several inches—*my kingdom for a ruler!*—stood at the ready, commanding me to reach out and touch. Let me assure you, I gave his shaft its much deserved attention.

I wrapped one hand around his massive member, loving the way it jerked at my touch. Obviously, it was thrilled to see me. My other hand went exploring for the golden nuggets of treasure by cupping his balls and weighing them to my satisfaction. His quick intake of breath drew my gaze away from his lower regions to meet the sultriest eyes I've ever seen. They grew darker with my every stroke, fascinating, mesmerizing me.

He moaned and covered my breast with his palm. Granted, I'm not the most endowed woman in the world, but I'm no pancake-baby, either. My breast fit his hand without any leftover to spare and nothing missed. It was as if my boob had been made for his palm.

I wondered. Would he fit inside me as perfectly?

I started to speak, but he held up one finger and pressed it against my lips. I obeyed him only because his lips followed his finger to my mouth. Taking me by the nape of my neck, he positioned my head backward, lifting my mouth to his. His tongue swiped over my lips, asking permission to enter. I opened my mouth wide enough for him to push his tongue through and sucked to capture it for as long as I could.

Although the tenderness of his approach was wonderful, I needed more. Slipping my arms under his, I slid my fingers over the water-slicked muscles of his back and pulled him to me. Our bodies crushed together and I gasped. His hand fondled the curve of my bottom and his fingers teased the crack between my cheeks. I shoved my breasts against him, wanting his rock-solid pecks against them. He grabbed my ass with both hands and lifted me.

I hooked my legs around his trim waist and he rammed against me, placing me against the shower wall. I sighed and led his shaft inside my welcoming cave.

"Jenn."

I grinned at the familiarity of the name and answered back. "Blake."

He kept his hold on me and I kept mine on him. Working with every thrust, I moaned and clenched the walls of my vagina. He groaned in satisfaction and shared his breath with me in a kiss to end all kisses. The water tunneled between us, mixing with the juices flowing down my legs, and climax after climax tore me apart. I struggled to stay up with him, dragging the musky taste of his mouth into mine as if it could give me sustenance and stamina.

He released my mouth, leaned away to look at me, and continued to pound into me. Molten gray eyes met mine and we held each other, both of us waiting for his release. I'd lost count of mine. When his came thundering through him, I held him and shouted with him in pleasure. I stared, wanting to see his climax on his face. Yet along with his climax, I caught a flash of red blazing in his eyes. Lost in lust, I dismissed it as an illusion my tired mind had decided to play on me. After all, demons, not sexy men, have red eyes and after my five recent mistakes, I knew better than to trust myself.

Minutes later, we collapsed on the bed and rolled to our backs, panting our happiness. Naked and sated, I turned my head to him and asked the question I had to ask. "Are you real?"

He laughed, a dark rich sound, and pivoted toward me. "Am I real? Real what?"

I giggled and followed the way he'd twisted my question. "Are you still real horny? 'Cause I sure am." I dropped my gaze to his probe which was already pointing to the ceiling and saluting a definite "yes".

"What do you think?" Blake tugged me on top of him and I guided him into me again.

Thirteen days of fun and sun later, we were married on board a cruise ship sailing toward America. Later on, I'd learn the truth.

I'd married a demon.

Some Like It Warm—Others Like It Hot

"Blake! Hey, Blake!"

"Yeah?"

My gorgeous new husband of nearly four weeks stepped out of the bathroom wrapped in one of our flimsiest bath towels. I could see his jewels almost as if he didn't have anything covering his lower torso. He'd asked me repeatedly to buy new towels, but I'd always found an excuse to keep the old ones. And why not? I'm a red-blooded American woman and I'm not about to give up my daily peep show. Or, as my dear old dad always said, "If you can see a show for free, sit down and enjoy it." I don't think he was talking about a peep show but, with my old man, ya never knew.

Blake's body had me inhaling a quick gulp of air to replace the one I'd exhaled in stunned delight. This hunk of hunks, this man of men, this sexy piece of male animal was my husband. All mine. Every day and every night.

Ain't life grand?

I caught the sparkle in his eyes and knew a session of hot sweaty lovemaking was on his mind. I lifted my hand to the buttons of my blouse, already thinking of tearing it off my body and jumping into bed with him. But the vacation was over and today was my first day back at the job as a struggling real estate agent, and I was already running late.

"No, Blake. Behave." He swept his arm out to drag me to him, but I feinted to the left and barely escaped his reach. I skirted around him, out of the bedroom and into the living room with him right behind me. "Some of us have bosses who would not be happy if we arrived late for work—especially since I took extra time off after my scheduled two-week vacation." Like I really cared what Herbert Swindle thought.

"Like you really care."

The man knew me well, which is why I had no choice. I had to lie. "I do care."

"Quit your job. Tell Old Swindle to kiss your ass."

"Oh, shit, Blake, I can't. Old Herbie might take me up on it." The image of Swindle pressing his thin lips to my cheeks burst into my mind and I shuddered. *Yuck.* "Thanks for the visual."

Running with shoes in one hand, I positioned the love seat between us and tried to stop giggling. I'd never giggled—I mean really giggled—until I'd met Blake. "Excuse me, but I like my job. I'm a modern woman and I want a career. You may as well know it now, bucko, I have no intention of doing the barefoot and pregnant thing."

"What? No home-cooked meals when I walk through the door at the end of a long day?"

"Not unless you've got another wife hidden in the basement."

He paused, cupping his hand to his jaw in the time-honored sign of contemplation. "Now there's an idea."

"Damn, he's not married a month and already talking about other women. Take heed, lover-man." I squinted and pointed a finger at him. "Play and you'll pay." I dropped my sight to the bulge under the towel. "And pay big time. If you know what I mean."

"No worries, hon. You're more than enough woman for me. Two wives would be one too many."

"You've got that right." I stuck out my tongue at him and wiggled my ass for an added little tease. Then again, maybe *little* wasn't the correct description.

He pointed at my butt. "Which reminds me. Can you pick up some hot sauce on your way home?"

Having a butt that reminds my hubby of hot sauce is a good thing, right? Better hot sauce than pork chops, I'd say. A smidgen of concern popped into my head, but I forced it away.

Demons love hot sauce. But lots of good mortal men like it, too. Besides, Blake's from Texas, which makes it natural for him to love hot sauce. In fact, he likes hot sauce and my rump, both at the same time. I gave serious consideration to the tantalizing idea, swallowed a lump of desire and forced my thoughts back to the matter at hand. Sure, I'd choose sex over work any day if I could, but I needed the paychecks to keep rolling in.

He hopped over the love seat as if it were nothing. I hurdled the coffee table and headed for the island counter in the kitchen. "Why not let me help you start your own agency? I'll bankroll you. I can be your horny silent partner."

I slammed to a stop, stunned into immobility. "You'd do that for me?"

"Be silent and horny? No prob." He caught up, snared me within his arms and hugged me to him. He was all seriousness now. "Sure, I would. I'd do anything for you. I love you."

Could any woman ask for sweeter words?

His deep mind-melting kiss had me ignoring the fact that he was still dripping water and getting me wet. "Must be nice to have money you can throw away on risky businesses. I didn't know investment analysts were independently wealthy."

He nuzzled my neck, making me rethink going into the office. "Perhaps not wealthy, but well-off enough to provide for his beautiful wife. You don't have to work, you know."

"But I want to work." I pulled his face to mine and looked into the eyes of the man I loved. "Seriously, I do. You're a sweetheart for offering, but I don't have enough experience to own and run my own agency." I kissed him again, forcing myself to make this kiss a short one. "Anyway, thanks for the offer."

Sad eyes, more pitiful than a basset hound's, blinked at me. His puppy eyes were effective tools against my resolve and he knew it. "Do you really have to go to work?"

I opened my mouth to tell him I did, but couldn't get the words to come out. Instead, I sighed as if giving into him was the biggest sacrifice a woman could make and tipped my head toward the bedroom. Two minutes later, I was on top of our bed, naked and loving it.

"How do you do what you do to me?" He slid his tongue over my throbbing clit and I clenched the bedspread and held on. He pressed his mouth to me and sucked. If his silent action was his answer, then it was a damned good one.

I moaned and lifted my hips against him, wanting him to drink me dry. "Eat me, Blake. Suck hard." One thing about my man, he took directions well.

I bit my bottom lip, trying to relax, but the rush after rush of climax after climax tensed my body until I knew The Really Big O was near. Blake pulled my legs on top of his shoulders, placing his arms to my sides and his big hands on my breasts. Clamping my hands over his, I braced for a second, felt the intense pain-pleasure of the eruption coming and let go. He didn't miss a beat but kept lapping up my juices, ignoring my screams of delight.

I would have kept on screaming if the lamp on the dresser behind Blake hadn't lit up in a flashing iridescent green. In a split second, my scream changed from pleasure to annoyed surprise.

"Oh, crap!" Pushing away from Blake, I scrambled to the other side of the bed and did a somersault off the edge to land on my feet. Who knew my little acrobatic trick from childhood would come in handy one day?

"What's wrong? Come back here!"

Blake lunged across the bed, flying over tangled sheets and nearly missing me. I threw the comforter on top of his head to buy more time. He thought I was playing, but I actually wanted to cover his eyes so I could dash to the lamp and shut off the signal. Before Blake managed to get the comforter off, I'd pushed the switch at the base of the lamp and turned off the green alert signal from the Society's headquarters. Whirling around to face him, I plastered on a fake grin and fought the anxiety churning in my stomach. I started gathering my clothes and brainstorming excuses. Fortunately, I'm good at coming up with excuses.

"I'm sorry, sweet man, but I just remembered Swindle's having a meeting this morning. He'll go ballistic if I miss another one."

Blake, however, didn't care. Hooking me around my knees, he brought me down, thankfully catching me before I hit the floor. "You're kidding me. You get me going and *then* you remember the meeting? Nice to know my fantastic sexual allure didn't distract you from thinking about work." He latched his mouth on to my tit, muffling his words, making him sound like a buff Elmer Fudd. "No fwair."

I stopped the words, "You wrascally wrabbit, you," before I let them escape my mouth. Something told me he wouldn't appreciate the comparison.

He was right, of course. It wasn't fair. I'd gotten my jollies off, but his shaft was still primed and aimed for action like Elmer's shotgun. I grimaced at my own cartoon comparison and, again, kept my trap shut. (By the way, I can keep my trap shut a lot more than people give me credit for.)

Still, my trusting hubby didn't know the half of it. Blake, the love of my life, the man who shared my home and my life, didn't know my secret identity. He had no clue I was a Protector and, according to the Society's edicts, I couldn't tell him. Of course, I'd broken that same rule by telling my friend Myra, but something held me back when it came to confessing all to Blake. Which begged the question—did I really trust him or not?

"Blake, you don't understand. If I don't make this meeting, Swindle will make my life a living hell." A soft mewing sound escaped me. Couldn't he tell I'd rather stay with him than sit through a boring meeting with my boss? I struggled to gain control of my libido and tried to fib convincingly.

"You really want me to let you go?" The low growl he rumbled between my breasts almost convinced me to spread wide for Blake and screw my boss at the Society.

"I don't want you to, but I have to go."

His throaty groan of desire morphed into a loud growl of displeasure and defeat. Releasing me, he fell against the side of the bed and watched me hurriedly dress. "Fine, go on. Run off leaving your poor hubby tied up in a sexual knot. But I deserve a reward for being such an understanding husband."

I leaned over and gave him a quick kiss. If I lingered too long with the kiss, his other head would change his mind. "I promise I'll give you extra special treatment tonight."

Sending him a loving look, I turned and headed out of the bedroom. He struck out again, narrowly missing my leg. "I'm going to hold you to your word, you know."

"I hope you do." I hopped toward the front door, trying to shove my boring-yet-practical flats on my feet. I'd never catch a were-animal if I wore heels on the job. Granted, six-inch heels made great impromptu weapons, but I'd rather have the option of a speedy escape. No, sir, no Manolo Blahniks for this gal on the go. "Gotta run. I'll see you tonight."

I reached the door but, sensing eyes on me, quickly turned around and caught my husband checking me out. The gleam in his eye told me my gym membership was well worth the money.

"See ya tonight, babe, and don't forget."

"I won't." With a kiss thrown over my shoulder, I scurried out to hop into my biggest indulgence: my Jaguar convertible with custom silver finish and red leather interior. I figured since I spent my life protecting the world I ought to drive a cool car. After all, you never saw James Bond driving a family sedan.

Glancing longingly at my home, I threw the car in reverse and screeched out of the driveway just in time to catch my nosy neighbor, Mrs. Hardgrave, scowling her displeasure at me. I waved even though I knew it was useless to try and get on the old biddy's good side. She hated sports cars and the people who drove them, which of course meant she hated me.

But I didn't care. People who don't own a fast car simply don't get it. I understood why men loved fast cars because I loved them, too, although I never checked to see what was under the hood. I never cared about how many cylinders or spark plugs there were. Instead, I silently gave thanks for whatever made my silver bullet race down the highways. I loved the way the wind blew apart my hairstyle. I loved the roar of the engine and the glances both men and women gave me as I zipped past them. Forget the bulky minivans and square four-door SUVs the other wives in my neighborhood drove. My silver speed demon was the only demon I truly loved.

Or so I thought.

Whizzing out of the suburbs of Pleasant Hill and into the outskirts of Tulsa, I wondered what calamity was about to befall the world. Had some ghoul decided to go on a brain-eating rampage? Perhaps gargoyles had kidnapped a baby? Or maybe a gigantic mutant alligator was terrorizing sewer workers? Various possibilities ran through my mind, but I finally gave up trying to guess. My next assignment could be anything. Keeping my attention on the road, I maneuvered my way in between vehicles filled with unsuspecting people. The poor slobs occupying those cars had no idea of the dangers lurking in graveyards, dark alleyways or their own closets.

I braked at the next traffic light and smiled at a middle-aged balding man seated in the Buick next to me. He probably thought he had everything in his life under control. He had the wife, the two kids, the dog who slept at his feet and a nice pension plan for retirement. Little did he know a vampire could lie in wait for him and suck him dry. But as long as I was around, he wouldn't have to know. I waved at him and he plastered a surprised yet pleased grin on his face. The light turned green and I gunned my Jag across the intersection, leaving the man behind, probably feeling flattered at the unexpected attention from a pretty woman. Yep, that's my motto—to protect and serve in any way I can.

Minutes later, I merged onto the expressway leading to downtown Tulsa. I could already pick out the nondescript building in the midst of all the other buildings. None of the daily commuters on their way to work would have guessed that it held the offices of the first-line defenders against evil and supernatural criminals. Forget the national government, the Protectors of the Society were the real caretakers of homeland security.

I slowed down, pulled into the underground parking garage and flashed my security card at the ancient man guarding the gate. Snooker, as he was known to Protectors, was nearly one hundred thirty years old, but he could still take down a demon. I returned his grumble with a friendly wave and drove down the first row of parking spaces. Pulling into a good spot, I left my briefcase filled with real estate files on the front seat and headed for the elevator.

"Hey, girlfriend, wassup?" Benita Johnson wiggled her fingers in greeting and I returned the gesture.

Dumping the contents of my pockets into the small plastic tub she held, I passed through what looked like a metal detector. Oh, sure, it could detect weapons, dirty bombs and other devices of mass destruction, but the machine also incorporated a special technology to scan a human for any signs of supernatural hitchhikers. No unwanted or unseen visitors were allowed into headquarters. At the same time, the tub scanned my items for anything out of the ordinary.

"Hey, Benny. Not much. Though I got a call from the big

guy. Have you heard any scuttlebutt?"

"A lamp call from him?" She pointed upward, but I knew she meant the boss and not *The* Boss. "Girl, are you going around attacking innocent people again?"

I tried to keep the wince inside from showing on my face. How long would it take to live down my mistakes? "No. I've been away on vacation. Remember?"

"Uh-huh. I remember." A quick frown skittered across her features. "I ain't heard nothing about nothing. Maybe he wants you to check in, is all."

To quote my friend—*uh-huh*. I could see it now. Mac and I exchanging vacation photos and talking about all the fun in the sun. The detector's bells went off and I reversed direction out of the scan area, gritting my teeth against the obnoxious sound. "Shit. When are they going to get this thing to recognize keys? I mean, come on. It can find a microscopic succubus hiding in a person's lung, but it can't figure out keys are just keys?"

Benny caught the keychain I threw to her and motioned me through the scanner for another try. "Girl, don't you know it? But what's got your panties in a wad? The boss's call? Or ain't your new hubby taking care of you?"

I passed through the machine with no problems this time and picked up the keys from the table where she'd tossed them. "No. I mean, I don't know. Blake's treating me quite well, thank you." I remembered my hubby's head between my legs and couldn't help but grin. "Really well, if you know what I mean."

"Oh, ho, ho. Looks like someone got a little sumthin'-sumthin' this morning. Tell me, hot stuff. How was he? Come on, girlfriend, dish. I want all the deets."

Her delighted cackle made my grin spread wider and rushed the heat to my face. I still get embarrassed talking about sex. At my age, go figure. "Sorry. I don't kiss and tell."

"Do you screw and squeal?" She let loose with another guffaw.

Her laugh echoed around the garage and I checked for any onlookers. I liked the gregarious woman, but sometimes she made me want to hide inside a hole. "Uh, I'll see you in a bit, Benny. Take it easy."

"Hell, girlfriend, I'll take it any way I can get it. Easy or hard, it don't matter to me."

I entered the elevator, turned to face the row of buttons and found Benny still shaking her head, enjoying her own joke. She was one of those lucky people who lived life to the fullest and I had to envy her. Maybe since I'd found Blake I'd end up a happy-go-lucky person like her. Yet as the elevator whisked me upward to the penthouse, I knew the answer to my musing. Not a chance. Or as my dear old dad always said, "Girl, if sour was money, you'd be richer than Trump."

Don't misunderstand me. I am a happy person, especially since falling in love with Blake. But when one of your jobs deals with tracking down and eliminating—usually in some gruesome way—demons, ghouls, ghosts and otherworldly creatures, it's difficult to find the brighter side of life.

The doors opened to reveal the foyer to the penthouse. Lush navy carpet trimmed in gold welcomed me. Taking a deep breath, I stepped out of the elevator and into the watchful eyes of Security. It was security unseen by the naked eye, but security nonetheless. A dozen hidden cameras, continually monitored by six of the Society's biggest and toughest guards, were hidden around the small interior—within the large silk flower arrangement, in the one-way glass passing as a beveled mirror, and even in the walls. No one entered the penthouse and MacNamara's office without the Society knowing about it.

The intricate mahogany double doors to the suite opened wide and I stepped closer. Knowing not to wait for more of an invitation, I entered the huge room. I suddenly wished I'd checked my shoes to make sure they were clean, but it was too late. I gathered my confidence and crossed to the enormous desk where Mac sat with his back to me.

"Good morning, Randall."

Aw, crap. I hate it when he calls me Randall. I knew something was up whenever Mac used my last name instead of calling me the more familiar Jennifer—and I doubted he wanted a report about my nuptials. "Good morning, Mr. MacNamara." Hopefully, using the more respectful surname instead of the less informal name of Mac would help appease his dark mood. "How are you doing? Uh, and by the way, the name's Randall-Barrington now."

"Let's cut the chitchat, Randall."

Shit. I knew I shouldn't have added the part about my new

name. Something was definitely up. "You summoned me, sir?" I took a deep breath in an attempt to steady my nerves. Why was I worried? I'd been on vacation so how could I have screwed up?

He swiveled his chair around and didn't offer me a seat in one of the two leather chairs facing his desk. I accepted this as yet another bad sign, took another deep breath and got ready for anything.

"Have you ever heard of the Bracelet of Invincibility?"

At least he hadn't mentioned the word *fired.* I mentally regrouped and wracked my brain before shaking my head. "Can't say I have. What is it? A bracelet to protect a girl's virginity? Sort of like a chastity belt she can wear around her wrist? Which would explain why I haven't heard of it in this day and age." Personally, I thought my joke was pretty funny. Mac didn't.

"Knock off the comedy routine." He reached for the remote to operate the television built into the wall to his right, started to point and click, then dropped his hand. "The Bracelet of Invincibility is a fairly new weapon, considering no one had heard of its existence before the Big War."

"The Big War? Do you mean the Gulf War? Or Iraq?" Granted, I'd never been a student of history, but Mac didn't have to snarl at me for my ignorant question.

"Damn, your generation needs a good history education. No, not the Gulf War. The Big War. World War Two."

"Oh, yeah. World War. *That* Big War. Hence the term *world* used in its title." I grinned for a split second and quickly tucked my chin down at his second snarl. *Note to self: Do not make jokes around Mac.*

Mac snarled yet a third time and leaned against the rich leather of his chair. "Let me give you a lesson, Randall."

Aw, hell. He called me Randall again. Things are not looking up.

"Legend has it Satan created the Bracelet of Invincibility for Hitler. The Bracelet was said to give great power to the wearer. With the Bracelet a man, woman, or worse, a demon could rule the world."

"Great. Exactly what this messed-up world needs. Nuclear bombs aren't enough. Let's have a super weapon made by the Big Bastard himself."

Mac nodded. "Agreed. However, the legend states the Bracelet, although containing great power, has to recharge after big expenditures of its energy before it can be used again. In fact, if someone depletes all the power of the Bracelet at one time, the Bracelet is empty. No one knows if it can be refueled. The few historians who dare to acknowledge its existence have spoken with witnesses who remember seeing Hitler wear it."

"I guess when you're the boss man you can get away with wearing jewelry and not have the troops make fun of you. Or is invincibility from ridicule part of its power?"

Mac glared, silencing me with one look. "These same historians credit the Bracelet for causing Hitler to commit suicide at the end of his reign when the Allied Forces were kicking his butt. They say the Bracelet disappeared and Hitler went insane when he couldn't find it. Of course, most historians agree he was off his rocker to begin with, so it wouldn't have taken much to push him over the edge."

Mac laced his fingers in front of him, pressing the tips to his chin. "However, the Bracelet recently surfaced again and then, uh, disappeared. According to the rumors, a high demon lord—we don't know which one yet—is hot to possess it."

"We can't let that happen." I was all business now. No more jokes. Not when a high demon lord was on the prowl.

"Right."

"What's this Bracelet look like?" By the way Mac referred to the thing, the word *bracelet* seemed like a proper name with a capital *B*. I glanced at the blank monitor, expecting a photo of the Bracelet to brighten the darkened screen.

"The people who've seen it describe a solid gold bracelet with intricate detail on it, but they couldn't give enough specifics for anyone to draw a decent picture. In fact, many of them claim the Bracelet caused their memory loss."

"If no one can remember what it looks like, maybe Old Blood and Guts Adolf simply forgot what it looked like and misplaced it." A memory loss caused by a piece of jewelry? I'd heard of memory losses caused by trauma to the head, or from drinking alcohol to excess, or by overdosing with drugs, but never caused by wearing a bracelet. "But come on, sir. You're saying no one knows what this Bracelet looks like? First it appears out of nowhere and then it disappears? Are you sure you're not getting punked?"

Mac jerked out of his chair and hiked up his bushy eyebrows. "Trust me, Randall. Everything I'm telling you is true, including the memory loss." His demeanor shifted from one of irritated leader to one of slightly embarrassed mentor. "Once the Bracelet is gone, the owner can't remember what it looked like."

"Where did the Bracelet reappear?"

He cleared his throat and put his back to me to stare out the row of windows behind him. "For a short time, the Society had the Bracelet in its protection."

"Here? The Bracelet of Invincibility was here? In Tulsa?" His silence was my answer. "And it's disappeared again?"

This time he nodded and turned around to face me with his former blustery countenance restored. "Right from under our noses."

"Holy shit." Nothing had ever been stolen from the Society. The idea was preposterous. Yet judging from my supervisor's face this, too, was no joke.

"I'm counting on you to find it and bring it back, Jenn."

Damn. He shortened my name only when he wanted to stick it to me big time and use the old "we're buddies and we're in this together so do it for the team" tactic. He knew I couldn't refuse the assignment now. Not that I'd planned to turn it down. I mean, demon hunting and finding jewelry both in one assignment? Throw in a handsome hero and what more could a girl ask for? Since I already had the handsome hero at home, I was all set.

Still, I didn't want to appear overly enthusiastic. "How am I supposed to know when and if I see it?"

"There's an engraved inscription inside the Bracelet which reads, 'Eternal Power'. Fortunately for your purposes, Satan wrote the inscription in English and not in German."

"Why would he write the words in English if he made the Bracelet for Hitler?" Not being a history buff, I wasn't sure if Hitler knew English or not. But he damn sure had to have known German.

"Most historians believe he wrote the inscription in English to piss off Hitler."

Satan had a sense of humor? The image of Satan headlining at a comedy club with his long tail swishing back and forth and horns sprouting from his head zipped through my head. If an audience member didn't laugh at his jokes, he could jab them with his pitchfork. I giggled, garnering yet another scowl from Mac. Did this man ever smile?

"Terrific. I'm supposed to find a piece of jewelry without knowing what it looks like, after it disappears from the one place on the planet with the highest level of security ever known to mankind. I'm supposed to do this before an unidentified high demon lord finds it. Do I understand the mission correctly, sir?" He knew he'd asked the impossible and knew I knew it, too.

"You've got it." He faced the wall of windows again and his shoulders, always thrown back and kept rigid, sagged. With a voice heavy with the weight of responsibility, he nodded and added, "I'm counting on you, Jenn."

Terrific. Simply terrific. I opened my mouth wanting to tell him not to count on me too much, then decided not to add to his burden. But how would I get this weight off *my* shoulders?

Never Judge a Book by Its Cover— Unless There's a Naked Man on It

MacNamara worked in the building all Protectors called headquarters. Yet another building housed what we liked to call the main office, where those with even higher security clearances than MacNamara worked.

However, no Protector knew its location. In fact, none of us had ever seen the inside of the main office or met the few powerful beings who worked there. Before Mac handed me a post-it with the address scrawled on it, I hadn't been totally positive the place even existed. Yet here I stood, biting my lip and trying to ignore the nervous tickle running down my spine. Stalling, I checked the address for the third time.

"This can't be right." It's not like I'm plagued with obsessive-compulsive disorder or a diminished capacity for reading, but I had to check the yellow piece of paper a fourth time. I simply couldn't grasp what was right in front of me.

If the address was correct—and I had to believe it was—then the main office, the agency where the brightest minds running the most secretive and powerful organization in the known universe was ensconced, was a cottage. The high-level super-secure office was a quaint, white-picket-fenced, flowers-in-the-window-box type of house sitting in the middle of a street lined with shade trees. Children played on the lawns of similar suburban homes a few yards away and a poodle barked incessantly from the front porch of the house across the road.

Another home boasted a stenciled placard declaring *Children Are Always Welcome*. I figured either the old lady in the shoe had upgraded to the burbs, or Hansel and Gretel's witch was running a scam to lure unsuspecting twenty-first century children into her clutches. Based on my past experiences, my money was on the witch.

I pushed through the gate and walked up the old-world stone pathway to the front of the home. I studied the copper mailbox attached to the wall next to the door covered in painted flowers, unable to decide whether to barge right in or knock first. Luckily, someone made the decision for me.

The door flew open and a man reached out, grabbed me by the arms and yanked me toward him. I reacted, of course, in true Protector mode and used my body's momentum to throw him off balance. We tumbled onto the hardwood floor, banging my head and making the world go fuzzy for a moment. However, I could see well enough to know the bear-size man was already on his feet while I still fought to catch my breath. But I wasn't out of the skirmish yet.

Wrapping my legs around his, I rolled and brought Grizzly Adams's big brother down—thankfully not on top of me. This time, I was the first one off the floor. Scrambling to my feet, I drew back my arm in preparation to knock Bear Man flat again should he ever get off the floor. I may not have much body weight, but I do pack one helluva wallop, if I do say so myself. In fact, I was a bit disappointed when I didn't get to belt the lug.

An elderly lady, the epitome of a sweet grandmother, burst out of nowhere and held up her hand to ward off any blows I could land on my attacker. Her buxomly form stretched the seams of her workout outfit, and hot pink running shoes completed her look. She frowned and shook a finger at us. "Stop fighting this instant. I will not tolerate fighting in the foyer. If you two want to wrestle, take it downstairs to the gym."

The gym? How can a little cottage have a gym?

She glared at me, her expectation of my obedience obvious, and I lowered my fists. Still, I kept at the ready just in case the big guy wasn't listening to General Grandmother. "Fine by me. I didn't come here to fight." I tossed Grizzly Gus a fierce look. "But I won't shy away from one, either."

"Good. I abhor violence except as a last resort."

With Grandma between me and my attacker, I took a second to survey the entry. Instead of a staircase leading up to another level, the foyer consisted of one white unadorned wall

Beverly Rae

stretching in a nearly complete circle from the front door. Several doors, all exactly the same, with no names or numbers to identify them, were set into the wall. Whoever had decorated the place was into minimalism to a major degree.

She nodded her approval of my statement of non-aggression and offered her hand to my ex-opponent. For her to help this gigantic man to his feet would have proven a difficult task for an older woman had not one very strange thing happened. Once Grandma and Bear joined hands, he began to shrink. My eyes most assuredly popped out of my head, but still my brain refused to believe what I saw. The big guy transformed into a dwarf-sized man. Grandma made a few strange clicking sounds and the diminutive man nodded, glared at me once and exited through one of the doors.

"How the hell—"

"You'll have to forgive him, Ms. Randall, but his people take the job of security for our building very seriously. After what happened, he feels he's let the Society down. Although I don't know why he blames himself. He wasn't on duty during the time of the robbery. Now if you'll follow me, I'll take you where you need to go."

"Wait a sec. How the fuck did he..." Wouldn't you know my brain would freeze, leaving my mouth forsaken of the question I wanted to ask?

She paused and waited for me to get the super glue out of my mouth. She apparently decided, however, that I wasn't going to get mentally unstuck and decided to move on. "Really, Ms. Randall, I don't like to criticize, but foul language does not become you. You're such a pretty young woman, why make yourself ugly by using profanity?"

I ignored the recrimination about my language, intent on a more important topic of discussion. "His *people*? There are more of these incredible shrinking giants around?" Without saying a word, she unlocked and passed through the middle door in the wall, then started down a long narrow hallway. I hustled to fall into step beside her. "But how did he shrink?"

She paused to face me, folding her hands in front of her as if getting ready to teach an academically challenged child. "Oh, I forgot. You don't know, do you? You're a Protector Level Ten, right?"

At my nod, she pivoted and continued down the hall. "Harry—we call him Harry because earthlings can't pronounce his real name—is from the planet we call XP234-2935."

I stopped, unsure I'd heard her correctly. "He's from another planet?"

Again she halted, turned to me and clasped her hands. "Yes, dear. Harry is from another planet." She smiled at me in a patronizing way and I struggled to keep from telling her my IQ. "Don't they teach Protectors about the other races in the universe?"

Uh, no. "If they did, I must've missed the class." I started to laugh, but cut it short when I saw she was serious. "You're not kidding, are you? He really is from another planet? He's a real alien from outer space?"

She shushed me and put a manicured fingernail to her lips. "Please don't call him an alien. He's adopted Earth as his second home and you'll insult him if you call him an alien. In fact, he considers himself as much of an American as you or I."

"Wow. Talk about the great melting pot."

"Exactly." She motioned for me to follow again. I obeyed, trying not to trip over my jaw hanging to my feet.

We must have walked for more than five minutes but the hallway kept on going and going and going. I wondered how the length of a hallway inside the small building I'd entered could extend more than ten times the length of the entire house. Or at least, the length of the entire house as it had appeared on the outside. The whole place was fast leaving the boundaries of space and dimension behind.

I've hunted supernatural creatures for years and I'd thought I'd seen everything imaginable as well as some things I'd considered quite unimaginable. Man, was I ever wrong! I'd met my first alien from space and walked down a hallway defying the laws of physics. What would I encounter next?

At last, we reached the end of the corridor where the hallway split into a T-formation and came to yet another white door. Grandma winked at me, knocked and called to whoever was behind the door, "Reslind, she's here." After giving me a pat on the shoulder, she turned and continued down the hallway to the right.

"Hey! Where're you going?" All at once, I felt like a child on her first day of school and Mom was abandoning me to fend for myself. "I didn't catch your name."

Grandma pivoted again and assumed her regular pose. "No, you didn't because I didn't tell you. I'm sorry. I don't know where my manners are." She giggled and suddenly looked decades younger. "Jack always said I was an impertinent gal. I'm Marilyn, Ms. Randall, and it was very nice to meet you." With another wink, she resumed her pace away from me.

"Good to meet you, too, Marilyn." I glanced at the door and when I turned back to her, she was gone. "Wow. For an old chick, she sure can move fast."

"She's pretty quick on her feet."

I wheeled toward the door and took a ninja stance, ready for anything. An overweight, balding man held up his palms in defense. "Whoa, young lady. I'm sorry I startled you, but I don't believe my action deserves an attack." His face took on an odd expression. Was he trying to smile? From the pitiful attempt, I could tell the guy didn't practice the gesture often. "I see you met Marilyn. I'm Reslind."

"I did. Well, sort of. I didn't get all of her name."

"Oh, well, Marilyn's rather secretive. But who can blame her? After all the fuss about her relationship with John Kennedy, you can understand why she'd like to keep a low profile. Please, come inside."

"John Kennedy?" I took him by the arm, keeping him with me. "Marilyn has a thing with a guy named John Kennedy?"

"Had. She *had* a relationship with him. John is dead."

"Oh, I'm sorry. Still, they must've gotten tired of the comparison."

"Comparison? What do you mean?" Reslind pried my fingers off his arm. "Who would they be compared to?"

"You know. *The* Marilyn and *the* John Kennedy, the former President of the United States. Granted, she doesn't look much like the movie star bombshell, but I assume people would've made the jokes anyway. You know, because of their famous names."

Reslind scrutinized me and lifted his eyebrows. Why did everyone in this place make me feel as though I'd skipped school the day the brains were handed out?

"Ms. Randall, I fear you don't understand. Marilyn—*our* Marilyn—is *that* Marilyn Monroe."

Okay, so either I was going crazy or the people who ran the office were certifiable. Frankly, at this point, I wasn't sure which option to choose. "But Marilyn Monroe died a long time ago."

"Ah, I see. The Protector classes aren't covering much history, are they?" He tipped his head to stare at me over his horn-rimmed glasses. "My dear, at the request of President Kennedy, Marilyn's death was manufactured. Staged, as Marilyn liked to say. The real Marilyn came to work for us the day the news media reported her death to the nation. She's been an invaluable asset to the Society for over forty years. Now perhaps we can get on with the reason you're here?"

I just met the real Marilyn Monroe. Oh. My. God. "But what about the woman they buried?"

"Mary was an android." He pivoted, once more closing the discussion on Marilyn. "Ms. Randall, are you coming?"

An android? Holy shit.

I followed my new escort through the door and into a room much like any other living room in America. A television served as the focal point with a conventional couch, loveseat and ottoman facing the screen. Pictures of landscapes dotted the walls, while knickknacks sat on the two end tables and coffee table. This was the type of room I'd have expected to find in a cottage. Nonetheless, I frowned, unable to stop the disillusionment flowing through me. After meeting Harry the Alien and Marilyn Monroe, I guess I'd expected something more than a typical living room.

"I can see you'd hoped for something, shall we say, less ordinary."

"Oh, well, maybe..." I didn't want to appear rude, but knew I couldn't hide the truth. "Yeah, I guess."

Reslind surveyed the room as though trying to see it through my eyes. "I can understand your disappointment. But we wanted you to see where the Bracelet of Invincibility was kept. Er, at least until it was taken."

Had I missed something? I took another look around the room and tried to picture a rare and powerful weapon safely hidden away. But where? In between the couch cushions? Behind the painting on the wall? "No way. You guys kept a valuable piece of weaponry in here?"

Reslind studied me, making me feel like a bug under a microscope. "Ms. Randall, don't you see how one should never take anything or anyone at face value?" Accepting my silence as his answer, he crossed over to the lamp beside the couch and flipped the switch, filling the room with light. He dropped his hands to his side and waited for my reaction as if he'd revealed the Hope diamond and I'd called it a chunk of gravel.

"Am I missing something?" I tried to keep my tone level, without my usual sarcasm, and failed.

Within seconds, the furniture started dissolving *through* the floor. The walls to the room fell away, melting before my eyes, to reveal a room rivaling NASA's Mission Control. I glanced around, once again having to force myself to close my mouth. One large monitor after another lined the upper portion of the new walls, and machines of various descriptions and sizes blinked lights and fed information into the screens. The scenes on the monitors caught my attention. Row after row, the picture was the same. Exact duplicates of the living room we'd been standing in seconds before flickered on the monitors.

"Each of those rooms contains various articles of importance, power or wealth. Can you see where the objects are?"

I stepped up to the closest one and squinted. "Nope. Looks like the room we're in—or were in."

"Exactly. Yet each of those rooms contains many objects of value. For instance, watch the sofa on Monitor Seven." Reslind pressed a button on a machine below the monitor.

I followed his direction. To my amazement, the sofa flipped over, exposing a long cylindrical tube covered with red spots. "What is that thing?"

"'That thing' as you put it is a weapon from the planet SC29711-103. To activate it, the operator touches those red spots in a specific order. Then a laser beam of immeasurable power travels in a path of destruction for a distance of not less than one hundred light years, cutting a hole through anything and anyone in its way."

"And you're hiding this weapon under a couch?" I stepped away from the monitor in an instinctual reflex of alarm. I didn't want to accidentally push any button—especially the wrong button. "What did the people of planet SC-whatever do with such a powerful weapon and how did the Society take possession?"

Reslind's stern composure crumpled in what I surmised was a show of emotion. "The people of SC29711-103 used it to annihilate their enemies on the planet SC29711-104. We received this one from a weapons dealer who took it off their decimated planet after an equally horrific weapon, launched moments after their attack, impacted their world and wiped out their civilization. Many millennia's worth of progress and culture of two thriving civilizations were gone within seconds."

"Both worlds are gone?" Sometimes I wondered if any intelligent life existed in the universe—including on Earth. "And no one survived?"

"Both planets were obliterated, and no, no one on either planet escaped extermination."

I looked at the weapon with new eyes and the realization of the office's purpose struck me with a thud in my gut. "These are everyday living rooms in an everyday cottage in an everyday neighborhood. And this building holds all these rooms? In other words, you're telling me the main office is a holding house for intergalactic weapons of mass destruction?"

"Yes. Providing secure housing for unusual weaponry is one of many functions we perform."

"But why here? Why not in a place with more security, like cement walls, super-powered guards, or a frickin' army to keep them out of the hands of the bad guys? How about on an uninhabited planet? Why risk our world by keeping all this possible destruction here?"

Suddenly, I knew the reason. The idea seemed impossible but, then again, I'd already seen the impossible happen in this house. "Oh, I get it. You're hiding these objects right under the noses, in relatively plain sight, of anyone looking for them. Am I right?" I hoped to see an expression of satisfaction on Reslind's face and I got what I'd expected. Goodie for me.

"You are correct." He took a step toward me to take me by the arms. "Earth was chosen because of our commitment to the safety of all intelligent life forms. Ms. Randall, no other Protector knows of this mission and you must keep our secret. The Society, with its mandate to protect others from evil supernatural beings, is only one small subsidiary of a much larger organization."

"A larger organization? Holy shit." First I'd learned about aliens and now I'd found out the Society was a one cog in a big cosmic wheel. The whole idea boggled my mind which was why I chose to refocus my attention on my own mission. "Oh, hell. You're telling me you had the Bracelet of Invincibility hidden in one of these rooms, aren't you? Under an ottoman, perhaps?"

He shook his head, but gave a measured response. "Yes...and no. The Bracelet was hidden in the one of the rooms—but not under an ottoman."

I studied every monitor one by one until the answer came to me. "The Bracelet was in Room Five."

"Why do you think we kept it in Room Five?"

"Because Room Five is the only room without a TV."

"You're an observant person." He looked at the fifth monitor and his somber appearance returned. "The thieves took the television set which, of course, means they took the Bracelet."

My gaze dropped to the controls on the machines below each monitor. "But how? You've got better than state-of-the-art security. How could anyone break in and steal anything?"

"Unfortunately, we suffered a disastrous power outage when an individual from planet TY-2w3d2, a member of the race called Tyskians, dropped in unexpectedly. You see, the Tyskians are electromagnetic in nature. When she showed up, she overloaded our massive generators and blew out our power, including our backup power supply. The thieves choosing that precise moment to stumble into the cottage and happen upon Room Five is a coincidence of infinitesimal odds."

"Are you certain it was a coincidence? Maybe the Tyskian was in on the heist."

Reslind scoffed at my ignorance of the off-world race. "Not possible. The Tyskians are known for their honesty. In fact, they are mentally and physically unable to lie. If they try to lie, their faces turn a bright pink."

Not having a clue what a Tyskian was, I had to take his word for it. "Okay, okay. Don't get all snotty about it. I needed to ask, is all."

"Of course."

Could his agreement sound any less sincere? But I knew when to let an argument go.

"Of course, being petty thieves, they stole the only object in the room they considered to have any value." Reslind tapped on the monitor for emphasis.

"The television." I puffed out a breath and tried to imagine the odds of all those events happening at the same time. Highly unlikely was a gross understatement. "You believe these were ordinary mortal thieves."

"Ordinary, yes, until they stole the Bracelet." Reslind met my eyes and held me with their invisible grip. "Now, however, they are unwitting players in a war between the Society and the Otherworld."

"Oh, crap." My job just got a lot harder. "Then I guess I'd better get going."

Reslind crossed the room to another row of buttons. "I agree, Ms. Randall. You'd do well not to dilly-dally." With a farewell nod, he punched one of the buttons.

Dilly-dally? How old is this guy, anyway? "Actually, the name's Randall-Barringt—"

Without warning, the floor beneath me fell away and I shouted for help. I dropped, feet first, hair streaming upward arms flailing out, hoping for a handhold. Instead, the dark tunnel swallowed me.

Do You Need New Batteries?

I like roller coasters, fun houses, and all kinds of amusement park thrills, but my trip through the dark tunnel put all of those other rides to shame. Freefalling in total darkness gives a person a rush like no other. Even the few times I'd parachuted from an airplane didn't compare. Trust me, when you can't see where you're going, the ride takes on a whole new level of anxiety.

I dropped through the darkness for several minutes—*how big is this cottage anyway?*—until, suddenly, I changed direction. Switching from falling downward to flying upward, I burst through a hatch much like a large pet door and landed with a hard thump on my rear. Skidding a few feet with the momentum, I narrowly missed ramming into the tall oak tree shading the side of the main office.

"Ow!" I twisted around and yelled, hoping someone inside the house would hear me. "I guess leaving through the front door would be too easy?" Perhaps this was the Society's way of sneaking people out of the house without prying neighbors noticing. "You could at least warn a person, ya know. Maybe put some cushions on the landing pad?" Sure, I had plenty of my own padding, but that wasn't the point. I rose and wiped off as much of the grass stain from my pants as I could. "Dammit. My new pants are ruined."

As if reminding me of the more important problems of the world than my stained wardrobe, a metal object burst from a different escape hatch and landed near my feet. Once the object was through, the hatch disappeared. "What's this? I guess you're giving me this for the mission? Or is it a party gift? Ha-ha." I waited to see if I'd get an answer to my sarcastic question, but none came.

I bent over and retrieved the strange device. They wanted me to have a cell phone? Or was it supposed to be a PDA? Either way, I couldn't see what was so special about this thing. Besides, due to my love of gadgets, I already had a smart phone with a personal organizer, digital camera, text messaging, wifi Internet and every other bell and whistle known to the prolific communications industry. But the main question repeated in my head. Why did the Society want me to have this device?

I gave it a quick examination. If it was a new and improved version of my smart phone, I'd happily trade up. I studied it closer. Yup, it had a phone, a camera, an organizer and more. I spent a few more minutes trying to unravel the intricacies of the machine, then shoved it into the back pocket of my pants and headed for my car.

I started talking out loud. Yeah, I know it looks strange, but I talk things over with myself whenever I start a new mission. Since I never work with a partner, talking out loud is my way of running through all the facts about a case.

"Okay, here's what I know so far. Mortal thieves lucked onto the house and into Room Five. Being your average run-of-the-mill robbers, they took what they thought was the only object of value." I neared my Jag and reached for my keys to punch in the security code. "I'm thinking the best places to start searching for these losers are the pawn shops." I slid into the driver's seat, started the ignition and revved the engine. "Let's see. Marvin's Pawn Shop takes hot televisions. If only I could remember the address."

A beeping sound coming from my rear pocket interrupted my train of thought. Pulling out the new device, I saw the address for Marvin's Pawn Shop on the screen. "Well, I've gotta admit it. A built-in GPS is cool. Not exactly mind-blowing technology, but cool nonetheless."

The words were barely out of my mouth, when the device scrolled more information across its screen. A list of pawn shops showed which shop had received a television set in the past few days. "Now how do we know for sure? Did we tap into their inventory somehow?"

A red light at the top right corner of the instrument blinked at me. The bright red glow flicked on and off faster and faster as if working overtime to draw my attention. "If I didn't know better, I'd swear this thing is angry at me." I pressed the button next to the red light.

"I am not angry at you, Ms. Randall. My function is to help you in your search for the Bracelet of Invincibility."

The sexy manly-man voice emanating from the device startled me and I dropped the talking thing in my lap. "Is that you, Reslind?" I doubted the wonderfully sensual timbre could have come from Reslind, but who else could it be? The screen, however, remained blank. "Are you calling me?" Gingerly, I picked it up and held it out in front of me as if the mechanism might explode at any moment. In my line of business, you just never knew for sure. Playing it safe is always the best option.

"No, Ms. Randall. I am not Reslind. Let me introduce myself. I am your Personal Partner and I have been programmed to help you on this mission. Please call me P.P."

I almost laughed at the thought of associating the melt-my-knees voice with such an absurd name. "Are you shitting me? Who am I really talking to? Are you calling from the main office or from headquarters?" I debated calling Mac, then decided to see what "P.P." would say next. "And no. I'm not going to call anyone by such a ridiculous name." Who knew? This could be some sicko who got off on women talking about urination.

The screen darkened as if the instrument meant to scowl at me. I mentally chastised myself for attributing human characteristics to an inanimate object.

"As I said, you are talking to P—um, your Personal Partner. I am not a mortal being like you. However, I am a sentient being and I would appreciate you treating me with the respect you would give a human partner. If you like, you can call me Partner instead."

I glanced at the cottage and thought about going back inside to get the straight scoop. However, with the possibility of running into Harry churning my stomach, I figured I'd rather take on the techno-partner. "Okay, Partner. Since you volunteered, I'll let you do the choosing. Where to first? And the name's Randall-Barrington now."

"Thank you, Ms. Randall, for the respect." Why couldn't anyone associated with the Society get my new name right? "First, I'll sort the names geographically, then alphabetically within each region. Then I'll combine the lists to determine most efficient use of our time. Hold, please, while I perform these functions."

I held. Various colored lights flashed across the screen until, at last, one long beep signaled the end of the process.

"I believe the best choice is to begin in the eastern part of the city with Ace Pawn Shop. Shall we proceed?"

Did this guy have a stick up his butt or what? I frowned and wondered how any mechanical object could ever get a stick up the butt. Placing my new "partner" in the bucket seat next to me, I gunned the Jag down the quiet suburban street.

"We're here."

"I realized as much when you slammed on the brakes, Ms. Randall. Did you take the Society's Defensive Driver course? I would highly recommend you sign up at your earliest convenience."

I stuck out my tongue at Partner. Who was he to talk? Could he even drive a car? I doubted it, but didn't think I wanted to challenge him. Instead, I snatched him up and headed for the store. "Do you always sound like a British butler? With a voice like yours, I would've thought you'd speak more like James Bond with a country attitude. You know, suave, yet familiar."

"I am sorry, Ms. Randall. Do you wish me to speak less formally?" Partner made a couple of clicking noises. "Is this better? Do I sound more like a friend? Or how'd ya like a Texas twang, darlin'?"

Laughing, I stared at Partner's new cool blue screen saver featuring a shirtless, very buff cowboy grinning up at me. "Well, yee-haw, cowboy. Now you're talking. Woo-wee, talk about an improvement from a blank screen. So this is what you'd look like if you were human?"

"Darlin', I can look any way you want me to look. Does the wrangler in me tickle your fancy? I pulled the image from one of those romance books you like to read. Do you like my new accent?"

I froze, gripping the metal case until my hand hurt. "How did you know...? And keep your mouth sealed about those books. Or whatever you use for a mouth. Got it?" Only Blake knew about my passion for romance novels and I wasn't telling anyone else. I certainly didn't want my fellow Protectors to find out. I'd never put an end to the jokes.

"I don't know what all the fuss is about. I scanned one of them and found the story intriguing, as well as being quite well written. In fact"—he returned to his deep twang—"I'd hafta say it was dang excitin'."

It seemed Partner had a problem sticking to his new character, but I let the momentary lapse pass. "Really? Most people think romance novels are stupid and trashy."

Again, he slipped out of character. "Then they lack the necessary intelligence to understand the deep emotions involved in those stories." He coughed and dropped into cowboy character. "I'd say those folks are plumb stupid."

I laughed at the sincerity in his voice. Who knew I'd find a fellow romance lover in a rectangular piece of metal and batteries? "I agree, but since our mission isn't to set up a book club, we've got better things to do with our time than to discuss romance novels. And, yeah, I like your accent."

"Are you sure? Would you prefer something more on the edge of the latest culture like this?" The cowboy image disappeared, replaced by the stereotypical image of a rapper.

"Very nice, Partner. I like rap as well as the next girl, but I'll stick with the cowboy."

"Whatever you want, darlin'."

I pushed through the door and strolled into the pawn shop. Instead of an entrance bell, a loud teeth-gritting squeak announced my arrival, changing my nonchalant stroll into a jerky walk. An unshaven older man dragged his attention away from a small black-and-white television to glare at me. He rubbed the stubble on his jaw and I felt an overwhelming urge to scratch my own face, as if whatever this guy had hidden in his scraggly beard had jumped over to me. Who knew what kind of vermin lived in his unwashed hairs? Lice, roaches, and other disgusting creatures would shout "soup's on!" at the stains on his filthy undershirt.

"Yeah? What can I do you for?" He checked the area around me, looking for someone else. "Didn't I hear two voices?"

I held up Partner. "Phone." I continued my way to the counter and hoped the man wouldn't notice how different

Partner was to other phones. Glancing around, I noticed several televisions grouped together in one corner. None of them, however, matched the type of set snatched from the main office.

"Yeah? You itchin' to sell or buy?" The stub of a cigar he popped into his mouth completed his image of a pawn shop owner.

"Buy." Although what anyone would want with this junk escaped me. Still, I had a job to do and I'd do the job to the best of my ability—no matter who or what got in my way. "I'm hunting for a TV."

The old guy's eyes lit up with interest. "I've got a few nice ones right there. One of them is even cable-ready."

In a world obsessed with big screens and home theatre systems, the term "cable-ready" was a dinosaur, yet I pretended to act interested. "Yeah, those are good." I swiveled to the sets and pretended to give them serious consideration. "But I'm actually interested in a specific kind of television."

Partner beeped, alerting me to his presence. I checked him and saw a photo of the stolen television set on his screen. My partner was nothing if not helpful. I held the photo up to the shopkeeper and hoped Partner would keep his mouth shut. "This is what I want to find. Did you have anyone come in and sell you this type of unit?"

From his reaction, the old man had experienced his share of police interrogations. He literally growled at me, irritated when he realized I wasn't really a potential buyer. "Shit. You a cop? If you are, you're wasting your time because I don't deal with crooks. I told another cop the same thing the last time you guys harassed me. What's an honest businessman supposed to do to get you cops off his back?"

Uh-huh, I'd thought so. He was definitely dealing in stolen goods. "I'm asking you a simple question. And no, I'm not a cop. But I could offer you a substantial reward for information leading to my finding this." Substantial being whatever amount I had in my pocket at the time. Unfortunately, the amount of cash on me at the moment wouldn't buy him dinner at McDonald's.

"Hey, lady, what you see is what I've got. Still, how much of a reward are we talking about?" He tapped the ashes from the end of his cigar into a coffee mug. "In case I run across it."

"We'll talk about how much when and if we need to talk." I figured I'd leave him salivating over the idea of the "substantial reward" and hope the incentive would get him interested. Taking one last glimpse at the televisions he had on the table, I decided I'd better play both ends of the game. "How about a bracelet? Anyone hock a piece of jewelry in the past twenty-four hours?" If the thieves had discovered the Bracelet hidden inside the television, they would've tried to pawn it. Jewelry made for a quick grab of cash at a pawn store.

"Nope. No jewelry at all for about a week. Besides, I thought you were looking for a television set." He squinted at me, making his already beady eyes appear even sneakier.

"Both." I scribbled my name and cell phone number on a post-it pad and turned to go, wanting to get on to the next shop. The only business cards I had contained my real estate information. Working undercover, Protectors didn't carry cards. "Give me a call if you get either one."

His grunt was his way of not committing, but I knew the greedy old fart would call if something showed up. Pushing through the squeaky door, I slid my sunglasses off my head and onto my nose, pausing to get used to the glare of the sunny day. Another pawn shop on the other side of the street beckoned to me until I froze at what—or who—sauntered out of its front door.

Instinct kicked in and I quickly squatted in front of my car. Taking a deep breath and holding it, I peeked over the hood. Fortunately, Blake didn't look around. Instead, he strode over to his Mercedes and slid into the front seat. I grimaced and prayed he wouldn't notice my Jag. If he did and came over, what would I say? I'd started working on a plausible excuse when I heard him rev up his car and peel down the road. And then it hit me. I wouldn't be the only one needing an explanation. He'd have some explaining to do too, right?

"What the hell is Blake doing on this side of town?"

"I don't know, darlin'. Would you like me to access the computer system at the main office and see what I can come up with?"

"No, don't." I didn't want anyone else to know I'd seen Blake coming out of a pawn shop. "Nobody in this area can afford his services and I doubt he's hocking his wedding ring already." I tried to add a chuckle to my joke, but the sound fell flat. "Why would an investment analyst visit a pawn shop?"

Partner beeped, then highlighted the positive aspect of the situation. "At least he didn't see you. How would you explain why you, a real estate agent, visited a pawn shop, especially after you lied and told him you had a meeting at the office this morning? I guess you could always say you were selling your ring. Ha-ha."

I nearly dropped Partner in surprise. "How'd you know I lied to Blake?" I glared at the glowing Happy Face on the screen.

"Oh, sugar, the Society knows everything about you. You know how it is." Playing the song "La Bamba", Partner changed colors several times in an obvious, gadgety way to lighten the mood.

I cringed to think what else the Society might know. Like why I had a set of fur-lined handcuffs hidden in my underwear drawer. The idea of MacNamara knowing about my sex life was not a pleasant thought. But now was not the time to worry about a possible exposé of my personal life. "Be careful, Partner. No one wants their secrets exposed."

"Ain't that the truth." Partner shut off the kaleidoscope of colors and resumed his cowboy image. "Speaking of work, darlin', your other boss left several rather angry messages. I knew, however, you didn't want me to interrupt you while you were busy doing real work. Would you like to hear them?"

I groaned and knew I'd have to make an appearance at Swindle Real Estate. At least then I wouldn't have actually lied to Blake about going to the office. "No, thanks. I can imagine what he said. But how did he get your number?"

Partner responded with blinking lights which I assumed meant he was preparing his answer. Deciding not to sweat the small stuff, I cut him off. "Never mind. I'm not sure I want to know. Come on, Partner, I need to make a pit stop and get my weekly lecture on how I'm not performing up to Swindle agent expectations."

Taking the long route to Swindle Realty gave me time to consider other possibilities for locating the missing television and the Bracelet. With the introduction of the World Wide Web and online retailers such as eBay, fencing a valuable piece of jewelry to a pawn shop wasn't the only avenue a thief had to dispose of a hot item.

"Question, Partner."

"What 'cha need, darlin'?" Country music filtered out of the device's speakers.

Oh, man, talk about staying in character. This thing went all out in portraying his role. "Did the television work?"

"Work? Actually, no, I don't think it did. The rooms weren't functional. They only needed to appear as though they were." A very old song started, reminding me of the old westerns my dad used to watch.

"In all likelihood, the thieves, once they figured out the TV didn't work, probably dumped it. The question is...did they find the Bracelet before getting rid of the set?"

"Is this your way of telling me we're going dump hunting?"

I gagged at the idea of traipsing through a landfill, digging through spoiled food, rat droppings and worse, to look for a television set. "Not a chance. I can get some regular uniformed cops to check the dumps. Besides, I have a nagging hunch the crooks found the Bracelet and sold it."

"Then it's back to the pawn shops after you check in and get yelled at? I don't know why you put up with the jerk."

I pulled into a parking spot outside Swindle Realty and cut the engine. "Ain't that the truth." Sure, it was only a cover job, but couldn't I find a less demanding one? Blake had said he'd set me up in my own business. Of course, I didn't actually want to sell real estate, so I had no intention of taking him up on his generous offer. Besides, a job as an agent, with the flexible hours and time out of the office, made a good cover for a Protector. The perks of the position, however, would be lost if I was my own boss. With my own company, I'd have to produce and make money. Yet I'd bet Blake wouldn't have a problem with my quitting until I found something I liked better. I gave the fantasy of telling Herbert Swindle to shove the job up his ass a little play time in my mind's eye. Letting out a half-sigh, half-groan, I scooted out of my car.

"Partner, be quiet while we're inside. Understood?"

An angry-sounding whir answered me.

I ignored the mechanical protests. Searching through the big window in front of the building, I spotted my best friend and confidant, Myra Shuster, in her seat at the receptionist's desk.

Myra waved at me, instantly brightening the prospect of my work day. Myra was the only non-Protector who knew of my alternate identity. I knew without a doubt I could trust her with my secret and my life.

Funny thing, I still hadn't told Blake about my real work and I wasn't sure why. Sure, I'd known Myra for years and Blake for less than a month, but he was my husband. Didn't he have a right to know? Yet something inside me wouldn't let me tell him. I frowned at the thought. Obviously, I was the one with the problem. Striding toward the front door, I resolved for the hundredth time since marrying Blake to tell him the truth—then quickly realized I wouldn't. Was I simply listening to my gut? Or was I afraid of what he might say? Would any man want his wife living a dangerous life? Deciding I had enough on my plate, I shelved the Blake-problem away for later and shoved through the door.

Hiding behind the partitions dividing agents' cubicles, I quickly right-angled my way toward my own little cubby-hole and hoped I'd managed to stay out of sight. The murmur of agents talking with prospective clients in semi-private cubbyholes or on the other end of a phone washed over me. As a less-than-mediocre agent, I didn't rate one of the offices lining the sides of the building, but I was okay with my spot since my cubicle was a long way away from the den of the self-proclaimed lion, Herbert Swindle.

"Jennifer Randall!"

Apparently not far enough away. I scrunched my eyes together, held my breath, and braced for whatever might happen next. My boss's whiney voice slammed me to a stop as effectively as if a three-ton rhinoceros had roared to life, blocking my path to my sanctuary. For about two seconds, I tried to pretend I didn't hear him, but the fantasy didn't last long.

"Jennifer Randall! In my office. Now!"

Myra, the sweetest person in the world, came up behind me. "He's loaded for bear." She took my briefcase, which was feather light since I had no clients at the moment and, therefore, no paperwork, and replaced it with my favorite cup steaming with coffee. "Take a sip before you go in. He took a look at the Board this morning."

The Board. God, how I hate the Board. Away from client eyes, a large dry-erase board hung front and center on the largest wall in the agents' breakroom. Every agent noted their clients' names, the sales prices and the closing dates on this board. Every agent, that is, except me. When you haven't had a client in weeks, you can't put anything on the Board. And Herbert hated it when an agent's name wasn't on the Board with at least one pending sale and many more listings.

"You know you don't have to bring me coffee, Myra. You're the receptionist, not anyone's gopher." I blew on the steam rising from my Buffy the Vampire Slayer mug and sent her an appreciative smile. "But I'm glad you do."

Myra's dark eyes twinkled and she tossed her head, making her mousy brown hair bounce. Her generous bosom peeked out from her skin-tight blouse and her skirt hugged her womanly hips. She rolled her eyes at me and pretended we didn't have this same conversation almost every day. "You know I only fetch brew for my BFF and, of course, the boss." She glanced in his direction and back to me. "One of these days I'm gonna stop playing doting secretary for the Herb and tell him to use his coffee for his next colonoscopy."

Herbert H.—yes, the second *H* also stood for Herbert— glowered at me from the door of his office. He fisted his hands on the hips of his frail body and narrowed his eyes at me. Did he really think the stance would give him an air of intimidation? It didn't, but we all let him think it did.

Myra yanked the bottom of her pink shirt down over the roll of her stomach, creating a *clackety-clack* sound from the chunky jewelry she loved. "Better go and get it over with. Try not to vanquish him like one of those demons you hunt—unless you call me first and let me watch."

I shushed her and checked the agents sitting closest to us to see if they'd overheard. "Watch it, Myra. You know you shouldn't say anything about you know what."

"Sorry." Sensing I needed it, she placed her hand on my shoulder and gave me a little push toward Herbert. "Good luck."

Herbert saw me heading his way, retreated into his office and closed the blinds. All eyes, as well as a few sympathetic looks, turned my way. Everyone knew what the closed blinds meant. Those closed blinds shouted, "Hey, everyone! Get off the phone. Jennifer's about to get her weekly ass-chewing."

You'd think I'd have gotten used to the lecture by now. And, I guess, part of me had. Yet another part of me couldn't get over the fact of someone, especially Herbert Swindle, speaking to me as though I was a poor relative he had to keep on the payroll. I was no poor relative to anyone, much less to Herbert Swindle. Nonetheless, I took a big breath and stepped into his office. "Did you want to see me, Herbert?"

His beady eyes zeroed in on me, registering the use of his first name instead of the more respectful "Mr. Swindle" he told everyone to call him. "Close the door, Jennifer."

I followed his direction and pivoted to smile at him. I had to smile so I wouldn't lose control and clobber him. "Sure thing. How are you today? Everything going well at home? The little missus happy and healthy?"

I hated calling Mildred Swindle the "little missus", but I knew Herbert liked the phrase. Supposedly, he thought of it as a term of endearment. *Bleck!*

"Never mind my personal life. What do you think you're doing? Or should I say *not* doing?" He lowered his scrawny butt onto the huge leather chair and leaned his elbows on the enormous desk in front of him.

My gaze traveled to the framed picture on the wall behind him. Two mini-spotlights focused on the shrine-like photo of Herbert standing next to the Donald, shaking his hand and grinning at the world. I tried not to, but I couldn't help but compare his comb-over to Donald Trump's hairstyle. Would I soon be hearing those same fateful words "you're fired" from Herbert's mouth?

"You haven't had a listing on the Board for weeks. Have you decided not to pursue a career in real estate?"

Oh, how I wished! But I couldn't let him know I didn't care a lick about real estate. How could selling a house to an aging businessman and his young trophy wife compare to saving the world from bloodsucking, soul-taking predators? "I'm sorry, Mr. Swindle." He loved it when anyone played the deference card and addressed him by his last name. As if I actually respected him! I often wondered how such a big ego could fit in such a wimpy body. "I guess it's taking me awhile to get back in the groove. You know how it is." *Not.*

"If I'd known you'd go into such a major slump, I would've thought twice about letting you take the time off."

I clenched my hands together and silently repeated my mantra. *I don't kill mortals. I don't kill mortals. I don't kill mortals.* Yet even then my brain chanted back, "*Just this one time. Just this one time.*" He droned on and on, but at least the convo in my head kept me from hearing his words.

"However, I am a kind and fair leader."

The clue for me to pay attention jolted me out of my head and into the lecture. Whenever he started referring to himself as a "kind and fair leader", I knew the speech was almost over. He raised his eyebrows as if waiting for a response.

"Oh, uh, yes. Yes, you are."

One eyebrow lowered while the other one arched higher.

I knew he wanted me to say the words. "I mean, yes, you are a kind and fair leader." My mouth tasted as if I'd taken a bite of dog poop. I had to resort to my Protector training not to hurl on top of his desk. How I wanted to make him pay for my humiliation. Surely unleashing one young demon on him wouldn't cause too much damage, would it?

"Good." The stern employer morphed into a benevolent one, albeit an insincere one. "I'm sorry to have to speak harshly to you, Jennifer, but this is a business I'm running."

I nodded and turned to the door, but he wasn't ready for me to escape.

"Jennifer?"

I closed my eyes for a moment before facing him again. Shit, this couldn't be good. "Yes?"

"I've scheduled an open house for tomorrow. The details are on your desk."

When I opened my mouth to object, he beat me to the punch. "No, no, no need to thank me. As the owner of the agency, I feel it's my responsibility to help my agents whenever I can. This will give you a listing on the Board."

I clamped my mouth shut knowing I couldn't reject his offer. "I appreciate it, boss." I shot him a thumb's up and spun around for the door. Trust me. No one could have gotten out of the office faster than I did.

୬

"Damn, how I hate that place. Three hours sitting in a cubicle at Swindle Realty is pure torture. Herb wouldn't let me out of his sight until the clock struck six o'clock exactly."

"I understand old Herb put a bee up your butt, but it's no reason to get us both splattered on the pavement." Partner sounded a series of beeps as if sending out a warning signal. "Slow down, darlin'."

"How about calling me Jenn. I'm starting to feel like I'm trapped in a Clint Eastwood movie." I risked a quick glimpse at the device on the passenger seat even though I was surrounded by harried rush-hour drivers willing to risk an accident to get home five minutes early.

"Sure, Jenn. No pro-blame-o."

Within minutes, I'd pulled off the highway and navigated the neighborhood streets leading me home. The closer I got to home, however, the more I wondered—aloud, of course—about the message Blake had left on my office phone. "Blake has a surprise waiting for me at home. I can't imagine what it could be." I checked the screen. "Do you know?"

"Sorry, not a clue. Don't newlyweds give presents to each other during the first few months of marriage?" Partner's cowboy image twirled a lasso over his head. "Like a new dress or a pretty calf?"

Calf? Why would anyone want a cow in the city? "I guess so." I frowned. "Then again, how would I know? I've never been married before."

"I reckon you'll find out soon enough."

I whipped my Jag into the driveway, punched the garage door opener and pulled into my side of the garage. "Yes, I reckon I will." Hopping out of the car, I waited for the reaction I knew would follow.

"Hey! What about me?" A few clicks and beeps demonstrated his irritation.

"You're staying in the car. I don't want you talking out of turn. How would I explain a country-talkin', interactive phone to Blake?" Tossing my purse over my shoulder, I wiggled my fingers in a quick goodbye and started toward the garage entrance to the house.

"What if I'm afraid of the dark?"

Figures I'd get a neurotic machine as a partner. "Then you've got a long night ahead of you. Unless you'd rather I shut you down?"

An angry buzzing sound left no doubt how Partner felt about my question. "Never mind. I'll sleep in the car."

"Good thinking."

I passed through the laundry room and into the kitchen. "Blake? I'm home." When I didn't find him in the dining nook, I dropped my purse on the table and kept going. If he'd followed his normal routine, I'd find him in his office. I hurried in that direction but, hearing voices, I slowed my pace. I couldn't make out the words, but the tones were clear. I inched my way closer to the living room. Although I paused just outside the doorway, fully intending to snoop, guilt got my feet moving again.

"Jenn." Blake stood by the fireplace in the spacious yet cozy room, next to a man who bore an uncanny resemblance to my sexy husband.

"Oh, I'm sorry." The stranger and I stared at each other, sizing one another up. I waited for an introduction until, finally, I had to force one. "I didn't realize you had company. Are you a business associate of Blake's?" I stuck out my hand for the handsome man to take and moved toward him, hand still extended.

"Honey, this is my brother, Michael."

What Is This? A Soap Opera?

I'm not sure which one dropped first, my hand or my jaw, but it was a close race. *His brother?* Until now, Blake hadn't mentioned any relatives, much less a heartthrob of a brother. Who next? A long-lost alcoholic mother and a slutty twin sister?

"Honey, are you okay?" Blake left his brother standing by the fireplace and moved to my side. His touch on my elbow brought me out of my shock.

"Um, yeah. Yeah, I'm fine. I'm a little surprised is all." Oh, yeah, I was surprised. Surprised as in knocked off my feet. I've seen headless mummies, decomposing demons, gutted ghouls and other horrendous things in my career, but an unknown brother showing up out of nowhere beat them hands down. "Your brother. Who knew?" *Really. Who knew? Not me!*

Michael widened a familiar-looking grin and nodded. "I'm guessing Blake didn't mention me much."

Try not at all. "Nope. Not much."

His gray eyes sparkled with mirth, reminding me of Blake's. His dark hair, worn shorter than Blake's, had the same slight cowlick over the right side of his forehead. No one could mistake them for anything except brothers. Why I hadn't grasped the resemblance faster was beyond me.

"Our family's not big on get-togethers." He locked eyes with Blake, then dropped his gaze. Michael's smile weakened. "Plus, we haven't stayed in touch over the past few years, which I admit was mainly my fault."

The expression I caught on Blake's face made my heart lurch. Gone was the delight I'd noticed minutes earlier. Instead, I realized their past held a secret that had kept my husband from telling me about his brother. Yet how could I get angry at him for keeping a secret? Hiding my own secrets meant not having the right to get mad about his.

"Michael's going to join us for dinner." The happiness I'd seen earlier reappeared on Blake's features and in his body language.

"Oh, sure. Great." Like I could say anything else? Besides, I wanted time to get to know my new-found brother-in-law. I slapped on a pleasant expression and morphed into Susie Homemaker. "I can't promise the dinner will be tasty, but I'll do my best to mix up something edible. Of course, you may have to sign a release promising not to sue me when you get violently ill." I laughed at my own joke and Blake joined me.

Michael's expression told me he'd already guessed I wouldn't give Rachel Ray any cause to worry about her cooking empire, and he didn't care. Yet I kept the sappy smile on my face and turned toward the kitchen.

"How about pouring us some wine, honey?"

I stumbled a bit at Blake's unusual request, but managed to keep going. Well, what did I expect? Act like a dutiful wife and I'd get treated like a dutiful wife. "Coming up, sweetheart." The "sweetheart" was a nudge to let Blake know not to take this chauvinistic husband thing too far.

"Want some help?"

Ah, there was the Blake I knew and loved. My tone softened, letting him off the hook. "No, no. You stay with Michael. I'm sure you two want to catch up."

I hurried through the sitting room, pushed through the kitchen door and made for the refrigerator. Luck was with me. I opened the freezer section and found a family-size frozen dinner of lasagna. Silently thanking Blake for having added the item during his last trip to the grocery store, I tossed the plastic container into the microwave and punched away. Now all I needed to do was throw together a salad and I'd have dinner served in no time.

I selected a bottle from the wine rack over the counter, then took three of our best wine glasses from the cupboard. I removed the cork and poured the ruby liquid into the glasses. I didn't know if this wine was a good vintage or not, but I figured it couldn't be too bad since Blake had chosen it. He knew his wines and chose only the best. Me? I wouldn't know a good wine from a jug of food-colored beer.

I took a sip and wondered again why Blake had never mentioned a brother. Although I was fairly certain I owned most of the skeletons in our closet, I couldn't shake the feeling that Blake's total was adding up fast.

I tore into the lettuce, added peppers, onions and mushrooms to the bowl. Even though I felt I should make home-made dressing, I decided Brother Michael could settle for store-bought version like the rest of us. Still, I tried compensating for my bottled vinaigrette by placing the wine on a silver tray to add a bit of class to the presentation. I pushed my shoulder to go through the swinging door and headed toward the living room.

Again, hearing their voices brought me up short. Gone were the irritated tones of the earlier conversation. Now I heard the anger in their lowered voices and I abruptly changed directions, sloshing the wine onto the floor. A stain on my new carpet, however, was the last thing on my mind. Instead of rushing for the spot cleanser, I cozied up to the nearest wall to eavesdrop.

"Michael, you can't go on like this." Even in a whisper, I could hear the pain and frustration in his tone.

"Will you back off? This is why I don't visit you. You can't change the past, man. Nothing you do can change what I am."

"But it's my fault. I'm the reason it happened to you."

I could hear the tremendous guilt Blake felt about his brother's problem—whatever his problem was. Putting the tray on the nearby bookcase, I peeked around the corner. Blake stood with his hands held in front of him in an imploring manner. Michael moved away from him to stand near the window.

"How it happened doesn't matter any longer. I'm fine with what I am."

What he was? I frowned and tried to understand why he'd used those specific words. Was *what* he was more important than *who* he was? Or was it merely a slip of the tongue?

"No, you're not."

Blake approached his brother, making Michael move away from him and in my direction. I held my breath and flattened my spine against the wall, hoping I hadn't gotten caught.

Deciding to go on the offensive, I snatched up the tray and stepped around the corner, into the room and into the conversation.

"Hey, you two. Having fun catching up?" I forced a smile as I scanned from my husband to his brother. "Dinner's in the oven and here's the wine." I purposely moved between the two of them and offered a drink to Michael.

"Uh, I'm sorry, Jenn. I can't stay." Michael glanced at Blake and quickly returned his attention to me. "I forgot about an appointment. I was telling Blake the same thing when you walked in."

I didn't have to fake my disappointment since I really wanted him to stay. How else would I find out what the problem was? Placing the drink tray on the large coffee table, I threw my husband a quizzical look and put on my best disappointed-but-optimistic expression. "Are you sure? Couldn't you reschedule? I mean, I haven't had time to get to know—"

"No, I'm sorry. We'll have to get acquainted some other night. If you'll invite me back, of course."

"Of course you're invited. You're Blake's brother. You're welcome in our home anytime." I heard a sound behind me and turned to wonder if my hubby had actually growled at me. "Blake?" But he wasn't paying attention to me. I whirled around to see my brother-in-law's image waver. Instead of a handsome young man, the image of a sickly mud-colored ghoul flashed before me. His rolls of fat dripped with slime and the chiseled face morphed into a fang-incrusted mouth with two beady eyes glaring above it. The vision lasted less than a second, but long enough for me to reach into my pocket for the small knife I always carried.

"Are you okay, Jenn? You look like you've seen a ghost."

Nope. A ghoul. But the image vanished, replaced by my good-looking brother-in-law who stared at me as if I'd grown a third boob. I shook my head to deny the ghostly sighting and to clear my head of the vision. Could I be hallucinating? Could I be mistaking an innocent mortal person for an evil creature, as I'd done with the priest? Not wanting my new-found in-law to think I was crazy, I laughed it off. "A ghost? Nope. Not me."

"Good to know." His grin warmed me almost as much as Blake's always did.

I hadn't seen a ghost. But had I seen a ghoul? And if I had, I'd made a crucial mistake. I'd invited him into my house at a later time. Even though Blake had undoubtedly done the same, I felt stupid for my mistake.

Everyone knows a vampire can't enter your home without an invitation, but not many people know the same holds true for ghouls. Either I'd hallucinated or I'd invited a real ghoul into my home. *Great. Just great.*

"Well, I'd better get going." Michael gave me one last searching look before wheeling around on his heel and heading toward the front door. Blake rushed after him leaving me to plop down on the couch and down a glass of wine. If I'd known what was going to happen next, I'd have chugged the whole damn bottle.

"Can we drop it?"

Blake placed the glass of wine on his nightstand and I decided this wasn't the time to remind him to use coasters. "Sure. No problem. We won't discuss the white elephant in the room. We won't discuss your brother and the obvious problem between you two." I made my best frown and hoped it would work like it had many times before when I'd wanted him to see things my way.

"Thanks, I'd appreciate it."

His tone was even yet, unlike every night since we'd met, he didn't lean over me to kiss me and wish me sweet dreams. Was this our first lovers' quarrel? "Don't you recognize sarcasm when you hear it?"

"Don't you recognize when a man doesn't want to talk anymore?"

Damn, where had this jerk come from? This wasn't the kind, good-natured man I'd married. I started to complain, but decided it wasn't worth it. Besides, didn't most couples have times when they couldn't stand each other? I chalked it up to the honeymoon's demise and sat on the end of the bed. Had we rushed into marriage? Maybe, but I wasn't giving up yet. I still loved the big lug even though I felt like braining him with a lamp.

"I'm sorry, Jenn. I didn't mean to snap at you."

He ran his fingertips through my hair and lifted my face,

forcing me to gaze up at him. Those charcoal eyes told me my sweet husband had returned and wanted to placate me. I've always liked being placated.

"It's all right. I know I'm pushing, but from the way you two were talking, a blind man could tell you guys have a problem."

Blake sat on the bed next to me and wrapped his arm around my waist. "Well, sure, a blind man could tell. The question is...could a deaf man?"

His jokes were usually pretty lame, but I liked them. I smothered a giggle and leaned into him. "Okay, I know I'm new at this married thing, but I'm guessing this is one of those times when a wife ought to butt out."

He nibbled on my earlobe, which relaxed and stimulated me at the same time. Yup, it's possible.

"And you have such a great butt." His hand slipped from my waist to cup my ample ass cheek. "In fact, everything about you is great." Pushing with his body, he put me on my back and snuggled next to me.

"Even my nosy nose?" I tugged on his shirt and it was gone before I knew it. My pants followed shortly after, along with the rest of our clothes. He always did have a magic touch for getting my clothes off before I realized what had happened.

"Especially your nose." His thumb rubbed my erect nipple and scoured the rest of my body with his hot gaze. "Okay, maybe not especially your nose."

His mouth found mine and our tongues intertwined, making me sigh. Not being the shy type, I guided his hand to where I wanted his fingers to play. Spreading my legs, he obliged me, stroking my clit until my hips started squirming on their own.

"I need you, Jenn." He studied my reaction. "I'm not sure you know how much I need you."

Okay, it's a fact I'm not very proud of, but I'm not good in serious emotional conversations. Whenever a conversation starts heading down the paths of Serious Talk and Emotional Discussion, I tend to make a joke to lighten the mood. I mimicked Groucho Marx and glanced at his penis. "Uh, wrong, bucko. I can see how much you need me."

Sometimes my stupid jokes worked and sometimes they didn't. This time it worked.

"I sure do, Groucho." The somber expression in his eyes melted away, replaced by the twinkle I knew so well. "And let me say, you've gotten a whole lot better looking since you died."

"I guess being undead can do wonders for a person."

We both paused, caught off guard by my remark. One thing I didn't want to do was to talk about the undead. But what was Blake's reason for the strange expression on his face?

His odd expression didn't last long. Instead, he laughed and pulled me to him. Sliding on top of him, I positioned his shaft directly under the cleft in my legs and rubbed against him, teasing both of us. But, knowing neither one of us could withstand the temptation too long, I stretched my body over his and placed my breasts—the size of which I've already detailed—above his mouth. He took full advantage of their proximity.

I moaned and moved my breasts across his face. Like a man bobbing for breasts, he tried to catch one of my nipples with his mouth. Fortunately for me, he's very good at playing catch. I sat back, lowering myself onto his shaft and wiggled against his pulsating probe, rising far enough to make him think I would allow him entry.

"Stop teasing me, woman."

"Woman? Say my name the way I like you to say it and maybe I'll be your woman."

"You *are* my woman." He trailed his tongue over my nipple as if marking his territory. "Jenn." The low sexy growl of his tone banked the fire inside me.

"Then show me. Grab my ass and make me yours."

He growled and followed my order. Taking each cheek—the ones without the blush on them—he pushed me high enough for his oh-so-talented shaft to enter me. At the feel of him shoving deep inside me, I sat up, placing my hands on his chest to enjoy the sensation of his hard-muscled pecs. Our combined humping made my breasts bounce and jiggle and his gaze seared their mark on them.

I admit it. I like being on top. Riding a man is more fun, more pleasurable than riding anything else I can name. Even my jag. And Blake is one helluva ride.

I rocked back and forth, up and down, and clenched the muscles of my vagina. He decided tasting wasn't enough and took my bouncing breasts in his hands. Simply by watching the passion in his face, I climaxed more times than I could count. Blake, however, was a pro at holding his own and I could see the determination in his face.

Once again my juices spilled over him and I tensed up, threw my head back and shouted the Big O to the world. Blake climaxed along with me, his voice mixing with mine. Collapsing against him, I smiled like a happy female who knows her life can't get much better. Who could ask for more than a great man and a fulfilling job? Or was it a great job and a fulfilling man? Hell, put a horny, sexy man underneath me and I'm in paradise. Nope, nix that. Put *this* horny, sexy man underneath me and I'd never ask for another thing in my entire life.

"Jenn?"

"Yeah?"

"I need to get that."

"Get what?"

"The phone." With a kiss to the top of my head, Blake slid me off him, scrambled to his side of the bed and grabbed the phone.

Although I knew the Society would never contact me via phone, I began making up reasonable-sounding excuses for getting an emergency buyer-wants-to-see-the-house call after hours.

"Hello? Yeah, it's me. What?"

I crawled closer to him and tried to overhear the other side of the conversation. Blake, however, gave me an irritated look and stood to move away from the bed. Sending him an expression of mixed emotions—hurt and confusion with an ounce of annoyance—I stayed where I was. After all, chasing him around the room wouldn't solve anything.

"Now?"

"Now what?"

He ignored my question and crossed to the other side of the room. "Okay, okay. I'm coming. I'll be there in twenty minutes. I, um, need to wrap up a bit of business here first." He clicked the phone off, tossed the receiver on top of the bed and started putting on his clothes.

A bit of business? Scooting off the bed, I crossed to the side chair and snatched up my robe to wrap it around me. Taking a deep, hopefully calming breath, I turned to take issue with the way my husband had described our lovemaking. "Oh, I didn't realize. Our making hot lusty sex is business now?" Okay, I knew I was being overly sensitive, but I didn't care. Using the word *business* to describe our sex would never be okay.

Blake moved toward the door, pausing to question my overreaction. "You're kidding, right? Come on, Jenn, I wasn't about to tell him I'd was in the middle of having sex with my wife. My gorgeous, understanding wife."

"Don't try flattering me. Who was on the phone? Why are you getting dressed? Where are you going?"

He took a step toward me and then reversed his direction. "I've got to meet with a client who needs some expert advice."

Was he joking? Nope. Blake didn't joke about business. *His* business, anyway. "A client? What kind of investment advice happens at night?" I hid the cringe I felt when I realized he was using an emergency after-hours client call like the one I'd started formulating in my mind. "You're not taking a client to a strip club, are you?"

"A strip club? Hey, not a bad idea."

I tossed a pillow at him. "Think again, big guy."

He caught it and tossed it over my head. "He's a very important client. And hey, investing never stops. Remember, lots of investors go for the overseas markets." He paused at the door and tilted his head toward the front of the house. "Someone's at the door. Can you grab it? I'm going out the back way."

I heard his steps as he headed toward the back of the house. Pulling my robe around me, I went the opposite direction.

Being the cautious type, I first peeked through the side glass panels next to the front door. Satisfied no demon—or another unmentioned relative—lurked on the other side, I pulled the door open, turned my back on the person standing there and walked into the living room. Of course Myra followed. My mind kept running Blake's excuse through my head and alarms pounded an accompanying rhythm.

"I know it's getting late and all, Jenn, but I couldn't help it. Look!"

Although I wasn't in the mood and my mind was totally

occupied with Blake, I whirled around to scan my friend's plump figure, odd-sixties-type clothing and excited face. What did she expect me to see? "I give. What am I supposed to look at?" Why was everyone playing games with me tonight?

Myra clucked her tongue at my lack of fashion sense and stuck out her arm. "Check out my new bangles. The new twenty-four-hour flea market on West Street is an absolute treasure. I bought all of this for only four dollars."

Although fashion isn't my thing, I tried to appear interested. A group of brightly colored bracelets jangled on her arm and each finger sparkled with a cheap ring. Myra was into cheap stuff, even if it turned her skin green. "Oh, hey, yeah. I love the, uh, rings." But Blake was all I could think about. "Oh, yeah, cool. Great."

My response wasn't what she'd wanted to see. Yet, being a good friend—a better friend than I was being to her—she took it in stride and noticed my preoccupation. "Are you okay, Jenn? You seem distracted." She moved closer, took my hand and led me to the couch. "Sheesh, I am such a nut. Here I come barging into your home and I don't even notice how bummed you are." She wrapped her arm around me in a comforting move. "Is it the Society? Is it your boss, Max?"

"Mac, not Max. And nope, this has nothing to do with the Society, or Mac, or my job."

"Oh. For a minute, I thought maybe you'd had a bad run-in with a gargoyle, or maybe a ghost or goblin." She tried to hide her hopefulness behind a fake sad face, but I knew her better. Myra dreamed of becoming a Protector one day and loved hearing about my exploits. She was the only non-Society person who knew about my alternate identity.

"No. Nothing that fun." My mind flashed to the glimmer of ghoulism Michael had shown, but I dismissed it again. Maybe I needed more time off. "Blake took off a minute ago. Supposedly, he's meeting with a client."

She bit her lip in consternation. "Sounds like you don't believe him."

The rush of uncertainty passed through me, putting my heart in a vise and my stomach in knots. "Which bring us to my problem. I feel like the worst wife in the world *because* I don't believe him."

Honey, Is That Lipstick on Your Collar?
Or Blood?

Blake came home around midnight, sneaking into the bedroom like a cheating husband who thinks he's fooling his wife. Turned away from the door and his side of the bed, I tried to tell myself pretending to sleep was my way of avoiding an argument. But the real reason was more *what if we do argue and I find out he really is one of those cheating husbands?*

Sleep, however, declined my invitation. Instead, I studied the shadows on the wall and contemplated the shadows lingering in my husband's life. I'm not sure how long I lay in the dark, listening to Blake's breathing and trying to decide if the dark shape at my window was made by a tree branch on the big oak outside, or from a goblin scrambling along the newly-installed aluminum siding on the house. Goblins loved aluminum for a reason unknown to the Society. However, the branch theory seemed more reasonable and I finally fell asleep for what amounted to a long nap.

As I said, I don't like having serious emotional conversations and would rather kick supernatural butt, so I woke up before daylight, took a quick shower, dressed and headed out of the house before Blake awakened. With a sinking heart, I slipped into the driver's side of the Jag and hit the garage door opener. I don't know why I thought I might wake up Blake. The man sleeps the sleep of the dead.

"Good morning, darlin'."

My responding jolt sent me toward the roof of the car. "Shit!"

"Are you all right? I didn't mean to startle you." Partner's flickering lights blinked a fast succession of red and green as if trying to decide if I was okay (green light) or not (red light).

I rubbed my head and picked Partner up to see the cowboy riding a beautiful black stallion. "I'd forgotten about you."

"Well, shoot. Thanks for making a pardner feel needed." His lights blinked off and the screen filled with the image of storm clouds.

Resting him on the passenger's seat again, I concentrated on maneuvering the car out of the garage and into the street. At the moment I started to cram my foot down on the accelerator, I noticed the curtains in Mrs. Hardgrave's house move, flashing a brief slash of light onto her front yard. "Oh, crap. How does she know when I'm about to gun my car? Doesn't she ever sleep?" Call it a professional hazard, but I immediately wondered if the old nosy body was an Otherworlder. Yet, aside from behaving much like Mrs. Kravitz from the old *Bewitched* television show, she seemed perfectly normal. "Naw, she's just weird and a pain. This one's for you, Madame Nosy!"

I squealed the tires knowing full well the old biddy would spread the word of my careless driving around the neighborhood by the time I made it home. Yet instead of telling everyone the time was five a.m., she'd no doubt say it happened at high noon with scores of children crossing the road. I didn't care. Saving the world took priority over squelching the scandals of Rose Hill Lane.

"Hey! Take it easy, darlin'. I don't have any hands to hold on for dear life, you know."

My snort was loud and clear. Although I realize a snort isn't the most ladylike reaction, it was the one that fit the situation. "If you're gonna ride shotgun with me, Partner, you're gonna have to learn to hang on."

"Easy for you to say. You get medical benefits. Me? I get thrown in the recycle bin at the main office."

"Yeah, but if your case gets cracked, all they have to do is download your information and upload it—you—into a new machine. If I crack my *case*"—I loved adding the finger quotes—"I'm out of commission for the long haul."

"True enough," he agreed with me and played a happy tune. "Darlin', you've got voicemail. Would you like me to play your latest message?"

Maneuvering my car onto the merge ramp, I watched for oncoming traffic, checked my blind spot and moved into the nearest lane. "Do I have a lot of messages? Never mind. Play the most important ones first."

"You have twenty-five messages, but they're all from the same person—your boss, Mr. Swindle. He wants—and I quote— 'your ass at the Madison Open House early this morning'. He said the Madisons left spur-of-the-moment on vacation yesterday and the place needs some cleanup before clients start arriving."

Normally getting stuck with an open house assignment would've ruffled my feathers big time, but I was actually glad for the excuse to stay away from my home and Blake. At least I was until I thought about how many pawn shops I could visit. Instead, I'd be stuck showing a rather average home to lookie-loos, unqualified buyers and neighbors who'd always wanted to see inside the Madison family home. Didn't they realize every house on the block was exactly the same?

"Dammit. I thought Wanda was the agent for this house." I pulled to the left, made a U-turn and headed back the way I'd come—away from all the pawn shops of Tulsa.

"She is. But Wanda's got a shitload of listings and, since you surveyed the home with her on the day it came on the market, he wants you to co-agent this one with her. He said you'd remember the lock box combination. If you sell the house, you'll get a portion of the commission." Partner made a whirring sound. "He said he's trying to help you get some money in your pocket and your name on the Board. He said you should thank him. He said—"

"Ack! Shut up. I don't want to hear another 'he said'." Taking a short cut I knew through a nearby subdivision, I tried to remember which road led to Piper Street and the Madison home. At last, a rooster-topped mailbox reminded me where to turn and I soon rolled into the driveway.

"Darlin', it's none of my business, but don't agents normally park their cars in the street? Leaving the driveway uncluttered makes the front of the house appear bigger, cleaner and more accessible. It's a little info I gathered from the database at the main office."

Picking him up and slipping him into my pocket, I

approached the front door, opened the lock box and retrieved the key. The first rays of the sunlight cast my shadow on the wall. "Are you seriously telling me how to do my job? My cover job, that is."

"'Course not, darlin'. I'm trying to be helpful, is all."

"If you want to help me, try calling some of my fellow agents to come and take over for me. I'm not spending a day here when I should be out scouring the shops for the Bracelet."

"Oh, are you making me your assistant?"

Partner's petulant tone put me in a sour mood.

Crossing over the threshold and into the foyer, I glanced around at the cluttered messy home. No wonder they wanted someone to clean up before the open house started. But since when did my job as a realtor involve working as a maid? "Start calling unless, of course, you've got a pair of hands to lend me."

I picked up a teddy bear and grimaced at the biggest wad of gum I'd ever seen stuck on the end of his nose. The disgusting stuffed animal could've passed for the underside of a school desk. "I bet Swindle volunteered my services as maid. I wouldn't put it past him to pull this kind of crap."

Somehow Partner made a few beeps sound like a chuckle before answering. "Too bad I can't help you with the hard labor. This is one time I like being a mechanical device and not a human assistant."

"Fine. Then if you'll excuse me, I've got some housecleaning to do." With a pat on my pocket for good measure, I went to work. Most of the time I stay as far away from housework as I can possibly manage. However, I have to admit I can wield a mighty vacuum when necessary and poor dust bunnies have no chance of surviving my onslaught. By the time the open house began, I had the entire house shipshape and more than presentable. My commission, as far as I was concerned, was already in the bank.

Five hours later, I was ready to use the overstuffed couch as a bonfire and walk away from the joint. I never again wanted to fake my excitement over the newly installed granite countertop or the matching stainless-steel appliances. And if I had to trot out the fantasy of the two staircases being the home's built-in stair-steppers, I'd end up barfing all over my freshly swept carpet.

Once the last unenthusiastic couple walked out the door, I flopped onto the sofa knowing I'd wasted an entire day not looking for the Bracelet. "Where the hell is Bellamy?" Partner had reached my fellow realtor, Bellamy, over two hours earlier and had garnered a promise to relieve me.

"You got me." A loud alarm rang out and lights flashed all over Partner. "Wait! He's here. I hear a car."

"It's about time." I launched my body off the sofa and dashed toward the front door. Swinging it open, I was ready to hug Bellamy. Instead, I nearly hugged a petite blonde woman whose surprised expression matched my own. "Oh! I'm sorry. I thought you were someone else."

She giggled one of those sweet little-girl giggles that was way too young-sounding for her age. A handsome man stood beside her with his arm wrapped protectively around her. "This is the open house, right? I hope we're not too late."

My heart thudded to my stomach. Not only wasn't this Bellamy, but I was stuck giving another tour. Oh, how I wanted to say, "This house is basically built like a box cut up into four rooms on the ground floor and three bedrooms on the second floor. It's like every house on the block—boring and unimaginative." Yet, being the good realtor I am—not a word!—I kept my trap shut and let the practiced smile spread wide. I'd kill my tardy associate, Bellamy, the first second he walked through the door. The he'd really be the *late* Bellamy.

"Hi. I'm Jennifer Randall-Barrington, the agent on duty, and you've come to the right place. Are you two looking for a new home?" Granted, the question was stupid and the answer was obvious, but it usually worked to get them talking. Right now I wanted them to talk fast and walk even faster—right out of here.

"We just decided to start house hunting this morning, in fact." He gave up his armrest around his wife to offer me his hand. "Hi. I'm Ryan Wallis and this is my wife, Judy." His smile said it before his words did. "We're newlyweds and living in an apartment, but Judy decided today was the day."

Judy looked past me and her eyes grew wide. Squealing, she scurried past me and into the house. "Ryan, it's wonderful. Look at the crown molding. Isn't it special?" She hugged herself and twirled. An almost maniacal gleam filled her expression, making me inwardly cringe.

I followed her gaze to the ceiling. Special? If a molding anyone could find at the local home improvement store could be called special, then I guess it was special.

Ryan grinned sheepishly at me and followed his wife. "Yeah, I guess." Judy continued to swirl around the room, exclaiming over almost everything. "I'm sorry. I know we're supposed to get pre-qualified and all but since I didn't know we were looking yet..." He shrugged and watched his wife moon over the ditsy flowered wallpaper in the dining room. "The idea came up rather suddenly."

"Don't worry about it. We can get you pre-qualified in no time." *Sheesh, how I hate people who don't get their finances in line before looking at houses.* Judy was still rushing around the house, but I couldn't get over how jerky her movements were. Could the woman have arthritis? Yet my mind wandered. Could there be another reason? I considered every option, trying to keep my suspicions in check, especially since my hunches had led me into making the wrong conclusions several times. "Have you two been married long?"

I tried not to, but I still kept coming back to my best guess. Judy was a zombie.

Forget what you know about zombies from the movies. Zombies can take on the appearance of ordinary humans. In fact, they can retain their human appearance for days at a time if they're an old and ancient mummy. Unless you get lucky and catch them in their decaying outer skin, the only way to tell if someone is a mummy in human guise is to watch their jerky, arthritic-like uncontrollable movements. Movements exactly like Judy's.

"Not long. In fact, only a few weeks. Judy and I had a whirlwind romance and she swept me off my feet." The loyal hubby must've caught me scrutinizing his wife, felt the need to explain and lowered his voice. "Judy has Parkinson's disease."

I turned to the young man, who seemed unsure of his decision to explain, and let him know he hadn't betrayed his wife by telling me. "I understand." Deciding to accept his explanation over my own suspicion, I hurried to change the subject to safer territory. "A quick marriage, huh? I hear those are getting more popular." Like my own quick marriage, in fact, but I didn't feel like sharing my love story with him or his oddball wife. I frowned and wondered why I didn't like the woman. Everything about her seemed very personable and friendly, and her odd movements were no longer a mystery. So why did she give me the creeps?

"Really?" Ryan ran a hand over the nape of his neck. "Yeah. We love each other. A lot."

The young man didn't sound as confident about his marriage as he obviously wanted to be. I gave him an encouraging smile.

He continued to follow his still-moving wife, but his smile faded. "She wants what she wants when she wants it and not a minute later. Right now, she wants a house."

Ah, there's the problem. Hubby got hitched before he knew wifey-poo was an overindulgent, selfish, high-maintenance bee-atch. But that wasn't my problem. I nodded, forcing myself to retain a steady smile on my face. Every chance I got, however, I glanced out the windows hoping Bellamy would show. Getting away from this woman and out doing my real job would make me very happy.

"Is there a basement?"

Judy's question brought me around to her again. "Uh, yes, there is. Although it's not finished." Swindler's voice echoed in my head, telling me to never point out the negatives in a home. Shoot, a house could have skeletons hanging from the light fixtures and he'd tell everyone to admire the "creative decorative style". I hurried to turn my negative statement into a positive. "But unfinished is good because it means you can fix it to meet your exact needs. Come on. I'll show you."

Judy clapped her hands and acted like I'd dropped the price of the house twenty grand. Oh, well, there's nothing like an enthusiastic buyer. Taking her reaction as a sign of my persuasive prowess, I motioned for them to follow me. If I was stuck at an open house, why not try to sell it?

I was at the door to the basement when Ryan's cell phone rang. He held up a finger and waved us to go on. With the perky bride in tow, I flipped on the lights below us and started down the steps. I ended up at the bottom in two seconds flat. Unfortunately, I hadn't intended to take the stairs in record time. But that's what happens when someone pushes you from behind.

Landing on the cold cement floor, I kept rolling straight into a supporting post. "Argh! Dammit!"

Fortunately, however, I glanced up in time to see sweet Judy throwing herself toward me. With a silent thanks to my personal trainer, I threw my body out of her path of destruction and scrambled to my feet. "What the hell?"

"Exactly. We'd love to have you join us in Hell, Protector."

Sweet little Judy went from future PTA Mom of the Year to Queen of the Damned in a split second. She let out an ear-splitting scream and slammed her body into mine with enough forward momentum to send us tumbling backward.

Her hands wrapped around my neck, cutting off my breath, and I struggled to breathe. For a second, I forgot my self-defense course and tried to yank her hands off my neck. She laughed a high-pitched giggle and held on. Fortunately, my training finally kicked in and I went into action. I brought my knee hard into her gut, then locked my hands together, bringing my arms up between hers and breaking her chokehold on me. She fell backward and I staggered to the side, trying to get away from her long enough to gather both my wits and my breath.

"Darlin', what the cowbells are you doing?" Partner's question reminded me of his presence in my pocket. "Are you trying to break me?"

"Shut up, Partner. I'm a bit busy."

Zombie Judy's screech of rage, however, warned me of her next attack and I launched a nearby box at her. She blocked the box and I scurried toward the corner of the basement where the lawn equipment was kept. She snarled at me. The dim light filtering into the room slashed across her transformed face. Gone was the innocent face of Judy. Instead, I stared at the decaying face of a zombie. Rotting skin hung from the skull and evil eyeballs clung to the eye sockets with thin tendons. Puss oozed from her mouth and her nose, or what was left of them, and a wicked smile let her toothless gums show.

"You're going to die, Protector, and I'm going to eat your brains with my bare hands."

The image of the perfect suburban housewife flipping through cookbooks for a quick and easy dish of Protector

Brains, then mixing ingredients into my chopped up cranium flashed through my mind. Sometimes my imagination is way too vivid for my own good.

"Jenn, you'd better take care of this thing before someone gets eaten and I end up in the hands of the Otherworld." Partner's cowboy accent was gone, replaced by an irritated, slightly frightened tone.

"Wha'dya think I'm trying to do?" Keeping one eye on the approaching zombie, I searched the area around me, hoping to find an axe or hoe of some kind. "Hey, maggot-face. Your skin's looking pretty dry. Maybe you should get some heavy-duty lotion." I feigned a dramatic gasp. "Are those wrinkles I see?"

"Ooh, me-ow. Good one, Jenn."

Her unworldly cackle raised the hairs on my arms. "Before you die, you're going to tell me where the Bracelet is. Then I'll break your gadget into a million pieces and see you in Hades."

"Hopefully, in that order, right?" Partner's voice pitched a little higher.

Her demand told me two important facts. First, the Otherworld didn't have the Bracelet. Secondly, they thought I knew where it was. But why? Hadn't they heard it'd been stolen from the Society? Why would they think I knew where it was? I'd been on my honeymoon at the time of the robbery.

I shook my head and edged toward a shovel leaning against the wall. "Uh, thanks, but no thanks. I'm not much on traveling, although I'd love to send your evil tight-ass back to Hell." My hands closed over the handle of the shovel at the same moment I heard Ryan.

"Judy? How's the basement look?" He had his head down, watching his steps as he descended the stairs. "Is it big enough to convert to a mother-in-law suite? I'm sure my mom would love to visit us in the—"

His gaze fell on his wife and his words died a quick death. Confusion, then horror, spread over his features. Watching his gaze travel from her face to her familiar clothes, then to her face again, I knew he was desperately trying to find a safe harbor on Denial Island. His boat, however, sank.

Zombie Judy screamed at him, spitting bits of phlegm in her rage. Yet even zombies can figure out who is the greater threat. Ignoring her nearly comatose hubby, she whirled toward me. I swung the shovel, striking the edge against the side of her neck. Thanks to the dedication of the homeowner in keeping his tools sharp, the shovel sliced through her skin and bones, decapitating her in one swift move. Zombie Judy's head flew off her body and thudded against the floor. A gargling sound accompanied the flood of bile spilling out the open end of her neck and onto her shoulders. Still screeching, the head rolled to the foot of the stairs. "Ryan, you asshole!"

Ryan shrieked at the talking severed head, his hands outstretched as if to ward off the gruesome sight his mind couldn't grasp. He must've shrieked for five minutes—at least two minutes longer than was necessary. Without warning, his body seemed to fold in on itself, slumping to a sitting position on a step and silencing the dreadful wailing. His glassy eyes locked onto his wife's head, but I knew he wouldn't have to stare at her for long. With one last screech, Judy's head and body exploded, sending zombie dust into the air. Gray zombie bits settled on his clothes and face, but Ryan didn't move an inch. The man was out of it.

I threw down the shovel and eased my way over to sit beside Ryan. "Mr. Wallis? Ryan?" Getting no response, I went for reinforcements. "Partner, send for the Psych Squad fast. I don't want Bellamy showing up to find a prospective buyer in a catatonic state. I mean, the house isn't great, but it's not bad enough to drive a buyer into shock."

"Oh, ha-ha, Jenn. Funny. Not. And I already called them. They should be here in a few minutes." Partner clicked and beeped in an excited electronic way. "Hoo-wee, what a fight. Does this happen to you a lot, darlin'?"

I slid him out of my pocket to check out his screen. Sure enough, the hunky cowboy was jumping up and down in glee. "Partner, most cowboys don't jump up and down like an overly spirited cheerleader. And yeah, these things happen, although I try to use my head more than my fists in defeating the scum of the world."

"Anyone down there?"

I looked up to where three people blocked the doorway. I assumed—okay, hoped—they were the Society's Psych Squad and not another group of lookie-loos. "Yeah. You guys are quick. Providing you're who I'm waiting for."

Without changing his dour expression, the bigger guy reached into his pocket and flashed a Society badge. "You can check with the main office first if you'd rather. I'm Agent Dumsy." He gestured at the man and woman behind him. "This is Agent Jones and Agent Tranton."

I smiled and nodded at them. Agents were Protectors who'd undergone a traumatic experience, rendering them "unreliable" in the field. As such, they were often very sensitive to any perceived slights from their fellow Protectors who remained on active duty. After the mistakes I'd made, I was lucky I hadn't been kicked down to agent status.

The other two agents nodded their greeting, but kept silent. Any other time, I probably would've checked their identities, but I was worried about Bellamy showing up at the wrong time. "Nope. You guys look good to me."

The two men moved toward Ryan, followed by Agent Tranton, who carried a metal briefcase.

I stepped aside to give them access to the shocked man. "Unfortunately, he saw his zombie wife go up in dust."

Agent Dumsy eyed me up and down. "Did you ever think about exterminating her where he couldn't see?"

What a jerk! I shot him the same condescending smirk in return. The jerk had obviously screwed up enough to get demoted and here he had the nerve to criticize me. "I didn't have time to choose the setting. She came at me and caught me off guard." Off guard was putting it lightly. She'd caught me totally unprepared even after my alarms bells had started ringing. I hadn't trusted my instincts and it had almost cost me my life.

He *harumphed* and glanced around the basement. "Did you two fight anywhere else in the house?"

I really didn't like this guy. "Nope, we kind of liked hanging out in the basement. You know, just us girls exchanging laundry tips." Ignoring his sneer, I gestured toward the pile of dust on the floor. "This shouldn't take much cleanup. Ryan's mainly the reason I called you. This is Ryan Wallis and his zombie wife's name was Judy. They are, er, were house-hunting newlyweds after a whirlwind romance."

Agent Tranton popped open her case and began taking photos of Ryan, the basement and the pile of Judy, er, dust.

"Good. The shorter the time they've been together, the easier it is to cover our tracks. But ya gotta wonder. How does a man not realize his wife is a zombie? She's got to have given him clues along the way. Clues and catching her out of her human form."

Agent Jones snorted. "I'll say. What kind of dumb-ass marries an Otherworlder and doesn't realize it? I mean, how stupid is this guy?"

Something inside me wanted to smack Jones upside the head. Ryan may not have been the brightest guy on the block, especially since he didn't know he'd married a zombie, but he deserved more respect than this. After all, the average man and woman of this world had no clue zombies existed. By the time I'd thought of the appropriate reprimand, however, they were all business.

"This should be fairly routine." Agent Jones passed me to squat next to the dust pile. After retrieving a test tube from his pocket, he scooped up some dust and recapped the tube. "We'll reconstruct his wife with this DNA—sans the zombie chromosomes, of course."

I paced to the side of the basement to get out of their way. I'd seen this situation all too often, yet I couldn't help but think of how Ryan's life had changed. Whenever a civilian witnessed an extermination, the Society would send them into reprogramming where all knowledge of the Society and the event would be wiped from their memory. Usually, it was an uncomplicated procedure. However, when a civilian witnessed the death of someone involved in his own life, the procedure got sticky. The Society had to replace the missing person without anyone noticing the switch.

"Be sure you get it right this time." Usually it wasn't a smart idea to tell the Psych Squad how to do their job—considering their easily bruised egos—but I wanted to make certain Ryan's new wife would be perfect. "The last clone you placed in a civilian's life went berserk and ended up killing the family's grandmother. Now we've got a clone inside a prison making license plates for life."

All three agents stopped their work to glare at me. But it was Agent Dumsy who snarled a response. "One lousy time. We get one wrong one frickin' time and you Protectors won't let it go."

I held up my hands in supplication. "Whoa. Sorry. I didn't mean to push your button. It's just, well, Ryan seems like a nice guy. In fact, maybe you could do him one better and make his new wife less demanding and selfish."

"We'll see what we can do." Agent Tranton finished with taking photos and held a small needle in front of Ryan's eyes. After one quick injection between his eyes, she pocketed the device. "Come on, Ryan. We're going to take care of you. Don't you worry about a thing."

Agent Tranton glanced at me and I was pretty sure she'd meant the remark for both Ryan and me. "Thanks." She and I shared another look. "Thanks for taking care of him."

"No problem." She started up the stairs with Ryan moving mechanically by her side. After shooting me a disgruntled sneer, Agent Dumsy motioned for Agent Jones to follow.

"Hey, Jennifer."

I glanced past the agents and saw Roger Bellamy at the top of the steps. "Oh, hi, Roger."

He stepped aside to let the agents and Ryan make it to the top and turn to head down the hallway. "I'm sorry I'm late, but traffic was a bitch. Were those potential buyers? Do you think they'll buy?"

I opened my mouth to speak and nothing came out. What was I supposed to say? *Yeah, you bet. I sold the house to a lovely man and his zombie wife.* Yeah, right.

He Loves Me for My Mind. Really!

"Blake!"

My husband grabbed me from behind and tossed me on top of the dining table, sending me into giggles.

"I'm hungry, woman!" Baring his teeth like some demented caveman—the real kind, not the Geico kind—Blake tore open my shirt and lightly bit my abdomen with his teeth. I tried, unsuccessfully, to stop laughing.

"Watch it. We're talking designer duds, mister." Yet I couldn't have cared less about my loss of wardrobe. Hey, I ain't not fool. If the man of my life wanted to wiggle me out of my pants, then I wasn't about to stop him. My lacy thong followed. "What do you think you're doing?" Grasping his shirt, I tried to rip it off, but with no luck. Instead, Blake tugged it over his head.

"I've been waiting for you to come home for hours. What's Swindle doing to you? Chaining you to a desk so clients can pass by and taunt you with unsigned contracts?" He ran his tongue over my breast and started shedding more of his clothes.

"Urgh. Do not—I repeat—do not ever say his name with your head pressed between my boobs. Such a mood killer." I swept a placemat off the table. "Want to find the bedroom?"

"Grrrr." Keeping his face at the hollow between my breasts, he shook his head in an unmistakable refusal. "No."

Table linens and the rest of the placemats flew off the table. Pushing me flat onto the cool, smooth surface, he groaned and kept his hold on me. My body, primed and ready for action, leapt to the call of his mouth on my nipples. And to think I'd stayed away from him all day.

After the incident at the Madison house, I'd spent the rest of the day checking a few more pawn shops, all with no luck. But at least now I knew the Underworld didn't have the Bracelet, and their massive army was one less zombie. Sometimes you have to take the small victories where you can.

His fingers toyed with my clit, making me squirm with a mixture of frustration and pleasure. I gripped his hair and pushed him down. "Eat me, Blake. I need you to suck me dry."

His chuckle answered me and he slid down to the end of the table, eager to please me. "Let me taste what's on your sexy plate." Landing on the end chair, he tugged me toward him until my "sexy plate" was ready to serve up to his mouth. Spreading my folds as he'd spread my legs, Blake raked his tongue over my wetness in a slow, deliberate move. "Hmm. Good."

Murmuring encouragement, I twisted to watch him. Then I reached around me and tried to grasp the polished mahogany. He buried his face in between my legs and I closed my eyes, focusing my attention on the sensation of his lips and hands on my body. "This is—oh, shit!—what I call a real—oh, oh!—meal."

He lifted his face long enough to quip, "A full-course dinner with dessert served first."

I started to laugh, but laughing is very hard when your whole body is pounding with sexual tension. Blake's hands found my breasts, squeezing them with each lick and nip. Loving the feel of his big hands possessing me, I closed my hands over his, keeping him there.

A shudder rippled through me with a climax and I yelled for more. Writhing under his control, I felt the fire of lust course through me. Vaguely, I wondered if my heart could actually beat out of my chest, breaking through bone and flesh to land on the floor. If it did, the loss would still be worth the ecstasy I was enjoying. "Now, Blake. I—I—can't take—it—any longer. Take me, Blake. *Now*. Please."

A growl escaped him—a deep, tortuous sound I'd never heard from him before—and he slipped his hands under my back to yank me to a sitting position. His nostrils flared and the heat in his eyes burned into me.

For a moment, I was afraid. Why? Because for a second, my husband's growl sounded a bit like the growl of a demon.

Okay, more than a bit.

His mouth traced a hot path from the tip of my shoulder to the soft spot at the base of my throat, and I tossed my silly thoughts aside. My instincts had been right about Judy, but this was different. After all, this was my husband. Still, a tiny spark of worry nestled into the dark corners of my mind.

Without waiting to grab some protection, Blake rammed into me and I forgot everything else except the feel of his shaft moving in and out in long strokes. I tugged him closer, wanting to be so close I'd fit inside his body, and clutched my hands to the hard muscles of his torso. My ridiculous suspicion reared its head again when, only for a split second, I thought I'd run my fingers over rough, scaly skin. Demon-like skin. Yet I knew my mind had to have imagined it because, once again, I felt the slick, sweat-soaked skin of my husband's back.

Knock it off, Jenn. Get a grip on yourself. Blake is your husband. He's anything but a demon. I kept the self-reprimand going for awhile until I pulled away from him to see his face.

Taking deep breaths, I managed to loosen the anxious knot in my stomach. I gazed into the face of my loving, sexy, very mortal husband right before he closed his eyes and tensed for his release. We met each other's thrust and climaxed together.

Afterward, we leaned on each other and supported our tired yet satisfied bodies. "We had sex on the dining table. Oh. My. God. Where will we end up next?" Since our return from our honeymoon, we'd christened the living room sofa, the kitchen counter, the shower and—well, you get the picture. Yet Blake kept coming up with other places to break our sexual bottle on to christen our new home. Hey, I wasn't about to complain.

"Want to jump in the shower together?" His sly smile spoke volumes for his rejuvenation abilities.

"You are insatiable." I wiped the sweat from his brow with my fingertip. "And I love it. And you, too."

"Ditto."

He grinned because he knew what I would think about his reply. I scowled at him. We watch one lousy chick flick together and he picks up that one-word response to use. Not "You complete me" or even "Love is never having to say you're sorry". Nope. He uses "Ditto". Thanks for nothing, Patrick Swayze.

Blake tugged me toward the bedroom. "Come on. Let's see

how much steam we can make."

As much as I wanted to heat up the shower with my sexy hubby, I figured I'd better get Partner out of my pocket and into the car for the rest of the night. Then I could really get busy with Blake. "I'll be there in a sec, but I've got to check on something first. You go on up and get things started. Hey!"

Blake swiveled around and I nearly forgot what I was going to ask when I saw his probe at full alert. The man was a sex machine. "Yeah?"

"Uh, I..." *What had I planned to say?* "Oh, yeah. I meant to ask. Have you heard from Michael?" After their meeting of the other night, I couldn't imagine Blake not trying to get hold of his brother to smooth things over. Smoothed over from what, I wasn't sure, but it had to be something major.

Blake's features clouded over and, unless it was my imagination, his ding-dong wilted a little. I forced myself to look at his face again.

"No."

"Are you going to call him?" My internal antennae searched for a clue and found nothing. Something was off with Blake and Michael, and I wanted to know what it was.

"Leave it alone, Jenn."

"But—"

"Hey, what about the shower? Let's get going."

Blake took off running and I tilted my head to watch his tight ass, strong legs and overall studly torso take long strides. I almost forgot about Michael and Partner, and started to follow Blake when his cell phone started playing *The Devil Went Down to Georgia*. Why he loved that particular song, I'll never know.

I grabbed his phone and yelled, "Blake?" But he was already through the door and into our bedroom. Probably even all the way into the bathroom.

Okay, I admit it. I'm a nosy broad. Following my naturally snoopy inclination, I checked the phone for a caller ID. Fortunately for me and my nose, whoever had called had left a message. I knew I shouldn't have punched the button to retrieve the message, but Angel Jenn who sat on my right shoulder had gone shopping for a new halo. Devil Jenn, however, was on my left shoulder and taking care of business. The words flashed at me. *Got your message. Leave it alone. I am what I am. No blame, no guilt. bro.*

"Never contacted him, huh?" My husband had lied to me. Grumbling a bit longer, I tugged on my clothes and hopped toward the front door. Although I'd much rather have joined Blake in the shower and demanded an answer to why he'd lied, I sensed I wouldn't get anything out of him. Therefore, since Blake wasn't giving me any answers, then maybe Michael would.

I was halfway to downtown Tulsa without realizing I didn't know how to find my brother-in-law. Turning to my PDA extraordinaire, I caught Partner up on the tense meeting between the brothers and the strange message from Michael. "I need to find his brother. Got any ideas?"

Partner's cowboy hunkered into a western version of Rodin's *The Thinker*. "I have it. If you had Blake's cell phone I could link with it and trace where Michael called from."

"Well, sheesh, Sherlock. Big deal. I'd assume he phoned Blake using his own cell phone. But so what? You can't tell a person's location by tracing a call made on his cell after they've disconnected."

"I can."

I slammed my foot on the brake to keep from running into the tailgate of the pickup in front of me. The driver tossed me an angry look through his rearview mirror and I waved my apology. "You can?"

"Sure can, missy. But only if you have Blake's cell phone. You left it at home, right?"

I pulled to the curb, picked him up and gaped at the cowboy. "Let me get this straight. You can use Blake's phone to find out where Michael is even though Michael probably used his cell phone and not a landline? And you can do this without going through a bunch of hassle contacting cell phone service providers?"

"Trust me, Jenn. I can. Or at least I could have. *If* you'd brought the phone with you."

I reached into my pocket with my other hand and pulled out Blake's phone. "Then I guess it's a good thing I brought his phone with me. I kind of accidentally shoved it in my pocket." A series of less-than-sincere beeps—I'd gotten very adept at beep interpretation—challenged my statement. "Really. I dashed out of the house and didn't look at whose phone I was grabbing."

The cowboy winked at me and chewed on a blade of wheat. "Oh, sure. An accident. Right."

Guilt by accusation gets me every time. Had I purposely taken Blake's phone by simply doing my subconscious mind's bidding? Yet whichever way it happened didn't matter now. One thing was for certain. I'd never admit to taking it on purpose. "Yeah, an accident. Now quit stalling and do your thing."

The cowboy threw down the wheat and hooked his thumbs in his jeans. "No problem, darlin'. Here's how it works. Turn on his phone and put it face to face with me."

I followed his directions. "Face to face? Don't you mean screen to screen?"

Partner let out a loud beep, startling me and making me almost drop both devices. "Ow! Are you trying to break my eardrums or what?"

"Jenn, quit whining and put us together." The cowboy wiggled his fingers at me in a hurry-up gesture.

"Fine. Here you go." I positioned the two machines together, screen to screen, and waited. After several minutes, however, nothing had happened. "Is it working?"

"Shush."

I obeyed not only because I didn't know what else to do, but because a couple of men walking by gave me a curious look after they heard me talking. If I'd had a free hand I would have touched my ear, pretending to have a phone earpiece. Instead, I decided to ignore them. If I was the oddest thing they saw all night, then they were very lucky people.

After five minutes, however, I became antsy and was about ready to ask Partner for an update when he beeped a couple of times. Separating them, I checked out Blake's phone for any damage and let out a sigh.

"His phone is fine." Another series of beeps and the cowboy's chiseled face appeared larger in a close up. "Nice to know you were worried about his simple tool and not me. And it's not even his important tool, either. If you get my drift."

"Uh, yeah. A deaf woman would get your drift. You are anything but subtle, my friend. Still, I can hardly return his phone if it's messed up." Why was I arguing with a piece of metal? "Well? Did it work? I'm tired of twiddling my thumbs."

"Then stop twiddling and mosey on over to the Night Crawler bar on West Hudson Street. The call originated from there." The cowboy disappeared, replaced by a map of downtown.

"Don't bother with the map. I know the place. It's a haven for all sorts of bad creatures, mortal and otherwise." I pulled the Jag into traffic and headed for downtown.

My mind whirled with questions. I navigated the dimly lit streets until I found a parking spot. Once I'd parked across from the bar, I grabbed Partner, then hopped out of the car.

"Jenn? Don't you want to take a weapon with you? After what you said about this place, I'd think you'd want to be packin'."

"Packin'? Are you a cowboy or a gangster?" I chuckled at my joke and continued across the road. "If anything goes wrong inside, I'd have to carry a damn machine gun to have a chance of walking out alive. Nope. It's better if I go unarmed. Hopefully, they won't see me as a threat if I'm not 'packin'." Taking a deep breath, I pushed through the door of the hole-in-the-wall joint, paused to strike a defensive stance, and got ready for anything.

A few heads looked up from their drinks to give me a glance, but no one bothered taking a second look. Moving to the nearest corner, I stayed put until my eyes adjusted to the dark, smoke-filled room and hoped I'd spot Michael before he spotted me.

Rock and roll played from speakers mounted on opposite walls. On the other two walls, one plasma television blared a football game and another flashed the latest episode of *Survivor*. Booths rested against the walls, and tables took up the mid-section. The mirror behind the bar showed the aftermath of bar fights in the cracks crisscrossed across its width. Customers occupied all the stools, with many appearing as though their bottoms had been glued to the seats since the last decade. In the back, down a hallway, I could hear the unmistakable sounds of men's low voices and billiard balls cracking together.

I scanned the nearest wall for an empty seat and spotted the occupants of the closest booth starting to get up. Not wanting to meet their eyes or draw attention to myself, I let them shuffle past me, then slipped onto the cushion and scooted as far to the other side as possible.

"What can I get ya?" The waitress, a poster girl for Goths R Us, leaned on the tabletop and cocked a penciled-in eyebrow at me.

"Excuse me?" Sometimes it's easy to sense a supernatural being and sometimes it isn't. Right now it was. This young woman had *vamp* written all over her.

"You want a drink?"

Of blood? I managed to keep my initial question inside my head before answering with the correct one. "Oh, yeah. A beer is good. Whatever's on tap." Was she staring at my veins? I put my elbows on the table and wrapped my palms around either side of my neck.

She smiled, telling me she knew what I was thinking, and moved off toward the bar. She returned faster than I'd have thought possible and plucked the money from my outstretched hand. Examining the ten-dollar bill as if it might be counterfeit, she arched the other fake eyebrow this time. "Should I keep the change?"

"Sure." If it kept her away from me, I'd give her another ten spot. She whirled around and sauntered over to a nearby table, leaving me to wonder which would be more dangerous, letting her suck my blood or taking a drink from one of these filthy glasses? I decided to play it safe and do neither.

Unfortunately, Partner decided it was time to chime in. Literally. Like the church bells on a Sunday morning, a soft lilting chime rang out of my pocket, drawing Ms. Vamp's attention. I shot her a small smile and silently wished I could pop out his batteries. "Oh, uh, it's nothing. Just a friend of mine." I patted my pocket for extra measure. Having more than likely seen her fair share of parasitic creatures catching a ride on her undead clients, she gave my pocket a cursory glance and returned to taking the others' drink orders.

"Be quiet, Partner, or I'll plug you into my car and let you mate with the cigarette lighter."

"Don't go kickin' up a fuss, I was just curious and wanted to know what was goin' on, darlin'."

"Curiosity can kill you as fast as it killed the cat."

I ignored Partner's snort and wondered if it was too late to pull his batteries without anyone noticing. Luckily for him a loud, familiar voice garnered everyone's attention.

"You motherfuckers are screwing with me. Did you finish them or what? Did you find it? Talk up or you'll regret your silence."

Michael's harsh tone drew my gaze to him. He, two men and a beautiful blonde woman were seated in a booth cattycorner from mine. The two men growled at Michael although the blonde appeared unconcerned by the men's aggressiveness. Instead, she swayed back and forth with the earplug to her iPod firmly in place.

I hunched down in my booth and studied Michael's companions. One was probably a ghost. His persona flickered once in a while—a dead (pun intended) giveaway—and left the telltale vapor outline of a younger man dressed in medieval clothing. Since his mortal exterior flickered, I knew he had to be a young ghost who wasn't yet powerful enough to maintain his outward appearance for long stretches of time. Young being less than a thousand years old. His friend, however, wasn't so easy to figure out.

"The master told you what to do." Michael's expression darkened. He uttered a low growl and pushed his body over the table to put his face closer to the two men. His action, swift and threatening, caused Blondie to look up, but she still appeared uncaring. If she wasn't a supernatural entity, she had nerves like one.

Poor thing is bored to tears. Is she Michael's girlfriend?

"We were told to find out where they were. That's all we were instructed to do—find them. No one said anything about killing them." The ghost's body wavered again. "It's not like we can't exterminate them any time we want. They're low-life mortals no one would miss."

I checked Michael's expression. He had to have seen the ghost shimmer. Therefore, Michael had to know his friend wasn't a normal human dirtbag, but something supernatural.

"Then go back and do the job right." Michael's ghoulish growl, deep and gravely sounding with a touch of terror in it, left nothing to the imagination and confirmed the suspicion crawling around in my brain since meeting him.

The implication finally hit home, and I swallowed the bile that had leapt up my throat. I'd seen his form change the night he'd visited, yet I'd tried to find another explanation. Now I couldn't deny what I'd seen any longer. It hadn't been my mind playing tricks on me.

My brother-in-law was an undead, a night creature, an Otherworlder. My brother-in-law was a ghoul.

Aw, shit. Family reunions are going to blow big time.

Finding out a loved one is an undead creature is hard to take. I'd seen enough families go through the awful experience to know. But I'd always been the sympathetic observer, not one of the family members. Still, I didn't know Michael well enough to feel sorry for him. It was Blake I was worried for.

No doubt this was the reason the two brothers hadn't seen each other in years. Most newly undead people break ties with their families. Michael was of the Otherworld and poor Blake hadn't found out about his brother's transformation. But what did Blake feel responsible for? Did he feel responsible for their estrangement? I could imagine the devastated expression on my husband's face when he found out his brother was part of the supernatural undead.

I downed my drink, hoping for a bit of liquid fortitude and praying I wouldn't catch anything from the filthy glass. Sometimes being a Protector sucked, and I had a bad feeling this was going to be one of those times. Leaving yet another tip for the waitress—trust me, the more you tip a vamp waitress, the safer you'll be—I slid out of the booth. Letting out a puff of relief, I made it to the door and outside without drawing attention from Michael's booth.

The cool night air was a welcomed respite after breathing the smoke-mixed-with-stale-beer air of the bar. I inhaled deeply, enjoying the fresh smell as well as trying to relax my nerves. The older I got—meaning out of my twenties—the harder it was for me to handle these kinds of surprises.

I crossed the road under the dim glow of the street lights and made it to within a few feet of my car. That's when the sensation of someone—or some *thing*—watching my progress hit me dead on. Whatever it was, it was close—too close.

Lions and Tigers and Werewolves, Oh My!

As a Protector, I have to make quick decisions involving life and death. I had no doubt this was one of those times. I could either move toward my car, putting me closer to the thing and probable danger, or I could run like hell and hope to reach the bar's relative safety. Neither option sounded very good to me, but I've never liked the idea of getting sliced and diced with my back turned. The idea of ending up torn into tiny Protector parts made my decision easy.

I leapt forward, clicking my remote to unlock the door. Tuning Partner in on my possible impending death, I yelled, "I'm under attack!"

The words were barely out of my mouth and answered by a high-pitched squeak from inside my pocket when a very large, very smelly object struck me from my right, knocking me three feet into the air. I hit the ground hard, knocking the breath from my lungs and Partner from my pocket. He slid, cursing, toward the storm drain near the curb. A flash of red lights covered his panel seconds before he fell through the grate and disappeared from sight. "Jennifer!"

Unfortunately for Partner, I had more immediate problems to deal with. A huge white werewolf with glowing red eyes snarled, exposing sharp, saliva-dripping fangs. The animal roared with glee at having me trapped. I tried to suck in more air despite the considerable weight sitting on my chest.

"Get. Off. Me. You. Asshole!" Although I'd put all the power and anger I could muster into my words, they still came out whisper-soft. And a very ineffectual whisper at that. I swear I saw the beast smile.

But I wasn't out of the fight yet. Bringing my legs up and around him, I prayed all my weight training had paid off. I rolled, clamping my inner thighs around its torso and locking my ankles together to hold on. The hell-animal snarled, struggling against my wrestler's hold. I managed to roll it onto its side for about two seconds before it had me pinned on my back again.

Have you ever heard the old saying, "I've got a tiger by the tail"? Trust me. Having a werewolf between your legs ain't no walk in the park either.

Recalling my last fight with a shifter, I made a fist and went for its most vulnerable spot. Its eyes. I screamed a karate yell and landed first one punch in its left eye, then another in its right. An angry roar nearly deafened me. Using its massive paws, the creature pinned both my arms down, effectively restraining me with its crushing weight. The only part of my body I could move was my toes.

My heart pounded against my chest and, although I'd never admit this to Partner, I wished I'd taken his advice and packed a gun. Enjoying my immobility, the shifter ran a rough tongue across my cheek. Laughing in a part-growl, part-howl, the beast lifted a paw, spread its claws wide, and prepared to slash my throat.

I closed my eyes, sent Blake a silent goodbye, and waited for death.

The werewolf's surprised growl opened my eyes in time to see it fly up and away from me, soaring over my car to land on the other side, out of my sight. Gasping for air now that the weight was off me, I pushed my aching body to a sitting position and started doing a crab crawl toward my car. I twisted around and leaned against the front tire. Sounds of fighting came from the sidewalk on the other side of my Jag, but I was too exhausted to move and check it out. I whispered a soft "Thank you" to my unseen hero and hoped he'd win the fight.

The struggle was soon over, however, and I readied myself to meet either my savior or another attacker. Putting my shoulder against my Jag, I forced my body to a half-standing, half-leaning position, and stared at the ground.

"Hey, lady. You okay?"

I lifted my head to see the biggest man I'd ever seen, including a few giants I could name. "Yeah, I'm okay. I think." My knees buckled with my answer and I started to fall to the street. Instead, arms the size of redwood tree limbs gathered me up like a child's doll and held me against a chest harder than the side of a mountain. Amazed, I pressed a hand to his chest to see if it was really as firm as I thought it was.

It was.

Big brown eyes stared at me from a face only a mother could love. I knew it was bad of me, but I couldn't get the image of Fred Flintstone and King Kong all rolled into one out of my head. This man, and I use the term loosely, was the largest goof-slash-ape I'd ever seen.

"You're sure-sure? If not, George can take you to a doctor." He sniffed twice.

Was he smelling me? Because if he thought I stunk, then he hadn't had a whiff of his own B.O. yet. The man must live with pigs and monkeys to smell this bad. "George?" I glanced around for another man-ape. Did these guys run in packs?

"Sure-sure. George." He removed one hand from around me long enough to pat his chest and grin—or at least I think it was a grin—showing off two-inch sharp teeth.

"Oh, you're George." I wiggled a little, hinting to let me go, but my clue went right over his head. Figuratively speaking, of course. "George?"

"Uh-huh?"

This guy was enormous, but he wasn't threatening. Instead, he seemed more like a big, tender-hearted bear. Still, I wasn't taking any chances. "Could you put me down, please?"

"Oh, sure-sure!" George dropped me without warning but, thankfully, I landed on my somewhat stable feet.

I stepped away and surveyed the long haul of him. Not even Big and Tall shops would be able to clothe this guy. He probably had his clothes custom-made, although not by a competent tailor from the way they hung on his massive frame. "Were you the one who saved me from the werewolf?" Remembering my attacker, I scanned the area around us and found nothing. George's face darkened into a glower and I swallowed, admitting I was more than a little nervous.

"George ran the wolf off, but George didn't hurt her much.

She was bad." His scowl grew even meaner. "George doesn't like bad people. Or bad animals."

She? I hadn't realized the shifter had been female. Not that it mattered. "Me, either." I stuck out my hand and he took it before I had a chance to think better of my offer. His calloused hand, nearly three times the size of mine, enveloped my fingers. I waited for the sound of cracking bones and, when it didn't happen, marveled at how gentle the big guy could be. "I'm Jennifer. But my friends call me Jenn."

"George is only George." The face-splitting smile came again. "But you already know George's name. Is George your friend? Can George call you Jenn?"

"I'd say saving me from an ass-chewing would make you my friend." I pulled my hand away from his. "Thanks for saving me, George. And yeah, call me Jenn."

"Awesome! You're welcome, Jenn."

"If you two are finished getting all chummy, could someone get me out of this hole?"

Showing remarkable agility for a guy his size, George spun around, fists in the air, ready for anything. "Where is he? Is it another wolf?"

I patted the big guy on the shoulder and pointed to the storm drain. "No, no werewolf. But my, uh, friend got knocked down the drain when the shifter attacked me."

George followed me over to the curb and watched me get down on my knees to peer into the drain. Sure enough, Partner lay on the edge of a piece of metal protruding from the side of the concrete. "Hey, Partner, how ya doing?" I peered past the shelf into the darkness below it. "Judging from the looks of things, you got lucky."

Why I found this amusing I couldn't say. After all, knowing the number crunchers at the Society, they'd probably garnish my wages to pay for a missing or busted Partner. And something told me Partners didn't come cheap.

"Darlin', could you give me a hand?" The cowboy on the screen sat in the middle of a mudhole, arms raised above his head and waving them in an imploring gesture. "A little help, please?"

I tried to work my hand through the iron rods of the grate, but couldn't get more than a couple of fingers through them. I tugged on the drain, hoping to find it loose, and got a neck strain for my efforts.

"Is your friend in there, Jenn?"

His dark shadow from the street lights covered not only me but half of the sidewalk, too. I wondered what it must be like to be that huge. "Yeah, he is. But I can't reach him and I can't lift the cover."

George placed a hand on my shoulder and moved me away. "Let George see."

I nodded and moved out of the way, giving room for George to squat down. "Do you think you could lift the grate?" I twisted around to see a couple of the bar's customers come stumbling out of the door. Luck was with me, though, since neither one of them was Michael. "I really need to get going, but I don't want to leave him here."

"You mean the phone? The phone is your friend?" George's seeking eyes found me. "How can a phone be your friend?"

"Because I'm much more than a phone, you nitwit." The cowboy was out of the mudhole and stomping the slimy gunk off his jeans. "I'm a virtual partner with emotions and intelligence like anyone else. And more than some others I could name."

George took his hand off the grate. "He doesn't sound very nice. George isn't sure George wants him to get out. Is he mean to you, Jenn?"

The evil part of me wanted to say yes, to enjoy a little payback for all of Partner's verbal jabs, but I knew better than to mess around right now. "No, George. Partner's really very nice. He's a little upset right now. You understand."

"Are you sure he gets it, darlin'? He sounds like he's fallen on his head one too many times."

I opened my mouth to stick up for George, but he beat me to it.

"George isn't the one trapped in a drain, is George?" The big guy crossed his arms over his chest and frowned at Partner. "Now who fell on his head too many times?"

Way to go, George! Yet another couple of drunks exited the bar and I ducked behind the friendly lug, using his mass to shield me. "Please get him out. I need to get out of here and get home."

The disgruntled giant nodded and lifted the grate off the drain as easily as if he was picking up a sheet of paper. George reached down to scoop up Partner and held him up with his short, stubby fingers for my inspection. Muck and debris clung to Partner's metal and plastic. "Here you go, Jenn. But he sure is dirty. Sure-sure."

I again ignored George's own odor, deciding not to insult my rescuer. "You'd be dirty, too, if you'd fallen in there." I pinched Partner between two fingers and shook some crud off him. "I'll clean you off when we get home. Speaking of which, I need to get moving. Blake's going to have questions about where I ran off to. I kind of left him in the lurch." I didn't have a clue what I'd tell Blake about deserting him and the good time he'd had planned for us in the shower. But I had the drive home to figure it out.

"Are you going to eat dinner, Jenn?"

Dinner? Was he asking me out? "Uh, no, George." I held up my left hand and wiggled my ring finger. "I'm, uh, flattered and everything, but I'm married." *To a man whose brother is a ghoul.* I scowled and banished the unwanted thought from my head. How would I ever tell Blake what Michael was? Of course, I already knew the answer in my heart. I couldn't tell him. I mean, why break his heart needlessly? Besides, if I told him what Michael was, I'd have to tell him the truth about me. See? I can rationalize almost anything.

"Oh, shoot, George isn't asking you for a date, Jenn." George waved me off as if dating me would be a disgusting experience. "No, no. George is asking about food. Nothing more. You know, like friends do. They eat food together sometimes. Sure-sure."

He *sure* liked the word *sure* a lot. I wasn't "sure-sure" if I felt insulted or not. Sheesh, now he had me saying it. Yet I decided to give him the benefit of the doubt and forget the possible slam to my ego. "Oh. Dinner as friends. Yeah. Got it."

"Well, invite yourself over, why don't ya?" Partner whistled low and gave a couple of warning beeps. "Pushy, isn't he?"

"When someone is his size, they can afford to be a little pushy." And when a person saves your life, it's extremely hard to say no to feeding them a decent meal. But I didn't have a choice. "Gee, George, I'd love to have you over for dinner"—I hurried on when I saw the excited light in his eyes—"but not tonight. My husband and I have things we need to discuss. Without company around. Maybe another night, okay?"

George's face looked like the droopy mug of a Basset Hound. "Oh. Okay. Sure-sure. George understands. Another time."

"Sure, George. Another time." I couldn't help it. He looked so forlorn I had to hug him. Partner, however, didn't appreciate getting squished between us.

"Hey! Gotta breathe here!" A series of loud beeps echoed against my chest. "Are you *trying* to kill me?"

George and I parted, and I lifted Partner's cowboy image close to my face. "Drama queen, knock it off. You don't have lungs, which means you don't breathe, right?" He started to answer, but I shook my head. "No, don't go there."

George watched us in fascination. "George would like one of those things. Where did you get it?"

I stuttered, trying to think up a good excuse and, instead, pulled my car door open. I needed to get out of there. "Oh, a friend gave it to me."

"Awesome."

"Yeah. Awesome." I started to sit in my seat, but George wiggled his fingers at me, bringing me up short. "Bye, George, and thanks again. I won't forget you."

Heavy eyebrows dived between his bulbous nose. "'Course you won't. George is coming for dinner soon."

Thinking George might be the oddest surprise guest I could ever bring home for dinner, I nodded, tossed a complaining Partner onto the other seat, and started the engine. George waved goodbye again and I returned his wave, grateful to have met the big guy. I squealed the tires and aimed the Jag toward home.

I killed the engine, letting it coast into the driveway. No way was I going to open the garage door. Blake may sleep the sleep of the dead, but he had the hearing of a dog when he was awake.

"I see someone's using her stealth abilities tonight. Afraid to let the new hubby in on your fun-time excursion? Or don't you think he'd be interested? After all, your trip to town turned up rather revealing information about his brother."

Oh, how I hated a smug know-it-all. Especially one that ran on batteries. And especially when he's right. "I'm being considerate, if you must know. Why wake Blake up? I can tell him everything in the morning." Or not.

The long, lean cowboy whipped off his hat and whooped it up. "Hoo-ee! I need to get me some knee-high boots with all the manure you're slinging. Sure you'll tell him. Or to quote your new friend, 'sure-sure'."

I shot Partner the finger, then pushed my car door open. "Well, you'll never know, will you? Have a good night in the car, Partner."

Slamming the door on his protests, I glanced around the street before hurrying up the walkway to my front door. Almost getting torn apart by a werewolf makes a person jumpy—especially after getting attacked by a perky zombie. I didn't waste any time getting into the house and punching in the code to reset the alarm.

Glancing around, I knew the house was empty. Not even the kitchen light was on. Had Blake gone out when he'd found out I'd left? If he had, where had he gone? I frowned, not liking the idea of my husband roaming the streets looking for me. Yet I could hardly admonish him to keep safely locked behind closed doors when I didn't take my own advice.

I dropped his phone on the desk by the front door where I knew he'd find it in the morning, and made a dash for the bedroom. Again, I was greeted by a dark room. "Blake? Are you home?" But my whispers received the response I'd expected. None. Deciding an empty house was actually a silver lining, I shed my soiled clothing, headed into the bathroom, and switched on the shower. With any luck, I'd get into bed and fall asleep before he came home with questions.

Dark patches where the bruises were already forming greeted me in the mirror. Some minor scratches crisscrossed my abdomen but, for the most part, I looked pretty damn good considering I'd spent part of the night mixing it up with a werewolf. After all, when I can tangle with a shifter and manage to come out of the battle still standing and without any bites, I count it a good day. Thanks to George, I'd managed to do both.

I stepped into the shower, luxuriating in the respite it gave me from the outside world. The water streamed down my back, easing the soreness threatening to set up shop. Besides the soothing comfort, I needed to get the smell of shifter off me. Shifter stench is unbearable and I was afraid Blake would get one whiff and pledge never to touch his wife again.

After a few minutes—I could have stayed in the shower for an hour—I toweled off, threw on my most comfortable and least attractive pajamas, and crawled between the sheets. Blake, however, still hadn't made an appearance and I was more than unhappy. I'm no financial whiz-kid, but I knew midnight was too late for any investment counseling. Where the hell was he?

Exhausted from my rumble with the wolf, I closed my eyes and drifted off to sleep. But I didn't get to sleep for long. Instead, I jolted out of a great Brad Pitt dream and checked the alarm clock's yellow glow. "Three in the morning?" My hand flew to Blake's side of the bed and found it empty. "Where the hell is he?" The Worried Wife morphed into the Irritated, Pissed-Off, Just-Plain-Fed-Up Wife in three-point-two seconds. *Game on, baby.*

And wouldn't you know it? Blake tiptoed into the bedroom at that exact moment. Instead of demanding answers, however, I closed my eyes and tucked myself under the covers. Carefully, I slid the comforter over my head and hoped he hadn't noticed the movement.

Although I knew he was trying to be quiet, I could hear him dropping his clothes to the floor. He coughed a few times, quietly, restraining himself, and I heard the familiar *clink* of money dropping into his change jar.

Should I peek? Will I see anything that might tell me where he's been? I'd decided not to risk it until I heard a different, yet familiar sound. But this wasn't a familiar hubby-type sound. Oh, no. This was definitely not a Blake-like sound.

The clicking sound I heard was the sound of a demon having difficulty maintaining his human appearance. I was one of a few Protectors who'd ever heard the sound. Yet, although I'd only heard it once before, I remembered it well.

The clicking sound happened again and I opened my eyes to peer through tiny slits. Blake stood in front of the television set with his back to me. What was making the sound? Silently,

I prayed it wasn't my husband. Denying any possibility, I shoved the idea away. My husband wasn't a demon! He couldn't be. But if not, why did he sound like one?

Without warning, Blake pivoted quickly and I shut my eyes again. Another *click* happened, sending urgency rushing through me. Whether I liked it or not, I had to risk his knowing I was awake. I held my breath and peeked again.

What the hell?

Honey, What Big Bruises You Have!

The announcer punched the buttons on the gadget. *Click. Click-click-click.* "Folks, if you pass up this amazing new food processor, you're going to regret it. The Mix-O-Master does everything your old food processor does in half the time, half the mess, and takes up half the space."

Blake moved a little to the right, revealing more of the television set mounted on the wall. I couldn't help it. I gawked at the screen. The smiling man on the show continued to punch more buttons. *Click-click-click-click.* Was *that* the clicking sound I'd heard?

Relief washed through me and I tried not to giggle. Of course! I'd programmed the set to record the show. The recording shouldn't have turned on the television, yet sometimes, for some unknown reason, it would. Tonight was one of those times. Blake had threatened to disconnect the digital recorder after several nights of being awakened in the middle of the night, but I'd stopped him. You got it. I'm an infomercial junkie.

Blake cringed at the sound of the show's music, frantically doing his own share of punching buttons on the remote. At last, he managed to switch the set off and turned toward me, almost catching me in the act of clamping my hand over my mouth.

Biting my tongue kept me from laughing and I pretended to sleep. I could sense him leaning over me, checking on me. I regulated my breathing, making myself take deeper breaths and, figuratively, held my breath. His sigh told me I'd earned an Oscar for Best Actress in a Sleeping Drama.

I contemplated whether I should pretend to wake up or not, and decided I'd missed my window of opportunity. Waking up now wouldn't play right. Instead, relieved my foolish suspicion of demonizing my husband was wrong, I executed a perfect roll to my other side. I'd get some sleep and tomorrow I'd ask Blake where he'd gone. At least that was my plan—until I heard Blake whispering.

"Yeah, Michael, it's me."

I had to remember to keep breathing deeply and in a regular rhythm. Why call Michael at this time of the night? This was the second call to his brother he obviously didn't want me to know about. Yet this time it was worse. This time I knew Michael's secret identity.

Okay, I admit it. I'm a pro at denial, although I didn't realize it at the time. But isn't not recognizing you're in denial a part of being in denial? I started reassuring myself, trying to spin my new knowledge about Michael away from anything to do with Blake. Simply because Michael was an Otherworlder didn't mean Blake was one, too. Shoot, he might not even know about his brother. Right?

"No, bro. I don't care what you say. I'm not giving up. What you did tonight doesn't change anything."

Blake paced to the other side of the room, listening to Michael. "No, I don't believe it. Trust me, if she was, I'd know about it. They're wrong."

If who was what? Who was this woman he'd mentioned? What were these two up to? The relief I'd felt moments earlier fell away, crunched by the knot forming in my throat. I bit the inside of my mouth to stay quiet, but part of me wanted to jump out of bed and demand answers. Yet another part of me had set up house in fantasy land, declaring it all a horrible dream.

"Come on, man, don't you think I'd know?"

Normally, I detest speaker phones, but I would've loved to have had one for this conversation. Either that or superhero hearing. Blake listened for several minutes before the exchange came to an abrupt end.

"Look, Michael, you've got to give me a chance to—"

Blake's grumbles signaled his frustration and the *crack* of him slamming his cell phone down on the dresser made me jump. I waited for him to say something like, "Are you awake?" but luck must've stayed on my side and he missed my surprised jerk.

At last, I felt the bed move beside me as Blake crawled under the sheets. Unlike he usually did, he kept to his side and didn't touch me. Did his distance mean something had changed between us? I waited for his snores to begin, although I knew sleep wouldn't come to me. Too many questions kept barreling through my mind without any of them running into an answer.

Why had Blake lied to me about contacting his brother? If Michael was in trouble, why didn't he ask me to help? Why keep it a secret? Yet the biggest nagging question was...did Blake know more than he let on?

I knew I'd fallen asleep when Blake's arm slipped over my hip and his hand grasped my breast, making me stir into semi-sleep. I also knew this possessive gesture was his nonverbal signal of "Me want sex".

Why is it men want sex in the morning and women prefer to get busy at night? After a night's sleep with no makeup, no breath mints, and hair sticking up at odd angles, a woman hardly feels like a sex kitten. But men don't seem to care. Which, I suppose if you think about it, is a good thing.

"Hey, darlin'."

The endearment he used—one he'd never used before—thrust me from my twilight slumber mode to full alert. I sent a silent emergency call toward Heaven. *Please, God, tell me Partner hasn't grown arms and hopped into bed with me.* Thankfully, Blake's lips on my neck identified my husband.

"Darlin'? Since when have you ever called me darlin'?" Could he have found Partner in my car, forced the communication device to spill the beans, and blown my cover as a Protector? Or had he been dreaming of a saloon gal straight out of the Old West?

His chuckle warmed not only my earlobe, but the chill lingering inside my heart. How could such a sweet guy have anything to do with the Otherworld? Answer? He couldn't. To think he could was simply ludicrous. Maybe I needed another vacation. I wouldn't mind another week sipping pink-colored drinks if Blake was there to rub suntan lotion on my legs.

"Roger Wheatland talked about this new western movie he'd seen the other day. He said it was horrible because every other word was 'darlin'."

I leaned into his next chuckle, enjoying the sensation of his warm breath on my skin. I quickly cleansed my mind of the cowboy images popping up and pictured white sands and soothing waves instead.

"Like real cowboys actually speak that way. I guess maybe the word stuck in my mind and I also guess you're saying you don't like it?"

Suddenly, Partner's cowboy waved from the beach chair next to me. *Ack.* "From you? No, I don't."

He rose on his elbow, leaned over my shoulder, and gave me a look. "What do you mean, from me? Do you have someone else who calls you darlin'?"

Oops. Yes. Sort of. "Of course not. I, uh, like the other names you call me better." I flipped onto my back and tugged my pajama top down over my abdomen. I couldn't let Blake see any bruises or scratches. He'd ask too many question if he did. However, that didn't mean I couldn't do a little survey of my own.

Protectors know that once someone becomes a demon, his body gets branded with a set of numbers. You know. Like Damian's *666* number in the movie *The Omen.* Yeah, people think screenwriters make up all that stuff in the movies, but I know better. Personally, I think it's God's little way of getting in the last word. Satan may rule the demon, but the Big Guy—not George—but the *really* big guy still has His finger in the mix. Sometimes, if you caught the demon in a vulnerable position you could find a hidden sign buried under hair and folds of skin.

Oh, sure. I'd seen Blake's naked body plenty of times both in the dark and in the daytime. And I'd never seen any numbers or letters on him. He had one small panther tattoo on his butt cheek, but lots of people had tats nowadays, right? Still, I'd never cared to explore some of the deeper, um, less attractive crevices—if you get my meaning. At least, not with my eyes.

Trying to seem normal about it, I kicked off the sheet covering his body and cast my gaze along his long sexy torso. I paused my survey for a more in-depth perusal of his bat and balls, and the heat started rising. Having a hubby who likes to sleep commando-style comes in handy sometimes.

Okay. A lot of times.

"Are you enjoying the view?"

I blushed, not from his words but from getting caught checking him out. Of course, he didn't know the reason for my attention wasn't what he thought it was. "Sure." I sought his eyes and wiggled my eyebrows. "In fact, I was thinking I hadn't seen enough of you. Not nearly enough. I think it's time for some exploration."

Blake caught my innuendo and I scooted down the bed. I was about to give the meaning of the word *exploration* a whole new twist in the line of duty. Fortunately, this was the type of exploration he would love.

I cupped his jewels in my hands and received an appreciative groan for my efforts. Playing with them in a sexy way, I made sure I saw every centimeter of their testicular glory. Blake's breathing became more labored and I became more engrossed in my examination of his package.

"Jenn, babe, don't stop. Don't ever stop."

A moan escaped him, giving me encouragement to continue my voyage around his body. I fondled one ball after the other, checking for anything abnormal. Reaching down to me, he tried to grab my hair, but I shook him off. "Knock it off. I'm busy here."

"No shit. Please. Don't let me disturb you."

"Trust me. You won't." Deciding I needed to do more to keep him under my control, I licked his shaft from the tip to the bottom while scanning every inch of his skin.

"Oh, man, Jenn. You're killing me. Killing me good."

He started to sit up, but I pushed him back down. "No. Stay. Let the professional realtor examine your prime property." Yeah, I know. Pretty lame, but my concentration was on the search at—in—hand.

He obeyed, reaching over his head to grip the slats of the headboard. "Hey, we both have needs, you know. How about me helping you with yours?"

I mumbled a negative reply and slid my mouth over his organ. I'd seen no signs of demonic possession which meant I could stop looking. Instead, I giggled and made the not-so-tough decision to keep the hunt going. Thoroughness, thy name is Jenn.

Blake was definitely in the thick of things with his panting

I Married a Demon

growing louder. He kept reaching for me and I kept pushing his hands away. I was good at my wifely duties and wanted no interference.

With careful execution, I brought my delectable hubby to the brink of release. In fact, I'd managed to bring us both to the brink when I suddenly looked down at my bagging PJ top and spotted a big purple bruise on my chest. Letting Blake see the bruise was not an option. Therefore, sexual release—at least for me—would limit my options, if not make it totally impossible.

This time when he gripped my head, I let him hold on. After all, I wasn't leaving until the job was completed. He groaned a deep guttural sound and watched me suck and pull.

"Jenn, come on. Take your pajamas off and get on top of me. I—"

I loved my power over him. "You what?"

"I. Want. You. Now."

"Sorry, Blake. This is my blow, er, show."

I renewed my massage of his shaft, delighting in his cries of pleasure. Although he said no words, I knew what he meant. *Warning! Warning! Eruption is imminent! Mount Blake is about to pop his lid!* I congratulated myself and waited for the volcano to explode.

After witnessing what could arguably be called the Eighth Wonder of the World, I suddenly realized I hadn't searched every place that needed checking. Taking his leg in my hand, I ordered him to flip over.

"You want me on my stomach?"

He did as I'd told him, but I could see he had his reservations. And why shouldn't he? I'd always been a bit squeamish about doing anything with his backside. I'd always preferred sex front and center, and had never ventured near the crater of any moon—even Blake's.

"Yeah, I need to check your butt hole." The words were out of my mouth before I knew I'd said them. Those words had to rank in the Top Ten of the What Not To Say To Your Lover list.

"Huh? What for? Are you getting kinky on me?"

I faltered, trying to think of something sexy I could do with his ass without actually having to do something sexual with his ass. I tried and failed. "I'm going to check your body for moles."

Talk about verbal ice water!

"Moles?" He twisted to gape at me. "Now?"

"No better time than the present."

"I can think of a lot of better times than the present."

"Not me." I tried to meet his confused stare with a confident glare of my own. "I read a man needs a full-body check at least once a year. Stop arguing." Although I didn't say the words, my meaning was clear in the tone of voice I used. *You owe me. Flip.*

Blake searched my face for a moment, then complied. If he was a demon—which I was ninety-nine-point-nine percent sure he wasn't—then he was a very cooperative demon.

Since I no longer needed to hide my examination behind sexual play, I didn't waste a second with subtleties. I pushed his cheeks apart and did a thorough examination. One which, I might add, I never want to do again.

"Are you satisfied?" He shifted to lie on his back again and gave me the strangest look.

"Almost."

"Almost?" He slid his gaze down his body, visually conducting his own search. "Where else do you need to check? You've seen every inch of me. How the hell did fun in the sack turn into a medical exam, anyway?"

"Not every inch. Sit up." Reluctantly, he obeyed my order and I maneuvered my body to sit beside him. "Now hunker down a bit and give me your head."

A typical Blake smile lit up his face. "I'd love to give you my head." His smile grew wider. "Or give *you* head."

"Ha, ha. Very funny." Taking hold of his rich dark hair, I yanked his head over to see his scalp better, then paused to reconsider what I'd passed up. "But I'll take a rain check on your offer."

I fingered through his thick hair, checking each inch of his scalp. Once I was finished, I hugged him to me and let the relief sweep through me. "You're clean. Thank God, you're clean."

He laughed right before he crushed his mouth to mine for a lingering kiss. When we parted, I was breathless and horny.

"I may be physically clean, but I've got a very dirty mind."

"Don't I know it." I stretched out my body, conscious of his gaze running over me. Looking sexy in PJs wasn't easy and keeping my top on during sex would be even harder, but I was up to the task. Besides, I figured it was time for a little doggy action, anyway. I'd already ventured into untried sexual territory, so I figured I might as well keep going with the experimenting. "Hey, do you hear what I hear?"

He paused to listen, his hand poised over my tit. "No. What do you hear?"

I wiggled my eyebrows to let him in on the joke. "I hear rain. Now how about cashing in my rain check?"

My friend Myra once said, "Satisfy a man and you can get away with anything—including hopping out of bed right after sex." Myra's quip kept running through my brain as I dashed out of the house, revved up the Jag and headed toward the office. Partner, however, wasn't the type of *man* I knew how to satisfy.

"Darlin', unlike someone who's been taking it easy, I've been doing research."

I curled my lip at him and pressed harder on the gas. "Hey, I've worked today. Just because I wasn't bent over a keyboard or striking down a shifter doesn't mean I haven't been working."

"Oh, right. You've been putting yourself out—ahem—in the pursuit of finding the Bracelet." Maybe it was my imagination, but his beeps sounded like snickers.

I grumbled under my breath, not wanting to go into detail about my morning's work.

"Anyway, I found out the following fun facts about the Bracelet. Remember the Bracelet? The powerful weapon you're supposed to be looking for? Or have you forgotten about your job in your quest to satisfy your libido?"

I guided the Jag around a sharp corner, purposely making him slide across the leather to hover near the edge of the seat. "I haven't forgotten." Who did this glorified cell phone think he was, anyway? He hadn't even gotten his first batteries by the time I'd managed several years of topnotch Protector assignments under my belt. "And how the hell do you know anything about my libido?"

"Puh-lease. I have my sources. Suffice it to say a lamp is not always just a lamp."

I started to ask for an explanation and decided I didn't want to know. At least, for now. But later, my house would get a big-time surveillance cleaning along with a new lamp in the bedroom. "You said you had info on the Bracelet?"

"Well, then, pretty woman, listen up."

Pretty woman? Did he mean like Julia Roberts? Or Miss Kitty? Nonetheless, I listened up.

"You know the usual things, correct? Like how it's a gold bracelet with an inscription inside?"

"Yeah. Tell me something I don't know."

I slammed to a stop at a red light. The man in the next car caught me talking to Partner, but he didn't seem interested. Ever since the invention of handless cell phone sets in cars, I could talk to an unseen anyone—or anything—without my fellow commuters thinking I was as wacky as the local bag lady who talked to her toes.

"Well, how about this? An agent who tracks energy sources and the corresponding output picked up a reading like the one the Bracelet makes."

I got a little excited. "Yeah? Where did it come from?"

A happy whirring sound preceded Partner's answer. "Here. Right here in Tulsa."

My excitement level doubled. "Here? Great. The thieves didn't take it out of town. Did he pinpoint a location?"

"Yes and no."

I glanced at Partner before turning back to the road. Biting my figurative tongue to resist yelling at him, I even managed to keep my tone calm. "Would you care to explain?" I tried to hang onto my optimism, but it sagged anyway.

"He picked up the reading at a flea market."

"You're kidding." I pulled into the Swindle Realty lot and parked. Picking up Partner, I watched the cowboy tip his hat to me in a gentlemanly fashion. "And?"

"And they did a thorough search of the market and turned up nothing."

"Which means we're back to square one," I scoffed. I slipped Partner into my pocket and made quick time into the office. "Great work—not."

"Jenn!"

For a second, I contemplated hiding under the nearest desk. If Swindle wanted to chew my ass out again, he'd have to find me first. Instead, I returned Myra's wave. She hopped up from behind the receptionist's desk and inconspicuously headed my way. Knowing she'd follow, I diverted into the Blue Room, one of the many rooms we used for private client-agent discussions.

"Jenn, I have stupendous news." Myra shut the door and bounced up and down, barely able to contain herself.

"Cool. You passed your real estate licensing exam, right?"

I knew Myra couldn't care less about selling real estate, but Swindle insisted all his support staff take a real estate course and pass the test. Everyone had, except Myra. Contrary to Herbie's belief, not everyone wanted to be an agent. But since the super-tight Swindle paid for the courses, his employees signed up figuring it was a good way to make the boss happy and possibly earn a raise.

"Puh! What do I care about passing some stupid exam? And no, I didn't pass. Again. I want to give up, but Swindle won't let me." She rolled her eyes before getting back on the original tack. "Besides, I don't need to sell houses to make money. I won money yesterday."

I brought up a list of houses on the computer and pretended to scope them out for a prospective client. "Yeah? You won? Terrific."

Myra was a lottery scratch-off ticket junkie, but as long as she didn't go berserk and gamble her life savings away, I was okay with it. After a year of playing and an indeterminate amount of (in my opinion, wasted) money, she'd won a grand total of fifty-three dollars. "I guess you can buy me a cup of coffee today."

"Girl, forget the coffee. I'm buying you lunch or dinner at Ragino's."

I stopped pretending to look at the house descriptions on the screen and spun my chair around to face her. "Wow. Dinner at Ragino's. You must've won a bunch. Like maybe as much as a hundred?"

"Think more. Think five hundred."

I clapped in delight and high-fived her. "No kidding? You did this with a scratch-off ticket?"

"I sure did."

I hugged her to me, absorbing some of her excitement. "Amazing. I need to try my luck sometime. Where did you buy the ticket?"

Myra kept hugging herself even after I let her go. "You know the big flea market out on Interstate Forty? They have a booth selling lottery tickets now. Cool, huh?"

"Yeah, cool." Could this be the same flea market Partner had mentioned? "By the way, did you happen to notice anything unusual while you were there?" I didn't know what I expected, but if someone had used the Bracelet at the flea market maybe Myra had noticed.

"Nope. Nada. People milling around looking for bargains like usual. Why?"

My hope deflated faster than a man's penis in ice water. "Oh, no reason."

"Darlin', I hate to interrupt, but you've got mail."

Myra jumped and twirled around, searching for the owner of the deep voice. "Who was that?"

I took Partner out of my pocket and held up the screen for her to see. Cowboy Partner twirled a rope with one hand and tipped his hat with the other. "Howdy, ma'am."

"Sheesh, Partner, don't you think you're taking this cowboy theme a bit far? I mean, 'howdy'?"

Yet Myra was entranced. "Oh, my God. What or who is this?"

"This is my Personal Partner who helps me out with information and more. The Society gave him to me for this assignment. I call him Partner." I laughed at the expression on her face. "I know. I know. It's hard to fathom at first. But you get used to him. Trust me, he's no big deal."

"Hey! I resent that." Cowboy dropped his lasso and tipped his hat up to glare at me.

"Then it's not a fancy cell phone?" Myra peered closer, reached out a finger, and touched Partner on his screen-crotch.

"Hey, pretty woman. Don't you think we need to know each other a bit more before you start playing with my family jewels?

And I prefer to be thought of as a him and not an it."

Myra continued to admire Partner and his chest seemed to enlarge. *Great. More ego for the electronic version of God's gift to women.* I let them take stock of each other until I couldn't stand it any longer. "You said I had mail?"

Partner broke the stare he and Myra shared to roll a text message along the bottom of the screen. I knew right away who had sent the message. The Society had an agent working as a policeman and he did a great job providing information and leads. As always, his message was cryptic. *Call me. Urgent.*

Attention, Buyers! Price Reduction on a Fabulous Blood-soaked Bungalow.

"Talk. What's the word?"

Herbert Swindle stalked by the Blue Room and scowled at me. Catching my look of warning, Myra grabbed a printout from the nearby printer and started studying it as though her life depended on it. Since I'd finally gotten hold of my informant, Jim Sterling, at the stationhouse, I wasn't about to hang up on him. Instead, I held Partner closer to my ear, plastered on my best suck-up-to-my-boss grin, and shot Swindle a thumbs up.

"Know who robbed the main office." Jim lowered his tone. "And took you-know-what."

With the news still ringing in my ear, I was glad I'd sat down to make the phone call. "Yeah? Give me the details."

"Petty thieves. *Were* petty thieves."

My pulse beat a little faster. "What do you mean, 'were'?"

"Dead. All five."

An image of Michael in the bar with his undead companions flashed through my mind. Hadn't they talked about killing someone? A cold shudder whipped along my spine and I had to clamp down on my teeth to keep them from chattering. "How did they die?"

"Someone shot them execution style."

Sometimes even one word tells a tale. I let out a rush of air because he'd said *someone* and not *something*. Maybe someone else had gotten to the thieves before Michael's gang could. "I'm coming to check it out."

"No use. Can't get in today."

Swindle continued to watch me and I widened my smile for his benefit. "Are you there right now?" Swindle, apparently mollified, nodded at me and continued on his way to hassle the other agents.

"Yeah, but can't get you inside the place. Not ranked high enough."

His stilted speech was getting to me, but that was his style. "Stay put. I'll be there as fast as I can. In the meantime, try to dream up some excuse to get me a look around."

"Fat chance."

I ended the connection and glanced at Partner. "Well, at least now I know I can use you as a phone."

Partner's cowboy persona returned to spit tobacco on the virtual ground in front of him. "Haven't you figured it out yet? I can do most anything. Especially anything a PDA or phone can do."

Myra gave the mechanical egomaniac the admiration he craved. "Partner is fabulous, Jenn. Do you think they'll eventually have Partners for the general public? Or at least Protectors' assistants?"

Grabbing my purse, I slipped Partner into my pocket and peeked around the corner of the door into the hallway. Swindle was at the far end of the main room with his back to me. *Perfect timing.*

"Myra, if old Herbie asks where I am, tell him I'm off checking out a home. Considering the occupants are sleeping with the proverbial fishes, I think the house may be coming on the market soon."

"Will do!"

I scampered like a rat escaping a trap to zip through the main office and out the front door. With any luck, Swindle would spend the next hour tormenting some other poor employee.

The thieves' house was located in a decent neighborhood on the edge of town. Steering the Jag onto the street, I took in a typical crime scene investigation in full force. Neighbors who'd probably not spoken to each other for months gossiped on the sidewalk and tried to get close enough to hear the juicy tidbits. Uniformed cops kept them from crossing into the yard. Yellow crime scene tape stretched across the steps leading up to the front porch—a clear sign of trouble waking up a normally quiet street's inhabitants.

Parking down the block, I patted my pocket, making certain I had Partner. I got out of my car and strolled toward the action, hoping I looked like just another crime scene investigator. Plain-clothed detectives talked in a small huddle outside the front door. The medical team leaned against the coroner's vehicle, going through the usual paperwork. Their bored expressions said it all. Judging from the number of cops and coroner's assistants at work, I knew they'd seen something awful inside the house, but apparently it hadn't appeared supernatural. I strolled up to the nearest cop, my informant. "A multiple murder, huh? Execution style, you say?"

Jim, a veteran of the Society for eleven years and a cop for seven of those same years, kept facing forward and scanning the growing crowd. "Right. Gunshots to heads. Lined up. Shot one after the other."

I tried not to smile. Of course I wasn't happy when any human died, but I definitely found the silver lining when they'd gotten whacked in a traditional, human way. "Good. No supernatural involvement?"

"Actually, yes."

My breath caught in my throat at his remark. "Are you saying there was?" I took a quick glimpse at him and returned to watching the crowd. "What do you mean? Exactly." Why did he have to go and tarnish my silver lining?

"Arm and leg. Gone."

"Yeah? Still, dismemberment isn't exclusive to the supernatural." What did I have to do to get this guy to stop talking like Tonto?

"Seems like the killer used the severed parts as a warning to others."

Wow, a long sentence. I tried desperately to get my silver lining polished. Hell, at this point, I'd take a tin lining. "You don't sound like you agree." *Come on, man. Agree.*

"Don't. Someone snacked."

Ah, crap. Bile rose to my mouth even though I was used to hearing this sort of thing. "Damn. But cannibalism doesn't necessarily mean this is an Otherworlder killing. Ever hear of

Hannibal Lecter?"

"Fictional character."

He was? I hated the heat flowing over my cheeks and scrambled to regain a snippet of my professional dignity. "Yeah, I know." *Liar!* "Anything else?"

"Ghost residue on sofa. Cops didn't notice." One of the detectives glanced our way and I positioned my body at an angle to him, keeping my face averted.

"I suppose it's a good thing." His brow wrinkled in confusion until I added, "About them not noticing the residue."

"I guess."

"Did anyone see the thing we're looking for?"

"Nope."

"No jewelry at all?"

"Nope. Television."

I tried not to get excited at the prospect of a clue. "Working?" Sheesh, I was starting to talk like him.

"Nope."

"Dammit, Jim. Was it the one stolen from you know where?"

"Reckon."

"Did anyone check it for you know what?" This twenty-question game was wearing very thin—like my patience.

"Nope."

"Why not?" I wanted to kick this guy in the balls just to hear him say more than a few words. Even if they were cuss words.

"Smashed."

"But we know it was our TV, right?"

"Uh-huh."

"So someone must've found the item. Problem is, we don't know if it was the thieves before they got whacked or the killer, right?"

"Uh-huh."

I kicked a stone and tried to distance myself from him without going too far to hear. Still, I had to try one last time. "Any chance of my getting in there?"

"Nope."

"Gee, Jim, I bet you talk the bad guys to death, don't ya?" Even though I'd turned my face away from his, I could hear his lightened tone.

"Uh-huh."

So much for getting more details without pulling his teeth out. I'd do it, too, if I had to. "Don't we have a connection high up in the police force? A man very close to the Police Commissioner?"

"Uh-huh."

Granted, patience is not one of my virtues, but this guy could frustrate Ghandi. "Jim, I swear I'm going to turn around and start screaming rape if you don't stop playing Mr. Ziploc with me. You know what I'm asking."

"Uh-huh."

I whirled on him, mouth open, ready to wail.

Jim held up his hand, stopping me cold.

Who did he think I was? A curious onlooker stepping too close to the crime scene? I needed answers.

"We do have a person with connections, but he's out of town on other business."

Finally. Real information. "Wow. You can say more than two words at a time. And you can't think of any other way to get me inside? Maybe you could *talk* them into it."

The corners of Jim's mouth twitched upward. "Nope."

I took a deep breath, closed my eyes for a moment to regroup, opened them to stare at him, and tried again. "This looks like an ordinary robbery with the victims not being anyone anybody cared about, right? Which means a quick investigation and not anyone hanging around tomorrow, right?"

"I guess."

I gritted my teeth and took the plunge one last time. "Okay. I'll be back tomorrow. All right?" Meeting Jim's gaze, I waited for his normal response. Instead, he broke his routine again—but not for the better.

Jim shrugged and walked away.

I knew I shouldn't have, given where I was and what had happened, but I couldn't help it. I laughed, loud and long, all the way to my car.

ᔥ

"Watch out. Swindle's out for bear and you're the one he wants to skin."

I rolled my eyes at Myra's warning and, because I had my eyes on my friend, I ran straight into Swindle. "Oh, crap! Sorry." My attempt to scoot away got blocked by a fuming Swindle.

"Jennifer, what happened at the house on Madison?"

I froze. Had he heard something about the team and Ryan Wallis? Or worse, about Judy Wallis' disappearance? "What do you mean?"

"I set you up with the perfect home to sell and an Open House to boot. Yet, instead of getting an offer, you hand it over to Bellamy. If I'd wanted Bellamy to have it, I'd have given it to him to begin with."

Wanting to suck in a deep breath of relief without getting a drag of Herbert's aftershave, I opted for turning my head to the side and coughing. Myra scooted over to us to stand slightly behind Swindle and held up a crudely drawn picture of Swindle hanging me from a gallows. I started to giggle which only made the prick angrier.

"I fail to see anything funny in you losing a sale to Bellamy." Swindle scowled at me, morphing his two bushy eyebrows into a single long one.

"Bellamy sold the house?" Figures. I sit there all day, then Bellamy lands a deal in the last couple of hours. "Good for him."

"Look, Jennifer, if you want to keep your job here at Swindle Realty, you'll start performing. I don't have room for dead weight."

I opened my mouth to assure him that the only dead weight in the office was his head, but Partner beeped, sounding exactly like a cell phone announcing a missed call and effectively cutting me off at the verbal knees. Still, a bright spot did appear. I held up my finger, silencing Swindle before he could start yet another round of criticisms. "Could be a client." Relishing my little victory, I checked the screen and punched the symbol for voicemail.

Jim Sterling's voice echoed in my ear. "Get there now.

Hurry." After leaving Jim earlier today, I hadn't held out any hope of getting into the house until tomorrow. This green light boosted my spirits and my determination. No way would I miss this opportunity.

I beat Swindle to the punch. "I couldn't agree with you more, Mr. Swindle." I started moving toward the front door with Herbert following along. "In fact, I'm off to scope out another home."

"Now wait a sec."

But I kept moving, knowing he'd stop at the door. He did and I continued on. "Gotta run," I called to him over my shoulder and didn't slow my pace. "Like you always say, 'Time is money and money is great!'" Hopping into my car, I kept my face averted and didn't given him a glance to wave me back. Laughing, I hurried out of the parking lot.

I stood in front of the house where the robbers had met their fate and wondered how many of the neighbors had their eyes glued on me. Although not one of them was in sight, I knew their attention would stay focused on the scene of the crime for days to come. Question was…if anyone asked, how would I explain my trespassing past the yellow crime scene tape left across the front door?

I decided to cross that problematic bridge if and when I came to it. Hopefully, anyone watching would assume I was a plain-clothes cop and not ask me anything. Right now, I needed to see what was inside. Forcing myself not to glance around and, thus, add to the suspicious nature of my visit, I strolled up the steps and reached through the several strands of tape to turn the doorknob.

To my surprise and delight, the door opened. "Perfect. The cops put up Do Not Cross tape all over the place, then fail to lock the door." However, I wasn't one to knock a gift horse in the mouth. Playing a short game of Twister, I dove under one piece of tape and over another to half-fall, half-slip inside the house.

I shut the door, scanned the room and knew I'd wasted my time. The broken television wasn't there any longer and even the ghost residue had been cleaned from the couch. Although I hadn't really expected to gather anything of great value from the place, I'd let myself hope. Yup, that's me. The eternal optimist.

"Darlin'? What do you see?"

Partner's irritated tone made me more anxious than I already was. Contrary to what others might believe from my past actions, I don't like disobeying police blockades, much less trespassing onto crime investigations. "Nothing. Now shut off or I'll shut you off myself."

"Oooh, darlin'. What got you all cranky and out of sorts? Is it Aunt Flow?"

Unlike many times before, I had no desire to quarrel with Partner. Therefore, true to my warning, I reached down and switched him off. His surprised expression was the last thing I saw.

I took in the blood on the walls and furniture, as well as the dried pool in front of the couch. Half-cooked food sat on the stove. Obviously, the victims hadn't expected company. From Jim's description, the unexpected company had preferred to feed on the thugs rather than the chili congealing in the pot.

Why I'd thought this trip would give me any help in locating the Bracelet was beyond me. But after scouring all the pawn shops in town, I wasn't sure where to start looking. I'd gotten lucky overhearing Michael with his Otherworldly cohorts and figured they were involved in the murders. But did they have the Bracelet? And if they did, which high demon lord would they give it to? Where and when would they pass it on? And, worse of all, was I already too late to stop them?

I decided then and there I needed to contact my snitch. But first, I'd check with the neighbors. With a bit of luck, I'd find a nosy, talkative one.

Grateful to be outside again and away from the blood-soaked site, I looked around the neighborhood. No children played outside and no dogs barked in the surrounding backyards. Were the frightened neighborhood moms keeping them tucked safely behind doors? "Weird."

"Weird is what happened over there."

I whirled around, ready for action. "Who's speaking?"

"I am."

I followed the sound of the gravely voice to an elderly gentleman rocking on the front porch of the house next door. "What was weird?" I tossed my hair in my best flirty style and sauntered over to him. "Did you see what happened?"

"I did." He popped his unlit pipe into his mouth and made sucking noises.

My radar shot up. Had he really seen something? Or was he merely a lonely old man using any excuse to talk? I batted my eyelashes and tilted my head coquettishly. "You do know your pipe isn't lit, don't you?" I planned to get friendly with the survivor of the Greatest Generation before diving into the tough questions.

"'Course I do." He took out his pipe, gave it a once over, and clamped his lips around it again. "I'm trying to quit. I wouldn't want to get cancer in my old age."

I studied him and tried imagining him getting any older. The Ancient One was well beyond old already. Unless he was an Otherworlder. I narrowed my eyes, searching for the signs. Yet, I had a hunch that he was all mortal.

"Good plan. My name's Jennifer." I started to take a step up to the front porch where he sat and hesitated. "Do you mind if I talk to you, Mister...?"

A toothless smile was my answer. Taking his gummy grin as an invitation, I joined him and sat in the rocker next to his. "I love rockers. I'm always wanting to sit on my patio at night, but I never have the time."

He nodded, the rolls around his neck wrinkling like an old hound dog's. "Call me Clem. You best make time to enjoy life, girlie. It comes and goes really fast." He stopped rocking to tip his head and peer at me over his bifocals. "Especially in your line of work."

In my line of work? Did he think I was a cop? "I'm not a policewoman." I frowned, unsure why I'd told him the truth.

He snorted, escalating the sound into a fit of coughing.

"Are you all right?" I stopped rocking to lean toward him, but he waved me off.

"I know you're no fuzz face, girlie. Don't you think I can tell a Protector when I see one?"

I gripped the arms of my chair and decided trying to fool him wouldn't work. After all, I'd already let part of the truth slip out. Nope, this guy knew too much for me to try and deny anything. "How did you know?"

"Hell, girlie, you don't get to be ninety-nine years old without learning a few things." He popped his pipe out of his mouth and pointed it at the victims' house. "I know who—or should I say what—killed those scum buckets, too." A hacking cough, the kind that makes you cringe to hear it, accented his statement. A wad of spit followed and I bit back the urge to criticize his lack of manners.

I hadn't expected to find a windfall, but I had. Who cared if it was in the form of an old geezer with half a foot in the grave? I hoped his mind had held up better than his body. I tried to remain calm and kept my excitement hidden. "Oh, yeah? Really? Can you tell me about it?"

"I suppose I could." His eyes twinkled with my attention and he began to rock his chair a little faster. "T'weren't regular murderers what done it."

"No? Then what kind of murderers do you mean?" I noticed a younger couple taking a stroll coming up the sidewalk. Nearing the house, they picked up speed and hurried past it.

"Don't play games with me, girlie. Like I said, I know what you are."

He was a cool old coot. I hoped I'd be that cool when I reached his age. *If* I reached his age. "Sorry. Why don't you tell me what you saw?"

"Good 'nuff. I saw a ghost, a vamp, and some other man I think was a ghoul go inside. Then I heard a whole lot of shouting and banging going on."

A ghost, a vamp, and a ghoul? It had to have been Michael and his friends. What irked me the most was how this old sod had spotted Michael for a ghoul within a few minutes of seeing him and I, a trained Protector, hadn't believed my own eyes. Had I overlooked Michael because of his relationship to Blake? Why else wouldn't I have recognized him for what he was? Shit, I'd given a whole new meaning to the phrase "blinded by love".

"Was there a beautiful blonde female with them?" If the murderers were the Otherworlders I'd seen at the bar with Michael, then I wanted to know if his girl-*fiend* had come along for the fun.

"No. No females." His dark eyes, sunken into his wrinkled face, locked onto me. "Was there supposed to be one?"

I shook my head and guided him back to his story. "Not

necessarily. Go on."

"Well, I could hear them even with my pitiful hearing. Deaf in one ear, I am. At any rate, I heard them shouting about a bracelet of some kind. Then I heard screaming and saw blood splattering on the window. After it got quiet, I saw the ghoul-man pick up a television and smash it to the floor. Damn shame to waste a fine television set."

Was Michael the ghoul-man? From what Gramps had said, Michael had known the Bracelet was in the set. But had he found the Bracelet? "What did the ghoul-man look like?"

Clem coughed up another wad of gunk. "Good-looking fella with dark hair, muscled body. In fact, he looked a lot like the photo you have on your keychain."

I'd forgotten about my keys and keychain I still held in my hand. In a sentimental move, I'd attached a small photo charm with Blake's picture to the chain. "He looked like this man?" I held the picture closer to Clem in a desperate hope of changing his mind.

"Girlie, my hearing may be bad, but my eyes are as good as they ever were. The ghoul-man wasn't this man, but damn close. Brotherly close, if you know what I mean. The man on your keychain came later on. A little while ago, in fact."

My throat clogged and my stomach sank, leaving barely enough room to get air in and out of my lungs. Again, I held up my keychain for him to study, but I could tell by the expression in his eyes he wasn't mistaken. "This man? He was here today?" I swallowed and asked the question I didn't want answered. "He wasn't with the others you saw before?"

"Nope. He wasn't one of them." Compassion wafted from Clem to me and I knew he was happy to confirm Blake's absence at the murders. The nearly hundred-year-old man could read me like a signpost. "He strolled around the house like you did. Like he was searching for something."

I stood quickly, unable to bear hearing anything more. "Thanks, Clem. I appreciate your help." Without shaking his hand, I bolted down the steps.

"No problem, girlie."

I was halfway down the sidewalk when I turned to ask a final question. "Did you tell the police all this?"

His gravely chuckle was low and soft. "What for? Would

they have believed me?"

The old man was indeed a wise man. "Not a chance."

His gaze darted away from me. Something behind me had caught his eye. "Girlie, did you mean female human or female creature?"

The message in his eyes was unmistakable. "*Turn around. Now.*" I whirled around in time to see a white werewolf—the white werewolf that had attacked me outside the bar—dart around the corner of the house and out of sight.

Honey, Whose Blonde Fur
is on Your Collar?

Lots of people have hard days at work. But I doubted their worst day was ever as bad as the day I'd just experienced.

What had happened to my life? I'd been enjoying my new role as a newlywed with a stable, financially and physically well-off, handsome investment analyst. A few short days later and my world had flipped over, turning everything I knew upside down.

Instead of wondering what to feed my wonderful hubby for dinner, I had to wonder if my husband was mixed up in an Otherworldly murder. Instead of scouring the sexy lingerie at a trendy new boutique, I was searching for the powerful weapon a high demon lord could use against mankind. And, as if that weren't enough, I had a brother-in-law who was not only a ghoul, but a dismembering cannibal. Could things get any worse?

Unfortunately, they could.

Not only did I have the pressure of trying to stop a demon from gaining world-wide control, I had to come to terms with my less-than-acceptable new relative. On top of that, I no longer trusted my husband and wondered if he might be a preternatural being like his brother. I pictured the upcoming holiday season and couldn't help but feel a bit anxious. With Brother Ghoul and drunk Uncle Lou at the same table, Thanksgiving dinners were bound to get ugly.

My life sucked. Big time.

I pulled into my driveway, debated my options, and wished

I could pack away all my troubles once I walked into the house. Even Partner picked up on my mood, remaining silent on the way home instead of complaining.

Slamming the driver's side door, I stomped around the rear of the car. But I didn't get very far.

"Yoo-hoo, Jenny, honey!"

I paused for a second, gritted my teeth at the sound of Mrs. Hardgrave's voice, and started walking again. Unbelievably, my life had taken yet another nosedive. Could I ignore her? No doubt the busybody had something juicy to tell me and wouldn't let me get away. Otherwise, she'd never have bothered to speak to me in the first place.

"Jenny! Jenny, I know you heard me."

Had I thought my life sucked before? Well, now it sucked double time. I closed my eyes and gathered my strength, forcing myself to be polite. I faked the biggest smile I could manage and turned around to find her dashing across my yard, full speed ahead.

"Hi, Mrs. Hardgrave. How are you?"

She grabbed my arm and nearly pulled me over, then tugged me to the other side of my car. Taking me with her, we ducked down.

"What the hell are you doing?" So much for politeness. I knew I shouldn't lose it, but this broad had a way of bringing out the worst in me.

"There's no need to cuss at me, Jenny."

God, how I hated being called Jenny. Only my mother could get away with calling me by my childhood name. "I'm sorry, but I'm really tired and I want to go inside. Please excuse me—"

Instead of letting me go, however, she held on tighter. "No. You can't."

"I can't what? Go inside my own home?"

"Exactly. You can't go inside right now. Not before you know what you're walking into, and not unless you plan on confronting him"—the look she gave me was fifty percent pity and fifty percent glee. Actually, make that twenty-five percent pity and seventy-five percent glee— "about *her.*"

Her? "Her who?" Okay, she had me. I didn't want to go

anywhere until I found out more information.

"Yes, her. Your handsome hubby is inside with a very exotic, very *beautiful* woman." The glee part rose to ninety percent.

I couldn't help but feel like she'd put extra emphasis on the beautiful part of her description. But I didn't have time to worry about Mrs. Hardgrave's personal digs at me. "Yeah? She's probably a client." Shit. My explanation sounded hollow even to my ears.

Mrs. H. snickered at my suggestion. "Oh, Jenny, honey. No client ever looked liked she does. Why, her gorgeous white-blonde hair is enough to pull men's eyeballs right out of their sockets. Not to mention her incredible body."

Blonde? I shook my head, wanting to get rid of the idea creeping its way from my head to my heart. Mrs. H., however, took my refusal to mean something else.

"Oh, I'm sorry, Jenny."

I couldn't be sure, but I had the uneasy feeling that an unspoken *not* hung in the air after her sentence.

"I'm sure there's a logical explanation. Perhaps she's his sister?" If my explanation sounded hollow, hers sounded downright contrived.

I continued to fight the idea of the blonde woman with Michael being the same blonde visiting Blake. After all, the world was filled with gorgeous blondes. Unless... "Is anyone else with Blake?"

"Like who?"

"Like another man. One who looks a lot like Blake. He's Blake's brother and he has a blonde, um, lady friend."

Mrs. H. wasn't convinced. "I didn't see anyone else with them."

"Why are you peeping into my home, anyway?" I'd never challenged her about her snooping before now, but this was as good a time as any to start.

Mrs. H. stammered for a second before apparently deciding indignation was her best option. "I wasn't peeping! I merely happened to be working in my garden and I happened to glance over at your house. Can I help it if the curtains were open?"

"You still didn't have to watch, you know. You could've

turned away and ignored what you'd seen." My tone was harsh. I knew I was using her as a target for my frustration and my shot-to-hell-and-back nerves, but I didn't care.

"Well, since you obviously don't appreciate me warning you about your husband's wandering ways, I'll let you handle it as best you see fit. Humph!"

She stormed off across the street to her house and I made no attempt to stop her. "Good riddance, you old snoop."

A few weeks ago, if someone had told me I'd be sneaking up to my house to spy on my new husband entertaining a beautiful blonde woman, I'd have chalked their story up to one helluva night's partying. Yet here I was tiptoeing up to the big window in the front, peeking around the window frame to catch Blake and Blondie together. Hopefully, not together-together, if you know what I mean. But after the events of recent days, I steeled myself to get ready for anything.

Blake and the woman were in the living room and, judging from the way she flung her arms around and their angry expressions, this was either a lovers' quarrel or a business deal gone terribly wrong. My greatest wish at the moment was to have better hearing or single-paned windows. Neither one was about to happen, so I concentrated on trying to read their lips.

The blonde Angelina Jolie body double was fed up. About what, however, I had no clue. She moved around a lot, motioning with rapid arm and hand gestures.

Blake, on the other hand, stayed in one place. It seemed like he was imploring her to do something. Surely my sexy husband wasn't begging her to sleep with him? Nah. After watching awhile longer, I dismissed my greatest fear. These two people weren't sleeping with each other. In fact, I could tell they didn't even like each other. But if I was right, what were they doing?

Blondelina turned toward the window. I gasped, ducked, and pressed my body against the wall. A newspaper landed at my feet, causing me to pivot enough to catch our newspaper man staring at me in concern.

"You okay, Mrs. Barrington?"

Startled, I pretended to search for something on the ground. "Oh, sure. I'm fine. I, uh, lost my earring." When his brow furrowed more, I hurried on with my ruse. "In the garden.

Uh, the last time I worked in my garden." I tried adding a pitiful smile.

"Uh-huh." He definitely hadn't bought my story. "Want some help?"

"Oh, no, no. I'm fine." Taking care to scoot to the other side of the window, I palmed a pebble off the ground, stood, and waved at him. "Found it."

He nodded and continued on his way.

"I am such a liar."

"That you are, m'dear. That you are."

I jumped again, away from the window, and landed on my butt. Which also had me nearly landing on a scowling imp. "Ow! Dammit! What are you doing in my yard?"

His tiny body was no more than the size of a leaf on my rose bush. In fact, he stared up at me from behind a red rose. Wiggling his elfish ears, he shook his finger at me. "Watch where you sit yer big ass, why don't ya?"

Could this day get any worse? I definitely wasn't in the mood to mess with one of the tiniest demons-slash-faeries around. The imp spread a mischievous grin across his face and danced around me, naked and flashing every part of his body. "Go away, little man, before I sit on you again," I hissed. I checked again just to be sure. Yep, that was a very miniscule and very erect pee-pee, all right.

"And what if I don't?" He twirled, then darted between my legs. "I'm thinking I'd enjoy a bit of fun with you."

"Trust me, squirt, I'm not in a fun kind of mood."

"Oh, no? Because yer oaf of a man is fooling around with the blonde bitch?" He whooped and hollered, accentuating his remarks by jabbing a finger into my ankle. "Not married even a year and already yer man's cheating on ya."

I reached out to scoop him up and missed. "He's not cheating on me."

"Then what's he doing with *her*?"

The way he'd said the word "her" spoke volumes. "Do you know her?"

His titters set my already frayed nerves on edge. "Do I know her? Do I *know* her?" Skipping, he continued his harangue. "Of course, I know her. The puzzle is that you don't. Especially since yer husband sure does. Hehehehehe!"

I'd had enough. Scrambling to my feet, I left the imp jumping over a twig, singing his heart out, and headed for the front door.

"Hey! Where ya going? I'm not finished discussing yer lover's straying!"

Later, when the mystery of the Bracelet was solved and my life returned to normal—or what used to pass for normal—I'd exterminate every single imp in my garden. One thing I knew for a fact. Where there was one imp, there were a hundred more you didn't see. Like cockroaches, they bred quickly and infested gardens.

When I burst through the door and into the living room, I was ready to call Blondelina out at high noon. With or without pistols. I'd built up a solid head of steam and was ready to boil her alive. Unfortunately, I didn't get the fight I wanted.

Instead, I found Blake relaxing on the sofa with a book I'd bought for myself—like I could ever find time to read—but which he'd already picked up and started reading a week earlier. Unlike most men, Blake was secure in his masculinity and had no problems reading a romance novel.

He paused and glanced up at me. "Hi, Jenn. How was your day?"

It was a joke. It had to be. I inspected the living room and checked behind the sofa. Blondelina was gone. "Uh, fine. And yours?" Confused, I headed for the kitchen, hoping I'd find her hiding under the sink.

"Good. Hey, where're you going?"

I darted into the kitchen, looked in the pantry and under the sink, but she wasn't around. Instead, a blur caught my eye outside the bay window and I drew closer to see. Blondelina whisked across the yard, heading for our privacy fence.

I had her now. Only an Olympic athlete with a pole could jump our tall fence. Believe me, I've tried. Yet I was in for a surprise.

Her body morphed, dropping onto all fours and elongating. Blondelina changed into the white werewolf I'd seen twice before. In a fluid motion, she crouched and leapt over the fence.

I didn't confront Blake about the woman shifter. After watching her transform, I returned to the living room and studied my husband. He was still reading the book, completely entranced with the story. As though nothing unusual had happened, he lay spread out on the sofa, laughing. Worn out mentally and physically, I plopped down on the arm chair next to the couch.

"Good book?" I couldn't have mustered up more than those two words if I'd needed them to save my life. Slumping into the comfort of the cushions, I closed my eyes and willed myself to think. Not only was my brother-in-law a ghoul, but my husband had something going on with the werewolf who'd tried to kill me. This begged questions I wasn't sure I wanted answered. Did my husband know the woman was a shifter? Did he know she'd tried to kill me?

"Yeah, it is. It's really good. This book has humor, action, and a love story."

"Hmm." The book sounded like my life except the heroine would more than likely have a happy ending. Me with a happily ever after? Far from guaranteed.

Blake, however, took my less-than-enthusiastic response and ran with it. "Yeah. And it's a paranormal story, too."

"Oh?" Anger started boosting my energy level again. I narrowed my eyes, hoping Blake would see *the look* and ask what he'd done wrong. Then I'd confront him. *Oh, nothing much, Blake. Unless you count cavorting with a shifter who tried to rip out my throat as doing something wrong.*

"You'd like it, too. The story involves an intuitive matchmaker. She can tell a person the name of their soul mate simply by touching them." He held the cover up for me to see. "It's called *Touch Me.*"

"Yeah, I remember." Was he trying to bait me? Give me a hint? The churning inside me wanted him to confess everything. Yet another part of me didn't think I could handle it. I decided on a compromise. "How's business, Blake?"

He lowered the book to gaze at me with those sensual, emotional gray eyes. "Fine."

"Did you have anything unusual happen today? Like maybe a visitor?"

Those deep soulful eyes clouded over with worry.

134

"Unusual? No. I go to my clients, not the other way around, remember?"

"Oh, right. Silly me." For the life of me—*sheesh, there's a crappy phrase*—I couldn't dredge up a smile. Instead, I simply nodded. Unless I wanted to explain to him where I'd seen the woman before, I had to keep my yap shut. "No one came here today, huh?" *Great, Jenn. Great way to keep the trap shut.*

"No. No one was here. Why do you ask?" The worry in his eyes deepened, but his expression remained neutral.

If I wanted to confront him, now was the time. But I couldn't do it. "No reason." I shrugged and glanced away.

Suspicion in his voice echoed the worry I'd seen in his eyes. "Oh. O-kaay."

The questions I didn't want to ask him kept pounding in my head, giving me one helluva headache. Blake had lied. Not simply by omission and not by mistake. He'd lied by choice. I had to wonder...what else had he lied about?

Granted, I've done my fair share of lying to my husband, but only to honor my commitment to the Society and to protect my fellow Protectors. I lied about business, but never about anything personal. "Do you love me, Blake?" The words were out of my mouth before they'd ever made it to my brain.

"Of course I do." Blake pushed off the couch and kneeled at my feet. Putting his arms on either side of my legs, he leaned closer to my face. "Don't you know how much I love you?"

"I thought I did." *Before Michael. Before Blondelina. Before you'd lied.*

His eyes were solid black and capturing mine without any resistance from me. "I love you more than anything or anyone else. I'd fight for you until my last breath."

One truth about me is that I'm a good judge of character. I can tell when strangers lie to me. I can also tell when someone I love is telling me the truth. Or at least I thought could. Yet even with my recent failures to recognize Blake's earlier lies, I knew, without a doubt in my heart, Blake was telling me the truth. He loved me, plain and simple. Okay, maybe not so plain or simple, but true enough.

I sat up and hugged him to me. Forget Michael. Forget Blondelina. Forget the lies. I knew what I knew. And I knew Blake Barrington loved me. As for all the rest, he'd tell me when he was ready. I had no doubt he'd have a reasonable answer for my questions when the time was right. Until then, I'd have to trust him.

A few minutes later, however, I realized the seeds of doubt had been planted and had started to grow. With our fast and wonderfully wild courtship and marriage, how much did I really know about the man I loved? Answer? Not much. Yes, Blake Barrington loved me. But who was the real Blake Barrington?

I'm not a computer person. Don't get me wrong. I like gadgets like Partner, digital cameras, video phones, iPods, and even some kickass video games. The more bells and whistles, the better I liked it. However, I hate sitting at a computer to do research. Usually, I get on the computer to check email, balance my checkbook, and nothing more. But I needed information and I didn't want Partner sticking his gossipy cyber-nose into my personal business.

I waited until Blake announced he was off to bed, then stayed up claiming I wanted to research the housing market for a new client coming in from out of town. We kissed goodnight and I soon heard his snores coming from upstairs. For once, I was glad Blake snored like a polar bear with sleep apnea.

I'd done research on other people before and I knew which websites to access. Surfing through the Web for information about Blake Barrington, I kept pulling up the facts I already knew about my husband. Facts I'd already obtained during the first week we'd met.

Yup, the Internet is a wonderful invention. I'd already Googled him back then. Hey, I believe in love at first sight and falling in love in light-warped speed, but I'm not stupid. Not then and not now. Besides, what red-blooded American girl doesn't Google her dates?

However, I did notice one thing different this time. No matter how hard I looked, the Web had no information on Blake Barrington before September, 2000. No business entries, no news items, and no birth certificate. From everything I could find—or more accurately what I could *not* find—Blake Barrington didn't have a life before the new millennium.

Trying to ignore the butterflies-turned-bats in my stomach, I tried something I hadn't tried the first time I'd scoped him out.

I plugged in his name and requested the search to include sound-alike names. The computer went through its search mode, rummaging through the data out in Cyberland. I waited, telling myself everything would be all right, and hoping what I dreaded might happen, wouldn't happen.

Demons often rose from the bowls of Hell to walk the earth by means of possessing the body of a mortal already born, bred and living on the planet. They could even repair the body if tissues, lost limbs, or other injuries had disfigured it. Yet instead of taking over the person's life, the newly entrenched demon would take their new body on the lam, away from family and friends who might notice a difference in his personality and, especially, in his actions.

Much like their mortal counterparts who decide to make a new life in a new place, the demon-possessed human creates his own version of the Witness Protection Plan. Often, he fakes his death—usually in some gruesome way that doesn't leave any remains to positively identify—and fabricates a whole new identity. In essence, he makes a new life for an old body. Strange thing, however, is how the demon usually chooses a name very similar to his victim's name. It was almost as if some of the victim still resides inside the body and wants to retain at least a thread of familiarity with his old life.

All at once the streaming information across the page halted and listed ten sound-alike names. I ran through them, finding none of them familiar, and decided to start at the top. Somehow, I had the terrible feeling I was headed toward the bottom with both my list and my life.

"Blake Blair." I clicked on the first name and the ever-helpful computer presented Blake's information. "Shoot. No photo." I kept scanning and, after the first few lines, I knew Blake Blair wasn't the man I was looking for. "Born 1973 and still living. No demon possession here." One down, nine to go.

The next three men were easily discounted. Each one of them had maintained a continuous presence in their birth body. No trespassers were indicated.

"You'd think I'd breathe a little easier since I haven't found anything demonic. Maybe Blake's earlier life information hadn't gotten plugged into the universal database," I mumbled to myself, knowing what I'd said wasn't likely. The more men I rejected, the closer I came to finding out the horrible truth my gut knew lurked right over the next superhighway hill. I continued my search.

My gut is usually right. But for once, I wasn't happy it was. Holding my breath, I clicked on the next-to-last name and let out an agonized groan. Smiling at me from the monitor was a picture of my husband. Yet the name under the photo wasn't Blake Barrington, but Drake Barrinson. To add to my growing horror, I noted the year of Drake's death—the year 2000.

A Rose by Any Other Name is Still a Rose—And a Skunk Is Still a Skunk.

I stared at the man leaning against the hood of a red convertible and fought to keep my tears in check. After examining the picture for several minutes and trying to conjure up any logical reason my husband would be in the newspaper—could this man be Blake's long-lost twin?—I let my gaze lower to the headline beneath the photograph.

Local Businessman, Drake Barrinson, Lost at Sea.

Drake Barrinson was Blake Barrington. Yet did it mean Blake was a demon? Reaching for any hope I could find, I suddenly remembered Bob Morton. I'd been completely wrong about Bob and maybe, with any luck, I was wrong about Blake. *Please, God, let me be wrong about Blake.*

A few years ago, I ran into a mild-mannered Pillsbury Doughboy who I thought was a demon. Like with Blake, I'd scoured the Web and found Bill Marton—deceased—who looked an awful like Bob Morton. The way I figured it, Bob Morton hadn't existed until after Bill Marton's death. But I'd gotten almost every other conclusion wrong.

I'd found out Bob was indeed Bill, but not until I'd nearly beheaded the terrified man. More investigation revealed the whole truth. Bill Marton, wanting to escape a loveless marriage and an IRS investigation, had faked his death and reinvented himself. Presto-chango and a few falsified documents later, enter Bob Morton. Thankfully, I'd found this out before I'd lopped off his head with a chain saw. Yeah, I'd learned my lesson and also realized I could never watch the *Saw* horror movies again.

"Maybe Blake changed his name the old-fashioned way, legally with an attorney." Could I let myself hope? I studied the face of Drake Barrinson one last time and knew I stared at the face of my husband. Even if Blake was able to explain the name change and the new history, would I ever trust him again?

"Dammit all. My life just keeps getting suckier."

It's a good thing I don't need much sleep because I sure didn't get any. Hours later, I cleared the history log on my computer, shut down the computer and made my way to bed. Unfortunately, a thing like seeing my husband's photo with a different man's name—a deceased man's name—has a tendency to give me insomnia.

Lying awake next to Blake gave me time to think. Time to find other excuses and time to go into deep denial. Still, I have to plead my case. How many newly married women wouldn't have done the same? By the time the alarm clocked buzzed, I'd thought up a whole list of reasons why Drake was Blake.

"Morning, possum-pussy."

"Yuck. Not a pretty image." The man I loved with every ounce of my soul placed his hand on my hip and snuggled closer. I sighed and twisted onto my side. "Morning, sugar-booger."

Since our first morning waking up together, we'd had this ritual of greeting each other with slightly ridiculous and often unflattering endearments. Nothing put a smile on our faces like being called a silly name. Blake, however, had made me promise never to repeat them to any other living male. Perhaps I should have asked him about any non-living male? I shoved the thought aside, renewed my determination to get to the truth this morning, and ran my hand over his cheek.

Blake copied my loving gesture. "You look like a woman who didn't sleep well. What's up, poopy lips? Bad dreams?"

A hazard of living the life of a Protector often meant nightmares, but they rarely kept me from getting my solid eight hours. "No. Just restless, I guess." I smiled at Blake and ran through my plan once more.

Somewhere around three in the morning, I'd come up with a scheme to get Blake to confess his deception. Not about being a demon—which, of course, he wasn't—but about his fleeing from a past he couldn't handle. Worst case scenario? He was a violent felon fleeing the law. Best case scenario? He was a polygamist who'd wanted to dump his frumpy, fat first wife and hook up with a sexy young lover. (Which, by the way, was me.)

"Blakie-Poo?"

Blake touched the end of my nose with his fingertip. "Yeah, stinky-stew?"

"Stinky-stew?" I made a face of disgust.

"Hey, it's early. Give a guy a break."

The twinkle in his gray eyes lit a fire in my belly. "I had time to think last night."

"Yeah? What were you thinking about?" He batted his eyes at me in perfect coquettish fashion. "Moi?"

Sometimes the man was such a ham, but I had to love him for it. "Uh, yeah, oh, self-centered one. *Both* me and you. And a will. You know. The thing that starts out with 'Being of sound mind and body'?"

The twinkle vanished, replaced by a scowl. "You're kidding. A will? Why are you spending time thinking about a will?" The scowl, however, was quickly replaced by a worried frown. "Is something wrong? Are you okay?"

Of one thing I was sure. This man loved me. The warmth of knowing real love washed through me. "I'm fine. You don't have to get sick to have a will. In fact, having one before something bad happens is a good thing. You're an investment analyst, for Pete's sake. I would've thought you'd have recommended one to your clients."

"Nope. I leave the money-after-death side to the lawyers and insurance agents. You know, the bloodsuckers."

Bloodsuckers? Oh, Blake, don't go there.

Blake pushed up to lean over me and plaster kisses on my neck. Tugging my ragged T-shirt over my head—I'm not the teddy kind of girl—he continued kissing his way down to my breasts. "Trust me. Nothing bad's going to happen."

I might have agreed with him except for the small fact that Protectors have a much higher mortality rate than either real estate agents or investment analysts. "Blake, anything can happen. I could die in a car wreck this morning or you could drown in a boating accident. Shitty shit happens."

He stopped tweaking my ever-ready nipples to raise his head and search my face. "Me drown? Thanks a lot."

"Stranger things have happened." And I definitely knew about strange happenings. "Don't you want to be prepared?"

Blake ignored my question and rolled over, pulling me on top of him. In one swift motion, he had my sleep shorts off me. "Jenn, can't we stop all the gloom and doom talk and have some fun?"

I tried to keep my mind on getting him to confess his secret past, but his teeth nibbling on my tits made it a superhuman feat. True, I'm a determined woman, which is almost like having super powers, but I'm also a true patriot and Blake's flag was flying sky high. I tugged his boxers off him and decided to salute the flag. Nothing says a girl can't have a little fun *and* keep searching for answers, right?

"Sure. But why can't you tell me about your life? For a wife, I know very little about you. For instance, what were you like as a boy? Where did you go to college? Have you been married before?" *Or are you still married?* "For all I know, you could have a criminal past, faked your own death, and gone on the run from the law."

"Wow, woman, you do have an imagination. A felon on the run, huh? Not bad." Blake lifted my hips, positioning me over his shaft. He rubbed against me and turned up the fire inside me. "Sorry to disappoint you, but I've led a pretty boring life. I had the typical childhood, the typical college experience, the typical six previous marriages."

Trying to listen while he stroked me was a skill all its own. "I'd still like to hear about—hey, six marriages?"

His hands fondled my breasts and I decided I couldn't wait any longer. Lifting my bottom up, I grabbed his shaft and slid it into me. We moaned in unison and he pulled me down to take a nipple into his mouth. I promptly forgot about the six marriages joke—*I hope!*—and concentrated on fulfilling the need in each of us.

Sex before meeting Blake was just sex. But sex with Blake? Now *that* was mind-blowing, earth-shattering, life-changing, amazing sex.

We rocked together, his hot mouth devouring my breasts as I clenched and unclenched, pulling him deeper inside me. His hands, first on my breasts and then on my ass, molded my body to him, making me his with every touch. His words of love poured over me, almost tangible in their strength.

"Jenn."

My name never sounded so sweet. With Blake loving me, I was more than I could ever be alone. I wanted to give him as much as he'd given me in the sound of my own name. "Blake."

With the morning sun filtered through the blinds, we renewed our devotion, our trust, and our love.

Most people love weekends. Saturday and Sunday gave them two whole days to play sports, make love any time of the day, or catch up on doing nothing at all. I hated weekends. Weekends meant open houses, last-minute calls to show a home, and catching up on the endless paperwork I'd neglected throughout the week.

Yet no matter how much my job as a realtor interfered with my free time, I always managed to carve out downtime with Blake. Except today. Today I needed all the extra time I could find to meet with one of my Otherworld informants.

Pulling on my power suit for the open house I had to man this morning, I struggled with my own special demons. Granted, informants were valuable in helping a Protector with information about the evil activities happening around town, yet a part of me would never get used to dealing with these scumbags. How much could I trust them? After all, if they'd sell out their own kind for money or favors, how much faster would they sell out a Protector?

But I'd run out of options in locating Michael and his cohorts. Even Partner couldn't find him, which meant Michael had gone undercover into the gritty, dirty Otherworld. I was desperate and knew I'd run out of time. I had to find the Bracelet before the High Demon found it first. My questions about Blake would have to wait.

The open house went smoothly without too many lookie-loos taking up my attention or zombie housewives attacking me. By the time my afternoon replacement arrived, I'd managed to wrap up my paperwork and text-message a love note to Blake. I tossed the house keys to the second shift, and was off and running toward the rendezvous location.

"A gargoyle? Damn, darlin', how do you stand it? Those things smell worse than a stall with a foot of manure."

I popped Partner into my pocket—an action fast becoming a habit—and scoured the perimeter of the picture-perfect neighborhood park for any sign of my informant. "I gotta do what I gotta do in this job. No thanks to you."

"Can I help it if I can't find your brother-in-law? I don't know why you don't force Blake to tell you where he is."

I headed toward the grassy center, skirting the taller bushes to avoid a possible ambush. Hungry, vicious gnomes loved hiding in bushes, waiting to attack the unsuspecting park jogger. In fact, over half the dog bites joggers reported to the police were actually bites from a faster-than-the-eye gnome. Strangely, no one ever noticed the difference in the teeth marks.

"Oh, sure. I'm going to make Blake tell me where his ghoul brother is. Can you imagine the conversation? 'Blake, honey, I need to find your brother. Why? Oh, no biggie. He might have the world's most powerful weapon in his hands and I've been ordered to recover the weapon at any cost. Oh, and if it means exterminating your brother and his friends, then sor-ry. By the way, what would you like for dinner, honey?'"

I smiled at an elderly couple as they walked past me. Without letting on, I kicked a gnome away from their heels. Those irritating things were always underfoot. "'Oh, and by the way, Blake, did I forget to mention? Michael's a ghoul and I'm a member of a secret society sworn to protect mortals from evil supernatural creatures like demons and flesh-eating mummies.' Yeah, he'll definitely out his brother then."

"Darlin', there's no reason to get your tail in a bunch of knots."

"Partner, I'm getting kind of tired of the cowboy bit. How about something different for a while?" I opened my pocket to see his reaction.

The cowboy dropped his lasso and threw down his hat. "Something different? After the hours of the research I did about the Wild West? I've put a lot of time and energy into making my persona as authentic as possible. And now you want me to change?"

Who knew Partner was an actor-wanna-be? I shrugged and made a face. "Would you mind? Think about it. You'll have fun researching your next role, er, character."

"Hmm, well, maybe. Do you have any preferences?"

"Anything mortal—or as mortal as you can get. Now hush. Keep quiet and let mommy talk business."

I continued past the grassy area, across the street, and up the steps of one of the oldest churches in the city. I examined the architecture of the building and its lack of any gargoyle ornamentation, and yet I knew at least one gargoyle lived at the church.

It wasn't long before I noticed the first sign of a gargoyle's presence. The stink almost overwhelmed me. Clamping a handkerchief over my nose and mouth, I tried to take in as little air as humanly possible. Partner, however, forgot my earlier admonition for quiet and piped up in a distinctive Southern Belle voice.

"Oh, my Lord Almighty. Do tell. What is that horrid smell?"

I peeked at Partner and almost dropped my protective mouth covering. Instead of the hunk cowboy, a diminutive woman, with petticoats peeking out from below her long red gown, stood atop a grassy knoll. She waved a delicate lace hankie at me and promptly positioned it daintily over her nose.

"Shut up, Scarlett O'Technoid!" I tried to hiss my order, but it came out louder than I'd expected.

A pouty expression changed Scarlett's features from disgust to indignation. In perfect imitation of the famous Southern character, she stomped a foot on the ground and protested, "Well, I never! Is that any way to talk to a lady?"

"Beats the hell outta me because I'm not talking to a lady." I glanced around me, searching for my smelly, still-hidden informant. "I'm talking to a machine."

"I'll have you know I was born and raised in Georgia where I attended the finest finishing school. I am a lady, you yellow-belly Yankee, and you will speak to me with the proper respect due a lady of my position."

Could a machine have a mental illness? Sort of like blowing a psychological fuse? Perhaps Partner was a Sybil of the synthetic kind? "Fine, Miss Scarlett, but for right now I need you to keep quiet. Gargoyles don't like crowds and with you in my pocket, three is definitely a crowd."

A waft of rank odor hit me, nearly cutting off my last gasp for clean air. I heard the growl of Gargeyan behind me and I whirled around in time to see the grotesque creature dart behind one of the church's white columns. "Gargeyan?" I didn't want to, but I moved closer, hoping to see him skirting among the bushes next to the column. "Come on out."

The familiar nasal voice greeted me, sending out another puff of putrid air. "Have you what?"

Gargeyan—aka *Gag*-me-yan—stuck his nose out of the bush long enough to sniff me. I correctly interpreted his question, knowing Gargoyles mix up the words in their sentences. Gargoyles loved cheese. Not just any old cheese, but moldy, expired-for-weeks cheese. Give them a fresh slice of cheddar cheese and they'd tear your throat out in anger.

"Come and get it, old man." I pulled the thickly wrapped rotten cheese out of the bag I carried and opened the foil. Immediately, the stink of cheese gone way off filled the air around me and tears stung my eyes at the stench wafting into them.

"Want me. Now want me." Gargeyan thrust out a bone-thin, scaly gray arm for the cheese. "Gimme. You cheese now."

I fought the urge to upchuck all over the decaying lump in my hand and slowly, temptingly folded the foil over the cheese. "Not so fast, handsome. Do you have information for me or not?"

Gargeyan grabbed for the bundle, but I was quicker. Jerking the treasure out of his reach, I tisked-tisked and shook a finger at him. "Uh-uh-uh. No play, no pay."

Snarling, the ancient gargoyle peered through the leaves of the bush. Irritation radiated from his dense, pudgy body and reflected in his squinty black eyes. Although it wasn't safe to get a gargoyle upset, I had to make sure he'd tell me everything he knew before getting his reward. Gargoyles were notorious for wanting payment for doing nothing.

"Me what tell?" His voice shook with either need or hatred, or a combination of both.

"Word around the street says a high demon wants a certain powerful weapon. True?"

Gargeyan grunted which in gargoyle language, is a big yes. Aside from dragons who love to offer up riddles instead of giving direct answers, gargoyles are the best at keeping secrets and information. Unfortunately for me, my friend Gargeyan—inserting tongue-in-cheek—had to be one of the toughest of all gargoyles to get to spill the beans.

"Good. Word also has it that this weapon is a special bracelet and that a ghoul by the name of Michael and some other Otherworlders may already possess this weapon. Do they?"

"Have, shit, no, no have, yes."

Even after years of dealing with these difficult creatures, I had no idea how to interpret his answer. I tried again. "Does the ghoul Michael have the Bracelet?"

"Have, shit, no, no have, yes."

I tried one last time, using all my patience to keep my voice mellow. "Gargeyan, listen carefully. Say yes or no to the question. Does the ghoul Michael have the Bracelet?" If he answered in gibberish again, I'd have to figure out another way to get the answer.

"Have, shit, no, no have, yes."

All the frustration from the past days—finding out Michael was a ghoul and learning my husband, or at least his name, was non-existent before the new millennium—burst out of me before I could cram the words back down my throat. "Dammit, you stupid ugly troll, just say yes or no!" I clenched my hand over the cheese, mushing the mound of yellow-gray mold.

Gargeyan's eyes bulged open and we stared at each other—me waiting for his reaction and him simply frozen in stunned misery. I didn't have to wait long. Opening his fang-filled mouth, he screeched in horror and lunged at me. I jumped at the last second, hitting him with the balled up fist of cheese. However, I knew I couldn't hurt him. Gargoyles have an amazing capacity to take a punch and feel no pain. A steamroller could flatten one and they'd pop right back up like a cartoon character.

Gargeyan rolled toward the column on the other side of the steps. The clouds parted above us, sending a shaft of light to land directly on Gargeyan. Although sunlight can't kill a gargoyle—they aren't like vampires, you know—the gargoyle still detested feeling the warmth of the sun's rays on his skin. Gargeyan screeched again, his ear-piercing wail setting off all the dogs in the neighborhood. He dashed into the bushes lining the building.

"Listen, Gargeyan, I don't have all day. Just say—yes—or—no."

Mimicking my own stilted sentence, he snarled and answered again. "Have. Shit. No. No. Have. Yes."

I gave up. How the hell would I get this moron of the granite set to answer this one simple question?

"Oh, for the love of mercy. Don't you understand him?"

Great, all I needed was to have the Confederate Cell Phone chime in. "Not now, Scarlett."

"I see. Then you don't want me to tell you what he's saying?"

I peeked into my pocket to find one very smug Princess of the Plantation waiting for my answer. "You're telling me you understand him?"

"Well, of course, I do, honey-child. Any idiot with half an ear could." She flipped her hair at me and pointed her snooty nose into the air.

Why was everyone from gargoyles to glorified and, not to mention, insane PDAs giving me a hard time today? "Well?"

"Well...what?"

I groaned. "You know damn well what. What's he saying?"

"I don't think I should tell you." Her dainty nose shot higher into the air and stayed there. "I don't like helping people who are rude to me. I, for one, was raised with the civility and manners becoming a young woman."

I squelched the urge to pop Partner's batteries out and let him—her?—die a slow, powerless death. "Partner, bring me the cowboy." Anything and anyone was better than dealing with this genteel diva.

"No. I like being a girl." Strains of West Side's Story's *I Feel Pretty* echoed from Partner's speakers.

Gargeyan whimpered, causing me to look up in time to see his imploring eyes. "Tell I."

At least I understood one comment. "I know you told me the answer, Gargeyan, but I don't understand what you told

148

me. Someone's not helping me."

"All you have to do is be polite." Partner-turned-Southern diva sang along with the show tune.

I gritted my teeth and forced the words through thinned lips. "Miss Scarlett, would you please tell me what the nice little gargoyle is saying?" Another whine from Gargeyan pushed me over the edge, making me add a plea. "Pretty please?" I swore right then and there I'd return Partner to Reslind—in a million pieces.

"Ah! There you go. See? Isn't a polite question much better than rude command?"

I wanted to ask her if a rude command was better than coercion, but decided I'd better leave well enough alone. "Uh-huh. Now, could you please tell me what Gargeyan said?" *Before I stomp all over your face with my big fat foot?* I smiled at my thought knowing Partner would consider the gesture a friendly one.

"Of course. I'd be happy to. But it's really quite obvious."

Easy, Jenn, easy. Hang on until she tells you. Then you can kill her. "Well, I guess I need a little help." Again, I smiled and pictured Partner spread over the top of the recycle bin.

"You have such a nice smile, Jennifer. You really should smile more often. The gargoyle said this. 'Have? Shit, no. No have. Yes?' Meaning in grammatically correct sentence form, 'Do they have it? Shit, no. They don't have it. Do you understand?'" Miss Scarlett batted her eyelashes at me. "In other words, Michael and his evil friends do not have the Bracelet."

Relieved to finally get an answer, I promptly forgot the hassle I'd gone through to get it. "Good. Good to know." Now I remembered. Gargoyles had no inflection in their speech. Therefore, his question hadn't sounded like a question to me.

I turned to Gargeyan, held up the yucky lump of cheese, and tossed it to him. "Here you go. Enjoy." Gargeyan's face lit up in what I assumed was a grin. Crying something akin to a cheer, he reached out his skinny arm and caught the cheese. All I wanted was to get away from the combination of gargoyle and bad cheese smell. But Gargeyan wasn't finished.

"Demon husband. Demon marry why?"

Stunned, I froze with one foot on the lower step and the

other planted firmly on the porch. "What did you say?"

"Demon husband. Demon marry why?"

I stared at Gargeyan and heard Scarlett whisper to me, "Do you understand what he's saying, Jennifer? Or do you want me to interpret?"

If someone had dropped my brain in quicksand, I couldn't have gotten my thought process to move any slower. I shook my head, feeling like my body had joined my brain in getting sucked into the bog. Yet though he'd spoken in the mixed-up gargoyle language with a hunk of cheese shoved in his mouth, I knew what Gargeyan had said. The problem was, I couldn't get my brain—much less my heart—to believe his words. Gargeyan had said, "Your husband is a demon. Why did you marry a demon?"

The Care and Feeding Of a Big Galoot

"Jennifer, don't you think we should talk about what he said? I mean, about Blake?"

"My husband is not a demon. Don't you know you can't trust a damned gargoyle?"

"But you believed what he said about Michael and the Bracelet, right? Okay, then, why not believe him about Blake?"

Because I don't want to. He had a point, but this was one question I wasn't ready to answer. "Turn off or keep quiet, one or the other. I'm not talking about this, Partner, so you'd better shut up and let me be."

"But if your husband is a—"

"Are you deaf? Shut the hell up!"

I went into autopilot mode on my way home, making turns, merging onto the highway, and pointing the car toward home. Could I trust what Gargeyan had said about Blake? Gargoyles were notorious liars unless you gained their trust. Did Gargeyan trust me enough not to lie to me? I'd believed him about Michael not having the Bracelet. Which begged the question...shouldn't I believe him about Blake being a demon? Hadn't I had my own suspicions?

I pulled my car into the drive and switched off the engine, unable to do anything more. The truth of what I'd subconsciously known hit me in the gut, taking away my stubborn denial. The events, the clues, the outright signs came rushing back to me. How had I missed them?

Yet, I knew the truth. Hell, I'd known the truth for several days. But who wants to admit such a truth when they've fought so long to keep it at bay? Even a half-witted gargoyle knew what a trained Protector didn't want to admit.

How could I have married a demon and not known it?

"Jenny, honey? Are you all right?"

I jumped at the tapping on the window and twisted toward the sound. Mrs. Hardgrave, hair in curlers and wearing her pink housecoat with the purple flowers running down one side, studied me with a worried, furrowed brow.

Not now. Please, not now. Not today.

Mrs. Hardgrave circled her hand, motioning me to roll down the car window. For a moment, I couldn't remember which button to push. Yippee for me—not—my memory came back before she'd given up.

"I can't talk right now, Mrs. Hardgrave." Oh, how I wanted to tell her to fuck off. Oh, how I wanted to tell the whole world to fuck off. Calling on my Protector training, I fought against the tears I wanted to free and smiled at the nosy woman.

"I know, honey. Except you've been sitting in the car for a long time and I thought maybe something was wrong. Is it about the large man in your house? I'm not one to pry, of course, but I couldn't help seeing this enormous man go inside. And, frankly, from the expression on Blake's face I don't think he knew the man or wanted him around. Really, honey, shouldn't you two be more careful about who you let into your home? You know me, I don't want to pry...but are you okay? You look ill."

"I'm fine." In a moment of weakness, I let my emotions take over. "You'd know if I wasn't fine, too, wouldn't you? After all, you know everybody's business all the time, don't you? Why don't you set up a chair in my living room, huh? It would make your constant prying easier. Or maybe we should give you an itinerary of our plans every morning? Think of the time you'd save not having to stand behind your curtains, peeking at your neighbors."

I knew my mouth vomit was a result of my shock over Blake's true identity but, like real upchucking, it's hard to stop once you start. Even the hurt wiping out the worry on the older woman's face couldn't stop me.

"Hey, don't forget our bedtime activities, too. I bet you'd get a kick out of watching us get it on, wouldn't you? You could get off on all your little fantasies about him, couldn't you? Don't deny it, Mrs. H. I've seen you watching him, staring at him."

She mumbled, but I didn't care to try and understand her. I wanted payback for my stupidity, for Blake's not telling me, for my loving a demon. I wanted it now and I didn't care who I used to get it.

I got out of the car, sending Mrs. Hardgrave into a backward shuffle. Shock at my outburst stiffened her limbs faster than years of rheumatoid arthritis ever had.

"Go home, Mrs. Hardgrave, and mind your own damned business." The terrified woman didn't budge and I knew I had to give her the incentive she needed. "Go! Get the hell out of my yard!"

Mrs. Hardgrave shrieked, threw up her hands, and scurried across the street. When she reached her front door, she turned, looked at me once more with those stricken eyes, and dashed inside her home.

No doubt about it. I was a shithead. I'd been really mean to an elderly lady and now the remorse swamped me. Mrs. Hardgrave was a snoop but she was a harmless one and I'd just tongue-lashed her to within an inch of her life. I felt like shit. No, not like shit. Like a shithead.

"Dammit. I don't need this." Groaning, I started toward her house, ready to trample my dignity to save hers.

"Jenn? Hey, Jenn!"

What now? *Who* now? I shifted direction toward the voice. Myra stood at other side of my drive, hopping up and down with excitement. "Jenn, you did it. You sold the house."

My confused mind couldn't understand her words any more than it had understood Gargeyan's. "What? What are you talking about?"

She rushed up to me to give me a big hug. "Swindle called me trying to get hold of you. He said one of the couples you met at the open house made a terrific offer and the sellers accepted."

The open house seemed like a thousand years in the past. Still, a sale was a sale and I was on the Board at work. At least something good had happened today. "Terrific news. Thanks for telling me. Is that why you're here? To tell me I made a sale?"

"You don't act like it's terrific news." Obviously, Myra thought I'd lost my mind. "And since when do I need an excuse to drop by?" She shuffled her feet and raked a ring-laden hand through her hair. "If you want me to call first from now on..."

I pulled her to me. "No, no. I'm sorry. I'm in a mood, is all. I railed on Mrs. Hardgrave for no real reason, too. Other than the fact her snooping is about to drive me crazy, of course. I'm sticking my tail between my legs and going to apologize."

Myra searched me for another explanation, but decided to accept the one I'd given her. "Why don't you give it a little time? I think you need to get yourself together first."

I laughed and heard the tremor in my voice. "Yeah, maybe you're right."

"Besides, it looks like you have a guest."

I followed the direction of Myra's attention to see Blake standing at the window with a man larger than any man I'd ever seen—except for one. George, my rescuer who'd beaten off the white werewolf outside the bar, raised a hand big enough to put a Christmas ham to shame, and waved to me.

"George? What're you doing—" Before I could finish the sentence, George engulfed me in a huge bear hug, mashing my face against his round stomach, and making me glad I'd left Partner in my car. He'd have gotten squashed to bit after broken bit. I gave up trying to talk and listened for the sickening *crack* of my ribs.

"Hi. I'm Myra."

At the sound of her voice, the giant man went stock-still, then turned, thrusting me away from him. He stepped closer to my friend, bent over and ogled her. Nothing else in the world existed for George and his eyes glazed over in an unmistakable look of love at first sight. "My-ra." A low sigh drifted after her name.

Yep, the big galoot had it bad.

Myra giggled and held out her hand in greeting.

"No! Don't!" I started to intervene, but stopped when I realized how gently George took her hand in his huge mitts. I glanced from the big guy to the little woman and saw an identical look of worship come into my best friend's eyes.

"Wow. I think your friend is smitten."

Blake's wonder reflected my own. Turning toward him, I

narrowed my eyes and demanded an answer. "Why is George here? How do you know George?" Could the big lummox be mixed up in this Bracelet mess?

"George."

The way Myra stated his name was an exact copy of the reverential way I'd heard George say hers. If this was love at first sight, then at least they'd both hitched a ride on the same love train.

"I don't know him. He showed up looking for you." Blake shook his head at the new couple. "He said you invited him for dinner."

Dinner? I'd forgotten about my less-than-sincere invitation for dinner. After all, I'd figured I'd never see George again after the attack. How had George found my home?

At last, the longest love-gaze in history came to an end. "Right! George came for dinner. Jenn invited George the other day when George helped Jenn—"

Afraid he would spill the beans about the white werewolf—aka my husband's newest friend—I jumped in and headed the conversation away from dangerous territory. "Retrieve my phone. It, uh, fell into a storm drain and George helped me get it out."

"Yeah, right. Then Jenn said George was her friend and George could call her Jenn. Jenn said George could come to dinner." The biggest smile spread across his face. If his smile got any wider, he'd have a mouth in the back of his head. "George is here for dinner."

"He sure-sure is." At Blake's quizzical expression, I added, "You'll see." I shrugged at Blake and hoped he'd get my message. *I had no clue he would show up like this.* "I don't suppose anyone's hungry for pizza? Because, frankly, I think the cupboard is bare." I turned to my husband. "Unless Blake went shopping for us."

"Actually, I did. In fact, George, you picked the perfect night to, uh, drop in. I made my incredible—even if I do say so myself—lasagna. Let me heat up the French bread and dinner will be ready in ten minutes." He cocked his head toward the kitchen, taking me by the arm and dragging me along with him. "You two get acquainted while Jenn and I get supper on the table."

I let my husband guide me into the kitchen and prepared to confront him. Blake, however, had culinary problems on his mind.

"Thank God I made a big pan of lasagna. I figured I'd save some to eat throughout the week but, by the looks of your big friend, we'll be lucky to get any of the food for ourselves."

Was he kidding me? Was he really worried about food? He lifted the pan from the oven, then retrieved the French bread. In the meantime, I grappled with a rush of conflicting emotions. Could this man really be a demon? But how could I have missed it? Why hadn't I noticed any of the signs? What was wrong with me? First I saw demons where there were none, then I missed one right in front of me. How could this have happened? How could I have fallen in love with a demon? But, no question about it, I did love this demon. No! I love this *man!*

I hate to admit it now, but when I saw my old friend Denial knocking at the door, I couldn't wait to let him in again. I needed to give Blake a test to be sure. Once he passed, I could forget what the gargoyle said and relax for the rest of the night. Either he'd have to pass, or I'd have to believe.

"I can't tell you how relieved I was when you walked through the door. George has talked both my ears off." My loving hubby turned to me after placing large portions of the entrée on our best china. "He's a bit strange, don't you think? I mean, he talked about living in the forest, for Pete's sake. And his habit of referring to himself in the third person is driving me crazy."

"Yeah, he's different." *But he's not a demon.* I bit my tongue and decided not to challenge him until I'd tested him with water. Holy water, of course.

"Oh, sure. I didn't mean bad different. Funny different." Blake lifted two of the plates and paused to scrutinize me. "Are you okay? You look like you've had a rough day. Is Swindle on your case again?"

I shook my head to force away the image of my husband-turned-demon. "No, everything's okay. I even sold a house this morning."

"Great! I'm proud of you, honey." He put his shoulder to the door and pushed. "Are you coming?"

"In a sec. I need to get something first."

The shaking started right after the door closed behind him. The signs had been there and I'd ignored them like an ostrich with her head stuck firmly in the ground. Now, however, I couldn't ignore them any longer.

How many times had I seen a flash of red in his eyes and resolutely swept it out of my mind? Instead, I'd concentrated on his captivating gray eyes, letting myself get sucked into them.

How often had I marveled at how much hot sauce Blake could eat? Lots of people like hot sauce, but he dumps tons of it on almost everything he eats. He swamps his eggs in hot sauce, covers his pancakes in hot sauce, and dips his pickles in hot sauce. Hell, he even likes including hot sauce in our more playful, tasty love sessions. If anyone else had eaten their food drenched in tongue-searing, throat-flaming sauce, they'd have screamed in agonizing pain. But me be suspicious of Blake? Nope, instead, I'd chalked it up to men having iron stomachs.

And what about the odd growling sound? If I'd heard the same sound from any other man, I'd have known he was a demon. Yet coming from Blake, I'd thought it sounded sexy.

But the most condemning fact was the lack of a history before a few years ago. Sure other people like those in the Witness Protection Program changed their names and relocated, losing all their prior history, but my gut told me Blake wasn't a star witness for anyone.

How could I, a trained Protector, have missed or ignored all the signs? How could I have been blind to Blake's true nature? Talk about getting swept off my feet! Hell, I'd gotten swept out of my right mind.

I crossed to the cabinet on the far side of the kitchen, and wiped away my tears. Reaching deep into its recesses, I brought out a small vial of holy water. With this test, I'd know the truth once and for all with no way to deny or ignore it. Taking a deep breath, I said a quick prayer, slipped the bottle into my pocket, and joined my husband and the others in the dining room.

"Jenn, you are one lucky woman." Myra took a seat next to George. Blake, playing the perfect host, passed the food around and offered to pour everyone a glass of wine. George mumbled a happy sound, grabbed the French bread and tore the loaf in half. With a satisfied sigh, he placed one of the halves next to his plate. Blake sent me a conspiratorial glance and added,

"Yes, please. Help yourselves."

I decided the best course of action was to play it cool. Remember? I'm good at playing it cool. "Uh, yeah, Myra, I'm a lucky girl. But why do you think I am?" I diverted my gaze from Blake. Until I did the test, I didn't think I could look him in the eyes.

"Because Blake's not only good-looking and successful, but he cooks. Does he do housework, too?" Myra took a small piece of bread from the remaining half of a loaf and laughed. Yet, although her praise was for Blake, her eyes were on George.

"Not much. And I don't do windows." Blake walked around the table, brushing his hand along the tips of my shoulders, and sat next to me. "However, I do love to make those patterns in the carpet when I sweep."

Maybe it was my way of preparing for the disappointment of a lifetime, but I tried pointing out a flaw in Blake's entertaining skills. "Before we make him a saint, I have to admit he does make mistakes. Like, for instance, we don't have a salad for this meal. I mean, what's lasagna without a good salad first."

I knew I'd thrown him a pitch out of left field, but Blake shook off his initial surprise and easily caught the verbal ball. "Hey, I'm trying to keep everyone safe."

"Safe?" George crammed a huge chunk of bread into his mouth and followed it with a bite of lasagna only Godzilla could have fit into his mouth.

I met Blake's eyes and saw the twinkle I loved. Stifling the pain it struck in my heart, I tucked my head and studied my plate as though I'd never noticed the gold pattern around the edge.

"Yeah, safety first. I'm terrible at putting together a salad. I tend to throw in just about everything including the kitchen sink. Trust me. It can get pretty scary."

"Along with a lot of other things at this table," I muttered.

Blake leaned closer to question me, his warm breath tickling my neck. "What'd you say, Jenn?"

"Nothing. Ignore me. I've had a long day." I gave Myra a weak smile, one she would have normally interpreted to mean *I'm tired. Go home, friend.* But tonight her attention rested with our other uninvited houseguest. "George, how about telling us about yourself." I needed time to think.

"George?"

Although he spoke with his mouth full of food, Myra stared at him with adoration. "Yes, George, tell us about yourself. I bet you lead a fascinating life."

Somehow the words "fascinating" and "George" didn't seem to go together, but who was I to judge? I leaned forward, making a show of giving him my full attention. Meanwhile, my brain stuck with the problem at hand. Was my husband a demon? If so, what would I do?

"George's life?" George reflected Myra's sappy, love-sick grin. "Do you want to know?"

Myra hung on his every word. "Oh, yes. Tell us everything. I want to know all about you. Don't hold anything back."

I shifted in my chair to watch Blake more closely. Surely, if he was a demon, I'd see the signs now that I'd pulled my head out of the sand. Carrying on a conversation with someone seated across from me wasn't easy since I was more preoccupied with the person sitting next to me. But I was determined not to miss any signs of demonic possession.

"George lives in the mountains of Wyoming."

I heard Myra's gasp and knew she was already working out a plan to move to Wyoming. Blake nodded to keep our guest talking.

"George lives by himself in the woods. George doesn't like people much." His goofy grin grew bigger and he once again looked longingly at my best friend. "Except special people."

I glanced at Myra and nearly giggled at the sappy expression on her face. "Special? Like in handicapped?" Although I'd directed the question at George, I returned my attention to Blake to see him pour a river of hot sauce over his lasagna. Did any normal human ever put that much hot sauce on their food? Blake, on the other hand, kept listening intently to George, oblivious to my perusal.

"No, not special in a different way. Special like Jenn. Special like Jenn's friend, Myra. George likes Myra."

Myra inhaled and held her breath before blurting out her feelings. "Myra, uh, I mean, I think you're special, too."

If I hadn't been focused on Blake I might have gagged on

the copious amounts of love coming from the other side of the table. Still, I felt the need to inject some common sense into the situation. "I'm happy you two are hitting it off, but let's hear more about George. I mean, *we*"—I shot a pointed look at Myra—"don't know a thing about him. I've only met him once before."

Myra rolled her eyes at me like a besotted teenager and put her hand on George's arm for encouragement. "Go on, George."

"George likes fish."

"To eat or for a pet?" I couldn't have cared less if George ate fish or played Scrabble with them, but it kept the conversation going.

Blake gave me one of his *what are you doing?* expressions which I pointedly ignored.

"Eat. George eats fish."

"Oh, I love fish, too. I especially love tuna, swordfish and shark. Have you ever eaten shark, George?"

"No, Myra. George eats what George catches in George's river."

"Wow, you have your own river? You must have a great place in the woods."

If Myra got any giddier around this guy, I'd have to pour Blake's hot sauce on her to cancel out all the sweetness. Hopefully, I could use George's autobiography to get answers out of my hubby. "Blake, honey, would you like to live in the woods of Wyoming? It sounds wonderful, doesn't it? Think of all the snuggling we could do by the fireplace."

Caught off guard, Blake laid his fork down and gaped at me. "Wyoming? Me? You're kidding, right? You know how much I hate cold weather. I'd probably end up in the fire trying to get warm. You know the only reason I moved here with the cold, icy winters is because your work is here. Even though I'm sure you could sell real estate anywhere you wanted to."

"You do get chilled easily. I don't know why, but I never asked you. Do you come from a warm place? A very, *very* warm place? Like maybe *down* under? *Way* down under?" I leaned toward Blake, glancing down to the floor and back, half-hoping he'd see the real meaning behind my questions.

"Huh?"

"Sure. Everyone is acclimated to their hometown's weather. Then, when they move, they have to adjust."

I almost growled at Myra's interference. "What do you do for a living, George?"

"George hunts."

All three of us turned to George. "Oh, so you hunt? For a living? Are you a tracker or a hunting guide?"

"George hunts for a living."

Yeah, like that answered my question. I leveled my gaze at Blake who appeared uncomfortable with my line of conversation. "Do you like to hunt, Blake? Like maybe at night?"

Blake pushed away from the table, his brow furrowing at my strange question. "What are you talking about? I don't even own a gun."

"Who says you need a gun?" Hunters don't need guns when they have the fangs and claws of a demon. I started getting into the questioning. "You could use your, uh, natural weapons."

"You mean kill with my bare hands?" Blake laughed along with Myra. "I'm hardly the aggressive type, honey. Unless, of course, you're talking about beating out my competition for a new client."

"George, what kind of weapon do you use when you go hunting?" Myra derailed my questioning of Blake to continue her exploration of George. "I bet you look amazing in hunting clothes. I love a man who knows how to come home with the bacon."

"George doesn't bring bacon home. George likes deer meat best."

"Deer meat? I've never eaten venison before." She batted her eyes at the big lug. "I'd love to try it sometime."

Could Myra's hint get any clearer? I had a bad feeling warning me to watch out for my friend, but I needed to keep my attention on the bigger problem. "You know what? I don't remember where you told me you were born, Blake? Here in the states or someplace exotic like Brazil?"

"Brazil? You know I was raised in Florida." Blake reached over to take my hand in his and I welcomed the touch. How could the touch of a demon make my insides quiver with lust?

"George, do you have a family?"

I cringed, knowing what Myra's real question was and asked it for her. "Yes, George, do you have a wife? Someone you don't keep any secrets from? Someone who knows you like no one else does?"

"Jenn, are you upset with me?" Blake whispered.

Instead of responding, I popped a forkful of lasagna into my mouth and faced forward, pretending that George's recounting of his life had suddenly become incredibly fascinating.

"No. George doesn't have a mate. Not any longer. George's mate died. In fact, George came here to find a mate."

"Oh, no. I'm sorry for your loss, George." Myra placed one hand over her heart and the other hand on George's gigantic arm. "If I can help you in any way, please tell me."

"You'll help George?" George clamped Myra's hand between both of his. "Even though George is…"

"Is what, George?" Myra had apparently forgotten about Blake and me.

"Even though George is a Big—"

Myra flung her body out of the chair and hugged George. Or rather tried to hug him since her arms couldn't reach around his massive body. "I don't care! I know you're big, but you're wonderful."

I gaped at the new Mutt and Jeff sitting across from me. "Myra! What are you doing? You hardly know the man."

"I know. But I can't help it. George is everything I've dreamed of. Big, handsome, self-sufficient, and lovable." She sighed and renewed her hug.

"Myra is special, Jenn. Very special."

I could see that George was enamored with Myra too. So who was I to get in the way of true love? Besides, at least George wasn't a demon. "Promise me you'll take things slow, okay?"

"You and Blake didn't."

Although Myra's statement was true enough, I couldn't think of a way to let her know about Blake. Not without blurting it out. Instead, I hopped up and headed for the kitchen. "I'll be right back. I forgot the cheese. I love extra cheese on lasagna." Pausing at the door, I waited for my usually helpful friend to offer her assistance, but she didn't seem to notice I'd left the room.

Giving up on saving Myra—for now—I pushed through the door and grabbed the cheese shaker from the refrigerator. Granted, the cheese was in a plastic container, but no one in this group would care.

"Jenn? Do you want my help?"

"No!" I'd wanted to keep him in the other room, but my refusal came too late.

"Okay, no need to snap at me." Blake let the door swing behind him, took a hard look at me, then placed the empty wine bottle on the counter. "I think we're going to have to hose those two down to get them apart." He took one of his favorite wines from the rack below the cabinet, then uncorked it and started to leave.

With a lump in my throat and a stone weighing heavily in my stomach, I called to Blake. "Wait a second, okay?"

The man I loved spun around and set the bottle down. "Yeah? So you do need me?"

Understanding his underlying meaning of "need", I turned away from Blake, moved toward the stove, and pulled the small vial of holy water from my pocket. It was time to find out once and for all. "Yeah, I do."

His arms slid around me and, pulling my back to his chest, he kissed my neck. Facing the stove, I turned on the two front burners. If my husband was indeed a demon and if he'd never loved me, I wanted to be prepared to defend myself even if that meant slamming his head down on a hot burner. I held my breath, popped off the rubber lid to the vial and tipped it, aiming a drop at his hand.

Burn, Baby, Burn

Blake leaned too close to the stove, struck the burner with the edge of his palm and jumped. A second later, I poured a couple drops of the holy water on the side of his hand. He yelped, cursed, hit the burner with his hand a second time and, jerking away from the stove, knocked into me, sending the vial flying. The bottle and its precious contents smashed on the tiled floor.

"No!" I twisted around and grazed my elbow against the second front burner. "Shit!" I hurried away from the stove to stick my aching elbow underneath the water faucet.

"Dammit, dammit, dammit, dammit!"

"Shit, fucking shit, this hurts!"

"Crap, crap, crap, crap!"

Our verbal tirade ran together making it impossible to tell where one word ended and the following word started. I could almost see my mother turning in her grave even though she'd had her own fairly colorful mouth. Forget the holy water. Forget whether or not Blake was a demon. All I wanted was relief to the pain searing through my elbow.

Blake joined me, sticking his ugly burn mark underneath my arm to catch the water flowing off my skin. "Crap. What the hell happened? How did we both end up getting burned?"

The cool water eased the pain throbbing from my elbow to my shoulder and, at last, I could get my mind back on business. I checked out the red mark on Blake's hand. Although I could see the outline of where the burner had scorched his hand, I couldn't tell where the holy water had hit him. Dammit.

Had I seen the whole thing correctly? Had he jumped because he'd touch the burner or because the holy water had scalded his skin? Had his double whammy on the burner been a freak accident or an attempt to cover the evidence from the holy water? Had he covered the burn of the holy water by intentionally scalding his hand again? I'd have to redo my test to be certain.

I frowned at the small puddle of holy water on my kitchen floor. Maybe if I could get him to help me clean it up, he'd blister himself on the water and I'd have the proof I needed. "Blake? Help me clean up the spill—"

I stopped in mid-sentence as a dishtowel plopped on the floor, covering the holy water and soaking up the precious liquid. Myra squatted down to wipe up the remaining splashes on the stove and floor.

"Don't worry about it, Jenn. I've got it." She stood, towel in hand, and widened her eyes at us. "How in the world did you both get burned?" George stood behind her, his hands placed possessively on her shoulders. "At least we know you've both been to sea."

"What?" I stared at the towel, certain Myra had mopped up my last chance for happiness. "Sea?"

"Yeah. Because you both know how to cuss like sailors." She giggled at her joke until she started to inspect our wounds. "George, you'll find a first aid kit in the right hand drawer over there. Would you get it for me?"

George nodded and started digging around in my junk drawer. "George thinks they'll need band aids, too." He brought the kit over to Myra who was already busy cleaning the wounds under the cold water.

"I think you're right." Channeling her best motherly instincts, Myra warped into high speed, spreading cooling ointment on Blake's hand and my elbow. With one last Mom-knows-best blow, she covered our burns with a clean bandage.

"Myra, you're really good at taking care of people, aren't you?" George watched my friend at work, his eyes lighting up in wonderment. Hell, you'd think he'd never seen anyone perform minor first aid.

Myra blushed at the compliment. "It's nothing. What caused the accident anyway? Or should I say accidents?"

Blake leaned into me, giving me a comforting and apologetic hug. "I'm not sure, but I think it was my fault. I got too close to the burners and, since we were hugging, I pulled Jenn too close at the same time." He pressed his lips to my cheek in a tender kiss.

My gut clenched and I tried to think of this kind, caring man tearing an innocent's heart out. Granted, demons are well-known for their ability to fool people, acting like normal humans to trick victims into their evil traps, but I had a hard time believing the love coming from this wonderful man was false.

"It doesn't matter how it happened. Let's finish our meal, okay?" I walked out, determined to get through the dinner. How I would get through the night was another problem. Could I sleep in the same bed as a demon? My Protector instincts had kicked in, confirming what my head already knew. Blake was a demon. Yet, my heart kept sending me another message. My heart, ignoring the warnings going off in the rest of me, chanted its own refrain.

I love him. I love him. I love him.

By the time the others had joined me in the dining room, I'd decided to stick it out until I could find the nerve to confront Blake. Was I afraid of him confirming what I already knew? Was I afraid to lose the man I loved once he changed into the demon inside him?

For the rest of the evening, I remained stoic, pretending to listen to Myra and George prattle on about everything from dog collars to apple pie. At last, Myra declared she had to go home and get ready for work in the morning. Fortunately, George took the hint and said goodbye. Being a gracious hostess, I wished the stranger-than-fiction couple well and watched them stroll down my sidewalk together. Odd, however, wasn't how Blake saw them.

"They make a good couple, don't you think?" Blake waved at George and Myra until they turned the corner and was out of our sight. In what normally would've been an easy gesture of familiarity, Blake started to slip his arm around my waist. His touch, however, left me feeling lost and alone.

Without warning, I left him standing in the doorway and escaped to the bedroom. Blake, playing the role of caring and helpful husband, took care of the cleanup job in the kitchen before walking into the bedroom. I was already in bed, covered to the tip of my nose with the comforter.

"Jenn?"

I didn't answer, but he knew I was awake. Truth was, I didn't think I'd ever fall asleep. Not until I could figure out what to do.

"Are you all right? Do you feel well?"

Was his concern real or a demon ploy to keep his stupid wife in his control? I wanted to believe the worry I heard in his tone, but cautioned myself not to trust him. Hadn't I played the part of the fool long enough?

I ran through several options in my head, trying to decide if I should sleep in the same bed or not, and decided to stay put. Blake, unaware of my dilemma, went through his usual bedtime routine of brushing his teeth, changing into his pajamas, and pumping through fifty sit-ups. He joined me in bed and I pulled the comforter tighter around me. Even so, he managed to run a hand down my back.

"Did I do something wrong? Are you angry with me?"

I shook my head, hoping my non-verbal response would end the conversation, yet knowing Blake wouldn't let a problem go unresolved if he could help it.

"Then what?"

I had to give him a reasonable answer. "I'm tired. Nothing else. I just want to go to sleep, okay?"

"Sure, honey. If you're certain there's nothing you need to tell me."

I could ask you the same thing, buster. But I didn't. Instead, I sighed with relief, closed my eyes, and tried to sleep.

"Jenn?"

I moaned a half-answer, hoping he'd take the hint.

"I love you, Jenn. You believe me, right?"

A tear traveled down my cheek to wet my pillow. Part of me wanted to keep quiet, knowing he'd interpret my silence to mean I wasn't sure of my own love for him, but a greater part of me couldn't do it. I had to tell the truth.

"I love you, too."

❧

The sun shining brightly through the window did nothing to lighten my dreary mood. My husband, the man I'd trusted with every ounce of my soul, was a demon. Amazingly, my heart still fought a battle with my brain, wanting to sweep what I knew about him under the mental rug in my head and go on, pretending life was the same as the day I'd met him.

"Jenn? You awake?"

I rolled onto my back and called out to Blake. "Yeah, I'm awake."

Hearing his normal morning sounds coming from the bathroom, I knew he was almost ready to go to work. Work? Did he really work as an investment analyst? The higher a demon climbed on the demonic ladder of success, the more the inhabitants of the Otherworld paid him for his services. Like in the mortal world, advancement had its perks.

"How're you doing?" Blake peeked around the corner of the bathroom wearing the skimpy, threadbare towel I loved. "Feeling better? Do you need to see the doctor?"

My gaze fell from his smiling face to the part of him eager to help get me over my foul mood. Doctor Dick was ready to make a house call. I sighed, wanting to let everything I'd learned slide away and give my libido control. Yet I knew I couldn't.

"I'm fine. I think the good doctor's services aren't needed."

Blake's disappointment registered across his features, but he didn't allow it to seep into his cheerful tone. "Great. Glad to hear you're feeling better. But if you need physical therapy…"

"I'll pucker up and blow." We both loved the old Bogart movie, but had changed the famous quote to mean something totally unrelated to whistling and more to do with Dr. Dick.

"Oh, okay. Well, I've got an early morning meeting, anyway." He disappeared into the closet.

By the time he'd sauntered over to kiss me on the cheek, I'd come up with a plan. If Blake was a demon—and logically I knew he was—he had to be involved in demonic activity. Perhaps even involved in the Bracelet problem. Either way, I had to find out.

With Blake downstairs eating a quick breakfast, I dressed

in jeans, a T-shirt and my favorite knee-high boots. To complete the ensemble, I grabbed a couple of knives and stuck them in the sides of my boots. Then I waited until I heard the door leading to the garage close. Not long after that, Blake pulled his car out of the driveway and was zipping off toward the highway. I wasted no time in flying down the stairs to the garage and hopping into my car. Revving the motor, I backed out of the drive, and propelled the Jag down the street.

"Partner, wake up."

"Yo, bitch. Whassup? I ain't never totally asleep."

Halting at the stop sign for a few seconds longer than usual, I glanced over at Partner's screen to find Scarlett gone and a young man dressed in black with jeans hanging precariously on his hips. "Where's the Southern lady? And who are you supposed to be? A gangsta?" Where did he come up with these personalities, anyway?

"A gangsta? No, bitch. I'm a homegrown home boy." He started strutting and rapping. "Partner's a boy, a man who can. He hangs with his bitch and he ain't no snitch. Protectin's the game and Partner's my name. So get off my back and cut me some slack." Finished with his song, he crossed arms in the way rappers do on MTV and glared at me.

"A home boy *and* a rapper, huh?"

"That's right, b—"

I jabbed my finger against his two-dimensional chest. "You call me bitch one more time and I'm going introduce you to a new term. Forget drive-by shooting, I'll show you drive-by flying—as in flying out the window. Get it?"

"Ow!" He clutched his chest, dropping the tough expression on his face. "Watch it. I have very fragile circuitry, you know."

A honk from the car behind me got me paying attention to my driving and I gunned it through the intersection. "Sheesh, why can't I have the normal texting and driving problem? Instead I have to deal with a cell with an attitude. Switch back to the original Partner. Immediately."

"Very well. If you insist. But I must protest. You're not allowing me my personal growth."

I knew the B-boy Partner was gone without having to look. "If you want personal growth, work for the Dalai Lama. Now tell me if you can locate Blake." I darted in between cars on the highway, heading for Blake's office. If luck was with me, he'd gone to work and not on a demonic mission.

"Task completed." Partner's gears whirred a little before he added, "A check at his building shows he used his identification card to gain admittance to his office." Another whir and he came up with the question I knew he'd ask. "Why are we tracking Blake?"

I had no doubt he knew the answer to his own question. After all, he'd been with me when the gargoyle had outed my hubby's demon persona.

A new dilemma raised its ugly head. Should I confirm Blake's probable demonic identity to this machine? If I did, would Partner wifi the news to the main office's central computer? I decided I needed to confide in someone before I went crazy, but I wanted a person with human emotions, human experiences, and a couple of boobs attached. Somehow talking to a machine didn't seem right. I decided to lie.

"I think Blake is having an affair." I kept my eyes straight ahead on the road, giving Partner less chance to see the lie in my eyes.

"Uh-huh. You're kidding, right? Blake's cheating on you?"

"You heard me. It's too true."

"And we're following him to catch him in the act of cheating? And not because of what the ugly troll-thing said?"

The underlying sarcasm in his tone was far too evident to ignore. "You know gargoyles lie. What he said is ridiculous. Don't you think I'd know if I was married to a demon?" I snickered, trying to sound confident in my answer. "Sorry. No demons to blame here. Just a cheating husband and the end of my marriage. Oh, and thanks for the rush of compassion."

"Uh, sorry. Right. Oh, you poor thing."

"Too little and too late." Not that I really cared. I pulled into a parking spot across the street from Blake's office building. "We're here."

"We are indeed here. What now, oh, lovely one?"

I risked a glimpse at Partner and saw he'd changed into the ugliest man I'd ever seen. I pulled away from him in a knee-jerk reaction. "What happened to you? Halloween isn't for another few months."

"Well, you know how it is. The tired old wifey gets dumped by the handsome hubby and ends up falling for the first sexy guy she sees. I thought I'd better ugly up to keep your lonely hands off me. We wouldn't want one of those awkward co-worker relationships, would we?"

The giggles bubbled over making it difficult to speak. "Oh, my. You're"—giggle—"kidding, right?" Giggle. "Ugly up? To keep me from wanting you? Wow."

A dark cloud swept over Partner's screen, turning the brightness level down to pitch black. "Don't laugh at me."

Clamping a hand over my mouth, I tried to stop chuckling. "I'm sorry, but you're kidding, right? I mean, you and me? Together? Don't you think our having an affair would rank right up there with the chances of my winning the lottery?" The screen didn't lighten, making me wonder if he'd turned off. "I mean, come on, Partner. We're not even the same species. Hell, we don't even have the same basic elements in common. I'm flesh and bone, and you're metal and plastic. It would never work out."

In a flash of light, the screen lit up with the image of the cowboy. "Darlin', can't you tell when I'm joshing you? Us as a couple? No way."

Could a machine get embarrassed? I stole another look at Partner and knew the answer was a big-time yes. I decided to go with the flow. "Oh, sure. Wow, you really had me going. Good one, Partner."

The cowboy pushed his hat back on his head and grinned at me. But the grin never reached his little mechanical eyes. "Yeah, I do love a good joke. However, we'd best mosey on back to business 'cuz your hubby's in his car in the basement garage and heading out."

Blake's car exited the underground garage and turned into the traffic. Hitting the gas pedal, I slid into the same lane a couple of cars behind his. Although a Jag isn't an easy car to blend into traffic, I didn't think Blake would suspect anyone of following him. With any luck, he wouldn't see my vehicle tucked behind the van ahead of me.

"He didn't stay at work long, did he?"

I knew what Partner really meant and I said it for him. "I guess he's hot and horny to see the slut he's messing with."

"Hey, how come I can't call you a name, but you can call her one?"

"Because if she's screwing with my husband, I can call her anything I want." I hated lying to Partner, but I couldn't confess what I knew about Blake. At least, not until I had to.

"Good point."

I followed Blake's sedan through downtown and out into the commercial area of town. The traffic thinned out and it got harder and harder to stay out of sight. I was about to call it quits rather than get busted, when Blake did a hard right-angle turn and pulled up outside an old warehouse. I slammed on the brakes, sending Partner sliding toward the edge of the seat, and caught him in mid-air, sailing toward the dashboard.

"Where are we?"

"Shh!" I slouched down in my seat and peeked over the side of my door. Blake left his car and approached the metal door of the building. "He stopped outside a warehouse."

"Hurry. Let's go after him."

Without thinking of his possible interference, I agreed. "Okay, but keep quiet until I tell you it's safe."

"Of course. This isn't my first mission, you know."

"It isn't?" I knew even whispering was dangerous—demons have great hearing—but I couldn't help myself. "Who did you work for before me?"

At least Partner answered in a similar quiet manner. "Lots of people including the best of the best at Interpol, the CIA, and Scotland Yard."

"Scotland Yard?" Blake waved his hand over the door, opening the large metal obstruction without touching it. "Oh. My. God." If I'd wanted more evidence, I'd just gotten it with a single gesture. Blake was definitely not the normal mortal man I'd hoped he was.

"I can tell you're impressed. Yes, I have had a rather illustrious career."

Blake entered the warehouse, wiping the retort out of my mind. Instead, I snatched up Partner, shoved him into my pocket, and raced down the alley.

"I'm getting squished in here. Couldn't you have worn looser pants?"

"Partner, shut the hell up. Right now."

"Look, Jenn, I'm getting pretty fed up with being told to shut up. I don't like it one bit." By the time I'd reached the door, Partner had gone through a series of complaints. In the end, however, he went silent.

I stepped into the dimly lit warehouse, knowing I might have to make a tough decision. Would I stop Blake from doing evil? And if so, how far would I go to stop him? Could I exterminate the man I loved to save countless lives? Would my feelings for him get in the way of doing my job?

The lump in my throat refused to budge, but thankfully, didn't transmit that same refusal to my feet. I moved forward, taking care not to bump into the many boxes stacked toward the ceiling. None of the boxes had any markings, giving me more concern. The boxes could contain almost anything from cotton balls to nitroglycerin, and I didn't want to find out the hard way what was inside. Carefully, I skirted around them.

"Oh, lord and master. Oh, Great One. I beseech you. Come."

I stopped, frozen in my tracks. I knew the summoning of a demon and, from the sound of it, the demon Blake called was a powerful one.

"Ah, Shytuman, my faithful servant. Have you news for me?"

The deep voice echoed through the building, sending a shiver through me. Shytuman? Was Shytuman Blake's demon name? Would using his demon name make my duty to rid the world of him any easier? I bit my lip and forced my feet to keep moving toward the sound of their voices.

"Oh, my word, Jenn. You *are* married to a demon! Dammit, why couldn't the stupid gargoyle have lied?"

I slapped my hand over my pocket and hissed at Partner. "Quiet before you get us killed. Or worse."

Blake's sultry tone, the same tone he used to seduce me, rang out loud and clear. "Yes, Master Demogorgon, I have news."

I held my breath, preparing for what I would see, and peeked around the corner of stacked boxes. *Demogorgon?* I stared at the vile being standing with my husband in the center of the room and felt the blood drain from my face. Demogorgon was a High Demon. His power was undeniable. Many Protectors had fought Demogorgon, yet none had survived.

"Tell me. Have you found the Bracelet?"

I bent over, crawled to another row of boxes closer to Blake, and peered over the top. Struggling not to cry, I pulled a knife from my boot. Why hadn't I thought to bring a gun?

A giant of a demon, towering four feet over Blake's six foot, two inch height, stood in front of him, engulfed in a strange murky mist. Long writhing tentacles covered the demon's obese body and rolls of fat hung from him, glowing a sickly green. Three red eyes protruded from his face, oozing a milky substance down his wart-covered cheeks amd over his three chins to fall in loud splats on the floor. A tail much like an enormous rat's tail swished back and forth.

I'd seen my share of demons but this guy made the rest of them look like cover models. I took in his mounds of lard before noting the evil on his face. I couldn't help it. I had to lower my gaze so I could choke down the bile bursting into my mouth. Below his rolls of fat, sticking out hard and long, his wart-encrusted penis extended a solid three feet beyond his belly. Worse, the demon's huge dick moved with every word his spoke.

Blake, however, didn't seem to notice. Bowing his head in submission, he answered his master's question. "No, my master. I have not."

The roar from the demon lord reverberated around the room for several seconds. Blake raised his head to look straight at the creature and held his ground. I smiled, taking a strange sort of pride in seeing my husband stand firm and strong against the hideous creature.

"You displease me, Shytuman." The monster shuffled forward, opening his mouth wider to reveal sharp, stained teeth. "Do you offer an excuse before I tear your heart from your chest? Why have you failed me?"

"I'm doing my best, master. I can, however, tell you that my brother, Michael, and his subordinates are close on the trail. We'll find it, I promise you."

"Ha! Your brother, the lowly ghoul, shows more promise than you. Mark my words, Shytuman. Find the Bracelet and bring it to me, or both you and your brother will pay dearly for your failure." A low growl shook Demogorgon's body. "What about the Protector? Have you eliminated her?"

Me? Demogorgon knows about me? His words sunk in and I inhaled sharply. Blake was supposed to eliminate me?

"I promise you, Demogorgon, my wife is no Protector."

A cruel laugh rumbled in his massive chest. "I've heard otherwise. No matter. Kill her and be done with it."

I couldn't believe my ears. Demogorgon wanted me dead. Worse, he wanted my husband to kill me. Would Blake follow his orders?

"Master Demogorgon, please trust me. If my wife is a Protector, she could prove useful."

"How?"

"If the Society finds the Bracelet first, I can torture her to find out where they took it."

Demogorgon considered Blake's argument. "Very well. But once the Bracelet is in my hands, you will dispose of her." With a wave of his hand, the mist started to grow thicker, hiding his monstrous body from view.

"Yes, master." Blake bowed before the demon lord. I decided now was a good time to get the hell out of there. Hey, I was good, but I knew my limits. I couldn't fight a High Demon Lord alone.

"Please wait. There is the other matter, my lord."

The mist dissipated, exposing—in the worst possible way—Demogorgon playing with his shaft. "What now? You bore me with your questions."

"Once I've brought you the Bracelet, will you keep your end of our bargain?"

The gigantic demon moved so quickly I wasn't prepared for the shock of seeing one of his tentacles surrounding Blake's neck. "You dare question me?" He roared again and his foul breath drifted over to me.

Instinct kicked in and I gripped my knife tighter. I knew a knife was no protection against such evil, but I would've tried anyway. Blake may have orders to kill me, but I still loved him. I loved him enough to die for him at his master's hand. Fortunately, I didn't have to.

Blake, however, remained unmoving and calm. Again, I couldn't help but admire his strength. "Of course not, master. I know you will reward me when I've fulfilled my mission. Yes?"

Demogorgon's fat pink tongue raked over Blake's cheek. "I like you, Shytuman." Another tentacle reached between Blake's legs and clutched his crotch. "You've got balls. Real balls. Yes, I'll give you what you want. *If* you bring me the Bracelet." He squeezed Blake's crotch and Blake clenched his fists. "If you don't, I'll have your balls for a snack."

I couldn't see Blake's face but, judging from the strain in his voice, Demogorgon had a hard hold on him. "Thank you, m-master."

Once Demogorgon released Blake, I whipped around, retracing my steps quietly and quickly. Not only was my husband a demon, but a demon planning on killing his wife.

I pushed out of the warehouse with my eyes stinging—and not from the bright sunshine. Running like a bat out of hell, I still couldn't get away from the images flipping through my mind's eye. Blake standing before the High Demon Lord, Demogorgon. Blake bowing before the monster. Blake promising to kill me.

The mind is a strange thing because, even though those horrific images pounded me, other images fought to find their place in my memory. Blake kneeling before me asking for my hand in marriage. Blake kissing me and fondling my breasts. Blake telling me he loved me.

"Jenn, are you all right?" Partner gave a loud beep. "Jenn, do you hear me?" His beeping grew louder. "I've been calling for you since I noticed we were outside again. Did I hear correctly? Is Blake supposed to kill you?"

Pulling Partner from my hip pocket, I tossed him on the passenger's seat and started the car. "Hey! Careful. I'm valuable and easily broken." After a few more squeaks and beeps, he continued his questioning. "What are you going to do? Jenn? Jenn? You know what you have to do, don't you?"

Yeah, I knew what Partner thought I should do. According to the vows I'd taken when I'd entered the Society, I had to destroy my husband and his demon lord. Could I keep those vows? Or would I keep the ones I'd made to Blake?

I didn't bother looking at Partner. Instead, I wiped away the tear rolling down my cheek. I'd cried a lot lately and I didn't like it one bit. "I'm fine. Now—"

"I know, I know. Shut the hell up."

Forcing the visions of Blake away, I fought against my own personal demons. I needed help. More help than Partner or Myra could give me.

I needed help from another Protector.

Diamonds Are a Girl's Best Friend…
But Gold Makes a Great Sidekick.

"Mrs. Wipp, I need your advice."

Mrs. Wippingpoof placed the tray of cinnamon rolls on the display rack, keeping her gaze on them instead of looking at me. At first, I wasn't sure she'd heard me. Mrs. Wipp, as the younger Protectors liked to call her, was of an indeterminate age, refusing to let anyone know when she was born. However, I knew she'd been with the Society for many decades and had recently retired. Retirement for Mrs. Wipp, however, did not include a rocking chair and watching daytime talk shows. Instead, she'd gone straight out of active duty and into owning her own bakery shop.

"Mrs. Wipp, did you hear me?"

Partner beeped a series of short blasts, catching the attention of the two customers sitting at a small bistro table. "Did she hear me?"

I pulled my front pocket open to hiss at Partner. "You! No talking or beeping."

"Why not?"

"Because I said so."

"Oh, I see. Now you're my mommy?"

"Partner, either you stuff it or I stuff you. Take your pick."

The two people at the table, obviously a romantic couple with their fingers entwined, watched me with curious expressions. I rolled my eyes at them and punted. "Oh, uh, new cell phone. I haven't figured out all the bells and whistles yet."

By the look they gave each other, they didn't buy my story.

Yet, obviously deciding I might be crazy but not the dangerous kind of crazy, they left me alone and returned to gazing into each other's eyes.

At last Mrs. Wipp pivoted to face me. "Of course I heard you, Jenny." She pointed at my pocket. "Both of you. My hearing is as good as it was when I was your age."

Why did older women always call me Jenny? "Which was how many years ago?" I couldn't resist an opportunity to find out her age.

She laughed one of those warm, comforting grandmotherly-type laughs. "Oh, Jenny, sweetie. Are you trying to trick me into telling my age? Shame on you."

No one could ever accuse Mrs. Wipp of diminished mental faculties. She was one sharp lady. "Sorry. I couldn't resist."

Partner, however, had no qualms about taking up where I'd left off. "Since Jenn won't ask, I will. How old are you, old girl? Are we talking Barbara Walter's, Eleanor Roosevelt's, or Helen of Troy's time period?" I slammed my hand over my pocket, but I was too late to silence him.

"Tell your new glorified walkie-talkie to mind his beeswax. A true gentleman never asks a lady her age."

"Beeswax? Talk about dating yourself." Partner executed a series of happy-sounding beeps.

"Knock it off, Partner, or I'll dump you in water and let you rust."

"Never mind him." Mrs. Wipp waved me around the counter and nodded to her assistant. "Take over for me, Lucy. I'm taking a break."

"Okay, Mrs. W." Lucy, a cute blonde cheerleader-type noted Mrs. Wipp's order before returning to flirt with a boy sitting across the room.

Mrs. Wipp motioned for me to follow her into the back room. "The poor girl doesn't have a brain cell in her body, but she's good eye candy. Since I hired her, I've had the entire high school football team in here buying donuts and cakes every day. Makes for good business since those boys eat like horses."

She rounded an old desk and took the big leather chair behind it. "I always did want one of these executive chairs and now I've got one." Settling into the smooth leather with a sigh, she offered me the plastic chair beside her desk.

"Shoot fire, Jenn. Where are we? Take me out of your pocket and let me see what the dang-all is going on. How can I be a good partner if I can't see what's happening?"

"Here. Give him to me."

I handed Partner to her and waited for the fun. *This ought to be good.*

She held him up, studied the cowboy on the screen, and laughed. "Those geeks at the main office keep coming up with better and better tools, don't they?"

"Look woman, I ain't no gall-darn tool. I'm this here lady's partner."

She laughed, full and throaty. "If *you're* not a tool, cowboy, I'd bet your boots you *have* a good tool. My God, Jenny, I think he's blushing."

"No, I'm not. I have a swarthy complexion from all the cattle drives I've ridden on. Real men don't blush."

Yet I could hear the embarrassment in his tone. "Partner, I believe you've met your wisecracking match."

"Humph." Partner whistled, long and low. "Mrs. Wipp, I'd be obliged if you'd hand me over to Jenn."

"Sure, pretty boy. In a sec. I wish we'd had these gizmos when I was on the books. We had to improvise a lot and supply our own, uh, tools." She handed him back to me.

"And you walked ten miles in the snow, right?"

"Partner!" I punched a button in warning. "Watch your mouth or I'm turning you off."

"Never mind, sweetie. He doesn't bother me. And, by the way, it was eleven miles in a blizzard, uphill, with no shoes and fighting demons the whole way."

I waited for the two to continue their quarrel. Instead, Partner and Mrs. Wipp started chuckling.

"Do you think we should tell her?" Mrs. Wipp thumbed in my direction.

"I reckon we ought-ta. Seeings how you've already said something, we have to. Otherwise, she's gonna bug me like a varmit watching a hen house."

"Hey, what's going on? Do you two know each other?" I felt like the odd man out in their verbal game of Keep Away.

"Mrs. Wipp was one of my creators. She, along with

Reslind, invented the first Partner several years ago."

"Really?" I gazed at Mrs. Wipp with even greater respect.

"Guilty as charged and proud of it. Partner's some of my best work."

"Ah, you old sweet talker, you." Partner swirled bright colors across his screen.

"I'm sure Jenny's not here to gab about my inventions, are you? What are you here for?"

I started to answer, but she stopped me with the palm of her hand. "Hang on. We can't get down to serious discussion until we have a little something to wet the throat and loosen the tongue." She withdrew a bottle of Jack Daniels from the bottom drawer along with two shot glasses. "How serious is this?"

I squirmed in my hard chair. "Serious. The worst kind of serious."

"Oh, my." The wrinkles in her forehead deepened. She took a second to study my face, then poured an inch of booze into each glass. Taking hers, she chugged the shot. "Ahhh. I always said there's nothing better than Old Jack to put the heat in a woman." With a twinkle in her eye, she added, "Unless Jack's a man with a six-inch pole."

Partner whistled. "The woman is obsessed with dicks. And I ain't talking about the Dick with Tom and Harry."

"Again. Guilty as charged."

I saluted her with my drink and followed her example. "I'll take Old Blake over Old Jack any day." Yet an image of my husband standing before Demogorgon made me blow out a hard breath. "At least, I would've before I found out."

Mrs. Wipp poured another round and leaned back in her chair to mull over her glass. "Oh, I see. Is this advice you're asking for about your personal life? Have you two had a falling out?"

"I think the situation is much worse than a lover's spat. It involves Society business, too."

"I'll say."

"Partner, stay out of this conversation or I'll call you the new Gameboy, and give you to the biggest brat I can find."

She ignored our banter, pursed her lips, and swirled the liquid in her glass. "Does this problem involve the Bracelet?"

Mrs. Wipp was full of surprises. "You know about the Bracelet?"

"Of course I do. I may be retired, but I still keep an ear to the ground. Once a Protector, always a Protector."

I downed the second dose of the fiery liquid before deciding to jump in all the way. "I'm looking for the Bracelet, but I ran into another problem. Blake's brother, Michael, is involved. He may have the Bracelet or he may not. However, I'm ninety-nine percent sure he's involved in the murder of the mortal thieves who took the Bracelet from the main office." I swallowed and choked out the first difficult confession. "Michael's a ghoul."

"I see. And you're worried about telling Blake after you bust his brother. Am I right?" She started to pour a third drink, but I'd had my fill. Any more and I'd end up sloshed. "Are you sure about his brother?"

"Michael is definitely a ghoul. I saw him shimmer and he hangs out with ghosts and shifters."

"Ah, not a pleasant thing to tell your sweet man, is it?"

"It's worse, Mrs. Wipp. My sweet man is a demon." I blew out a big breath, thankful to have gotten the worst admission out of my mouth.

Mrs. Wipp paused, took her third drink, and set it on the table. "You're telling me your husband is a demon." The kindly grandmotherly type changed into a hard-nosed Protector. "Did you know this when you married him?"

"No." I winced at the incredulous expression on her face.

"Then when did you figure it out?"

"Not until recently."

Her expression grew harder. "I find this hard to believe. Oh, I can believe he's a demon, all right. Yet I can't get my head around you not realizing until now."

"*I* would've known, but she hardly ever takes me inside the house. And when she does, she keeps me hidden away. If I'd seen Blake, I would've known for sure." Partner's muffled voice continued to drone on even after I covered his speaker with my palm.

Ignoring Partner, I kept going. "Trust me, you're not the only one who finds it hard to believe."

Mrs. Wipp's bright blue eyes darkened. "Hmm." She rested

on her elbows and gave me a penetrating look. "Couldn't you tell what he was after you married him?"

"No." Did she think I'd married a demon on purpose? "I had no clue."

"Really? No clue at all?"

"Okay, maybe there were a few clues." The flush of warmth running up my cheeks wasn't from the alcohol. "What can I say? I fell in love and I didn't want to recognize the signs when I saw them. I guess love messes with a girl's senses. Besides, I searched for his demon numbers and didn't find any."

"Does he have a tattoo?"

The image of Blake's black panther tattoo flashed in my mind, making me lose my breath. "Oh. My. God. How could I have been so stupid? Oh, shit, I'm dumber than I thought I was."

Mrs. Whipp took a sip and gave me a sympathetic smile. "Don't be so hard on yourself, honey. Until recently, tattoos weren't socially acceptable and demons didn't like to draw attention to themselves by sporting a tattoo. But now, it's the easiest way to cover the numbers."

I shook my head, amazed and more than a little embarrassed at how easily I was fooled. "But after today, I can't deny the truth any longer. Blake is a demon and he's working for the High Demon Lord Demogorgon." A cold relief washed through me. I'd finally gotten the words out.

Mrs. Wipp grew quiet, barely speaking above a whisper. "Demogorgon and your husband. Oh, Jenny, I'm sorry."

I slumped into the chair, defeated by the weight pressing on my heart. Unsure of what to say next, I let the silence take over, giving us time to think about my situation.

"Do you still love him?"

Mrs. Wipp, one of the toughest Protectors to ever work for the Society, was asking if I still loved my demon husband. Lying, I knew, would be useless.

"Yeah, I do."

Again, we let each other mull over the problem.

"Jenny, sweetie, you know what you have to do. We can't afford to let that bastard, Demogorgon, gain control of the Bracelet. I know how powerful he is. With the Bracelet, there'll be no stopping him. The world, our world, would come to an end."

"I know." I knew what she said was the truth, but it didn't make it any easier to swallow.

"No person, not even the man you love, is worth the loss of thousands of lives and who knows how many souls."

"I know." Didn't she realize how much pain I was in? I glared at her, angry at her for making me say out loud what I didn't want to even think in private. "I have to stop them."

"You may have to do more than stop them."

Her meaning was clear enough. I might have to kill my husband.

She must've seen the understanding in my face because she nodded, picked up a bank pouch from the side of her desk and stood, as steady on her feet as a sober judge. "Come on. I have to make a deposit at the bank and we need to talk more."

"What more is there to discuss? I know what I have to do." Was the old Protector planning on drilling my duty into my head? Was she afraid I wouldn't choose duty, honor and the safety of the world over my own happiness?

I followed her from the room and out into the sunshine. I glanced around, noticing the people going about their lives with no idea of the evil around them. Instead of enjoying life they way they did, I ached, my heart twisting against the thought of what was to come. "Why couldn't I live like these people do? Why can't I have a normal life?"

Mrs. Wipp looked at me as though I'd grown a third arm. "Because you're special, Jenny. You're a Protector." Giving me a comforting hug, she whirled around and hurried down the street. For an old woman, she sure could move!

She jaywalked across the street, heedless of my running to catch up with her, and waltzed into the bank. She was already in front of the cashier when I slid in line behind her. "What do I do? How do I take care of...of him? Of them?"

Mrs. Wipp thanked the teller for her help and started for the front door. "You keep doing what you've always done. You're his wife and he doesn't think you do what you really do, right?"

"I don't think so. Or at least, he told his master he didn't think I was a Protector."

"Then make him believe his own words. Keep acting like a loving wife." She glanced at me, then hooked my arm in hers to rush us around the corner.

I swallowed and forced out the question I hated asking. "Including in the bedroom?"

"Including in the bedroom." She laughed before sending me an apologetic look. "Honey, most men don't know anything's wrong unless the fun in the sack stops. That's why you have to keep up the act—especially in the bedroom."

I skidded to a stop before hurrying to catch up with her again. "How can I pretend I don't know?"

"You simply pretend." She confronted me, taking my hand in hers to pull me near. "Haven't you known, down deep, what he was before now?" She gazed into my eyes, forcing me to tell the truth with my nod. "You say you still love him, right? So what's to pretend? Besides, you can't tell me you haven't hidden things from him before this. Like how you're a Protector sworn to exterminate his kind?"

She was right. I'd lied enough times to Blake about my secret life and my real job. What were a few more lies? "I guess I can do it."

She started her fast pace again. "You can and you will. However, your primary focus should be finding the Bracelet. I doubt you've done your best in your search, what with learning about Blake."

Mrs. Wipp was right. I'd spent too much time worrying about my husband and his brother. I was a Protector with a job. I owed it to the Society and my fellow citizens to get back to work.

"Jenny, sweetie?"

I snapped out of my short-lived pity party at the tone in Mrs. Wipp's voice. "Yes? What's wrong?"

"I trust you've made a tour of visiting all the pawn shops in town, correct?"

Although she kept walking in the same direction leading us to the bakery, I had the sudden impression her destination had changed. "Sure I did. But I didn't find anything."

"And the television set the Bracelet was hidden in was found in the thieves' house, correct?"

She already knew the answers to her questions, but wanted me to come to a conclusion by myself. What the conclusion was, however, I wasn't sure. "Right. But it was broken into lots of little pieces with no sign of the Bracelet."

"Have you checked the flea market?"

"Other agents did, but with no luck. What're you getting at, Mrs. Wipp?"

She stopped walking, hit the button on the traffic light to cross the street, and didn't look at me. "Where else would you find a bracelet?"

"Can I play? I love playing detective, but Jenn never lets me play."

"Quiet, Partner." I stumbled at her question, knowing I should have the answer, but I didn't. "I'm not sure." What did she want me to say?

"Check out the store over there."

I followed her gaze to the nearest store on the other side of the street. A smile widened her mouth and she waited for me to get up to speed.

"A jewelry store?" Although I understood part of her reasoning, the rest of the answer was still lost in limbo. "I don't get it. A jewelry store manager wouldn't take stolen goods, would he?"

Mrs. Wipp gestured toward the store again. "You're correct except for one fact."

I racked my brain to come up with the one fact and failed. When had I turned into such a mush-head? "Okay, I give up. What fact?" Studying her face didn't give me the answer, either.

"You should have said no *reputable* jewelry store manager would take stolen goods. However, a crooked manager might."

Again, I followed her gaze to the store. "You think this manager's a crook?"

"Those two demons make me think he might be."

"Demons?" Partner beeped a series of excited beeps. "Let me out, Jenn. I want to help."

Ignoring Partner's request, I kept my attention on the two men, one dressed in a business suit and the other dressed in casual, low-riding jeans and torn T-shirt. Demons? "How do you know they're demons? I mean, how can you tell from this far away? Without seeing any signs first?"

Mrs. Wipp chuckled. "Trust me, sweetie. My demon radar has never failed." She shot me a soft smile. "Stay alive in this job for a couple more decades and you'll be able to spot one quickly, too."

"I'll take your word for it." I knew she wasn't putting me down or anything, but I still felt like a new recruit right out of the Society's academy.

Mrs. Wipp patted me on the shoulder. "Don't worry about it. Sooner or later, everyone goes through a period of being off. What with all you've been through and who you're married to, your radar is bound to be out of whack." With a wave of her hand, she bolted across the street, defying anyone's definition of an elderly pace.

"Mrs. Wipp! What're you planning on doing?"

She scooted against the wall of the building and gestured for me to press close to the bricks on the other side of the entrance. "We're going to take a couple of demons down, Jenny. And maybe, if we're really lucky, we'll find the Bracelet at the same time."

"You think those two have it?" I peeked around the corner and saw the two demons speaking with an attractive redheaded saleswoman. From the perplexed expression on her face, the woman was obviously thrown by the odd couple. At last, however, she nodded and went through a rear door, leaving them waiting at the counter.

"What other reason would those two have for being at an upscale jeweler like this? If they have the Bracelet, they know it's too valuable to sell at a pawn shop."

Why I hadn't realized the same thing instead of spinning my wheels running from one pawn shop to the next was a mystery. I groaned at the mistakes I'd made with this case. In fact, I'd screwed this up so badly I wondered why Mac hadn't called me into his office and booted me out of the Society.

"Don't get down on yourself, sweetie. Like I said, you're off right now." Mrs. Wipp leaned around to spy on the demons. "Well, well. It appears our two boys do have something valuable to sell."

"Really?" Excited, I peeked again. "I think you're right. But I can't see what it is they're showing the manager."

"Then I guess we'd better get a closer look."

I nodded and punched a button on Partner. "One word and you're on eBay."

Before I knew it, Mrs. Wipp pushed through the front door of the shop and I hurried to catch up. *Seems like I'm always hurrying to catch up with her. Where does she get her energy?* I grabbed her elbow and whispered, "You'd better let me handle them, Mrs. Wipp. After all, you're retired." I nodded at the manager and the two men who'd turned around at our entrance. In a loud voice, I added, "Don't let us interrupt you. We're just looking."

The manager, a slim middle-aged man of Asian ancestry, gave me a haughty look. He called behind him without taking his eyes off us. "Melissa, you have customers."

"Coming, Mr. Yang." The redhead shuffled out from the rear of the store and swayed over to where Mrs. Wipp and I were pretending to look at men's watches. "Hello, ladies, may I help you?"

Mrs. Wipp put on her best "I'm a vulnerable elderly lady" expression and tipped her head to peer over her glasses. "Oh, aren't you nice? And pretty, too. Isn't she pretty, Jenny?" Without waiting for an answer, she explained, "Jenny's my granddaughter and she's looking for a special bracelet for her mother's birthday. Would you have anything special, dear? I'm thinking something in gold?"

I smiled a dutiful granddaughter smile. "A gold bracelet would be great. What do you have?" I swiveled away from Melissa, pretending to head for the case across the room containing bracelets and necklaces. On my way, I stole a glance at the piece of jewelry the demons held in front of Mr. Yang. The middle-aged demon in the suit kept his hand on the gold bracelet and I trembled with excitement. Could this really be *the* Bracelet?

"Ooh, I likey!" Breaking between the two demons, I reached out to snatch the bracelet, but the older demon moved faster, yanking it away before I could get my hands on it.

"Excuse me, lady, this is our bracelet. It's not for sale."

"Don't you mean it's not for sale yet?" Mrs. Wipp sidled up next to the grungy young demon and gave Mr. Yang a pointed look. "Aren't you gentlemen attempting to sell this piece to the store? Because I'd love to make a counteroffer."

"Hey, you stay out of this!" Mr. Yang was not happy at her interference, especially when the demon holding the bracelet decided a possible bidding war was brewing. "These gentlemen are handing the bracelet over to me."

The older-looking demon's eyes glistened with greed. "Hang on a second, Yang." He turned to give his full attention to Mrs. Wipp. "You want to make me an offer, lady?"

An offer? Why would we want to make an offer? I tried to get Mrs. Wipp to look my way, but she stayed focused on the demon holding the bracelet. I had to wonder why we didn't bang these two on their heads and take the Bracelet. The Society could take care of Mr. Yang and Melissa later.

"Perhaps I do. Do you mean to say you're giving the bracelet to Mr. Yang? For free?" Mrs. Wipp held up her purse, pretending to dig out her checkbook. "Instead, could I persuade you to change your mind by asking you to name your price?"

A phone rang in the rear of the store and Melissa, who up until now had done her best to act busy in front of her employer, headed into the other room.

"Mrs., uh, Grandmother, what're you doing?"

Mrs. Wipp sent me a comforting smile before crooking an expectant eyebrow at the demon.

The demon nearly salivated at the prospect of pulling a huge number out of thin air. "How about you suggest a price, lady? Make it in the five figures or we're not doing business."

"Now hold on a second, Grimsley." Mr. Yang reached out for the bracelet, but Grimsley slapped his hand away. Mr. Yang, however, wasn't about to give up. "You-know-who wants that bracelet. Do you really want to disappoint *him*?"

"He's right, dude. I'm not double-crossing Demogor—"

"Shut up!" Both Grimsley and Mr. Yang yelled at the skuzzy demon.

"Okay, okay. Calm down." The young demon slouched, pulling his backward cap lower on his forehead. "Don't get all wound up, man."

The demon's acceptance appeared to placate Grimsley. "Maybe we can do better than letting you-know-who have it. Besides, if we keep our mouths shut, he'll never find out."

Grimsley pointed at the other demon. "You're always spouting off about how you'd like to stick it to him. Well, here's your chance, Buzz."

"Ah, I see. You, Grimsley, are a shrewd businessman who recognizes a good deal when he hears one. With my price for the bracelet, you could purchase several nice pieces for your, um, friend. How about I write down a number and you tell me if you want to give this lovely piece to your friend...or sell it to me? Hmm?"

Not knowing what Mrs. Wipp had in mind, I kept my mouth shut. Did she really want to buy the bracelet? But why buy it when we could just take it? Mrs. Wipp had to have something up her sleeve. I wished, however, she could tell me what her plan was. Under the circumstances, however, I'd have to go with the flow.

"I'm starting to see the logic behind your thinking, lady. Remember, make the number with lots of zeros or no deal." Grimsley held the bracelet up as though to adore the sheen from the gold. "It's a wonderful piece of work and I'm not taking a lowball offer."

"Dude, we're fucked big time if you do this." Tiny beads of sweat broke out along the top of Buzz's upper lip.

"I understand. Now if I can find a pen and paper..." Mrs. Wipp lifted her purse, opened it, and rummaged inside as if hunting for the elusive pen. After a couple of minutes digging around in her purse and placing a knitting needle, keys, and her makeup case on the counter, she stopped abruptly, snapped her purse shut, and shook her head.

Grimsley, who'd been peeking into her purse, jumped at the *snap* the closure made and snarled, "What's the holdup?"

Keeping in her grandmotherly character, Mrs. Wipp *tisked* at him. "Don't get your tail all twisted. I have my offer right...here!" She struck out with the force of a professional boxer, knocking the demon in the head with her purse and sending him crashing against the glass display case. The bracelet flew across the room. Grimsley slumped to the floor but, thanks to the protective safety glass, the case remained intact.

Taking her lead, I executed a roundhouse kick and shouted a loud, "Kee-ah!" My aim was dead on, striking Buzz's balls exactly where I'd intended. My tae kwon do instructor at the Society would have been proud. Buzz folded into a fetal position, hitting the floor next to his friend with a satisfying thud.

Mrs. Wipp yelled, "Geronimo!" and shoved Grimsley to his back with her foot resting on his chest. She grabbed her knitting needle off the counter and fell on top of him, hitching up her flowery dress and straddling him. "Get the bracelet, Jenny."

Heeding her call, I landed another kick on Buzz's mid-section for good measure, then raced to the other side of the room and grabbed the bracelet. "I've got it!"

"Good." Mrs. Wipp's smile left her lips. She glared at the demon who struggled under her weight, which was planted firmly on top of his chest. "Say goodbye, Grimsley." He screamed, emitting a terrible high-pitched sound. With a warrior's cry, she jabbed the needle into his throat. The scream changed into a gurgle and she hopped off the quickly morphing body. "Oh, my, how I've missed this. Don't get me wrong. Baking is a wonderfully creative outlet, too, but it can't compare to the rush I get when I take one of these vermin out of the game."

Grimsley's body changed, going through a rapid metamorphosis, adopting one body image after another of all the humans he'd possessed during his existence. I counted at least seven people of various ages and ethnicity until his body finally became the skeleton of the very first person he'd ever possessed. The bones shortened, shrinking to a petite-size skeleton, and finally crumbled to dust.

"His first victim was a child." The tone in Mrs. Wipp's voice matched the pain in my heart. "At least her soul can rest easy now."

"Yeah." Spotting Buzz attempting to crawl behind one of the counters, I rushed over and grabbed his foot. He shrieked and tried to kick my hand away. "Sorry. I hate to be a buzz-kill, but it's your turn...dude." Weaponless, I called for help. "Mrs. Wipp?"

She correctly interpreted my need and tossed the knitting needle my way. I caught it in mid-air and flipped it around to put the pointed end in between Buzz's shoulder blades.

"Actually, I lied. I'm gonna love being a Buzz-kill." Using all my strength, I jabbed the needle into the back of his neck. Listening to the hissing sound of air leaving his body, I sprang out of the way and watched him disintegrate. Unlike his friend, Buzz's body didn't morph into the remains of different victims, but quickly changed to skeletal form and into dust.

"He was a young demon."

I nodded. "Good. Better to get them young before they work their way through too many people. Hey! Where'd Mr. Yang go?"

Mrs. Wipp took the needle out of my hand, picked up a jewelry cloth from the counter, and wiped it clean. "The scumbag ran out of here so fast he broke the sound barrier. Never mind. We'll send reinforcements to take care of him later. Let's take a look at that bracelet."

I'd almost forgotten about the bracelet I still clutched with my other hand. Holding it up, I checked for an inscription and felt my pulse throb faster when I found one. Squinting, I read the message out loud.

Peek-a-Boo, I See You!

"To Gloria from Alex."

I had to reread the inscription several times before it finally sunk in. This wasn't the Bracelet. "Dammit, dammit, dammit, double dammit."

"Really, Jenn. A lady shouldn't curse."

"Oh, ho! I see Partner's still the same conservative at heart. You dream of a wife in the kitchen, pregnant and barefoot, don't cha, Partner?" Mrs. Wipp laughed. "Jenny, don't let this minor bump in the road bring you down. Even if we didn't find the Bracelet, at least we've rid the world of two demons. It beats the hell out of baking brownies."

I tossed the useless bracelet on top of the counter. Fighting the frustration building inside, I rubbed the toe of my shoe in Buzz's dust and pondered my situation. If push came to shove, could I do the same to Blake? And what if he found out I was a Protector? Would he understand and accept my role as a demon exterminator? Would he have any remorse killing me?

"Go home, Jenny. You need to find out what Blake and Demogorgon have planned. If you can't kill Demogorgon, you need to stop him from getting the Bracelet." Her arm slid around my shoulders to lead me out of the store. "As for Blake, you can't let him in on your secret. Not until we have the Bracelet in our possession. Once you've completed your mission, it's your call, but a Protector married to a demon? It simply can't work."

We walked out of the jewelry store, leaving it in almost the same condition we'd found it, except for a couple piles of clothing and ashes. The Society's Psych Squad could take care of Melissa—providing she was human and not demon—but I was ready to bet Mr. Yang was already gone and would never show his face around town again. After all, not only did the Society know about him now, but he'd failed to get the Bracelet for Demogorgon.

Pulling me around to take both my shoulders, Mrs. Wipp looked me in the eyes, making me aware of the seriousness of the situation. As if I didn't already know! "You're going to have to make a choice. Either you stay on with the Society or you stay with your husband. You can't go on as you have. Not once headquarters finds out what he is."

She hugged me to her, smothering me with the mixed aroma of cinnamon and demon dust. "Take care, Jenny. I'm sure you'll make the right choice." With one last squeeze, she turned and walked away.

The ride home was both the longest and the shortest ride I'd ever taken. Although I wanted to get home and find some quiet time to reflect on my next move, I dreaded the possibility of seeing Blake. Could I do what Mrs. Wipp suggested? Could I pretend not to know about Blake and act naturally around him?

I pulled into my driveway to find Myra sitting on my front porch. Leaving the strangely quiet Partner on the passenger seat, I left my car and shuffled over to sit next to her.

"Long day, huh?" She leaned into me to push against my shoulder with hers. "Anything exciting happen?"

Myra desperately wanted to be a Protector and loved hearing about my missions and the Otherworlders. Most of the time, I enjoyed telling her about my adventures, but tonight was different. This mission hit too close to home for an easy tell. "I'm sorry, Myra, but I'm wiped out. I don't have it in me to talk shop. Do you mind?"

She bumped me again. "Of course not, as long as I get a rain check."

A vision of the rain check I'd gotten from Blake was in and out of my mind in a flash. "Deal."

"I went shopping." She lifted her large tote bag and jiggled it. "I bought a whole purse full of great costume pieces."

"That's great, Myra." I knew I wasn't being a very

supportive or interesting friend, but I was simply tuckered out. My mind just wouldn't kick into gear.

I shook my head, letting my mind wonder to thoughts of Blake. How could I have married a demon without knowing it? And now that I knew he was a demon, how could I find out what he had going with Demogorgon? Myra continued to rattle on about who knew what, blissfully unaware of how off-kilter my life had gone.

An image of Blake sauntering over to me on the beach shot raw emotion through me, twisting my gut into a tangled mess. I sighed, remembering the blazing sun making his skin glisten when the light hit the water on his body to create sparkling beads. Oh, how I'd wanted to lick those drops before they could shimmy along his tight abs. Thing is, I'd gotten to lick them off, along with his thorough licking of my body. Had I been too consumed with sex, making me miss the signs of demonic possession?

"Anyway, I have bigger news."

The part of my consciousness keeping track of Myra's ongoing conversation alerted the rest of my mind to the change in topics. I broke free of my remembrances of Blake and did my best to concentrate on my friend's words. "Yeah?"

Myra reached over and pulled the hair on my arm.

"Ow! Since when did you get violent?"

"Since you deserved it. I knew you weren't listening to me blabber on."

I made a guilty face and tried to beg forgiveness. "Shoot, Myra, I'm sorry. You know I like hearing about your life, but the—"

"I know. I know. The weight of the world is on your shoulders."

I smiled, thankful she had no clue how close she'd come to the truth. "Yeah, the weight of the world right here, sister." I patted my shoulder and slumped over.

"No problem. I understand. But listen for a sec, okay?"

The excitement in her eyes piqued my interest and I forced my full attention her way. "Yes, ma'am. Spill. What's the big news?"

"You remember George, right?"

The grin spreading across her face reminded me of the one I'd had when I'd first met Blake. "Hmm. Let's see. Big guy, right? Lives in the woods? Likes fish? Eats more than ten men?" I placed a finger on my chin in the classic Jack Benny pose. A pose I knew Myra wouldn't connect with the well-known older comedian. She never watched the black-and-white shows like Blake and I did. The cozy picture of Blake and I snuggling under the covers, laughing at the old movies, threatened to send a pain to the center of my heart, but I pushed it away before the emotional dagger could strike its mark. "Nope. Can't say I remember."

"Jenn, stop kidding around." She gave me a playful slap. "Come on. I can't wait to tell you."

"Okay, okay. What's up with the big guy?" I hadn't thought to check with Myra after the impromptu dinner party the other night. "I guess you two have gotten together since the other night?"

A pink hue flushed into her cheeks and added to the happy glow on her face. "Uh-huh. In fact, George came home with me and never left. He's staying with me."

I paused, letting her startling news sink in. Myra was Ms. Proper Behavior. For her to take a man home within hours of their meeting was amazing. I glanced up to the sky to check for any signs of winter weather moving in. Hell had to have frozen over.

"Wow. George is staying at your place. Wow." I squinted my eyes and dived in for the real dirt. "Myra Shuster, are you telling me you're shacking up with a man you hardly know? Myra, are you getting busy with George the Great?"

"If you're asking if we're having sex"—Myra tucked her head, peeking at me through long lashes—"then yes. I'm having sex with George." She giggled. "Funny you should call him 'George the Great'...because he certainly is."

I laughed and hugged her to me. At least someone's life didn't stink. "Wonderful, Myra! I'm happy for you. Shocked and amazed, but happy."

"And here's the best part." She took a big breath and waited for me to coax her.

"Tell me you're not getting married." Having a fun time in the sack was one thing. Marriage, on the other hand, was serious business. And rushing into marriage? Well, I knew how disastrous *that* could be.

She blurted out the rest with her exhale. "George wants me to come with him to his home in the woods. He says he wants to tell me something important."

Being a suspicious person by nature—except, I guess, for my lapse with Blake—I couldn't help but analyze her words. "He wants to *tell* you something important. Not *ask* you something important. I'm thinking he's not talking about marriage."

Myra's enthusiasm died a quick death. "Why are you picking apart everything I say? I don't know what George wants to tell me, but I'm damned sure going to go and find out."

I tried to backpedal without giving up an inch. "I'm sorry, Myra, but you've got to admit, you haven't had much experience in these matters."

"Oh, great. Now you're not only acting like my mother, but you're calling me naïve and gullible. Thanks a lot."

"I'm not trying to mother you or call you names. I'm trying to be your friend and watch out for you. You hardly know the man." Again, Blake's face flashed in my mind's eye and I knew I'd already done exactly what I didn't want Myra to do. "Why not slow things down a little? Take your time to get to know him better, here where you're safe."

The hurt expression on Myra's face didn't help matters. Yet it was better than the accusatory tone of her voice. "You've never liked George much, have you? I could tell by the way you acted the other night. You got all fidgety. Like he was one of those creatures you hunt."

The hair on my neck stood up, ready to call out reinforcements. Not all supernaturals were horrible creatures and Blake was living proof. Or at least, I hoped he was. "Not true, Myra. I like George. How can I not like him? He saved my butt. I'm only saying you might want to take things at a more leisurely pace and enjoy yourself. What's the rush?"

Myra was on her feet and moving down the sidewalk. "I can't believe you're acting like this. George and I found each other and I don't care if we haven't known each other very long."

She wheeled to face me, causing me to bump into her. "You don't understand, Myra. I'm trying to help."

She poked me once in the chest, let out a frustrated grunt, and whirled around again. "Shit, the kettle is calling the spoon black."

"It's 'the kettle calling the pot black'." Again, she spun to face me and, again, I bumped into her. "Give me some warning when you're reversing directions, will you?"

"What? What about a pot?"

"It's a pot. Not a spoon." I grinned, hoping to find the normally affable Myra inside this red-faced, spitting woman. Instead, I had to deal with Myra the Maniac.

With a snarl, she pushed me backward, pivoted and stalked several feet away before I realized my peaceful friend had shoved me.

"Calm down." Out of the corner of my eye, I saw Mrs. Hardgrave doing a piss-poor job of pruning her rose bushes. Pruning is hard when your concentration is on the fight going on across the street. "Myra, you're causing a scene. Mrs. Hardgrave is eating this up with the spoon you mentioned." Okay, so maybe I should've shut up about the spoon.

I realized a little too late this wasn't a good time for a joke. She backtracked to tear into me. "If you don't watch out, I'll give you a spoon right up your nose. I will not calm down. Not until you apologize. Just because you're a big-time Protector doesn't mean you can run other people's lives."

Enough was enough. I grabbed Myra's arm. Putting my thankfully spoonless nose close to hers, I hissed my words, hoping to bring the volume of our argument down. "Dammit, Myra. Do you want everyone to know what I do? Knock it off. You're not thinking. Will you come inside and let me explain?"

Myra stopped to scan the rest of the street. I could almost see the steam coming off her. At last, she started to cool the fire of her rage. "You're right. I'm sorry. I shouldn't have said...you know what."

I let out a huge breath of pent-up air and emotion. "Me, too. Could we please talk about this rationally?" I moved my eyes in a quick motion toward Mrs. Hardgrave and back. "Away from eavesdropping neighbors?"

Myra nodded and let me pull her along with me. A shout startled us, making Myra jump. A man wearing a hooded mask bolted from behind the bushes separating my yard from my neighbor's. He shouted again, brandishing a long dagger at me.

The Protector in me took over and I leapt in front of Myra, pushing her out of range of the lethal-looking knife. Executing a roundhouse kick, I doubled the man over. (*When I tell this story later, I won't mention how I'd missed my real target—his knife.*) At least I'd connected, but he wasn't down for the count. Growling my frustration, I tried to parlay my kick with a blow to his head, but he thrust out his other hand, blocking my attempt.

I went down hard, striking my shoulder against the sidewalk pavement. The stun gun he'd used grazed my hand. Pain shot up from my arm, forcing me to stay on the ground, trying to regain my senses.

The attacker, seizing the opportunity, snatched Myra's purse before throwing the knife at me. I rolled seconds before the blade pierced the ground beside me.

"Thief! Help! Thief!"

Managing to push up on my throbbing elbow, I waited for the world to stop spinning. But even my addled mind couldn't have dreamed up the sight of Mrs. Hardgrave streaking across the street, intercepting the fleeing robber. She struck out with her rake, but he sidestepped her. Like the desperate-housewife version of a knight of the Round Table, she swung her garden-sword into action. I had to admire her spunk and skill. Without a regard for her safety, she chased the man several yards before he sped around the corner and vanished from view.

Puffing, Mrs. Hardgrave joined Myra in helping me to my feet. "Jenny, are you all right?"

"Yeah, I'm okay." My dignity had taken more of a bruising than my body. Although I was loath to admit it, I'd been saved by Mrs. Hardgrave. Still, the woman deserved praise. "Way to go, Mrs. H. You ran him off, but good." With my unhurt arm, I patted her on the back, giving her one of the few genuine smiles I'd ever shown her. "And about the other day..." I was working my way up to a belated apology, but Mrs. H. headed me off at the pass.

"Oh, piddle-poop, honey. Don't worry about it." Mrs. H. gave me a pat of my own.

"You were amazing, Mrs. H." Myra cast me an apologetic look. "You, too, Jenn. You totally took the brunt of the attack by shoving me out of the way." She wrapped an arm around both of us. "You're both my heroes."

Mrs. H. grinned and waved off Myra's tribute. "Shouldn't we call the police?"

"No!"

Myra and Mrs. H stared at the crazy woman—me.

"Why not? We need to report the robbery. The thief took off with your friend's bag." Mrs. Hardgrave's tone sounded less concerned than smug. Too bad I couldn't let her bring the police in on this, but something about the man had seemed familiar. Familiar like in one handsome hubby's brother. But why would Michael want Myra's purse?

"I meant Myra should call them." I shot Myra a look I hoped she'd interpret. "After all, it was her purse."

"Jenn's right. I'll report the robbery." I tipped my head toward my house and she caught my silent message. "I'll take Jenn inside to lie down and call them."

Mrs. Hardgrave, however, wasn't about to give up on more drama. "I truly don't mind. Besides, I'm sure they're going to want to speak to me."

I tugged Myra along with me, starting for the house, and got the last word in. "No thanks, Mrs. Hardgrave. We'll take care of the report. Thanks again for your brave assistance."

Myra and I hurried inside, leaving a sputtering and disappointed neighbor on the front lawn. I headed for the phone on the desk in our entry hall.

"Are you really calling the police?"

"Absolutely not." Instead, I dialed Blake's cell phone number. It rang several times before he picked up. "Blake, I need you home. Now."

Myra silently questioned me with gestures which I silently ignored. Instead, I listened to him try and make excuses. "No, Blake, no excuses. It's time to set the record straight once and for all."

After Blake agreed to meet me at home, I replaced the receiver. Was this a huge mistake? Could I confide in him? "Blake's on his way."

"I'm confused. You're calling Blake for help? What's he supposed to do? The thief's already long gone."

"Yeah, I'm sure he is. I called Blake because I want to quit hiding my identity." What little strength I had left flowed out of me and I slipped into the seat next to the phone desk. I leaned against the chair and closed my eyes.

"You're kidding. You're going to tell him you're a Protector?" Myra crossed her arms and planted her feet in front of me. "Isn't telling anyone against the Society's rules?"

"I told you." I opened my eyes and lifted an eyebrow.

She lost a good dose of her bravado, uncrossing her arms to link her thumbs in her pockets. "I see your point. But the fewer people who know, the better, right? Why tell Blake now?"

I sighed and prepared myself for whatever reaction she gave me. "Because it's time for the truth to come out and it's only fair we both spill our guts. Figuratively speaking, of course." Yes, it was definitely time for our own version of Show and Tell. Especially since I had a sneaking suspicion that Michael was our mugger. But that was more than I wanted to think about right then. The bigger problem still remained. "I have to tell Blake about me...because he's going to tell me he's a demon."

I'll Show You Mine,
If You'll Show Me Yours.

Myra took the news better than I thought she would. After explaining how I hadn't known Blake was a demon at the time of our marriage, she was all sympathetic hugs and tears. I knew she could understand how I felt. Myra had my back like she'd had it all the years I'd known her.

"Oh, Jenn, I can't fathom what you've gone through."

"I haven't had a good night's sleep since I found out." I managed a weak smile and shrugged. "Maybe I could go on Oprah or Dr. Phil. I bet I'd get better ratings than the wife who found out her husband was a closet transvestite with a secret family living right next door."

Myra didn't crack a smile at my joke. "Honey, what are you going to do? Do you still love Blake? Even after finding out the truth about him?"

"Well, you've nailed the two million dollar question on the head."

"It's the sixty-four thousand dollar question, Jenn. Not two million."

"Trust me, Myra. This question is definitely worth two million."

After a moment of silence, she reached over to take my hand. "Whatever you decide, I'll stick by you."

I squeezed her hand, grateful to have a friend like her. "Thanks. I know you will. I may need you to keep me sane."

The sound of the garage door opening signaled Blake's arrival. I grimaced at my friend and stood, ready for action. "If you don't mind, I need to do this without any witnesses. Okay?" I managed a weak grin. "Not that I'm planning on exterminating him or anything."

Myra accepted my request, but not before checking. "He's not dangerous to you, is he? I mean, we are talking about a demon."

She was right, of course. You never knew what to expect from demons. Yet, instead of using my head as my training had taught me, I went with my heart. "No. Blake won't hurt me. I believe he loves me and I still love him."

I could hear him in the kitchen now, dropping his briefcase by the back door like he did every evening. "You've got to leave, Myra."

"Jenn? Where are you?"

He rounded the corner sooner than I'd expected, meaning he must've moved with demon speed. "Are you two all right? Mrs. Hardgrave stopped me outside and told me about the mugger. Shit, a mugger on our street? It's hard to believe, but I guess it's a sign of the times." He glanced between us, searching for an answer. "Did anyone get hurt? Are you two okay?"

Leave it to Mrs. Hardgrave to bushwhack Blake with the news. Yet, unlike I usually did, I didn't feel any animosity toward her. I couldn't get mad at her any longer after she'd helped me fend off an attacker. "We're fine."

"Have you called the police?" He kept running his gaze over both of us, trying to make sure we were uninjured. Yet I couldn't help but think I saw something else in his eyes. What it was, however, eluded me.

"Not yet. I'll explain why in a minute." I started for the door, taking a gawking Myra along with me.

"He's really a demon?" Myra whispered and I hoped Blake was too preoccupied to hear her.

"Later, Myra, okay? Do you have your car keys?" Myra always carried a purse for her purchases along with a fanny pack. It wasn't fashionable, but it did come in handy—like now. She nodded and patted her pack. "Good. I'll call you, okay?"

With one quick hug, Myra opened the front door, paused for a last questioning look, then left after my quick nod. I knew my world would change before I saw her again. The only question was...how much would it change?

"You're sure you're okay?" Blake drew me to him, wrapping his strong arms around me. I snuggled against his chest and prayed this wouldn't be the last time I'd feel like getting close to him. "You're not trying to hold anything back, are you?"

I tensed, wondering what he meant. Yet, instead of questioning him, I shook my head and took it as an opening. "No, Blake. I'm not holding anything back any longer." I knew he didn't recognize my reference to my secret—his secret—but he'd find out soon enough.

"Good. I'm relieved. Still, you should've reported the robbery to the cops. Mrs. H. said he got away with Myra's purse, right?"

Again, I nodded, breaking out of his embrace and turning away from him to shuffle through the mail. I hated procrastination, but this time was different. "He did, but she never carries anything valuable in her purse. Mainly junk. Not even a credit card or money. She wears that fanny pack for those important things, remember?"

Blake's deep laugh made me tingle. Would I hear him laugh after I told him the news? Or would he turn violent once I revealed his secret?

"I'd forgotten about her fanny pack. Yeah, she's one of a kind, our Myra."

I struggled to keep the tears in check and was glad he couldn't see my face. His calling her "our Myra" nearly broke my heart.

"Let's lighten the mood, okay?" Blake's arms encircled around my waist and pulled me close. "Hey, good-lookin', whatcha got cookin'?"

For a second, I allowed myself to pretend nothing had changed and he was still my very sexy, very mortal husband who liked to tell lame jokes. "You are such a cornball. Who says that kind of stuff nowadays?"

"What? Men can't call their wives good-lookin'? Or are they not supposed to assume she's got something cookin'? Am I being a male chauvinist pig?"

I closed my eyes and enjoyed the touch of his lips against the nape of my neck. After tonight, would I ever feel those lips against my skin? "Blake, we need to talk." I knew it sounded cliché, but I didn't care.

He dropped the playful attitude and turned me toward him. "Okay, I give up. What's wrong, Jenn? I get the impression you're upset about something besides the mugging. Am I right?"

My laugh sounded more like a hacking cough. "Yeah, I am." I decided to get straight to the point. "I have a secret."

His gray eyes melted my heart with their surprised concern. "You do? Is it a bad secret?" His arms slipped down my torso to lock together at the base of my spine. "You're all right, aren't you? I mean, you're not about to tell me you've got a horrible disease, are you?" He bent down to get an even closer look at me. "But if you are, don't worry. We'll get through it together."

How could I not love this guy? And yet, how could such a good man be a demon? The whole idea of Blake as a demon didn't make sense. Yet I knew the truth now and I wasn't ready for another trip to Denial Land—no matter how much nicer it seemed there. "No, Blake, I'm fine. Physically, at least."

"Good. But you're making me think you're not fine. I mean, other than physically."

I broke apart from him and tugged him along with me to the living room couch. "Sit with me."

"Oh, this can not be good." He chuckled, still trying to lighten the mood, yet I heard the nervous tone behind the words.

I released his hand and scooted farther away from him. He noticed, but didn't try to close the gap.

"Let's have it, Jenn. What's bothering you?" The lines in his forehead wrinkled. Yet, instead of making him appear older, they made him even sexier than before. "Do you want a divorce?"

"No." The word was out of my mouth before I could think. Was my answer the right one? Even if I didn't want a divorce, would the Society insist on one? I gazed into the face that meant everything to me and spoke the truth. "No, I don't want a divorce." He grew serious and deadly calm. *Deadly or undeadly? Urgh. Jenn, you really need to choose your words more carefully.*

"Whew, what a relief. Then what's up? Go on and spit it out, babe. Like I said before, whatever it is, however bad it gets, we'll tackle it together. Please, tell me what *it* is."

I took the biggest breath of my life and let *it* out. "I'm a

Protector."

Blake's expression didn't change which, of course, confirmed he already knew my secret identity. He may have fooled Demogorgon into thinking he didn't know, but he couldn't fool me. He cleared his throat and kept up the pretence. "You're a what?"

I resisted the urge to shout, then gritted my teeth and kept my voice even. "No, Blake, don't. Don't pretend you don't know what a Protector is."

"I'm sorry, babe, but I don't. What's a Protector?" His poker face adopted a sincere, yet confused expression.

"Blake Barrington, I know you know about the Society, the Protectors and everything going on."

"Jenn, I swear—"

"Don't!" I grumbled a few choice words, stalked across the room to expel more of the energy boiling inside me, and whirled to confront him again. "Don't lie to me, Blake. I'm sick of the lies. I'd rather know the whole truth, no matter how ugly it is, no matter how it changes our lives. I'm finished living a lie and hiding what I am." I glared at him, letting him know I knew everything. "And so are you."

He stood and faced off with me, neither one of us blinking, neither one of us wanting to be the first to break the heated silence. But, as always, someone finally did.

Blake took a step toward me before apparently changing his mind and backing up. "Are you sure? Are you sure you want to bring all of this—everything—out into the open? Because once it's out in the sunlight, we can't shove it into the dark again." His eyes deepened and I swear I saw a flash of red in them. This time, unlike the previous times, I didn't ignore the telltale demon color in my husband's eyes.

Was I sure I wanted the truth to come out no matter what the consequences? I swallowed and forced myself to say the words. "I'm sure."

"You're a Protector." Again, his eyes flashed fire and I knew he was fighting to maintain his human form.

"How long have you known, Blake? Did you marry me knowing I was a Protector? Or maybe *because* I was a Protector?" *Is our marriage part of your scheme to help Demogorgon?* I wanted to ask the question, but couldn't bring myself to reveal that secret yet. I wanted him to confess to me.

"I found out right after we returned from the honeymoon." Blake let out a rush of air, walked over to the liquor cabinet, and poured a stiff drink. "I didn't know who you really worked for before I married you."

He downed the drink and reached out for me, but I refused to take his hand. Frowning, he dropped his hand to his side. I knew it hurt him, but I just couldn't go to him. Not yet. Not until everything was out in the open.

"I had a friend of mine at high levels of the government check you out." He grinned sheepishly. "I'm sorry, Jenn, but I knew you couldn't be a realtor. You hardly ever sell a home and you're really lousy at the job. I'm surprised Swindle keeps you on."

I stood where I was, keeping my hand firmly on the nearby bookcase. Without something to hold on to, I'd fall to the floor. "Are you kidding me? Are you going to stand there and act like you're the average married man who happened to find out his wife works for a top-secret organization?"

"Well, I wouldn't consider myself average when I'm married to a spy. Besides, being married to you—no matter what your job is—makes me luckier than the average man."

Was he for real? Did he think I'd buy his flattery? "Blake, stop it. Are you trying to tell me you don't know what the Society does?"

"The Society? I'm sorry, Jenn, I don't. The best my friend could uncover was to say your job was very important and confidential. What is this Society, anyway? Wait." He held up his palm. "If you tell me, will you have to kill me?" The following chuckle lacked true warmth and I didn't laugh with him.

"You're full of shit."

He feigned a surprised look, tilting his head toward me as if wondering whether or not to call for the men in white coats. "I don't understand why you're getting all worked up. How am I full of shit?"

I clenched and unclenched my fists. Forgetting my Protector training on how to stay calm, I pulled a book from the highest shelf in the bookcase and grabbed the vial of holy water I stashed there for safekeeping. "Blake, you're going to knock off the bull or else."

"Or else what?" He acted as though he didn't know what I had in mind, but I saw the glint of alarm cross his face before he regained control. "Are you planning on throwing that on me? Is it acid perhaps? What's wrong with you, Jenn?"

"You know damn well what it is. This is holy water and it's going on your face if you don't cut the crap." I popped the lid off the vial and took a menacing step forward.

"Come on, babe. You're losing it. Take a deep calming breath." He sidestepped, keeping a safe distance between us.

"I'm going to count to three, then I toss it." I moved closer and Blake held his ground. "One. Two."

"Stop it, Jenn."

"I mean it, Blake." Raising the vial, I slowly pulled back my arm and prepared to fling the blessed liquid at the man I loved. Could I really do this? Fortunately, I didn't have to find out.

"All right. You win." Blake held his hands up, imploring me to stop. "I'll tell you."

Once I'd lowered the vial and replaced the lid, he poured another drink and downed it. He raised his empty glass to me in an offer to fix me one and lowered it at my refusal.

"I guess since this is confessional day at the Barrington household, I need to tell you something, too." The corners of his mouth curved upward. "You're right. You're not the only one living with a secret."

I nodded to encourage him.

"I'm not as successful as you think I am." Blake ran his fingers through his thick hair and averted his gaze from mine. "Business has gone down the tubes lately, which is why I've been working those odd hours. In fact, I'm sorry to have to tell you—"

"Shut up! Stop telling me lies." I removed the lid and moved to throw the liquid. "Quit messing with me, Blake. You have one more chance. Make it the truth or you'll regret it."

A shadow fell over his face and his gray eyes met mine. "In a way, I guess it's good you're a Protector." His chuckle sounded bitter. "If you were any other woman, you'd never believe me."

"Goody for me. Now tell me everything." I couldn't say the word *demon*. Instead, I wanted him to say it for me. For both of us.

"I'm a..."

"Yes?" I held my breath and said a silent prayer, hoping he'd say anything other than what I knew he'd say. I may have suffered through a long phase of denial, but no longer. My demon radar was on full alert and blaring out warnings.

"I'm a...demon."

We both released pent-up air with his admission as though he'd pronounced himself free from cancer. Like we were both somehow relieved to get the truth out in the open. At least I was for a moment. Then the vision of the world around me tilted. My loving husband, the man of my dreams, began to change.

Blake shifted, transforming into a person I'd never seen. His eyes flashed red and his body wavered, losing its human form. Strong, muscular arms contorted into scaly dark green skin with shreds of flesh dripping from his elbows and armpits. His handsome face morphed, altering into someone—some *thing*—I didn't recognize. I gasped, seeing my husband for what he really was, and the horror threatened to crush my chest. Long deadly teeth sprouted from his mouth. His silky black hair disappeared into tuffs of gray, leaving large areas of his scalp raw and exposed.

As though he wasn't certain I'd heard him the first time, he repeated his words. "Jenn, honey, I'm a demon."

Liar, Liar, Horns on Fire

The low growl of the voice coming from the creature standing before me was not the voice of my lover. Instead of Blake, a disgusting creature stood before me holding the shot glass. "Jenn."

"Blake?" I wanted my husband, not this demon. As hard as I tried, I couldn't reconcile the man and the demon as being the same person.

A sound resembling a groan came from him and he dropped the glass to the floor. "I know I'm grotesque. But it's still me. Inside this monstrous exterior, I'm still the person I always was."

Could his personality have stayed the same even though his body had altered beyond recognition? I'd never thought of a demon as being a person. The Society told Protectors the human part, the good caring part of the person, left the body once the demon had taken possession. Yet I had to wonder...could they be wrong?

"Jenn? Do you believe me?"

"But how? Why isn't the demon inside you controlling you?"

Blake shook his head. "I can feel its presence, but I don't let it take over. Not completely, anyway. It's like there's a battle raging inside me for supremacy and I have to fight to remain in control." The triumphant light in his eyes dimmed. "I'm winning. At least for now."

I guess demons are more like people than I'd ever thought. The demon who'd taken over Blake's body wasn't as strong as he was. Could other people conquer the demon inside them?

He took a step in my direction and I fought against the instinctive urge to toss the holy water on him. Letting out a small cry of despair, I lost the battle and lifted my arm to throw it on him—until I looked into his eyes.

I could see the torment in those beautiful eyes. Even if everything else about him had changed, the look in his eyes had remained the same. Behind the terrible pain lay the undeniable truth of Blake's love. Whatever he was, no matter how gruesome he appeared, the essence of the man I'd fallen in love with existed, fighting to survive in a body not solely his own.

I could barely breathe, yet I somehow managed to whisper the words, "Oh, Blake." I plugged the lid into the top of the vial and took my first step toward him. His gaze drifted to the bottle in my hand and I pocketed it. I took another step and held out my arms. "Blake."

His ghastly body shook as if I'd lifted a great weight from him. A spark lit in his eyes, dampening the ache there, and he moved into my arms. Yet although the stench of him was awful, I pulled him against me.

"I'm sorry, Jenn. I know I should've told you." His body shivered as if freezing from the pain of his guilt. "I just couldn't bear the thought of losing you."

"It's all right. We'll make it all right." I broke the connection with him although I knew he wanted to keep his body next to mine. "I understand. I lied, too." Tears sprang to my eyes and I hurriedly wiped them away. My sniff brought my finger under my nose—to stop my nose from dripping as well as to try and stifle his rank aroma. Unfortunately, it didn't work and love can only handle a certain amount of stench. Ask any mother of a ten-year-old boy. "I'm sorry, Blake, but could you revert to your human form?" I grinned, knowing he would understand. "Seriously, dude. No offense, but you reek."

Blake shifted, returning to the gorgeous male I loved. Thankfully, once he'd changed, his foul body odor also dissipated. "I know. Even I have trouble standing the smell sometimes."

I coughed a short laugh. "Damn, we're a pair, aren't we? Kind of like the Beauty and the Beast of Suburbia, huh?"

He attempted a weak smile and we fell into an uncomfortable silence. After pouring another drink, he asked one of the many questions racing through my mind. "Would you have married me? If I'd told you during our whirlwind romance, would you have stayed with me?" He cast a glimpse at my pocket where I'd stashed the vial. "Or would you have done what any other Protector would've done? Would you have exterminated me?"

I didn't want to, yet I had to answer him truthfully. "I don't know."

He laughed a sour, humorless sound and nodded. "Gee. Not the answer I wanted."

Two could play at the What If game. "Would you have married me if you'd known I worked for the Society?" After all, turnabout is fair play, although I really didn't care about playing fair at this point.

Blake's face dropped. "Do you really need to ask?"

"I guess I do. Besides, you did." Straightening, I fought to keep hold of my emotions. I wasn't sure what I'd do if I fell apart.

"In a heartbeat."

I gazed at my husband of a few weeks and saw the sincerity etched on his face. "Oh." Blake waited for more of a reaction, his features hopeful, but I couldn't give him what he wanted to hear. He would've married me, but I couldn't give him the same reassurance. *Sorry, no can do, Blake.*

His shoulders slumped when he realized what my silence meant. "What do we do now?" He sank to the couch and ran a hand through his hair.

I joined him on the couch, my mind a blur of images and questions, and flopped against the cushions. Even after his revelation, I didn't fear him. If I couldn't count on his love for me, then I was lost anyway. "I guess it depends on your explanation."

"My explanation of what?"

"Bla-ake." *Warning, warning.* "Don't act ignorant again."

"I'm not. I've told you what I am. What else is there?"

I sat up, anger giving me a new burst of energy. "Blake, I know about your brother. I know he's a ghoul."

He didn't hide his surprise very well. "You do?" His eyes took on a faraway look. "Yeah, he's a ghoul *and* he's also my brother. How did you find out?"

"Never mind." We could deal with the subject of Michael later on. Right now, I needed to know about the more important characters in this weird reality show called our life. "How about telling me what you're doing with Demogorgon?"

The features of his handsome face fell at my words. "Demogorgon? How do you know about him?"

"I saw you, Blake. I saw you talking with him."

Another conflict waged war inside Blake. I could see it in his tense body language and in the way he avoided my gaze. "Every demon has a demon lord. Do you expect me to be any different?" He leaned forward and covered his face with his hands.

"No. But I saw you together. I heard you talking about the Bracelet."

Blake jerked upward to glare at me. "What do you know about the Bracelet? Tell me you don't have it."

Suddenly, our adversarial sides came out and I wasn't happy to see the flash of red in his eyes. "What if I do? What then, Blake? Are you going to kill me to get it for your master?"

He rose and strode to the other side of the room as if he couldn't get far enough away from me. "Don't be crazy, Jenn. I'd never harm you, no matter what. But some Otherworlders believe you have it. I've told them you don't to keep them from harming you."

"Well, it didn't work."

The red in his eyes disappeared and he stared at me in shock. "What do you mean?"

"I mean I've had a couple of near misses." I couldn't help myself, I had to gloat. "Obviously, they failed and I didn't."

"I swear I didn't know."

Could I believe the relief I saw on his face? I considered the question, coming up with the answer in a second. "I believe you and thanks for looking out for me. But isn't watching over me and trying to give Demogorgon what he wants a conflict of interest?" Would he choose me over his master if he had to make a choice? I thought he would, but I didn't want to test my assumption, either. "Didn't Demogorgon order you to kill me?"

"He did, and I told him I hadn't found the Bracelet yet. I

213

made him think I needed to keep you around awhile longer."

"Gee, I appreciate the help. What happens to you if he figures out you lied to him?"

"I don't care. I'm not helping him." He moved with demon speed to sit beside me again. "However, I do need to find the Bracelet. Not for Demogorgon, but for me. For Michael. For us."

I tried to twist my mind around this new development and couldn't. "For us? Sorry. I don't get it."

He took my hand between his two. "Demogorgon wants me to find the Bracelet, kill you, and give the Bracelet to him. Not necessarily in that order. In exchange, he's promised to make Michael and me mortals again."

"I didn't realize demon lords made deals with their lowly subjects." The heat from his touch traveled up my arm and into my heart. The truth of my feelings washed over me. I didn't care what he was as long as he stayed my husband.

"They don't. Of course, I know he won't keep his end of the bargain, which is why I don't plan on giving him the Bracelet—or killing you."

I feigned a relieved expression. "Whew! That's a relief."

"No. I want the Bracelet for myself."

Having seen a lot of strange things in my job—both my jobs—I'd have bet my Aunt Hildie's prize-winning recipe for double fudge cake I couldn't be surprised. But with his declaration, I would've lost and someone else would soon be eating her cake instead of me. "Yourself? Are you out to rule the world, Blake? If you are, we're going to have a little problem."

"Rule the world? Not a chance. I've got enough problems." He squeezed my hand to reassure me. "I want the Bracelet to help my brother and myself. I owe Michael."

"Why? What happened between you two?"

His tortured expression tore my heart out for him. Yet I found I couldn't extend the same sympathy to his brother.

"I talked Michael into joining me at this new bar. He wanted to stay home, but I pressured him to come along. Later, after the place closed, we ran into trouble."

"The supernatural kind of trouble?"

"Yeah. We ran into a demon in the alley. I was drunk and picked a fight with him."

I'd heard similar stories throughout my career. Yet this time the victim was my husband. "And you came up on the losing end of the fight. But what about Michael? Demons don't have the means to change humans into anything other than another demon."

"It seems my not-so-friendly demon had a ghoulish friend. He took care of Michael at the same time the demon was taking care of me." Blake ran a hand through his hair. "Afterward, we faked my death, then his, and separated, disappearing from our old lives. We lost track of each other and I didn't hear from him until recently." He looked at me with a tortured glint in his eyes. "It's my fault Michael was there in the first place. We were both changed by my mistake, and I'm going to reverse the transformation."

Finally! He'd given me a reason to hope. "How? What do you plan to do?"

I sensed the tension in him before he released my hand to tunnel his fingers through his hair. "If I possess the Bracelet, I can make sure Michael and I return to our normal selves."

I took in Blake's idea and my heart began to pound faster. Blake would return to being a normal, beer-drinking, football-loving guy. I wouldn't be married to a demon any longer, which meant I wouldn't have to keep his secret from my friends and colleagues. Still, I needed more information before I could pop the cork on any champagne bottles. "Okay, let's say you get the Bracelet and you change Michael and you back into mortals. What then? What happens to the Bracelet?"

Blake pointed at me. "When I'm through with it, you take it to the Society where it belongs. Hopefully, they'll do a better job of protecting it the next time."

I blanched knowing the Society's screw-up and subsequent loss of the Bracelet had to have supplied a shitload of jokes for the folks in the Otherworld. We must've looked like big-time idiots. "Trust me. No way will it happen again."

"Actually, you're lucky mortal thieves stumbled on to it before an Otherworlder."

I nodded, agreeing, but didn't want to stay on the subject of the Society's mishandling of such an invaluable piece of weaponry. "I think you nailed it on the head. The security and sensors in place were made to catch Otherworlders, not humans. The humans didn't set off any alarms when they lucked onto the room."

"Yeah, yeah. Excuses." He hugged me to him, giving me exactly what I needed at the moment.

An awful thought clouded my happiness and I pushed away. "Hey, wait a sec. If you use the Bracelet to change Michael and you to mortals, won't Demogorgon take off your head? I'd hate to think you'd get your wish, only to die soon afterward."

"I realize it's a huge risk, but I'm hoping the Bracelet will have enough power in it to both help us and vanquish the big guy. Maybe it'll have enough time in between to charge up again."

"We need to find the Bracelet first, you know."

"We?" He tugged my body to him again, this time hanging on with more determination.

"Yeah. We." I cocked my head to give him a look. "What? Did you think once I knew about you, I'd throw you to the wolves, er, rather, the big, bad demon lord? Not a chance, bucko."

"Have you got an idea about how we can do this?"

"I kind of thought you already had a plan."

He shook his head. "Nothing concrete."

"O-kay. Not to worry. We'll come up with one. First things first, though. We need to find that damn piece of jewelry. Until then, I'll keep you safe."

His lips brushed my forehead. "Hmm. I think I like having a Protector of my own."

"And I think living with a demon might not be a bad thing." Wiggling my eyebrows at him, I broke free and gave him a hard look. "But stay in human form, okay? Your other side is just plain butt-ugly."

"You got it, sweet cheeks."

I basked in the Blake-grin I loved. "Sweet cheeks?"

He shrugged. "I thought I'd give it a try. Do you like?"

I scrunched up my nose for emphasis. "Uh, no. Not at all." Taking his hand in mine, I led him to the bedroom.

Sugar and Spice
and Everything Not So Nice

I closed my eyes, enjoying the way Blake slid his hands down my body. We'd already made love twice and here he was knocking on my door (ahem!) for more. Perhaps sexual stamina was a side effect of being a demon. If it was, being married to one definitely had its perks.

The odd thought echoed in my brain and I opened my eyes both literally and figuratively. Wow, had I changed or what? Before meeting and falling for Blake, I'd have checked myself into a psychiatric facility for thinking such an outrageous idea. Now, however, I was content to let my demon hubby—in his human body, of course—lick every inch of me.

Blake pulled my legs apart and discovered yet another area needing his attention. Grasping the rumpled sheets, I moaned with pleasure and wiped every thought from my mind and focused on him.

Enjoy me, Blake. Enjoy me hard.

As if hearing my unspoken command, Blake intensified his attention, slipping my legs over his shoulders for a better position. He nipped and sucked and I squirmed with delight.

His hands explored my stomach and I grabbed them to pull them to my breasts. He complied with my urgency, squeezing them and rubbing his thumbs over my tender nipples. Another wave broke over me and I cried out, a happy and sated woman.

Heaven was here in my own bed.

"Babe, I need you."

I pretended to not understand. "You do?" Arching my hips

up, I demanded he return to his work.

He lapped at me one more time before trying again. "You know what I mean, Jenn. I need you like I've needed you all night."

I started to respond, to tease him a little longer, but he wasn't into my game. Instead, he dragged me to him.

"Hey!"

"Hey nothing." Wrapping my legs around him, he thrust into me, primed and ready to go.

"Blake."

"Yeah?" He panted, synchronizing his pants to his rapid hip movement.

"Slow down." I lifted up, keeping him with me, and rested on my elbows. "What's the hurry?"

In an instant, he slowed, changing his quick, hard jabs into slow, agonizingly wonderful lunges. He paused, leaned over to take my tit in his mouth, and I moaned my approval. Stretching my neck, I lifted my breast and joined my tongue with his. Together we sucked on my raised bud.

He groaned, then began to pound into me with renewed power. "I love you, Jenn."

My climax exploded with his, but it was several moments before I could answer. "I love you, too, Blake."

He collapsed on top of me, mixing our sweat together. I held him, thankful to have the man I loved with me. *Who cares if he's a demon? Not me.* "Blake?"

"Hmm?" He nuzzled my neck, feathering the hollow at the base of my neck with light kisses.

I struggled to remember the question I wanted to ask him. "Oh, uh, yeah. When was the first time you became a demon? I mean, the first time the demon in you took someone? Oh, crap, you know what I mean. How many people has this demon possessed before he found you?"

He lifted his head to frown at me. "Do you really want to know?"

"Yeah, I do." I played with the damp curls at the tips of his hair.

"Not long. A couple of decades ago."

"A couple of decades, meaning two? How many decades

exactly?"

"All right. Four decades. The first possession was in 1940, then the demon changed bodies again when he took me in 1974."

Aw, shit. Bad news. If Blake's demon was an older demon, he'd have a chance against Demogorgon. Not much of one, but at least a better chance. "Hmm. You're actually thirty-four years older than you say you are." I rolled my lips under and acted coy.

"Well, sort of."

"Which means you're actually sixty-eight, not the thirty-four you claim you are, right?"

He shot me a "what are you up to?" look. "I'd have assumed, Ms. Protector, you'd know the body doesn't age as quickly after going demon." He plastered on a shit-eating grin and patted the top of his hand under his chin. "Hence, my youthful appearance. It's one of the few perks of demonic possession."

"Oh, right, sure. For a demon you're young." I tried to appear innocent, keeping my punch line to myself. "Yet talking in human terms, you're getting up there in years. In fact, some would call you a senior—"

He clamped his hand over my mouth, stopping my next words, but not my giggles. "Don't you dare say it. I am not a— one of those."

Without speech to aid me, I rolled my eyes, widened them in exasperation, and tried to speak anyway. "Mmmm. Err. Mmm-huh!"

"I'll take my hand off your mouth if you promise not to call me what you started to call me." He waited for my agreement which I gave by shooting him a thumbs up sign.

"Good." Slowly, he lifted his hand from my mouth.

"All I wanted to say was that you're a good-looking—"

"Jenn, I'm warning you." Yet the tips of his mouth lifting in humor took the sting out of his words.

"—virile, vital young man." *Vanity, thy name is Blake.* "Better?"

"Better."

"I'm glad I could make you happy. You old fart, you."

"Why you little—"

A crashing sound startled us from our playful conversation. Blake leapt up and headed out the bedroom door, yanking on his jeans. I followed, hot on his heels. He ignored the darkness, no doubt using his demonic night-sight ability. I turned on each light I passed, even though one second to flip a switch slowed me down. He'd already slammed opened the door to his study before I caught up with him.

"Blake! Wait up!" He roared and fear gripped me. Although my mind shouted at me, calling on my Protector training to proceed with caution, I threw that caution away and rushed on. With the dim moonlight shining through the slants of the blinds, I made out two figures, one holding the other against the wall, feet kicking above the floor. Switching on a nearby lamp, I gawked at the scene even though relief flooded through me.

A partially transformed Blake held a scaly gray gargoyle in place, his hand clamped around the creature's pudgy, wrinkled neck. The gargoyle clutched Blake's hand and tried spitting at him, spittle running down his snarling face in his wild attempt. I gasped at first, thinking of the acid in a gargoyle's saliva—*don't let him scar my handsome man's face!*—then relaxed once I'd remembered a gargoyle's spit was harmless against a demon's tough skin. Fortunately for Blake, he'd managed to change his arm into demon form. The rest of him remained human.

"Whatcha' got there, Blake, honey?" I swaggered over, taking care not to get too close. My skin would sizzle and shrivel in a flash if the gargoyle managed to hit me with his spit.

"We have an intruder. I found him rifling through the drawers in my desk."

I sidestepped over to the desk to find the drawers pulled out and their contents strewn across the floor. "Gargoyles are breaking and entering now? What the hell for? Rotten cheese?"

Blake pivoted to me with an exasperated expression on his face. "I'll give you three guesses what he wanted. Oh, and a special prize if you can tell me who sent him. Wanna play?"

"Ooh, goody, a game." *Pulease. I should turn in my gold Protector badge (yes, we actually have gold badges) if I can't figure this one out.* "The Bracelet. Final answer."

"Jennifer Randall-Barrington, you're a winner!" He shook

the creature when he tried to lash out at Blake's face with his long claws. "Knock it off, buddy, or I'll break every nasty bone in your body and crumble them to dust."

Stifled from his full voice by Blake's fist on his throat, the gargoyle screeched as loudly as he could. Even from a distance, I could smell the stench of spoiled garbage on his breath. Why couldn't this particular creature have stayed hidden away in one of the hundreds of underground tunnels beneath the city? Instead, he'd come to my house to hunt for the Bracelet. *Lucky me.*

"What's your name, asshole?" Blake changed positions, dropping the gargoyle to his feet. Once his feet touched the floor, however, the little beast attempted to run. Blake bent the long, skinny arm behind his back and held him in place. "I asked you your name." He twisted his arm again, sending the gargoyle into a squealing panic.

"Oh, get over yourself. We know you don't feel pain. Stop acting as if you're about to die." I took a wary step closer. "If you spit at me, I'll have my man rip out your guts. Maybe then you'll experience actual pain."

"Now answer me or I'll take the lady's suggestion and see what's inside your disgusting body."

"Name my Witspie."

Couldn't a gargoyle speak normally for once? "Witspie, who sent you?" Although I had a pretty good idea.

Witspie snarled at me and clammed up. Blake quickly lost his temper and whacked the little guy on the side of the head.

"Blake, what say we offer our guest a piece of cheese?"

"I'd rather torture him."

Witspie screeched again, making me cringe against the fingernails-on-the-blackboard sound. "Why? He doesn't feel the pain, anyway."

"I know, but I enjoy it."

"I can see that." I mentally jotted down another asset on the pro and con list running in my mind. *Perk number two for having a demon hubby. Let him do all the head-bashing.* "But let's try a different method." I gave my husband a pat on the arm and motioned for him to let the creature go. He let go, grudgingly, and I moved between the door and the gargoyle. "Now, Witspie, tell us who sent you." I used my best sing-song voice to entice him. "I'll give you a nice, big piece of cheese if you do. Granted, it's not rotten cheese, but it's pretty smelly nonetheless."

"Hey hold up, Jenn. You're not promising him my Limburger cheese, are you? You know I love the stuff."

I rolled my eyes at my sweet hubby, shooting him an "oh, come on" look, and crooked my head in question. He grumbled, but nodded his agreement.

"Can't tell I you. Will master get very my angry."

"I understand. And I wouldn't want to get him angry, either. Hmm, what to do, what to do." I put on a thoughtful, empathetic expression before raising one finger in the air in triumph. "By George, I think I've got it." An image of Myra's George the Great zipped into the forefront of my mind. *Urgh. Do not go there, my friend.*

Both Blake and Witspie locked onto me in anticipation. "You tell us who sent you to steal the Bracelet—"

"Which we don't have, by the way."

I wasn't too happy with Blake's admission, but I assumed he did so to try and protect me from any future break-ins. "Anyway, you tell us what we want to know, and you'll get your cheese and you can be on your way. No harm, no foul. Tell Demogorgon you couldn't find it."

"No. Say Demogorgon, you find and you kill."

I started to grin, having gotten Witspie to admit Demogorgon had sent him, until it hit me. Witspie didn't mean for *me* to find and kill anyone. In true gargoyle style, he'd jumbled the words. Demogorgon had sent the gargoyle to find and kill *me.*

Witspie panicked—he must've seen the realization on my face. With a fierce yell, he tossed all caution to the wind and puckered up, ready to spit on me. I dodged the wad of acid he sent flying my way.

Blake shouted, all anger and frustration. "Damn you! You're dead meat, you piece of shit!"

Witspie screeched and yanked out of Blake's grasp. He didn't, however, get very far before my husband managed to corner him behind his favorite battered recliner.

"The Bracelet master your brother has said. Killed thieves

and your took brother it. You and Protector brother to defeat him are working." Witspie tried feinting to the left to throw Blake off, but Blake was too smart. Witspie howled, scratching out with his long claws.

"Demogorgon thinks Michael killed the human thieves and took the Bracelet." I laughed even though I'd come to the same conclusion. "Your master is wrong."

"Lie you! Says master his brother you work with." Witspie dodged, darting under Blake's attempt to capture him. With a snarl, he slashed out at me.

His claws grazed my thigh and I yelped in pain and anger. Rolling away from him, I scrambled behind a small desk just in time to miss getting hit by a missile of spit.

With a furious roar, Blake grabbed him and lifted him over his head. The gargoyle screamed, uselessly clawing into the air. Blake, his face radiating a fury I'd never seen in him, readjusted his hold on the gargoyle. In one swift motion, he brought the creature's body down, placing it expertly over his knee, and bent the gargoyle's spine.

The *crack* of the gargoyle's back reverberated through the room. Blake pushed on his legs and chest, bending his spine even more. Satisfied the gargoyle was dead, Blake dropped the lifeless form to the floor.

Within seconds, the gargoyle's body disintegrated, leaving nothing but a pile of dust on my clean carpet. Blake's anger diminished quickly.

"Do you think he's right? Do you think Michael killed those humans?"

I could see the torment in Blake's eyes at the thought of his brother's involvement in the murders. Part of me wanted to assure him it was only a gargoyle's lie. The other part of me, the part that respected my husband, made me tell the truth. "Yeah, I do. I think Michael was involved. Whether he actually killed them or not, I don't know." *Yes, I do. The old man told me he saw him do it.*

"I hope not." Blake glanced at the dust pile on the floor and wiped a hand over his face. "Killing these creatures is one thing. But killing humans..."

"Are you saying you've never killed a human?" I hadn't given the idea any thought, yet being a demon kind of necessitated killing humans. Could my husband be different?

"I've harmed people, but I've managed to keep from killing one. So far." He saw the surprise I knew showed on my face and added, "I'm serious."

Wow. If I'm married to a demon, at least I'm married to a good one. "I believe you."

The relief relaxed his features and he smiled at me. His smile, however, didn't last long. "Do you think Michael has the Bracelet?"

I thought about it for a moment. "I used to think maybe he did, but not any more. If he had it, wouldn't he have used it already? If he didn't want to use it, wouldn't he have turned it over to Demogorgon?"

"Good points."

"Also, if Michael has the Bracelet, why would Demogorgon think we have it here?"

"Maybe because Michael was over here the other day and he thinks we're working with Michael? Oh, hell, I don't know." Blake stepped over the pile of gargoyle dust and headed toward the door. "I'm wiped out. Let's get some sleep and talk about what we do next in the morning."

"Uh, Blake?"

He stopped to question me with raised eyebrows.

I pointed at the pile of dust. "What do you think I am? Your maid? You kill 'im; you clean up the mess."

"Tell me you're joshing me."

I glanced at Partner who'd resumed his cowboy persona. Although I'd never admit it, the cowboy image was my favorite one. "Joshing?" I jerked up my head just in time to catch a blurred image with my peripheral vision. "Hey! Watch what you're doing, man!" An older gentleman driving an ancient Chrysler whipped his car in front of me and I laid on the horn. Swerving quickly into the other lane of the highway to avoid ramming into his taillight, I cursed again to the accompaniment of my heart tripping the light fantastic. "Damn, isn't there an age limit on how long people should drive?"

"Don't try and change the subject."

"Concentrating on my driving is not changing the subject. It's staying alive."

The Old Man in the Car darted in front of me again and I tossed out more expletives—my mother probably flipped over in her grave at least five times with this round of cuss words. For an old dude, he sure drove fast. The appearance of a blue pickup truck driven by a young woman with red streaks in her hair caught my eye in my rearview mirror. What was with drivers today? Why did these two want to hang around me? Didn't they realize they could use the other lanes?

"Stop jerking the car around. I almost slid off the seat and onto the floor."

"Pretend you're breaking a bronc, cowboy."

After a couple of grumbles, Partner took up his earlier harangue. "You and your demon husband—whew-ee, a demon!—have invited his ghoul brother over for a pleasant evening at home in the hopes of getting him to admit he has the Bracelet. Do you really think he's going to fall for the old family dinner ruse?"

"There's a bit more to our plan and you know it."

"Like what?"

"We're going to tell him I've changed."

"Changed how? Into a good cook?"

"Hey, watch the personal jabs, dude." *Why is Bitchie-in-a-Pick-'Em-Up Truck riding my bumper?* "And before you ask, no, you're not invited."

"Yet another mistake on your part."

"Like you can eat food."

"A blessing in disguise, little missy. Come on, let me ride on in to the party."

"Ha, ha. I'm signing you up for open mike night at the comedy club." I glowered at him before returning my attention to the road. "Little missy?" I swung my car into the left lane and Old Geezer mimicked my move. Without hesitation, Ms. Streak followed us. An alarm sounded in my head and my gut clenched with anxiety. "Uh-uh. I don't think so."

"I'm your partner, remember? I can't help you if you keep me turned off and locked away in your car. It's bad enough I had to stay here while you diddled with another stupid open house today. And for what? No sale."

I braked, forcing Streak to slow down. Geezer kept going several yards more before he noticed I wasn't right behind him. I tried for an exit off the highway and missed. I could see Geezer cussing, working hard to position his car in front of me again. *This is not good.* Once again, Geezer and Streak maneuvered me into the trap like a bug stuck between two roach motels.

Still, this bug wasn't about to check in and never check out.

"Partner, can we discuss your opinions, complaints, or whatever some other time? Right now, I think I need to focus on the shit about to hit the fan."

His tone changed from whining to all business. "What's going on? Talk to me."

I checked my speedometer and verified what I'd already sensed. With Geezer in front of me, he'd managed to slow me down. Streak did her part for the tag team and kept me pinned between them. "Get ready. We're going to play Demon Demolition Derby."

"Play what?"

I opened my mouth to give Partner more details when, suddenly, Geezer slammed on his brakes, lighting up his car's one working taillight. "Shit!" Knowing my only options consisted of (a) slamming on the brakes and staying trapped between two probable demons, (b) running into the rear of Geezer's car in hopes of hurting him without hurting me or (c) jerking the car into the right lane and hoping no one would broadside me, I made my choice.

I chose Option C.

I threw my vehicle to the right and braced for the possible collision. This time, however, luck was on my side. No screeching brake sounds. No loud crashes making steel meet steel. Well, at least, almost no sounds. A high-pitched screech signaled the left side of my car scraping Geezer's tank, leaving what I knew would be an ugly scar on my precious Jag. "Dammit!" I didn't, however, take time to complain about my poor Jag's unscheduled repair job.

"What did you hit?" Partner's lights flashed off and on, attracting my attention.

"Uh, not much. One of the demons tried to smash me between them. Do you think I can get their insurance information?" I chuckled mirthlessly, noting how Streak followed me, positioning her pickup inches from my bumper. Geezer, however, decided staying on my left side was better than taking the lead. Saying a silent apology to my deceased mother and her frequent grave-flopping, I shot Geezer the bird. "I'm thinking Demogorgon's two thugs don't want me to get home safely."

I stomped on the gas, jumping ahead of my pursuers and catching them off guard. Nonetheless, they didn't waste any time in catching up with me. Every time I tried to get away from them, Geezer proved himself the ultimate speed demon—pun intended—racing past me to slide ahead of my car. Time and again, I was trapped between them.

I yelled at the old man ahead of me. "Oh, for Pete's sake! If you want to have a threesome, just say so!" Geezer, however, didn't answer. "Hold on, Partner. I'm about to pull another fast lane change."

At the moment I swerved to the left, Streak's car bumped me from behind. I checked her out in my rearview mirror expecting to see her vicious, shit-eating grin and, instead, saw her cussing her head off and glaring into her own rearview mirror. Changing to my side mirror, I tried to see what was happening behind her.

A blue Chevy was fixed to her ass as close as she was to mine. Gritting my teeth, I made my sharp jerk to the left and checked my other mirror to get a glimpse of my unknown benefactor. But I couldn't see much. Whoever this person was, she didn't want to be identified. She sat low in the seat, crouched behind the wheel. A big floppy hat, the type gardeners wear, along with oversized black sunglasses hid her face from view. I waved a quick *thank you* and took advantage of the unexpected help.

Putting my foot to the pedal again, I zoomed past Geezer, who couldn't find his way around the truck in front of him, and showed him my middle finger again. He snarled, his eyes flashing red. His many wrinkles morphed into scaly, puke-colored skin.

"Goodbye, Gramps and good riddance." Using the skills I'd honed at the Society's driving course as well as the many hours

I'd spent drag-racing in my wayward teen years, I left the two demons behind me. Glancing in the mirror, I saw my rescuer ram Streak's car into the rear of Geezer's. The two demons' vehicles careened to the right, hit the gravel and flew into the air, landing in the deep ditch at the side of the road.

"Woo-hoo! Way to go, whoever you are!" Damned impressive driving, if you ask me. I just hoped I'd be able to thank the driver one day.

"What? Tell me what you're talking about?"

Taking the first exit, I slowed down, stopped at a crossroads and glanced to my passenger seat. *Huh?* "Where are you?"

"Down here. I told you you'd throw me off the seat."

Leaning over, I peered under the seat to find Partner stuck between an empty coffee mug and an assortment of crumpled snack packages. "Oh, quit bitching. I'm the one having to do the fancy driving. All you had to do was hang on."

The expression on the cowboy's face made me bite my lip to keep from laughing. He, obviously, didn't find this situation as amusing as I did.

"'Hang on', she says." He let loose with a stream of beeps and whistles loud enough to make me cover my ears. "Really? Is that what you suggest I do? Hang on?"

"Huh? Uh, yeah."

"Then tell me how I'm supposed to hang on with no arms."

I sputtered, caught with the truth of his statement. "Oh, uh, well..." My nonexistent answer trailed off.

"Oh, uh, well what?"

"This." When in doubt, do something. Any action is preferable to no action. Following those two rules of thumb, I sat up and threw the car into gear. "I guess you're stuck on the floor until we arrive home. Sorry, Partner, I've no time to chat. Gotta rush home and get demonized."

Aw, Hell. Cow's Brains Again?
Whatever Happened to Meatloaf?

At some point, I knew I'd have to give in and bring Partner into the house and out into the open. Besides, after telling him about Blake's and my plan to tell Michael I was a newly indoctrinated demon, thus convincing him to spill his guts—*not literally, please!*—I knew I couldn't leave Partner in the garage any longer. I made him swear to keep his sound turned off, then agreed to his recommendation to record the evening. Who knows? Maybe one day I'd teach a Society class on How To Trick a Ghoul and Partner's record of the evening would come in handy.

Yeah, I know. I'm justifying.

At least that's how I rationalized it as I sat down to eat with Blake to my right and a very suspicious Michael staring at me from across the dining table. I smiled for what seemed like forever before deciding to give my face muscles a break. Instead, I sipped my wine. One sip. Then two sips. On to three sips and I suddenly realized my sips had grown into long swigs.

"I'm glad you decided to join us tonight, Michael." Blake smiled at his younger brother and offered him the serving bowl of green beans. After all, even ghouls should eat their vegetables.

"Yeah, well, I promised I'd make up for the last time when I left unexpectedly." Michael took the bowl and dished a pile of green beans onto his plate. "You make sure you keep your promise."

At the mention of a promise I gulped, sending the smooth Cabernet down the wrong pipe. Coughing, I waved away Blake's

Beverly Rae

hand and eventually managed to speak. "Promise? What"—cough—"kind of promise?"

Blake waved away my question like I'd waved away his help. "Nothing much. I said we'd keep certain topics off the table."

Having no clue what he meant, I gave my husband a questioning look which he answered with a pointed one of his own. I interpreted his look as asking me to trust him so I closed my opened mouth, my brain storing the question for later. Unfortunately, sometimes my mouth works all on its own.

"So, Michael, what have you been up to lately? Still working for Demogorgon?"

Michael froze with his spaghetti-wrapped fork halfway to his mouth.

Blake let the piece of bread in his hand drop to his plate. "Shit, Jenn. What about my promise?"

I glanced between the two men and faked an innocence I knew neither one of them would buy. "Oops. Did I mention one of the off-topic topics?"

Michael cocked an eyebrow at me and lowered his fork to his plate. "I don't know what, or who, you're talking about."

"Oh, come on, Michael. We're all family here. You know, like the Addams Family or the Munsters. You can tell us. What's the old fart up to? Ow!" Blake's kick landed squarely on my ankle. "Hey, knock it off or you'll end up with noodles all over *your* noodle."

"I'll stop when you stop." Blake gave me another, albeit lighter kick on the shin.

"Maybe I should leave." Michael started to rise from the table, not giving me time to think. "Thanks for a less-than-yummy meal."

"Huh? You're leaving because I'm a lousy cook?" I reached over to lift the bowl of meatballs sitting in front of him. "Did you know I made the meatballs out of cow's brains? Do you know how hard it is to *find* cow's brains? They don't carry them at the local grocery, you know."

Cow's brains are a delicacy for Otherworlders. Granted, they prefer a human's gray matter over a cow's, but the bovine kind is a close second. I hoped he hadn't noticed the lack of meatballs on top of my spaghetti. My willingness to do anything

230

for the Society and the safety of the world didn't include eating gunk like brains.

"Come on, fratello, have some of my meat-a-balls-a. Like I said, we're family. Consider us the supernatural version of the Mob." I adopted a big grin at my politically incorrect imitation. *Italians everywhere, please forgive me.*

Blake's low growl told me not to push it.

"Cow's brains, huh? You definitely have one strange sense of humor, Jenn." Michael obviously shared his brother's opinion of my less-than-comical wit and stood to leave.

I hopped up, determined to save the night and our plan. "No. Stay. Please. I'll keep quiet, I swear." I crossed my heart and held up three fingers in the Girl Scout salute.

"Michael, stay."

Blake's heartfelt plea must have won the argument since Michael nodded and returned to his seat. He picked up his fork and resumed eating, although his eyes had grown darker, meaner. I gave him a little bow of apology and sat down, too.

"I think it's time to give my brother the good news. Don't you, Jenn? You've already given him enough hints."

I acted uncertain, but that didn't stop Blake from starting Phase One of our plan. "Oh, but wouldn't our news fall into one of those taboo areas?" I forced a mix of concerned and happy expressions on my face. "Still, it would be nice to get the good news out into the open."

Michael remained leery, stopping to check Blake's reaction. "What good news do you have?" His gaze fell to my stomach, even though the table blocked his view. "Are you...?"

I followed his gaze, searching my new silk top for spaghetti sauce stains. After all, it wouldn't be the first time I'd ruined a new outfit with my sloppy eating. But my top looked shiny and new. "Am I what?" Blake and I exchanged curious glances.

"You know." Michael's mood lifted for the first time since sitting down at our table.

I frowned at him and slashed my hand in the air space above the top of my head. "Nope. Sorry. Your question flew right over me. Am I what?"

"Uh-huh. Okay, I'll play along. Are you two pregnant? Am I going to be an uncle?"

I shivered at the thought of a murdering ghoul for my child's uncle. Of course, having a father who's a demon wasn't the best start in life, either. I could already hear the conversation at our first parent-teacher conference. *"Mr. Barrington, we can't have your son sucking the brains out of the other children's heads. Little Lambs and Turtles Preschool simply won't allow unruly behavior of any kind."*

Blake's amused chuckle didn't help matters much. "Pregnant? Wow. Think of it, Jenn. Us as parents."

Me? A mom? Oh, wow. I wonder if there's a Young Protectors Program? "Trust me. I'm thinking, all right." I had to remember who my husband was on the inside. I had to hold on to the idea of his good spirit prevailing over his evil urges, despite having demon DNA inside him. Still, I didn't want the misconception continuing for a minute longer. "Okay, stop right now. Talking about my being pregnant—which I'm not—isn't my idea of pleasant table conversation. No, Michael, I'm not pregnant."

From the way he acted, I think Blake was as disappointed to hear I wasn't pregnant as Michael was. What was with these two? Did going ghoul and demon stir their fatherly instincts into high gear? Could twisting a man's head off and ripping his heart out go hand in hand with feelings of parental nurturing? Before this conversation, I would've doubted it.

"Then what's the news?"

Blake rose to stand behind me. He placed his hands on my shoulders and squeezed them, sending me a show of support. "Well, as you know, I'm a demon."

Michael's features didn't change a bit at Blake's announcement. "Go on."

"And I'm a Protector."

He remained silent and stone-faced. Did anything throw this guy for a loop? Unless, of course, he already knew about me.

Blake squeezed my shoulders again to urge me to continue. I guessed it was time to jump in with both feet. I said a quick silent prayer and hoped I didn't land in quicksand.

"Did you hear what I said, Michael? Blake's a demon, which you already knew, and I'm a Protector." *Come on. Earth to Michael. Say something.*

Blake stepped to my side and took my hand. "More

accurately, she *was* a Protector. Although she hasn't officially resigned yet, she will soon. She'll have to, of course."

Michael's cold assessment of me made warm sweat slide down my spine. I'd confessed to being his worst enemy and he didn't have a reaction? Too weird.

Blake gripped my hand tighter, then prompted his brother. "Say something."

"Let me see if I have this straight. You're a demon and she's a Protector which I'm assuming is some kind of special agent or hero type." Michael raised his glass in a mocking toast. "Quite the marriage you two have, what with making up stories together. But I always thought married people saved the pretend characters for the bedroom." He slumped in his chair, yet despite his nonchalant attitude, his body language conveyed one big challenge. "Tell me. Do you dress up in a monster suit while Jenn gets dolled up in a Wonder Woman outfit? Kinky, guys."

"Cut it out." Blake dropped my hand to move to his spot at the table again. But he didn't sit. Instead, he gripped the back of his chair and leaned toward his brother. "Jenn knows everything. Including the part about you being a ghoul." He gritted his teeth, straining to keep control of his emotions. "I know it's my fault. You're right to blame me. God knows I do."

Michael's laugh startled me. What did this guy find funny? At this point, I couldn't even force a smile.

"And there's more."

His mirth evaporated in an instant and the cold, suspicious Michael came back. "Okay, bro, I'll bite. What more is there?"

Blake's hard expression told me to take the lead and I did. "I *was* a Protector. But now I'm a demon."

Michael didn't laugh this time. Instead, he seemed to consider my words, weighing them with slow deliberation. "You're a demon."

I laughed and Blake's smile gave his brother confirmation of my statement. "Yup. I found out about Blake and you. Once I did, I had to make a choice between my work and my husband." I took a breath and said out loud the commitment I'd, until then, kept unspoken. "I chose Blake."

"Ah, how sweet." Michael feigned a saccharin smile for us.

Okay, now he'd pissed me off big time. A cold anger built

inside me. Fortunately for him, I resisted my urge to slap him silly. "Yeah, it is." I turned to Blake, who stood looking at me with all the love in the universe showing on his face, and I knew right then and there I would give up the Society for him. Hell, I might even become a demon—a good one, that is—for him. Maybe. Of course, my first choice would have him becoming mortal again.

"We want you to know you don't have to hide what you are from her any longer. We're all in the same company. We really are the same family."

Blake continued working the plan and I tried to squelch my desire to gut the ghoul smirking at me. Brother-in-law or not, he was one obnoxious jerk. "Agreed. Let's can the pretence, okay?"

Michael lifted his wine glass to his lips and downed every drop. "You two sure know how to throw a dinner party. I have to say, the entertainment is much better than the actual food."

"That does it." I got up and dashed around the table toward my rude dinner guest. "Granted, I've never claimed to be a good cook—"

"I'll say." Michael covered his mouth and puffed out his cheeks in a perfect imitation of someone gagging on a nasty bit of food.

"—but you could at least appreciate the effort involved. I mean, hell, I'm talking making meatballs out of cow's brains. Yuck and double yuck."

"I thought you liked cow's brains." Michael's narrowed eyes saved him from getting a fat lip.

"I-I do. But they're a lot of work."

"I take it you want a medal for your attempt?"

Could this guy get any more annoying? "I'm warning you, *bro*, if you slam my cooking one more time, I'm going to push your face into your spaghetti until you breathe sauce through your ears." I'd cooked for a damn ghoul and he wasn't about to get away with ridiculing me.

"Easy, Jenn." I reached for Michael, but Blake dashed between us, thwarting my move. "He's getting to you. Besides, your cooking isn't what we need to discuss. Remember?"

I let the steam inside me bubble from a simmer to a boil. "Yeah." I twisted around Blake to point at Michael. "But I'm not going to let some two-bit ghoul talk trash about my cooking in my own home."

"Babe, calm down. Can't you see he's trying to change the subject?"

Was Blake right? A rush of realization swept through my body. Michael had baited me in order to change the subject and I'd taken his lure like the last fish in a dried-up mudhole.

The flash of red in Michael's eyes said it all. "I say it as I taste it."

Blake kept his hold on me and pushed me backward. I flailed but not before I caught a glimpse of Partner, silently flashing his lights wildly in an attempt to gain my attention. *Dammit, not now, Partner. I knew I should've put him in a drawer instead of placing him behind the silk plant on the buffet table. I have enough on my plate without having to deal with an attention-seeking, glorified PDA.*

Letting go of me, Blake whirled on his brother. "Let's stay on track with the real conversation. We know who you're working for. All we want is a piece of the action. I work for the same high demon lord, you know, and I'm trying to find the same piece of jewelry you are. Why not work together?"

"I haven't got a clue what you're raving about." Staying calm—at least outwardly—Michael poured himself another glass of wine. "I think you two must've shared a few bottles before I showed up. Forget this crazy talk about ghouls and demons. Why would I care about some bracelet?" He held up his jewelry-free hands. "I've never liked jewelry."

I growled much like a real demon would do and made a lunge for him. "Let me at him, Blake. We don't need him for the Bracelet."

Blake, however, wasn't ready to have me take his brother out of this world. "Why are you denying you're a ghoul, man? It's okay to admit it in front of her. She's one of us now."

For a moment, I could see Michael considering Blake's words. Instead, his face grew even more guarded. "She'll never be one of us."

Was this his way of admitting the truth? I stopped fighting against Blake and waited. I should've known it was useless, though.

"I mean, she'll never be one of our class. You married

down, bro."

The top of the volcano inside me blew off. *First, he insults my cooking and now he insults me? Someone tell me this is not happening.* "Why you lousy, brain-sucking asshole."

"See how crude she is?" Michael took another sip of wine. "Need I say more?"

I was so flabbergasted I couldn't speak. Worse, Blake didn't say anything, either. *Why doesn't he stick up for me?* I glared at him, challenging him to say something in my defense.

Yet, instead of defending me, Blake kept trying to get his brother to admit the truth. "We can help you find the Bracelet. If you've already found the Bracelet of Invincibility, then great. We'll help you put it to good use. You're going to need our help if you plan on crossing Demogorgon."

"Admit it, Michael. You've got the Bracelet. In fact, I think you found it when you broke into the thieves' house." I had no proof, but who knew what a little bluffing might uncover?

Michael's laugh was anything but lighthearted. "You're something else. First you accuse me of being some kind of a monster. Then you go a step further by accusing me of breaking and entering into someone's house. What is with you?" He glared at me. "I read about those men in the paper. Are you accusing me of murder, too? When do the accusations end?" He pointed his index finger at his head and circled it around. "I think your little woman's gone off the deep end, bro."

Little woman? Where the hell does he get off calling me a little woman? Talk about insulting! I fisted my hands and forced myself to keep them at my side.

"We want to work with you. Help me get the Otherworlders off Jenn's back, and we'll use the Bracelet together. What could be better? Us back together along with my wife, the ex-Protector-turned-demon?"

Although he'd spoken in a soft tone, Blake's calm voice didn't soothe my rattled nerves, much less cut my anger. Not one bit. In fact, I was miffed he hadn't stood up for me, claiming me to be his equal in every way. Especially after the "little woman" crack. I opened my mouth to blast both my nineteen-fifties-thinking brother-in-law and my non-protective hubby. But Michael's demeanor shifted, throwing me off balance.

"Work together?" He paused to cast us a speculative look.

"All of us. Hmm."

Blake and I jumped on the opening he'd given us. "Yeah. Together." Was he about to admit he was a ghoul and working for Demogorgon?

Yet Blake moved in to seal the deal before I could. "Do we have an agreement or not?'

A knock at our front door jolted us and closed Michael's mouth.

"Damn, not now." Someone's timing for a visit was way, way off. I hurried to the door, planning on letting out some of my frustration on whoever was on the other side. "I'll get rid of them."

"Hel-lo? Hey, Jenn, is anyone home?"

I've Got Bracelets That Jingle, Jangle, Jingle

I skidded to a stop after I rounded the corner into the foyer and nearly ran into the massive man who had his arms wrapped around my best friend, Myra. Sappy grins highlighted both their faces. With a shout of glee, the big guy picked her up and hugged her to him.

"George! Stop it!" Myra squirmed in his arms but anyone could see she liked being tossed around like a gaudily dressed rag doll.

"Oh, sure-sure." George set her down gently and cupped her hand inside his gargantuan one. "George loves picking up My-my."

"My-my?" A blush washed over Myra. For the first time in the years I'd known her, my friend was in love. But with who? Or should I ask, with what?

"Oh, bite me, Jenn."

George sniffed the air and sighed. "Bite her? Why would Jenn want to bite My-my?"

I opened my mouth to answer, but he took off, eating up the ground with his long strides and dragging Myra along behind him. "Yummy. George smells food. Sure-sure."

George, with Myra huffing behind him from the exertion, made his way into the dining room before I could catch up with them. "George knew he smelled food." Letting Myra go like a bad case of the measles, the big guy grabbed a chair and plopped down at the table. He grabbed the bowl of spaghetti and set it down in front of him, without a care for how the rest of us gaped at him. Then he snatched up the serving bowl of warm spaghetti sauce—I don't make homemade sauce because store brands taste good to us (yes, believe it)—and poured the entire contents on top of the noodles. Adding a mountain of parmesan cheese to the mix, he clutched his fork like an enormous five-year-old and dug into his mound of food.

"Gee, George, help yourself." I shrugged at Blake and waved Myra to the seat next to her ravenous lover. "Don't mind us. Myra, I have more spaghetti in the kitchen. Give me a second and I'll fix you a plate."

"More?" George's elation wasn't muffled by the mound of food puffing out his cheeks.

"Georgie, behave."

Myra's quiet admonishment had the big galoot bowing his head in submission. "George sorry. Sure-sure."

I couldn't help myself. Something about the guy made me want to pet him. Compromising, I reached over and patted his arm. "Don't worry about it, George. Enjoy. Right?"

He nodded and continued to shove as much food into his mouth as would fit. "That's right! Enjoy. Sure-sure."

"Georgie, we didn't come here to eat."

George froze, his fork suspended in the air. He pouted at Myra, looking as though he'd lost his best friend. Which, I assumed, was food.

"It's okay, Myra. He's welcome to it."

George's features lit up. Emitting a happy sound, he opened his mouth wide for the food. Bowing his head, he resumed his attack on Spaghetti Mountain.

"I appreciate it, Jenn." Myra looked from me to the men silently staring at her. "I'm sorry, Blake, I should've called first. I didn't realize you had company."

"Jenn's right, Myra." Blake ran a hand through his hair. "You're always welcome here. You and George."

"Myra, this is Blake's brother, Michael."

The usually friendly Myra didn't extend her hand in greeting. I knew something was up when she didn't welcome a person with open arms. Worse, she actually edged away from Michael, toward the safety of George. Did she sense his ghoulish personality?

"Hi, Myra." Michael didn't offer his hand, either. "Nice to meet you."

What's going on between these two?

In a rare rude gesture, Myra ignored Michael to turn to me. "I need to talk to you about something." She shifted back and forth on her feet and snapped her fingers on both hands, her way of showing her excitement or nervousness.

"Yeah? Is Swindle ragging on you? Is he trying to track me down?" She kept snapping like a flamingo dancer gone mad. I figured her nervousness wasn't a result of anything dealing with the real estate office, but I couldn't think what else could get her agitated.

"No, nothing to do with him or the agency. It's—" She paused to stare pointedly at Michael.

"You can speak in front of me, Myra." Michael's shit-eating smirk made my skin crawl. This couldn't be good. "Blake, Jenn and I know everything about each other. In fact, we were discussing our possible partnership when you barged, er, dropped in."

In one slick move, he'd put us in a corner. If we wanted him to trust us, we'd have to show him we trusted him. I hated how he'd trapped us, but I had to admire him, too.

"Oh, uh, sure." Forcing myself not to glance at Blake, I did what I had to do. "You can say whatever you want in front of Michael. He's family." Although I'd said the words, I wanted to rush to the sink and wash my mouth out with soap. Preferably the foulest tasting soap I could find.

My declaration of trust surprised Myra, yet she accepted it at face value. "Oh. Okay." Her excitement overtook her wariness and she started telling us everything. "You guys are not going to believe this. I've gained magical powers."

I'd learned a long time ago not to take Myra literally. "No kidding? What kind of magical powers?" Blake couldn't stifle a groan and I shot him a warning.

"I'm serious, Jenn. I can do these incredible things now." Myra waved her hands around in the air for emphasis, but she still wasn't making any sense. For my friend's sake, I tried to appear serious.

Michael, however, didn't heed my warnings. "Wow. You mean like a witch or a wizard? Or, hey, maybe you're an alien!"

He was, in fact, having a delightful time egging Myra on.

Fortunately, Myra didn't pay any attention to him. "I can do lots of things."

I tried to ignore Michael by concentrating on my friend. "Like what? What kinds of things can you do?"

Myra puffed up her chest dramatically and waved her hand. "Like this."

A cloud of pink smoke appeared over her hand, quickly obscuring her hand from view. Within seconds, however, the smoke was gone and a beautiful red ruby rested in her palm. My mouth dropped open.

"Holy shit, Myra!" I reached out to touch the jewel, hesitated until she gave me a queen-like nod of her head, then gingerly lifted the stone from her hand. I'm not an expert, but when I held the jewel up to the light, I knew it was the genuine article. Myra, my normal, mortal friend, had pulled a ruby out of thin air.

Michael was beside me before I knew it. He snatched the ruby from me and examined it. "This is real. This is a real ruby." With an evil leer, he shoved the ruby in his pocket.

"Hey! Give that back to her." I started to dig in his pocket, but Myra stopped me.

"Don't worry about it, Jenn. I can always make more. Lots more."

George lifted his head from feeding to confirm her boast. "Myra does lots of things. She made lots of pretty stones. She bought George a new cabin in the woods."

Just when I'd thought I couldn't be more surprised. "You bought him a cabin?"

Myra motioned with her hands again. Granted, she'd always used a lot of hand motions to punctuate her stories, but she was really going to town now. "Sure. Why shouldn't I? And the man who bought the first fifty jewels wants more of them."

"Fifty? You've made fifty of these rubies?"

"Fifty-one now." Myra's smug expression bothered me, but now was not the time to worry about her attitude.

"What else can you do?"

I'd almost forgotten about Blake. I noted the tone of his voice and knew he had something in mind.

"I can make things disappear, too." Myra ran her hand over the salt shaker, keeping everyone's gaze glued to her. In the next second, my grandmother's crystal salt shaker disappeared in another pink cloud.

"Myra, you bring back my grandmother's shaker right this minute." My best friend had developed magical abilities and I was worried about a salt shaker? Yeah, I was.

"No problem." With yet another flourish of her hand, the shaker reappeared.

"When? How? What happened to you? Did a mysterious fog flow over you? How about a high-level dose of radiation? Talk, Mrya." How had she changed? When had she changed? Did George have anything to do with her acquisition of mystical abilities? I studied George for a second and nixed the idea. George giving Myra super-powers would be like a gnat teaching Batman to fly. It ain't gonna happen.

Myra giggled, enjoying my perplexed attention. "I don't know."

With my background in strange events and creatures, I should've taken the whole thing a lot easier. But I couldn't. I didn't. Irritation made me spit out my words. "Oh, crap, of course you do. Quit playing around and tell me."

"Yes, Myra, go on. Tell us. But keep making precious jewels, okay?" Michael's evil laugh had me spinning on him.

"Shut the fuck up, Michael." If I'd had a weapon in my hand, I would've taken him out, Blake or no Blake. Instead, I stamped down the urge and whirled to confront her again. "Myra, talk."

At last, Myra took me seriously and began her explanation. "I really don't know. One day, I'm plain old me and the next day—wham!—I'm Magical Myra."

"And nothing odd happened in between? No strangers casting spells on you? No little green men taking you hostage? Come on, Myra, something strange had to have happened."

"Sorry, but no. I spent some time in the woods with George, but nothing out of the ordinary went on." She giggled and ran a hand over the giant's shoulders. "Well, at least, nothing bad."

Eeww. Magical Myra and George the Great locked in lusty lovemaking in a thatched hut. Not what I consider a fairy tale. "When did you first notice this change in you?" I couldn't, wouldn't give up.

"The first time I did anything magical happened right after the mugger attacked us."

"You mean, the one in our front yard?" Blake skirted around Michael to stand next to me. He slipped his arm through mine, letting me lean on him.

"Right." Myra shivered, reliving the incident. "After the attack, I decided I didn't want to risk carrying my jewelry around with me. Instead, I wear as much as I can and hide the rest in my home."

I pictured Myra stuffing cheap costume jewelry underneath her mattress in her tiny studio apartment with her ample bottom sticking upward to the ceiling. The image wasn't a pretty one.

She circled her arms around in the air in front of her, letting the many bracelets clink together. "See? I'm making a fashion statement, don't you think?"

Not even Myra, the jewelry-loving diva, had ever worn this many bracelets, rings and necklaces. To top off the not-so-chic fashion statement, she'd added more piercings to her ears. The girl could've started a jewelry outlet with the garb she sported on her body.

"Uh, yeah. I guess so." To make up for the hurt expression I saw on her face, I quickly added, "Shoot, Myra, you know I'm not into fashion like you are. I wouldn't know Gucci from sushi."

She accepted my lame excuse like the true friend she was and the creases in her forehead smoothed out. After all, friendship means not having to have a good excuse. "Don't feel bad, Jenn. When you're as pretty as you are, you don't need any adornment."

Myra, my best friend. God, how I love the woman. My smile gave her the incentive to continue her story.

"I am amazing myself. Did you know I can turn on a television without using the remote? I don't even have to use my Clapper any longer." She clapped her hands together at an invisible television set.

"Cool. Although I'm thinking making jewels out of thin air is probably more amazing, but the TV thing is useful, too."

Myra reached over and kissed George on the head. "I

scared poor Georgie to death when I did my vanishing act."

"Vanishing act?" Michael moved closer to Myra and scrutinized the bracelets on her wrists.

Why is he staring at her costume junk so intently? He can't possibly think... Does he really believe my average-Jane Myra might be wearing the Bracelet? I almost laughed at the ridiculous idea. *My wonderful girlfriend possesses the most powerful weapon known to Mankind and the Otherworld. Uh-huh. Oh, poor Michael, I do believe you're a ghoul gone goofy.*

Following his lead, I studied the bracelets on her arms. Where the heck would she have gotten the Bracelet, anyway? The flea market? Yet I guess Michael didn't think it was such an outlandish idea. He moved in for a closer examination.

"Yes, I can vanish. I can make myself invisible." To prove it, she blinked out of sight.

"Oh, my God." I felt Blake tighten his hold on my arm. "Myra? Come back, Myra." A pressure against my cheek had me reactively jumping into Blake. "What the heck?"

"It's me!" Myra appeared again, jumping up and down in excitement. "I didn't go anywhere. I was right in front of you the whole time." She leaned over and pecked me on the cheek. "You felt me when I kissed you."

"Wow." Blake and I spoke at the same time.

"I know! It's a whole lot of fun."

Myra, her excitement growing into a fevered pitch, started to dance around Blake and me, making Michael hop out of her way. Nonetheless, he tried to stay close to her.

Myra finally stopped dancing and hugged me to her. Well, at least, she tried to. But Blake wouldn't let go of me, which made her hug end up being a half-hug from the side. "I wish I knew how and why this happened to me. Not only can I do all this fantastic stuff, but my luck has changed. Everywhere I go, something good happens."

All her news caught up with me, leaving me speechless. All I could do was gape at her, letting her take my silence as encouragement.

"For instance, when I went into the bank on Riker Street, I expected them to treat me as rudely as they always do. This time, however, I pretended I was very rich and had a million dollars in my account. And you know what?"

Michael filled in the necessary response. "What?"

"I did have a million dollars in my account."

Her declaration helped me finally find my voice. "You had what in what?"

She resumed her happy-dance, answering in a sing-song voice. "I'm not kidding. They pulled up my account information and showed me. I have exactly one million dollars in my account. Yippee! I'm rich, I'm rich, I'm very, very rich! Do you want me to make you rich?"

"Yes!"

"No!"

I glared at Michael for his greediness until Blake's sheepish expression let me know where he stood in the to-be-or-not-to-be-rich debate. He shrugged. "Maybe?"

Myra, however, giggled and kept on dancing. She started spinning, flailing her arms over her head, then sticking them straight out like a kid pretending to be an airplane. I grabbed for her and missed. George, full at last, stood and patted his already protruding belly. Stretching his arms wide, he let out an enormously disgusting belch, and bumped into her.

"Aiieeeeee!" Myra and George tumbled together to the floor, causing several of her bracelets to fly off her wrists and skate across the floor.

Blake and I picked up the bangles next to our feet. Michael, however, wasn't concerned about helping Myra, and instead, hurried after a gold bracelet on its way under the buffet. Cussing, he went down on all fours to retrieve the stray bracelet. Warning bells clanged in my head. Why had he gone after a cheap bracelet? No way would he help Myra unless he could gain something by helping.

He clutched the bracelet in his hand, stood, and studied the inside of the golden circle. I elbowed Blake to pay attention to Michael and held my breath, fearful of what Michael might now possess. Proving me right, my ghoul-in-law broke into the widest cat-who-caught-the-biggest-rat grin I'd ever seen.

"Jenn! It's the Bracelet! He's got the Bracelet!"

I don't know how Partner managed to turn his speakers on, but I was glad of it. Partner was eye level with the Bracelet and could see everything Michael saw.

And still I couldn't believe it. "You've got to be kidding me." Thankfully, Blake didn't have my denial problem.

"Who was that?" Blake waited for someone to answer and, when no one did, got back to the more urgent situation. He released me to stretch out his hand to Michael. "Give me the Bracelet, bro."

Michael's eyes flashed red, hinting at his ghoulish form. "Not on your life, brother. In fact, why don't you—"

"No! Don't!" I screamed at Michael to keep him from finishing his sentence. Didn't he realize that, with the Bracelet in his hand, anything he said might come true? "He's your brother."

"Hey! That's my bracelet." Myra and George still sat on the floor, staring at Michael as he morphed into his ghoulish body. George, however, didn't let his surprise keep him from getting Myra's bracelet. With an animal-like growl, he hopped to his feet and threw his body at Michael.

Who knew such a large man could move like a track star? Blake followed George's lead and aimed his own body at Michael. I yelled at them, cautioning them to watch out. But the ghoul wasn't about to go down without a fight. He jumped out of the way and shouted the one word able to slice through my heart. "Knives!"

A Demon's Gotta Do
What a Demon's Gotta Do

Long sharp knives appeared in Michael's hands. Brandishing the weapons, he spun out of the way of George's awkward leap. George crashed into the small table sitting in the corner of the room, crumbling the table under his weight, and sending the vase of flowers flying. Water, flowers and shards of glass lay strewn across the floor.

Dying flowers and broken vases didn't concern me. My brain noted and quickly dismissed George's collision. Looking like something out of a martial arts movie, Michael jumped, twisted his body in midair and threw the knives at Blake.

"Blake, watch out!"

"Look out!"

Partner's and my warning came too late. Blake tried to dodge the weapons. One knife zipped harmlessly past him to lodge in my freshly painted walls. *Yeah, I know it's weird to think of my walls at a time like this, but that's how my mind works.* The other knife, however, found its mark. I stared in horror at the hilt of the knife protruding from my husband's chest. Blood spurted from the wound, making a red irregular oval. Blake groaned and slumped to the floor.

"Blake!"

Michael whirled away and bounded over George, who sat, legs spread wide, glancing around him in confusion and holding one hand to his forehead.

I hesitated, torn between my duty as a Protector to race after the Bracelet and the ghoul, and my duty as Blake's wife to come to his aid. I chose my husband and hurried to his side. "Blake? Oh, hell, Blake."

He lifted his head from examining his wound and gave me a weak grin. "Hell? Let's not bring up Demogorgon's home, okay?"

I echoed his humor with a shaky laugh and yelled for help. "Myra, get some towels. Anything to stem the flow of his blood. George, are you all right?"

"George is okay." He grumbled under his breath before adding his signature line. "Sure-sure. George is okay."

Although I didn't turn away from Blake, I could tell George was okay by the sound of his voice. At least physically okay. Ego-wise, however, he was in a big hurt.

Myra stepped past us and shoved open the kitchen door. "I'll get some cloths. Oh, and some water. We'll need lots of boiling water."

Blake clasped my hand and brought it away from his wound. "What do I need with water? I'm not giving birth, for cripe's sake."

"Good to know this hasn't spoiled your sense of humor, but I think she's thinking of sterilizing the wound or something."

"Tell her not to bother. I'll be all right in a few minutes."

I gasped, however, and he gripped the shaft of the knife. "No. Leave it in. Let the doctors take it out." But Blake, being Blake, didn't follow my order. Instead, he pulled the knife out and dropped it onto the floor. I picked up a cloth napkin and held it to his chest.

"Jenn, I'm okay."

I pressed the cloth to his chest and was startled to find myself getting a little lightheaded. As a Protector I'd seen—hell, I'd caused—my fair share of bloodletting, but the sight of Blake's blood, the blood of the man I loved, put all those prior experiences to shame. "Yeah, I know. You're tough. I know." But I didn't want to take any chances. Not with my man. "George, call nine-one-one."

George mumbled something resembling a reply and fumbled to his feet. Slipping once on the water, he managed to make it to the nearest phone in the living room.

"George! Stop! Don't call." Blake took my hand to, once again, remove it from his wound. "Jenn, aren't you forgetting something?"

I couldn't fathom what he meant. I stared into his eyes and waited for him to clue me in. "What?" Maybe he wanted painkillers? I racked my brain trying to remember what kind of pain meds we had in the medicine cabinet upstairs.

"Aren't you forgetting what I am?"

At last, his words soaked into my fogged brain. "Oh. Uh, yeah."

"Yeah? And?" Myra dropped to our side with an armful of cloths and a kettle of water. "Demons do die, right? I mean, Jenn's exterminated plenty of—oops. Sorry, Blake."

"A kettle? Did you plan on making him some tea?" I grinned at my perplexed friend. "Tell me. Is chamomile tea better than green tea for puncture wounds?"

"Huh? No, of course not. What? I brought towels and water for the wound."

"Blake? Does George call now?"

George stood in the doorway, phone in hand.

I let out a relieved breath. At least until I noticed the cord of the phone dangling from the earpiece. "Uh, George, that's not a cordless phone." George held up the phone and fingered the broken cord. "Didn't you notice how the other end of the cord was connected to the other part of the phone, big guy?"

George's face scrunched together and he turned to look into the living room where the base of our retro-style phone rested on the coffee table. "George didn't notice. George is sorry."

"It's okay. I have my cell phone." Myra reached into her pants pocket.

"There's no need to call anyone, Myra." Blake placed his hand over hers to make her lower her phone. "I'm fine. See?"

Proving his words, he lifted the blood-covered cloth away from his chest. Our gazes met and he unbuttoned his shirt. "Have you ever known a demon to die from a shallow knife wound, Jenn?"

Blake wiped away the blood to show his chest. Although he did have a wound, I could see that it wasn't a very deep one. Relieved, I felt the knot of tension lodged in my neck starting to unwind. He really was okay.

I knew demons couldn't die easily—you really have to jab a

knife deep into them to kill them—but I guess the trauma of seeing Blake hurt had wiped everything I knew about demons out of my mind. When I'd seen the knife in him, I'd known how much I loved Blake. Whether he remained a demon or not was irrelevant to me. I loved him and nothing would change the way I felt. Yet now that the danger had past, I couldn't seem to stop shaking.

Allowing Myra to place a large bandage over his wound, Blake took my hand, ridding me of the shakes. "Don't you see? Michael didn't want to kill me. He didn't throw the knife hard enough to kill a demon. But he probably figured all the fuss would slow us down."

"A demon?" George dropped the phone, shattering it against the hardwood floor, and shuffled closer to our little group. "Blake is a demon? Are you sure-sure?"

A series of very loud and extremely annoying beeps broke into our conversation. "Excuse me! I realize no one actually cares, but I'm fine, too."

I stood up to peer at Partner. "Well, of course you are. You're a machine."

Partner's screen changed from bright white to a dark blue. "Machines have feelings, too, you know. Once, just once, I'd like someone to worry about me."

I rolled my eyes at his dramatics. "I'm very happy to know you're not, uh, damaged."

"Thank you. I was beginning to think—"

"Now get over yourself." I dropped to Blake's side again.

"—no one cared about me."

Even though he didn't want us to, Myra and I helped Blake off the floor, Partner's pitiful play for attention forgotten. Blake gave me a look which I countered with a promise to explain the mysterious voice later. We knew we needed to track down Michael as soon as possible, but first we had to fill George in on Blake's alter-identity.

Amazingly, George had bought into the whole "demons and ghouls in the world around us" fairly easily. "Blake is a demon? For sure-sure? But demons are bad and Blake isn't bad." It seemed he wasn't dismayed that demons actually existed; more that Blake was one of them.

After quickly regaining his strength, Blake left the rest of us to race upstairs and put on another shirt. Myra took George's arm and led him to sit on the couch. I sat on the edge of the armchair across from them and tried to find the right words to explain everything.

"Here's the deal." I stopped, hoping Blake would return and take over this chore. "Blake is, well, he's, uh, that is, he's not quite—"

"Oh, damn, Jenn, don't make it a big deal." Myra turned to George and spoke as though she couldn't get the words out of her mouth fast enough. "It's true, Georgie. Blake is a real live demon."

"Strictly speaking, I'm undead, not alive." Blake hurried down the rest of the stairs, buttoning his shirt and shooting her a grin. "Although it's actually a bit more complicated than that."

Myra shot Blake an irritated expression, effectively shutting up my husband faster than I'd ever seen anyone do it, including me.

George glanced from Myra to Blake to me, and back to Myra. "Blake's a demon? Really? Like the devil-made, come-from-hell kind of demon? Like the ones on television?"

"Well, sort—"

Myra's glare sliced into Blake, making him relent, holding up his palms toward her in surrender. He joined me and sat on the arm of the chair.

"Right, Georgie. Except Blake is a good demon, not an evil one." Myra's firm expression softened and she looked to me for support. "Right, Jenn?"

"Oh. Uh, yeah. Definitely a good one." I patted Blake's leg, hoping the gesture would prove his good heart to George. After all, would I pat a bad demon?

"Is Michael a demon, too? A good one, too?"

"No, George. Michael's a ghoul." Could George handle learning about the Otherworld and the creatures lurking there?

"Michael's a bad ghoul," added Myra.

"No, he's not!"

Myra and I jumped at Blake's forceful and very loud declaration. "You're kidding, right?" I gawked at Blake, trying to understand him. "I don't care if he didn't kill you. He's not exactly campaigning for Brother-of-the-Year, ya know." Blake lifted an eyebrow at me. "Oh, hell, you know what I mean. I don't care if you think he didn't want to kill you. He stabbed you in the chest and you're saying he's not a bad ghoul? If he's not bad, what the hell does a bad ghoul do? Rip out your still-beating heart for an afternoon snack?"

Blake matched his glare to my gawk. "Actually...yes. Now do you get my point? An evil ghoul would do exactly that. Michael wanted to get away with the Bracelet, nothing more."

George narrowed his eyes and leaned forward so far he almost toppled off the couch. "Show George."

"What?"

"Show George. I want to see Blake the demon."

I couldn't blame him. When faced with an incredible story like the one we'd told him, I'd want proof, too. Lifting my head to Blake, I seconded the idea. "Yeah, Blake. Show him. What better way to prove it?"

"I guess you're right." He glanced at Myra, then George. "Are you sure you want to see me? In my demon form, I mean? Some people can't handle the sight."

The odd couple nodded in unison.

"Okay. Here goes." Blake moved a few feet away. He faced us, took a deep breath, and began the transformation. The smell of sulfur struck me in the same instant Blake's eyes changed from a beautiful gray into a deep fiery red. I gritted my teeth, trying to keep the image of the man I loved firmly in my mind as that man disappeared. Deciding I'd seen enough of my hubby in his grossed-out form, I turned my head away from the sight. Instead, I watched horrified expressions cover my friends' faces. Yet, after a few moments of studying their reactions, I decided their looks of disgust were harder to bear than watching Blake morph into a vile demon.

Myra's quick intake of air signaled Blake's change and I felt her fear. Toned muscle melted into scaly, oily skin. His ears lengthened, growing more pointed at the end, and his facial features altered, losing the tight square jaw for the crusty, crag-filled, wart-covered face of a monster. A low rumble came from the bottom of his throat and his tongue elongated and forked. Acting in true demon style, he flicked it out like a gigantic lizard.

Blake bared his fangs and moved toward the couple. His

move didn't frighten me since I knew he'd never harm my friends, but Myra didn't know what I knew. She gave a frightened yelp, pulling her body onto the couch in a futile effort to protect herself.

"Myra, don't worry. It's still Blake. He won't hurt you."

George, however, didn't take my word for it. In an alarmingly quick move, he picked up Myra and settled her on the other side of the couch, right behind him. I stood, calling for both of them to calm down. Placing myself between George and Blake, I put my back to George, flattened my hands against my husband's chest, and forced him to stop. "Stay back. Can't you see you're scaring them?"

Blake stayed put, but I knew in an instant it wasn't because he'd obeyed me. Something else had stopped him cold. His mouth fell open to gape at whatever was behind me. An enormous, spine-tingling growl rumbled from somewhere over my shoulder and a foul odor—worse than a demon's or ghoul's—drifted over me. I fought the automatic reaction to gag. Slowly, I turned on my heel to see what had made the ominous sound and terrible smell.

I'd seen a variety of creatures during my time protecting the world. Some of them were beautiful, like the faeries living in the woods surrounding our city. Some of them were so vile in their appearance anyone gazing upon them wanted to scratch out their own eyes. I knew of demons, ghouls, gargoyles, dragons and even aliens. But I had never seen one of these creatures. Never...until now.

Behind me, standing guard over a cowering Myra, was a Sasquatch. The beast held up paws at least ten inches wide with long, razor-like claws. His growl made the air around us seem to waver, and he opened a mouth filled with viciously sharp teeth. I felt my jaw drop. Gawking at the sight before me, I lifted my head to stare at the animal whose head touched my ten-foot tall ceiling.

Blake and I echoed each other's words. "Holy shit."

Monster, May I?

"Oh. My. God."

Blake and I recovered from our initial shock in under a minute. After checking out Myra's stunned expression, however, I wasn't sure if she'd ever recover.

"Georgie?" Myra whimpered his name and tucked her body into a tighter ball. In fact, the evening had given us all opportunities to gawk.

Big Foot George stopped growling at Blake and dropped his huge arms to his side. His enormous brown eyes fell on Myra and his face, a mask of untamed animal fury, went slack. If I hadn't seen the fierceness in him mere seconds earlier, I wouldn't have believed the two creatures existed in the same body. Now he reminded me more of a big hairy teddy bear than a cross between mankind and the Missing Link.

With a moan, he went down on all fours and laid his head against Myra's leg. She flinched, started to edge away, then stayed where she was. Tentatively, she relaxed her body, reached out and placed her palm on George's head. A sigh rolled from him and she rested her other hand on his cheek.

I had to admire my friend's nerve. "And I thought we were the Beauty and the Beast of Suburbia."

"Yeah. Thankfully, it looks like this Beauty has tamed her Beast." Blake, returned to his sexy human body, pulled me into him for a comforting snuggle. "I can understand now why the guy has a never-ending appetite."

"Georgie?" Myra took his face in her hands. "If I hadn't seen it with my own eyes, I'd never have believed it." She stroked his cheek. Purring like a giant gorilla-kitten, he laid one large paw on her leg. "My Georgie is a Sasquatch."

His transformation back to human—albeit an enormous human—came quickly. Myra held his head during the entire process, never once uttering a sound or cringing. I had to give her credit. The girl definitely had balls. Within seconds, George had returned to normal. Or at least, *normal* for him.

After several more minutes where we all took our time to take in this new development, George finally got up off the floor and resumed his seat next to Myra. "Is Myra all right?"

She nodded, running her eyes over him. "I'm all right." She lifted the sleeve of his baggy shirt. "No wonder you wear such oversized clothing."

George, however, seemed to need something more. "No. George means...are you all right with George being...George?"

"Do you mean is she okay with you being a Big Foot?"

George snarled at me, no less a menacing sound coming from his human form. "George likes the word Sasquatch better."

Who knew the big guy had issues with nicknames? "Uh, okay. Sorry. I didn't realize Big, er, the other term wasn't PC. Sasquatch. Got it." Now I'd had everything imaginable happen to me. I'd been corrected by a Big Foot. Er, Sasquatch.

"Why didn't you tell me?" Myra touched his cheek, stroking it the same way she'd done when he was in his alternate form.

George tucked his head. "George wanted to but George was scared. George didn't want Myra to stop liking George." He raised his head to search her face. "Does Myra still like George?"

"No."

The stunned hurt in George's eyes almost punched a hole in my heart. Why had Myra said such an awful thing? If she didn't like the guy any longer, she could've at least let him down easier than with a big fat *no*. Sheesh, even a Big, er, Sasquatch has feelings, right? She'd verbally kicked him in his balls.

"I don't *like* George any more." Myra smiled and used both of her hands to hold one of his. "I *love* Georgie. And I don't care what you are. Sasquatch or man, I love you."

Now there was the Myra I knew and loved. Letting my girlie instincts run wild, I reveled in the love story playing out in front of me. Partner, however, wasn't ready to send out wedding invitations.

"For the love of Bambi, he's an animal. How can you even think about a life with Chewbacca's country cousin? Have you no pride, woman? No self-respect?"

Blake whirled, searching the room for the owner of the voice. "Okay, screw telling me later. Who the hell is that? Whoever you are, come out of hiding right now!"

Amidst Blake's protest, Myra's angry retort and George's snarl, I kept my mouth shut and strode into the dining room where Partner continued to trash their possible union.

"I'm telling you, this inter-species thing can't work. You don't see a cow mating with a horse, do you? There's a reason. It jest ain't natural. Think about the poor, not to mention, ugly babies they would have. It's worse than inbreeding."

I picked Partner up, flipped him over, and worked on the battery lid. "You need to keep your opinions to yourself unless we ask for them."

"What are you doing, Jenn? No! Don't do it! I'll lose important information. Yanking my power source could cause serious problems. Jenn, I'm warning you. Leave my bat—"

I held up the batteries I'd ejected from Partner and checked out his screen. The image of the cowboy wavered for a moment and disappeared. But not before he'd given me a not-so-cowboy-like gesture with his middle finger.

Taking Partner with me, I returned to the living room and held him high for all to see. "Partner's out of commission for awhile."

"Who or what the hell is Partner?"

I blinked at Blake. "I meant to tell you about him earlier"—*not!*—"but I sort of ran out of time." I handed Partner to Blake. "He's my partner called Partner and he's helped me out a lot." I sighed and searched for the words to describe what the mechanical-device-turned-friend meant to me. "But I'd still rather talk about this later. Okay?"

Myra and George rose together, their fingers intertwined like teenage lovers. "What do you think, Jenn? Is Partner right? Will our babies turn out...you know, not normal?"

Normal? Normal with a Sasquatch? Was she serious? I wanted to tell her everything would work out fine in the end, but I didn't want to lie, either. How did I know, anyway? "Gee, I don't know. I mean, on the one hand George is a Sasquatch." I studied the man standing in front of me, staring at me with imploring eyes. "But then, on the other hand, he's also human. I think it would take a geneticist to figure this one out. Not a Protector."

Blake took one final look at Partner and tossed him on the coffee table. "If we're finished sorting out their future progeny, we might want to get going on a more pressing matter."

I knew what Blake meant and had to agree. "He's right. We need to find Michael and the Bracelet before Demogorgon gets his hands on it."

"Ohmigod. Are you saying my bracelet is *the* Bracelet? And all the things I could do and my good luck was a result of my wearing it?" Myra fingered the remaining jewelry on her arms. "Figures. I'd hoped the good luck and powers had lingered inside me all these years and had finally broken out. But I'm still plain old Myra."

After what had happened to her, after she'd stayed a true and valued friend through good and bad, I couldn't let her get away with slamming herself. Besides, I loved telling the truth when it made someone else feel better about themselves. "Girl, you were never plain or old. You've always been and always will be fantastically special."

We hugged and I could almost hear the testosterone in the room groaning. Blake, for instance, couldn't stand the girl love-fest for a second longer. "If you two are through sharing a moment, we need to put our heads together and get our asses moving. Time's a-wasting."

Time's a-wasting? Breaking apart from Myra, I pivoted to Blake. Since when had he started talking like Partner's cowboy? I laughed and punched a button on Partner. "I used him once before to find Michael. Hopefully, Partner's locator will give us the lowdown we need again."

Frowning at the unresponsive machine, I let my impatience work my mouth faster than my brain could stop it. "What's wrong with this damn thing?"

Blake grabbed my hand and opened it up to reveal the batteries. "You killed him, remember?"

"Oh. Yeah. My bad." Feeling more stupid than angry—but not by much—I reinserted the batteries in Partner and hit the

On button. Partner slowly came back to life.

"I see. Not even fifteen minutes later and you already need me. Let me guess. You need me to cowboy up and help you. Am I right?"

I should've known he'd have an attitude once he woke up. I swallowed the biting remark I wanted to make. "Yes, Partner, you're right. We need to find Michael. Can you pick him up on your locator?"

A petulant cowboy glared at me from the screen. "I don't know. Maybe. What's in it for me?"

I had to have imagined his words. Was a machine bargaining with me? "What's in it for you?" I nearly choked trying to keep my retort inside my mouth. Yet a few of them slipped out anyway. "Hmm, let's see. Maybe the possibility of staying turned on? Or how about saving yourself from winding up in the town dump? Are those incentives good enough?"

Partner's screen went black. I shook him, wondering if something terrible had gone wrong. "Partner? Are you all right?"

The monitor wavered for a moment, running static across the screen, before the cowboy image reappeared. "Whoa! What the hell happened?"

"I thought you could tell me." Did I trust him? Was this a ruse to think I'd damaged him? Was this box of electronic mish-mash guilt-tripping me?

"I'm not sure." The cowboy gazed around him to check his internal workings. "I think maybe taking my power source—"

"Batteries. You mean your batteries. Right?" Blake leaned over my shoulder to see the screen.

"No, that's not what I mean. They may look like batteries, but they're actually a very sophisticated power source." Cowboy fisted his hands on his hips and rolled his eyes, acting like the first gay ranch hand I'd ever seen. "Should I continue? Hmm?"

I elbowed Blake in warning. We didn't need to antagonize the Wireless Wonder. "Yes, go on. Can you tell us where Michael is?"

"I don't believe I can."

Was this part of his bargaining ploy? "Why not?"

"You must've damaged some of my sensors when you did what you did. I can't get a reading on anything, anywhere.

Shoot, I can't even get a reading on you and you're standing right there."

I studied the image and knew with a churning of my gut he was spouting the truth. *Damn.* "Great. In other words, you're of no use to us."

"Hey, little lady, don't go blaming me. I can't work under hostile conditions. Have someone rip out your power source and see how well you handle it."

The thing did have a point. "Well, what do we do now?" I glanced around at my friends and lover. "Does anyone have any ideas where Michael could've gone?"

A silence fell over our group.

"George does."

Okay, I admit it. Out of the four—five, if you count Partner—individuals in the room, I wouldn't have expected an answer from George. Still, I couldn't pass up any suggestions no matter who—or what—made them. "You do? Great. Let's hear it."

George looked at the floor and shuffled his feet. I'm guessing he didn't have many opportunities where he was the one with the answers.

"Go on, Georgie. We're all waiting." Myra hugged his arm to her.

"Georgie sometimes sleeps in places where dead humans sleep."

"Huh?" *Can you say eewww? Do I want to know what he means?* Judging from the expressions around me, no one else understood what he meant, either. I swallowed and decided to go where no man, woman or creature wanted to go—inside George's brain. "What do you mean...sleeping where dead humans sleep?"

"I know people think they're spooky, but they're quiet. When George can't make it home to the mountains, George sometimes sleeps in a graveyard."

Maybe I shouldn't have supported his relationship with Myra, feeling the way I felt. I mean, the guy sleeps in graveyards, for creep's sake. I've said it before and I'll say it again. *Eeewww.* Right now, however, I needed to get him to stick with the problem at hand. We'd discuss his gruesome sleeping arrangements later—if we had to. "And this has to do with Michael's whereabouts because why?"

George gazed at me with his puppy-dog eyes and proceeded to floor me. "Michael's a ghoul."

I tried to remember not all people got to the punch line as fast as I did, but my tolerance level lowered another degree. "Yes, George, we've established that Michael's a ghoul." I threw out my hands in a *now what?* gesture.

George, however, was a Sasquatch who marched to the beat of his own slower-than-a-worm-snug-in-warm-mud drum. "Sure-sure. Everyone knows Michael is a ghoul."

Myra sensed my impatience and pushed him before I could open my mouth to yell at him. "And? We're dying here, George. Tell us, please."

George beamed at her. "Because George sees ghouls in the graveyards lots of times. Ghouls like graveyards. Which means…"

"Michael would like graveyards." Why hadn't *I* thought of this? George, the Big Foot, er, Sasquatch, might appear dumber-than-dirt, but he had some hardworking gray matter encased in that monster-sized head of his.

Blake grabbed my arm, turning me toward him. "I can't believe I'm about to say this, but I think your job in the real estate business can help us. You know this town better than the rest of us."

I checked the expectant faces around me. My mind zipped through locating the cemeteries in our area of town and came up with the one closest to our house. "Michael wouldn't want to waste any time in using the Bracelet. Plus, I think he'd want to get to the nearest cemetery where he could use it in the relative safety of his own kind. *Or* where he could turn it over to Demogorgon."

"But what would Michael use the Bracelet for?" Myra patted George's arm in a loving manner.

"I'm not sure." Blake and I exchanged a worried look. Obviously, Michael hadn't planned on using the Bracelet to regain his and Blake's mortality. Instead, I feared he would rendezvous with Demogorgon and hand over the Bracelet. "But I intend to find out."

"My thoughts exactly." Blake leaned over and searched my face. "And the nearest cemetery is…"

"Twin Oaks Cemetery. Ten miles from here."

My Gravestone or Yours?

Have I mentioned how I'd love for someone, once in my career, to say "Hey, great idea, Jenn!"? Maybe even give me a little pat on the back with an "'Atta girl" thrown in? But nooooo. Nothing of the kind ever happens and it didn't happen this time, either. I stood, arms crossed, and unmoving. Blake, Myra and George, however, dashed for the front door.

Proving once again big guys can move quickly when they want to, George reached the front door first and held it open for Myra. He blocked Blake with a tree-trunk-sized arm, and arched a bushy eyebrow at my husband. With a grunt of satisfaction, George followed after Myra.

Blake let his irritation seep into his tone, turned and arched his own, albeit well-groomed eyebrow at me. "Are you coming or what?"

Or what? Had he really given me attitude? Oh, no, he had-n't. But alas, he had. Still feeling sorry for myself at the lack of congratulations I'd wanted and didn't get—although George was the one who'd come up with the graveyard idea—I nodded at my snippy hubby and trudged grumbling after him.

"Hey, what about me? You're going to leave me on, right?"

Crap. I'd forgotten about Partner. "Why? Can you fight? Can you run? Why should I take you along? For comic relief?" I knew I shouldn't, but I took out my frustration on the person— *person?*—who was easiest to blame.

Partner let loose with a whirr of angry sounds. "Why should you take me along? Are you seriously asking me why you should take me along?"

I rocked my head to one side, then the next. "I'm seriously

I Married a Demon

asking you. Talk up or shut up." I cringed at my harsh remarks, but it was too late to retract them.

Partner shot different colored beams of light onto the ceiling, flashing on and off like an insane lighthouse. "Because, Ms. Pissy Protector, *I* can call for help."

His answer hit dead-on and blew my snarkiness to hell and back. Even though Blake and Myra had cell phones, Partner's direct line to the Society would get help faster. *And* without a bunch of explanations. "Good point." With Partner in hand, I followed Blake out the door.

The new Mutt and Jeff were already loaded into Myra's tiny Corolla. I took a moment to wonder how George could fit his massive form into the little car. But such mysteries would have to wait for another time. Another time when the fate of my brother-in-law, much less of the world, wasn't in jeopardy.

Blake and I slid into my Jag—I know, I know. I can't help it. I simply like saying the word Jag, so sue me—and I handed Partner over to Blake. I waved to Myra sitting in the driver's seat with George of the Jungle riding shotgun, urging her to follow. She pulled out of the drive and waited for me to take the lead. I swung my Jag—*shut up!*—out of the drive and noticed Mrs. Hardgrave sticking her head out her door. I waved at her, too, hoping she'd pay no attention to the animal-like man riding in my friend's car. With one eye on Mrs. Hardgrave and the other on the street ahead of me, I stomped my foot on the gas, zooming my Jag down the quiet suburban street.

Ten miles had never seemed farther in my entire life. Blake buckled and unbuckled his seatbelt in anticipation of jumping out of the car, hot on the search for Michael. But he was driving me nuts with his antsiness. Normally, I'm an easygoing kind of gal—really, I am!—but this time it was all I could do not to slap him upside the head. At last, I slid the car against the curb outside Twin Oaks Cemetery, bumping both the front and rear tires and jostling Partner off Blake's lap. He smacked against the glove compartment, fell to the floor and skidded under the seat.

"Hey! Watch it, Jenn! You call that parking?"

Neither Blake nor I took the time to retrieve him. Instead, we launched ourselves out of the car and headed toward the twelve-foot-tall wrought iron entrance gate. "Partner, quit griping. If we're not back in thirty minutes, call the Society for backup."

Blake beat me to the gate and called over his shoulder. "Thirty minutes? Hell, if Michael uses the Bracelet or gives it to Demogorgon, we'll be vanquished in less than ten minutes." With a snarl, he shook the heavy link chain and lock securing the gate.

"What if he already has?"

"Let's hope he hasn't had time to slow down and figure out how to use it. Maybe there's more to using the Bracelet than simply wishing with it."

"Myra didn't have any problems using it."

"I know." He paused a second to wonder, then shrugged the problem away. "Let's find him first, then worry about what happens next."

The two doors of the entrance were held together with the sturdiest chain I'd ever seen. No one would get into the cemetery at night. At least, no human would.

Myra's car squealed to a stop behind mine, barely missing rear-ending my car. I silently gave thanks for the small favor. George and Myra rushed over to us before I had time to greet them, but Blake was focused on the problem of getting the gate opened.

What's wrong with this picture? I studied the gate, trying to coax an answer to the surface of my tired mind. Although I could sense the answer hovering near the edge of my consciousness, I couldn't dredge it out of the swirling mass of circuits called my brain.

"Watch out, everyone." With a growl reminding me once again of his other identity, Blake grabbed the metal and yanked. Links separated, flying into the air. The lock and the rest of the chain fell to the ground and the gate swung apart. "Let's go."

Myra and George rushed by me, dead on Blake's heels as his long legs ate up the ground. I followed, still unable to let go of the elusive idea. At last, the thought broke free of my subconscious and swam to the surface. "Wait a minute!"

All three of my companions whirled to confront me.

"What? Come on, Jenn, we don't have time. I have to stop my brother from making the biggest mistake of his life." Blake bounced on the balls of his feet, keeping himself ready to go in any direction. "Both his lives."

"You mean worse than changing into a ghoul?" Okay, maybe worse for the rest of humanity, but I couldn't fathom how it would make anything worse for Michael. "You're talking about your brother, right?" I shook my head at him. "We'll have to have this debate later. But for right now, you need to stop. We're letting him get away."

"Standing here talking is letting him get away."

George nodded at Myra's words and reinforced them in his own unique way by picking her up and raising her above our heads. "Yeah, Listen to Myra." Did he think we couldn't hear her unless he held her up?

"Put me down, George." He placed her gently back on the ground.

The whole conversation would've seemed comical if I hadn't needed to get my point across. "This isn't the right cemetery."

"What?" They peered at each other after all three of them had uttered the word in unison.

"Cute, guys, but try it in harmony next time. Listen up. Michael didn't come here. We're at the wrong graveyard."

Now they remained silent—together. For a second, I thought I saw the human—partly human—version of Hear No Evil, Speak No Evil, See No Evil. I gave them one more chance to speak, but they were a mute bunch. "Okay, here's the thing. If Michael had come to this place, wouldn't he have broken through the gate like Blake did?"

They peered past me to study the gate. What was their problem? I knew they were smart enough to grasp my argument. Or at least two of them were.

"Oh. I get what you mean." Myra slowly nodded, yet I still wasn't sure she understood. But at least she'd given me a reaction.

The big guy's face drooped, the implication of my words finally sinking in. "George does, too."

Okay, those weren't the two I'd assumed would get me.

Blake, my wonderfully intelligent man, still didn't get it. How could he not? I frowned at him, urging him to accept the truth. I glanced at George and back at Blake. Was it an IQ thing? Naw, couldn't be. Maybe it was a man thing. Did he simply not want to admit we'd messed up? Instead, he pivoted on his heel and started running toward the middle of the cemetery.

"No. He's here. I can sense him."

"Blake!" I took off after him, zipping past Myra and George. However, they didn't take long to catch up to me. I huffed and puffed to keep up with my hubby and tried reasoning with him. Trust me. Running alongside a demon isn't an easy thing to do. Especially with a really fast demon. "Slow down. You're wasting time. This isn't the right place. Dammit, Blake, stop!" No matter how hard I tried to keep up, I soon fell behind him.

Blake kept running, hurdling over grave markers with the ease of an Olympic track star. Pumping my legs until they hurt, I couldn't match pace with him. He raced around the edge of a mausoleum and I lost sight of him. "Blake! Hold up! Wait for us!" I grabbed the corner of the cement building and checked to make sure Myra and George were close on my heels. My momentum carried me around the side of the building—and straight into Hell.

Or at least Hell on Earth.

Blake grabbed for me, pulling me down behind one of the bigger gravestones. Shushing me, he pointed ahead of him. Without bothering to look, I nodded and readied myself to catch George and Myra before they barged in on the scene. Fortunately, George surprised me again by peeking around the corner of the tomb instead of barreling around the corner. Myra's bouncing curls stuck out from below George's chin, her wide eyes asking questions I couldn't answer.

Motioning for them to get down on the ground and crawl, I decided to see for myself what Blake had found. Lifting my nose over the stone, I squinted into the dark cemetery. If it hadn't been for the full moon—*oh, crap, I'm missing my shift for werewolf duty tonight for the Society*—I might not have seen Michael standing in an open area surrounded by graves.

Michael held the Bracelet toward the sky, his face ethereal in its wonder and awe. Lifting his head, he called out the words no Protector ever wants to hear. Especially not from her ghoul brother-in-law holding the most powerful weapon in the world. I sensed Blake scrunching next to me and soon felt the warmth of George's breath on my neck. He and Myra scoped out the scene.

"Oh, master, come to me. I, Zeiwa, your faithful servant, have brought you what you seek. Demogorgon, High Demon Lord, I beseech you. Come to me so I might deliver what is rightfully yours into your hand."

I gave Blake a look. "Is he kidding? I mean, who talks like that? He sounds like an old black-and-white movie villain."

"Quiet." Blake tried to keep his dire expression, but couldn't help letting the tips of his mouth curve upward. "He always did go in for the corny bits. Besides, Demogorgon likes the old way of speaking."

"Oh, well, of course. Ya gotta make the boss man happy." My sarcasm could've cut diamonds until I remembered that Blake had spoken to Demogorgon in the same curious way.

Our collective foursome ducked when Michael shifted his body to face our direction, held up the Bracelet again, and repeated his words. "Oh, master, come to me. I, Zeiwa, your—"

I leaned against the tombstone, half-listening to him drone on and trying to think on my feet. "What're we waiting for? Let's get him. He's all alone."

"Uh-oh. No, he's not."

I caught Myra's horrified expression and followed her gaze. Several ghouls rose out of the ground to stand directly behind Michael. Without acknowledging their ghouly presence, he continued to summon Demogorgon. More ghouls continued to push their way out of the soil surrounding him. "Sheesh, how many minions does one ghoul need? Talk about overkill."

I fell against the cold stone and tried to wrap my brain around what I'd seen. Leaning over Blake, I saw past the hulk of George's frame to see yet another ghoul digging its way out of the grave behind us. "Oh, come on, already."

George swung around, a growl rumbling low in his throat. He started forward but I grabbed his arm, keeping him with us. The ghoul didn't appear to notice us and stalked past us without a glance in our direction.

"I didn't know ghouls lived in graves."

I had to hand it to Myra. Although she'd always dreamed of becoming a Protector, she'd never had to deal with any monsters or other supernatural beings. She was, however, taking it all in stride. "There's always something new to learn about the preternatural." I smiled at her, hoping to give her the confidence I didn't feel. "Actually, these ghouls are probably newbies being dredged up from the grave by Michael's summons to the High Demon Lord. They're like lookie-loos. They aren't buying, but they wanted to see what was for sale."

Myra's frightened features relaxed a little and I knew my little joke had worked. My job of Best Friend was fully intact. Now I could concentrate on my real job.

"I guess Michael has some groupies."

Blake kept his attention on his brother, nodding his agreement. Not exactly the response I'd hoped I'd get for my joke, but it would have to do.

"Demogorgon, High Demon Lord, I beseech you. Come to me so I might deliver what is rightfully yours into your hand." Michael kept his spiel going with another round.

Would Demogorgon make an appearance? Not that I wanted Michael's ritual to bring out the head honcho. Without Demogorgon around, the possibilities of getting my paws on the Bracelet went up. However, if the boss beast did show up, then maybe, just maybe we could get rid of him for good. And I meant for *good*.

"He should be here by now."

Apparently, my hubby wanted to see the High Demon Lord, too. "Does Demogorgon usually come when a subordinate calls? I mean, isn't his ego too big to answer a command from one of his flunkies?"

"Not when the Bracelet is a part of it. Besides, it's not a command. It's more like a high-level email needing the supervisor's signature."

Oh, sure. Demogorgon and the Enron execs. I could definitely see the comparison. "Okay, although the odds have changed a bit, I vote for taking Michael on and getting the Bracelet before the lead vermin shows up."

"Too late."

Catching Blake's meaning, I scrambled around to peer over the top of the stone again and almost fell over from the shock. Instead of the gruesome entity I'd seen in the warehouse, a skinny pimply-faced youth stood in front of Michael. "Holy shit, isn't that Buddy from the Food Mart?" What the heck was our grocery store stock boy doing in the middle of a graveyard surrounded by a bunch of ghouls?

"Ohmigod, we have to help him!" Myra might have made it past our hiding place if George hadn't caught her before she made it half a foot. He scooped her up with one arm, letting her dangle by his side, playing King Kong to her Fay Wray.

I was starting to like the big lug. I mouthed a silent "thank you" and patted his arm to release her. "Think, Myra. Buddy isn't really a stock boy." Again, I had to give it to the scrappy woman. She had more balls than some men I've known.

Confused, she glanced between Buddy and me. Slowly, I saw understanding dawn on her face. Understanding...then terror. I turned to see what had caused the change.

Although I'd seen him in his true state before, a flush of revulsion coursed through my body. Gone was rail-thin, big-eared Buddy. In his place was a creature of tremendous destruction.

In his place was the High Demon Lord, Demogorgon.

As supernatural beings went, this guy was uglier than a gargoyle and troll combined. The long, writhing tentacles covering the demon's obese body reached out to caress Michael's face, bringing a glop of bile into my mouth before I could steel myself against the sight. Rolls of putrid glowing green lard hung from his body, waving like the loose skin of a fat man's underarms. His three red eyes protruding from his face glistened with excitement and greed spread his lips in what I assumed was a smile. A smile made up of sharp stained fangs.

"Ugha." Myra's gargle of revulsion expressed her dismay. "Gross and double gross. Where does something so revolting come from?"

"Straight from the depths of Hell."

At Blake's whispered response, I checked his face, searching for any sign of emotion and found none. He stared at the creature, unable to take his eyes off him.

"Gross."

Again with the gross? I followed Myra's gawking stare to Demogorgon and nearly gagged. I don't know how, but I'd forgotten about the worst part of this freak. His long hard penis, extending from under the fat folds of his abdomen, aimed straight at Michael, making me think of the pointer used for a blackboard presentation. At that moment, I wished he'd been even fatter, although I'm not sure the rolls of flab would've been enough to hide his four-foot penis.

Wait. *Four* feet? Had it grown from the last time I'd seen it? Eew. "Oh, damn. Somebody gouge my eyes out."

"Don't ask too loudly. You might get your wish."

I swallowed, realizing Blake was right. "Thanks for the reminder. But when are we going to make our move?"

Supporting his massive bulk with his thick tail, Demogorgon stretched a tentacle out to take the Bracelet. Michael, however, had a different idea. "Excuse me, oh, Wise One, but I want to discuss our agreement."

Demogorgon shifted his cumbersome body closer, whipping his tentacles around Michael like bullwhips cracking at his face. "Give me the Bracelet first."

A couple of ghouls stepped in front of Michael, blocking Demogorgon's way. The High Demon Lord roared his displeasure and struck out, slicing the two ghouls in half with one blow. Within seconds, however, more ghouls took their places. Demogorgon bellowed again, but didn't strike out. "Watch your step, Zeiwa. You push your luck."

Michael, aka Zeiwa, bowed low, but kept a firm hold on the Bracelet. "I mean no disrespect, master. I only wish to confirm our agreement before I make you more powerful than you already are."

"Do not take credit for what you do not control."

Michael bowed again. "Yes, master."

Somewhat mollified, Demogorgon rested the bulk of his weight on his tail again. Tentacles floated around the two ghouls like watchful snakes ready to bite. "Very well. You have been a faithful servant and, for a reward, I will excuse your impudence—this time. I am, however, disappointed in your failure to eliminate the Protector called Jennifer. Both you and your brother had ample opportunities to kill her and didn't. Your brother made the mistake of caring for this mortal and he will pay for his mistake. You, however, have yet to receive your punishment for failing me."

"She will die in the next few hours. I swear it."

"Good. Be certain she does." Demogorgon rolled his thick black tongue out of his mouth to lick his protruding member.

"State our agreement."

"Yes, master."

I glanced at Blake who watched, transfixed by the exchange.

"Per our agreement, once I deliver the Bracelet to you, you will reward me. In return, I will rise from the lowly rank of ghoul to become a Demon Lord."

A rumbling sound rose from the ghouls surrounding him. However, I couldn't tell if they wanted to congratulate Michael or tear him apart for his defection from their kind.

"Do you believe this? Your brother's bucking for a promotion to demonhood. Don't you get it? You're trying to save his ass for nothing." Blake gave a slight nod of his head and kept watching. But I wanted to know more. "Is it better to be a demon? There's a pecking order in the Otherworld between the different species? And demons rank higher than ghouls?" I knew I shouldn't, but I couldn't help but feel a smidge of pride. My hubby was among the higher ranked Otherworlders. After all, if he had to be one of them, at least he was high up on the totem pole.

Demogorgon blew a gigantic wad of black snot from his nose, spraying the ghouls standing in front of Michael. Instead of despising the action, the ghouls wiped the filth off their bodies and into their mouths.

"Ughh." Myra's gagging sound echoed my own and I tried not to upchuck. Ghouls, I knew, were among the grossest of supernatural beings, but this was way too gross.

"What you say is the agreement we made." Demogorgon waved his tentacles around, slapping against one ghoul with a resounding thwack. "I honored you with this agreement because of your past service."

"Yes, master, and I appreciate your generosity." Michael stepped back, keeping his attention on the monster in front of him.

Uh-oh. His move signaled a possible problem to me. And to Demogorgon.

"Give me the Bracelet, servant." Demogorgon pushed the ghouls apart, tossing them into the air like toy soldiers.

Michael kept backing up until he'd gone through the crowd of ghouls and came to a grassy area where funerals often held their memorials. Demogorgon followed him, plowing down the ghouls who attempted to stand in his way.

"I'm sorry, master, but I'm not giving you the Bracelet."

The High Demon Lord tossed more ghouls into the air. One fell close to us and broke into a myriad of pieces, sending Myra clinging to George. But Michael, Demogorgon and the other ghouls were too busy to notice.

Michael held up the Bracelet, making a show of starting to place it on his wrist. "I'm keeping the power for myself. You, oh mighty big ass, can consider yourself replaced." With a sound equaling the shriek of a thousand banshees, Demogorgon raised his tentacles and slashed out at Michael.

"No!" Without warning, Blake dashed from behind the gravestone and raced toward his brother.

Brother, Pull Yourself Together!

At the sound of my husband's shout, Michael twisted toward Blake, lowered his arms, and forgot to place the Bracelet on his wrist. Blake rammed against him and snatched at the Bracelet, but Michael held on. The force sent the brothers sprawling to the ground, knocking down ghouls like decaying bowling pins.

Demogorgon lumbered forward toward the two men, yelling commands at each of them. Commands neither one of them obeyed.

Roaring, the High Demon Lord raised a tentacle, readying to grab Blake, Michael and the Bracelet. I lunged out of my hiding place with George and Myra right behind me. Aiming my body like a human missile straight toward Demogorgon, I lowered my head and visualized knocking over the giant. At the very least, I prayed I'd make one helluva dent in all that blubber.

To my right, a shrill call echoed through the night, overshadowing even the sounds of Demogorgon's bellows. I stumbled to the ground, causing Myra and George to trip over me. I took a quick glimpse toward the ruckus and saw a sight stranger than ghouls popping out of the ground.

Mrs. Wippingpoof and Mrs. Hardgrave, each carrying what appeared to be whale harpoons and shrieking like avenging angels, ran as fast as their stubby support-hosed legs could carry them straight at Demogorgon. Moving with the agility and speed of young women, they shot their harpoons at the giant demon. Their aims struck true and he hollered in pain, but that didn't stop them from rushing forward. Demogorgon gripped the harpoons and tore them from his body, breaking them in half.

Black-green pus oozed from the wounds, releasing a smell so putrid nearby flowers wilted.

Using their broken weapons to beat at him, Mrs. Hardgrave assailed him on one side and Mrs. Wippingpoof hammered at him from the other side. He laughed at their pitiful attempts to hurt him and grabbed Mrs. Hardgrave by her curly blue-silver hair to violently shake her. She opened her mouth wide to cry out, but made no sound. Instead, her dentures flew out, bopping Demogorgon in his crooked nose. Rubbing his huge nose, he grabbed Mrs. Wippingpoof, who made a valiant effort to stab him in the eye. She missed, but only by an inch.

Shaking both ladies like pesky insects, Demogorgon opened his mouth and started to shove Mrs. Hardgrave inside. She screamed a curse at him and jabbed her weapon into his mouth, knocking one of his fangs loose. "Twhere! How do wyou like losing *youwer* tweeth?"

With an ear-shattering roar, Demogorgon threw the women away from him. Unfortunately, he flung them straight at me. In the split second before impact, I had to decide whether to jump out of the way or try to catch one of them. I opted to catch one of them.

Mrs. Hardgrave landed on me with an *ooph*, flattening me on my back. She ended up sitting on top of me. The world spun in a dizzy circle for a moment as I tried to regain my equilibrium.

"Hi twhere, Jwenny." My meddlesome neighbor gazed down at me and gave me a toothless grin.

"Hi." I had to admit this was one of those rare times when I was at a loss for words.

"I dwo hope I dwidn't huhrt you." She put a palm to my forehead and told me to stick out my tongue.

"Uh, Mrs. Hardgrave, I don't think getting smashed gives a person a fever. Would you mind getting off me?" She obliged, scrambling up to dash over and retrieve her dentures. "What the hell are you doing here?" I pulled Mrs. Wippingpoof to her feet and Mrs. H joined us. "And how do you know Mrs. Wipp?"

The two older women exchanged knowing glances before pointing at the High Demon Lord who had turned his attention to my husband and his brother. "Mrs. Hardgrave is one of us. When the Society found out you'd married a demon and

Demogorgon was out to have you killed, they assigned her to watch out for you. We were lucky she already lived on your street."

Mrs. Hardgrave shrugged, reached under her flowery dress, and revealed a knife the length of a small sword.

For a moment, I forgot everyone and everything in my amazement. "Then you aren't really a snoopy neighbor? Instead, you're *my* Protector?"

Mrs. Hardgrave brandished the sword with a precision that would've made a pirate proud. "You've got it, honey. Now, don't you think we'd better get back to the party?"

"Duck!"

I obeyed Mrs. Wippingpoof's order and ducked. "Kee-ahh!" She kicked out, her leg whooshing over my head to neatly slice through the neck of the ghoul about to take a chunk out of mine. I spun around in time to see the ghoul disintegrate.

"Thanks, Mrs. W."

"No problem, sweetie." With a wink, she dashed across the cemetery to where Myra and George stood surrounded by a group of ghouls. George had transformed into full Sasquatch and had a screeching warrior Myra sitting on his shoulders. I gaped at him, astonished at how easily he eliminated three ghouls with one blow of his massive arm. Myra took out a fourth using a ghoul's dismembered arm. Mrs. Hardgrave patted me on the shoulder and took off after Mrs. Wippingpoof.

Since George, Myra, and the two senior citizen Protectors seemed to have the ghouls under control, I headed toward my husband and his brother who were still fighting with each other. With their attention squarely on each other, they didn't notice Demogorgon's slow shuffling approach.

"Blake! Watch out for Demogorgon!"

Blake, however, was too busying wrenching the Bracelet out of Michael's hand to notice my warning. Instead of hot-footing it out of there, he leapt to his feet, clutching the weapon in his hand and turned toward Demogorgon. "Run, Michael. Save yourself."

"Put on the Bracelet!" I figured he needed protection and since he had the most powerful weapon in the world, why not use it? But not my brave hubby. Instead, he shook his head at me.

"No, Jenn. I can't." Sending me a sad smile, he reached out to hand the Bracelet to the monster headed his way.

"No! What do you think you're doing?" Had Blake fooled me? Had he planned all along to give Demogorgon what he wanted? I rushed toward him not knowing if I'd end up fighting my own husband for the Bracelet or helping him exterminate the High Demon Lord.

I made it halfway to him when he laughed at Demogorgon and lowered his arm. Grinning, he shook his head at his master and laughed again. "Sorry, asshole. The Bracelet isn't for you. Besides, you don't look good in gold." He tilted his head to study the monster headed his way. "Actually, to be brutally honest, you don't look good in anything."

At least half of Demogorgon's tentacles whipped out, wrapped around my husband, and lifted him high into the air. The last tentacle enveloped him, causing Blake to lose his grip on the Bracelet. The Bracelet fell free.

"No!" Blake struggled against the monster holding him, but he couldn't get loose.

Michael dove after the rolling Bracelet, snatching it off the ground a split second before Demogorgon reached for it. "I've got it!" He turned to run, but the demon latched a tentacle around his ankle and pulled him off his feet. Once he'd snagged Michael and the Bracelet, Demogorgon lost interest in Blake and dropped him to the ground.

I started to take advantage of Demogorgon's attention to Michael, but Blake held up his hand, stopping me in my tracks. "Stay there, babe."

Confused, I obeyed and skidded to a stop.

Blake picked up one of the harpoons the demon lord had tossed to the ground and rushed him. Like a gladiator fighting for freedom, he launched his body at Demogorgon, shoving the spike deep into the creature's ear.

I clamped a hand over my mouth, both awed and terrified for my husband. The High Demon Lord screamed a shrill ear-splitting shriek, making Otherworlder and human alike cover their ears. He released Michael, who held the Bracelet to his chest and crawled a few feet away. Pushing himself up, Michael scrambled in the opposite direction.

Amazingly, Demogorgon grew several feet taller and wider,

adding to his immense form. With a terrifying growl, he faced Blake. "You have betrayed me! I will tear your heart from your chest and feed on it. Prepare to die, Shytuman."

How enormous could this creep get? The earth below my feet shook from the creature's weight and I struggled to keep my balance. "Blake, run!"

But my husband wasn't going anywhere.

The demon lord screamed again, but this time added a new feature to the evil sound. Black pebble-sized pellets shot out of Demogorgon's mouth, like a myriad of mini-cannonballs aimed directly at Blake. Horrified, I added my own scream to the chaos.

Everyone froze, including the few remaining ghouls still putting up a fight, their stares locking onto my unmoving husband. I called to him, hoping to spur him into movement. Yet my call only served to make him look in my direction.

The next few moments slowed down, making those seconds last minutes. I swear I thought the world had stopped moving and air no longer drifted around us. Blake's eyes met mine and I held my breath, reading the message in those deep gray oceans. He knew his message had been received, and the corners of his mouth lifted a little.

Without a doubt, I knew the man I'd married was a demon. Yet, without a doubt, I also knew the man I loved was more human than I had ever believed.

He was prepared to die to save mankind. He was prepared to die to save me.

I reached out even though I was several feet away, needing to touch him one last time. My heart sank to the hole churning in my stomach and I readied myself for my husband's death.

Michael, however, had other ideas.

Instead of running off as I'd assumed he would do, Michael changed directions, turning toward Blake and Demogorgon. Holding the Bracelet high above his head, Michael threw his body in between Blake and the black rain.

The pellets struck Michael, covering his body from his knees to his chin. The force of the strike altered the direction of his body, sending him flying over Blake's head to land in a shallow, open grave. He cried out, emitting a horrible sound filled with pain, rage and anguish.

"Michael!" Blake hurried to his brother and I was right behind him. Together, Blake and I leaned over the grave and stared at Michael's quickly dissolving body. What I'd thought were black pellets were actually tiny bugs. The scavengers scurried over Michael, eating away at his clothes and flesh. Bugs filled his mouth, muffling his screams.

And still he held on to the Bracelet.

Blake flexed, ready to hurtle his body into the grave to help his brother. I grabbed him, knowing his rescue attempt wouldn't work, and struggled against him to keep my grip on his arm. "No, Blake, don't. He can't be helped."

"But why?"

I shook my head at Blake, not understanding his question.

"Why didn't he use the Bracelet? Why didn't he save himself?"

I tried to answer, hoping an answer would come. But I was wrong. Why hadn't Michael used the Bracelet? He could have saved his life with it yet, instead, he'd given his life for his brother. I looked at Michael, this time with a new appreciation. "Maybe, in the end, he wanted the same thing you wanted. For you both to become mortal again."

Demogorgon's evil cackle interrupted Blake's reply. "Your brother is food for my little ones. They love a good ghoul treat. If he hadn't betrayed me, I would've given him a quicker death. One with a smidge of dignity. Unlike the death I'll give to your bitch." Demogorgon chuckled, making his blubbery belly shake. "Bring me the Bracelet, Shytuman, and I may let you serve me a little while longer."

I glanced down at Michael and immediately wished I hadn't. A sea of black bugs covered him, from his one remaining foot to the tufts of hair left at the other end of the grave. The bugs continued to feast. With a squishing sound, his torso fell apart, separating his body into two parts.

"I'm going to send you back to Hell, Demogorgon."

Blake's tone sent chills up my spine. Hate, pain and misery filled his words.

Demogorgon, however, thought his threat was humorous. "Really? Why, thank you, for thinking of my comfort. You know I'm a homebody, don't you? But alas, I must stay in this wretched world until my business is finished. Thanks anyway, old boy."

I held on to my husband harder, knowing he wouldn't quit until the High Demon Lord was dead. "It's you and me, Blake. We'll take this scum-sucking evil out of the world to..."

My words trailed off at the sight below us. Michael opened his eyes, bright lights amid the total blackness covering him. His eyes held no pain, no anger, only an urgency I knew wasn't meant for me. "Blake, look!"

He followed my gaze to his brother. In the instant their gazes met, Michael shifted into ghoul form, pulling the top portion of his body away from the onslaught of bugs. Seeping up from the muck, Michael used his ghoul strength to raise his nearly severed arm—with the Bracelet still clutched in his hand.

"Bro!" Michael groaned and forced his arm higher. With incredible effort, he tossed the Bracelet to Blake. The Bracelet sailed above us, spinning above Blake's head until he snatched it out of the air.

Life, Death, and
Fashionable Accessories

Blake's heartache spread over him, slumping his strong body.

"He's gone, Blake. I'm sorry." I searched his face, wanting to give him whatever he needed, yet feeling totally helpless to do anything. Michael's body fell apart, leaving only bits and pieces, dissolving under the slimy trails left by the ravenous predators.

"He saved me." Pivoting to me, Blake searched for confirmation. "He saved us."

Although I wasn't sure about the *us* part of the deal, I wasn't about to argue. "Yeah, he did." Off to the side, our friends were fighting against more ghouls rising from the ground, but I wasn't leaving Blake's side. Not now. Not ever.

"He was human inside. Even after all this time as a ghoul, he was human. He still cared."

Demogorgon's cackle pushed my last nerve. "Saved you? For a short time, perhaps. Long enough to enjoy seeing his body devoured." His laughter roared, shaking the ground beneath us. "Oh, drats. Is he gone already?" Demogorgon clucked his disappointment. "I had hoped he'd make a better meal. Now I'll have to find another snack for my pretty ones. Perhaps your wife?"

"Leave my wife alone."

"Shytuman, how touching." The smirk on Demogorgon's face died. "Don't be a fool like your brother. You know you don't have the power to stand up to me. Show me your loyalty. Follow my orders and give me the Bracelet. I'll grant your wish and make you mortal again. Although I don't understand why anyone would want to become one of *those* things."

Had Demogorgon ever been human? I found it difficult to believe this Heap from Hell had ever possessed a mortal soul.

Shifting his bazillion pounds of lard, Demogorgon pointed at George, who stood pounding his fist into one ghoul after another. The two older Protectors battled at his side and Myra fought from his shoulders. "Oh, ho! Now there's a good meal."

"Leave my friends alone."

"Friends, are they? Oh, how far you've fallen, little man." Demogorgon's black eyes blazed a fiery red. "Hand over the Bracelet. I grow weary of toying with you."

Blake took a step toward Demogorgon, stopped, and studied the Bracelet. "No." He cleared his throat, straightened up, and repeated in a determined voice. "No. I'm using the Bracelet for myself."

"Then you must be exterminated." Demogorgon's roar drowned out the sounds of fighting and shouts.

I couldn't take any more. Something inside me snapped. He'd killed my brother-in-law—okay, granted, I didn't know or care a lot about Michael, but he was still family—and his death had caused my husband a lot of pain. Would I let this putrid pus from purgatory go after my man? Hell, no.

I dashed toward the monster with nothing but my bare hands for a weapon. Myra, using George's shoulders as a diving board, jumped off and rushed the demon at the same time, which, of course, brought George hurrying after her. Acting like three very odd-looking ninja warriors, we attacked Demogorgon head on.

And I do mean *head on.*

George leapt into the air, making the highest jump I'd ever seen. If white men can't jump, then Sasquatch sure can. Michael Jordan had nothing on my Big Foot friend. George's body slammed into the side of the monster's belly and his hands clamped around Demogorgon's head. When I last looked at George he was doing his best to twist off the High Demon's head.

I had a different head for my goal. And from her actions, Myra and I had the same idea. Obeying the teachings of a millennium of mothers, we went after the most crucial part of a male's anatomy.

Myra dove, a perfect example of a baseball player sliding into home plate, and slid underneath the roll of fat covering his giant organ. "Penis or Bust!"

I laughed at Myra's boast and skidded right up to the end of his purplish penis. Never have I ever been so close to that big a dick. And trust me. I never want to be that close ever again. "Grab it, Myra!"

Myra used the pin from one of her many pieces of jewelry to stab into his shaft from below. I grabbed the head of his cock and started twisting. Using all my body to wrench it around and around, I felt like the Crocodile Hunter wrestling a three-hundred-pound gator. Except, unlike the mighty Hunter, I was losing the match.

Demogorgon's bellow deafened me and I flopped over from the top side of his penis to hanging on underneath it. Myra, who'd given up after making numerous slices to the thick, rubbery skin, pointed at the two older Protectors. They'd resumed their fight with the few remaining ghouls and were steadily working their way toward us.

But where was Blake?

I craned my neck around to see him standing where I'd left him. What the hell was he waiting for? "Hey, Blake! We could use a little help here, ya know. Use the Bracelet to destroy him!"

Blake gawked at me and I could see the whirlwind of his mind in his eyes. Why didn't he fight with us? When the reason struck me, I almost let go of the creature's prick. He was torn between two choices—to use the Bracelet to save us—or change himself into a mortal.

Anger flashed through me at his hesitation. Obviously the choice wasn't as easy for him as it was for me. I wouldn't have hesitated for a second to use the Bracelet to save my husband and my friends, and eliminate a major badass demon from the world. Anger, however, quickly morphed into hurt.

"Blake! Help us!"

Myra's cry echoed my own and when he didn't respond, I saw my anger and hurt reflected in her face.

"He can't use it to help us. If he does, the Bracelet might not have enough power to change him into a mortal again." I knew Myra would recognize the ache in my tone, but I had to stick up for my man. Right or wrong, I had his back.

Myra, my friend to the bitter end, nodded and increased her feverish attack on the demon. I, however, couldn't continue twisting his dick. Instead, I held on and searched my husband's face for an answer.

Love is a funny thing. It's a song, but it's the truth, too. Although I was disappointed in Blake for not coming to my rescue, I couldn't fault him. Wouldn't I want to be human again if I were in his place? Trust me, I would.

Once I realized the truth, I risked taking one hand off Demogorgon's long shaft and waved at Blake, making sure he wasn't in a daze. (Part of me hoped he was in shock and, thus, he'd have a good reason for not attacking the monster.) He shook his head, clearing it. "Blake. Use the Bracelet on yourself. Use it now!"

A smile spread across his face, sending me an unmistakable message of thanks. I smiled in return before going on the attack again. Weaponless, I did the only thing I could think to do.

I opened my mouth and—*urgh!*—bit the tip of Demogorgon's dick. The High Demon Lord shrieked in agony but, trust me, my agony was a whole lot worse. One thought came through loud and clear.

Kill me now!

If someone had told me I'd be chomping off the end of a demon's penis one day, I'd have bought them a one-way ticket to the funny farm. Yet, here I was, clamping down with everything I had in me.

Myra's mouth fell open right before the grimace of disgust wiped the shock from her face. "Oh, God, Jenn."

I didn't hear her whisper over the wails of Demogorgon, but I read her lips and understood her anyway. I closed my eyes, tried to ignore the dreadful taste of demon blood and who-knew-what filling my mouth, and thought about Blake. If he returned to mortal, the filthy act I'd committed would be worth it.

Death had to be better than this.

The monster wrapped a tentacle around my neck, pulled me off him, and my last thought disappeared. I sensed him lifting me into the air and blessed blackness encompassed me.

Death by Dick?

I wondered if my grandmother would meet me in Heaven. Would I even make it to Heaven? Or would God frown on a woman who died biting the head off a demon's dick? Plus, being married to a demon and having a ghoul for a brother-in-law probably wouldn't help my chance much, either. I sighed, hoping all my good deeds as a Protector would offset those rather iffy qualifications.

"She moaned. Did you hear her moan?"

Had Myra made it into Heaven? And George? But where was Granny?

Although my eyelids felt like paperweights rested on them, I managed to open them to find Myra and George watching me. I guess they'd made it to Heaven, after all. Swallowing the dust in my throat, I croaked out a greeting. "Hi, guys."

Their faces lit up with excitement. Myra leaned over to hug me—how had I ended up flat on my back?—and George patted me on the head. "Thanks goodness you're conscious." Myra stopped me from trying to sit up and pulled me into her lap instead. "Take it easy. We thought we'd lost you."

I heard her words and started to respond until I saw Blake. He stood in front of Demogorgon with the Bracelet held high above his head. When I recognized the evil on his face, I pushed Myra's hands away and sat up.

"He's saving us, Jenn. All three of us. He's using the Bracelet to save us."

He was saving us? But at what cost? Would he use too much of the Bracelet's power? Would he have enough to kill Demogorgon *and* make himself mortal again? Although my throat felt bruised from the strangling the demon had given me, I managed to yell. "Blake!"

He didn't turn to me. Instead, he kept his focus on Demogorgon and his voice rang out loud and clear. "Demogorgon, vile creature of the Otherworld, I command the power of the Bracelet. Die, devil's spawn, die!"

For a moment, all motion, all sound, everyone including the one remaining ghoul, the two older Protectors and my threesome froze, waiting for whatever might happen next.

Suddenly, the air around us thickened. The darkness in the graveyard deepened from the clouds covering the full moon above us. We waited, and Blake continued to hold the Bracelet high. His eyes blazed a deep fire red, telling me he was still a demon.

Little by little, I heard a faint ringing growing louder. The sound, which reminded me of the church bell on my grandmother's small church, continued, the reverberation growing steadily louder with each second. One church bell grew exponentially into a cacophony of sound. If I hadn't known better, I would've thought all the church bells in the world were being rung at this same moment in time.

"Where are the bells coming from?" Myra's question drifted over my shoulders. I didn't respond, but kept my attention glued to Blake.

"George likes bells."

I grinned, knowing George grinned, too.

Demogorgon wrenched back and forth as if his body was stuck to the ground. He growled, but he couldn't shuffle even a single foot forward. A snarl formed on his lips and his tentacles whipped around his head.

And the bells grew louder.

Blake took two tentative steps away from the High Demon Lord before turning and dashing over to where George, Myra and I now stood. He drew me into his arms, giving me the emotional and physical support I needed.

The joyful sound continued and a peaceful sensation passed over me. Peaceful, however, was not the sensation Demogorgon felt. He thrashed his tentacles about, striking himself in the eyes, on the head, and at his bleeding penis. His body jerked. Spasms racked him, shaking his blubber.

Shouting curses, he finally broke free and wobbled toward us. Our hardy little group planted our feet, ready to face whatever he would throw at us.

The ringing bells escalated until they were the only sound in the world. I couldn't hear my own words, so I told Blake I loved him by laying my head on his chest. If we had to die, at least we'd die together.

Yeah, sometimes I can be such a drama queen.

With a shout, Demogorgon stopped and fear settled over the anger in his face. His eyes bulged from their sockets and his body swelled up like a blowfish. Opening his mouth in a soundless screech, he exploded.

Clumps of blubber landed on us, sliming us with blood and sickly green-black pus. Myra cried out even though George covered most of her with his bulk. The rain of fat spread out, covering Mrs. Wippingpoof and Mrs. Hardgrave. Ghouls fell to the ground around us, dissolving into gray dust.

At last the terrible deluge ceased and the bells stopped ringing. I glanced at my pus-covered clothes and hair, and lost it. "Oh, come on! Isn't biting his dick enough? Now I have to get covered with his shit?" I looked around me at my friends and grimaced.

George, who'd gone from Big Foot to Big Human, seemed to take the whole thing in stride. "George doesn't think this is shit. George thinks this is—"

"No!" Blake, Myra and I yelled at him, cutting off his last remark before he could say anything to make this whole thing worse. He pouted, however, and Myra ignored the filth covering him to hug the big galoot.

"We're sorry, George. But we don't want to know what it is."

Holding onto her man, Myra sent me a pointed look. "Blake, George and I have a favor to ask you."

I have to admit I was a bit irritated at my friend. Hadn't Blake just saved their butts? And she wanted another favor?

"What do you want from him, Myra?" I wanted to tell Blake to forget it, but something about the way Myra stared at me with a plea in her eyes stopped me cold.

"We want you to make George human. He doesn't want to stay a Sasquatch. Please, Blake. We, uh, we want to have babies some day. Mortal, normal babies."

I couldn't believe my ears. She wanted Blake to help George with the one wish Blake had refused himself in order to save us? "No. George, I'm sorry, but you're asking too much. He used the Bracelet's power to save us. Now it's his turn to use it on himself."

Tears sparkled in Myra's eyes and I had a tough time steeling my heart against her. But Blake came first.

"I'll try."

I wheeled on Blake, stunned at his agreement. "No. You can't. You've already used a lot of power from the Bracelet. If you use too much, it won't replenish and you won't get to change yourself." I wanted to hit something, someone, but could only clench my fists.

"It's okay to think of yourself. Of Jenny, too." Mrs. Wippingpoof linked her arm through Mrs. Hardgrave's and nodded her agreement. "You could wait and see if full power comes back to the Bracelet. Then you might be able to change both of you."

"She's right, Blake. Give it time to recharge."

Blake took my hand in his and diffused the ire within me. "I have a sense I've already used too much of its power for it to fully recharge. I don't think waiting will do any good."

"But what harm is there in waiting?" I knew Myra might hate me for what I said, but I didn't care. Blake's mortal life was at stake.

"No. I know it's too late. Don't ask me how I know, but I do." He gave me a soft smile. "I have to help him, Jenn. How can I not?"

Easy. Just don't. But I couldn't bring myself to say the words. Instead, I nodded.

After a squeeze of my hand, he let go and held up the Bracelet in front of George's face. Remembering the bells and how loud they'd gotten, I placed my palms over my ears and prepared myself for any eventuality.

Yet nothing happened. Nothing except a small popping sound.

"What happened? Did the Bracelet run out of power? Did it blow a fuse?" Myra bit off the end of a fingernail and chewed on her lip.

"I think it was the sound of the Sasquatch in me leaving my body."

"Wait a sec. You said 'I' and not 'George'. What does that mean?" Myra placed her palms on his chest and searched his face.

Something was different about George. Although I couldn't see the difference, I could sense it. "George? Do you—are you human?"

George, the former Sasquatch, picked Myra up and answered her question. "I'm human! I can feel it." Whirling Myra around, George the human shouted his joy. "I'm human! I'm a man!"

After George and Myra calmed down, the rest of us congratulated him on his mortality. Although part of me was angry with them for using the power instead of Blake, I couldn't stay upset for long. I watched the happy *mortal* couple walk off with Mrs. Wippingpoof and Mrs. Hardgrave. If Blake couldn't return to his human form, then George becoming human was the next best thing.

I took a deep breath before facing my demon husband. "You didn't have to do what you did, you know. No one would've blamed you if you'd changed yourself instead of George."

Although his eyes held a sadness in them, a gleam of pleasure for his friend leapt out and he shrugged off my comment. "Let's go get cleaned up."

I agreed, taking his hand to start our march out of the cemetery. We walked without speaking, sensing we both needed this short time to think about all we'd experienced. Nearing the gate, two black vans squealed to a stop next to my Jag. "Ah, hell. What now?" Blake slid the Bracelet into his pocket and planted his feet. I gave him a quick look of support. Within seconds of the vans stopping, several men in black jumpsuits poured out of the vehicles and raced over to us. A young man halted the men's advance and scanned us. I was half-tempted to say we were aliens from the planet Slimeball. "Uh, Jennifer Randall?"

I raised my hand and stepped in front of Blake. No way did I want this group to realize he was a demon. Hopefully, they were what they looked like: newly commissioned Protectors who did backup duty for seasoned Protectors. "I'm Jennifer Randall-Barrington." At some point, people had to start using my new name.

He searched my face, obviously wanting to find something in it to verify my identity. "Uh, Ms. Randall-Barrington? Your Partner sent us a distress message. He said you needed a posse. He said you'd circled the wagons against the biggest baddest outlaw around." The young man raised his eyebrows, obviously hoping for an explanation of Partner's odd choice of words.

"I sure did." I waved a hand to indicate the goop on my body. "And yes, he was biggest, baddest and yuckiest outlaw, er, demon around. But you're a tad late for the showdown."

"Yes, ma'am. I guess we are." He shifted his weight from one side to the other. The boy was definitely a nervous newbie.

"What's your name?"

"Uh, Sherman Shanks."

Sherman? I wondered how often he'd gotten beaten up in school. I hated it when parents named their kids stupid names. "Okay, Shermie, listen closely." Not that I didn't like making their names sound even more stupid. "We risked our lives and saved not only your ass but everyone else's in the world, and we got a tad dirty doing it. Therefore, if you don't mind, we're going home to take a long hot shower."

His expression said he agreed with the necessity of a shower, but wasn't sure what else he should do. "Uh, ma'am?"

"Call me Jenn." I batted my eyelashes for his benefit. "Yeah, Shermie?"

"Uh, the boss said you might have something we should take to headquarters." He gave me the once over, checking for a clue to what that something could be. Obviously Mac hadn't filled him in on the details.

"Don't worry about it. I'll get it there."

He didn't appear too sure of my decision, but didn't want to push it. "Uh, okay. I guess."

The kid sure said "uh" a lot. "It'll be fine. But while I'm taking care of headquarters, here's what you and your buddies are going to do. We left quite a mess in the cemetery. In fact, if you think we look bad, check out the guys who lost the fight. They're falling to pieces—literally. You lucky guys get to clean 'em up." I laughed at their expressions of disgust. Hey, we all have to pay our dues, right? "Get to it, men."

Tilting my head to the side for Blake to follow me, I led my demon-killer hubby toward our vehicle. Blake slipped his arm around my waist and tugged me to him. Even with demon guts all over him, he mesmerized me with his touch.

"So, Jenn, how about it?"

"How about what?" I recognized the playful tone in his voice and faced him. Surely the man didn't want to get it on here? With this yucky stuff on us?

"Don't you think saving your life earns me a reward?"

"A reward?" What was my sneaky hubby up to? "Are you forgetting how long you waited before you used the Bracelet to save me?" *Come to think of it, why did he take so long?* "Were you choosing between me and mortality?"

Blake pulled me to him, trying to persuade me out of my sudden ill mood. "Not at all. The truth is I enjoyed watching you wrestle with his giant ding-dong. That's a sight few husbands ever get to see. Besides, you looked like you gave as good as you got. No sexual innuendo intended. At least until he grabbed you around the neck."

I took a moment to consider his explanation and realized it made sense. At least, it did for my Blake. "Oh. Then I guess you're off the hook."

"Great. Now let's talk about my reward. How about letting me drive?"

"Drive? You mean, *you* drive *my* Jag?" When I started to object, my gaze fell on my precious car and I realized I had a bigger problem than letting him drive. Either one of us getting into the car would mean getting this awful gunk on my seats. *Demon gook on my perfect, smooth leather interior? Uh-uh. No way.*

"Blake, I'm not letting either one of us dirty up my car. Which begs the question—how are we getting home?"

He laughed and whispered his solution in my ear.

Was this a joke? A quick glance said it wasn't. "Really? But what if someone sees us?"

"Then they're damned lucky, aren't they?"

I giggled and started stripping my clothes off.

ॐ

"Try it again, Blake." I couldn't believe it, and I wasn't ready to give up, either.

Blake shook his head and handed me the Bracelet. "It's no use, Jenn. The power is gone. Taking out Demogorgon zapped it of most of its power. Then changing George into a mortal used the last bit of it."

This wasn't fair. Blake was the one who deserved mortality. Nothing against George, of course, but I wanted my hubby to have his dream. I wanted him mortal again. After everything we'd gone through, after losing his brother, he needed this more than anyone else. "You can't give up."

"I can and I am." He stood and moved away from the couch where we'd both spent the better part of the morning trying to coax a miracle from the Bracelet.

After driving home in the nude last night without being seen by anyone—except, of course, Partner, who had had a field day whistling at me until Blake had silenced him by removing his power source again—we'd scampered upstairs and hopped into the shower together.

By silent agreement, we locked up the Bracelet in our safe and didn't say another word about it. I think we both hoped a night of not using it might give it time to regenerate. Like charging up the battery on a cell phone—albeit without the power cord. Besides, it's not like the local electronics store would carry chargers for the Bracelet. After a sensual time in our shower, we made love and fell into a deep sleep, spooning each other until the daylight woke us.

We hadn't mentioned the Bracelet until this morning. And now our hopes were gone.

"I don't want you to give up." I couldn't let it go. Not for his sake and not for mine.

Blake stood looking out the front window, his back stiff and straight. I sensed he was trying to physically fight off disappointment, but I never expected he'd say what he said next. He pivoted to face me. "Tell me, Jenn. Since there's no way I'm going to change into a mortal man, do you want to stay

291

with me? Tell me the truth. Can you handle having a demon for a husband?"

I tossed the Bracelet onto the coffee table and was up and moving toward him before he'd finished his last word. "What are you saying? Do you think I don't love you now? Do you think all I could offer you was conditional love?" I stood toe to toe with him and slapped him on the shoulder. "Damn you, Blake. Why don't you just call me a heartless bitch?"

"Hey! Watch it. I'm still sore from yesterday's party." He went from rubbing the spot where I'd hit him to taking my hands in his. "I need to be sure, is all."

His eyes met mine and I knew he had to have the reassurance. "Blake Barrington, you're my husband. For better, for worse. Mortal or otherwise."

"But wouldn't you rather have a chance at a normal life? One with a mortal man who could give you mortal kids?"

I know he didn't expect me to giggle, but I couldn't help myself. "Are you kidding me? First of all, we've never discussed kids before. The whole idea, whether they're mortal or not, scares the bejeesus out of me. But I think you may be able to persuade me to have one or two rug rats. Later. Way later." I giggled again. "And secondly, I'm a Protector, for God's sake. My life has never been normal."

His body relaxed and he brought me into his arms, leaning his chin on top of my head. I put my ear to his chest and listened to his heartbeat. "I guess this means my membership to the Otherworld has been revoked."

"Yeah, I guess." Closing my eyes, I kept my face against him, enjoying the warmth of his body next to mine. "I guess you'll have to find another organization to join."

"What's the old saying? Oh, yeah. 'I wouldn't join a club who'd want a member like me.' Or something like that."

The idea struck me, nearly knocking me over in its simplicity. Hell—excuse my use of that word—I couldn't believe I hadn't thought of it sooner. I let go of Blake's waist and took his face between my palms. "I've got the greatest idea. This is perfect." His mouth opened to speak, but I never gave him the chance. Instead, I whirled around to scoop up the Bracelet and, tugging him along with me, hurried out of the house.

"Where are we going?" Blake hopped into the passenger's seat and moved Partner to the floorboard.

"Excuse me. Didn't we have the discussion about this floorboard thing, Jenn? Are you going to let him keep throwing me on the floor?"

"Better get used to it, Partner. If I have my way, Blake's going to ride shotgun for me all the time."

Damn, I love my little Jag. Not merely because it's beautiful, but because it's fast and easy to drive. Going into automatic driving mode, I brainstormed, working out the kinks in my plan. We made it to the Society's headquarters in record time.

Once there, I took Benita, the Society's faithful garage attendant-slash-security agent aside, out of hearing distance for Blake. Using my best persuasive powers, I talked Benita into letting Blake enter the building without setting off any alarms. It took some doing, but, eventually, she gave in. Besides, I had a secret weapon. I knew Benita was a sucker for love and, once I'd told her a shortened version of what had happened, she agreed to let me escort Blake to Mac's office. Still, I was willing to bet she'd alert the guards to Blake's presence.

I herded Blake into the elevator and pushed the button for the top floor.

"What's going on, Jenn? Why are we at an insurance company? Are you thinking of taking out life insurance on me, then bumping me off for the payout?"

Blake had taken the whole drag-you-out-of-the-house act with grace, but I could see his patience dimming in the way he clenched his jaw. "Funny man. Blake Barrington, you have entered the home office for the Society. We're going to see my boss."

"Hey, hon, I trust you and everything, but have you forgotten how much Protectors dislike what I am?"

The elevator doors opened onto the foyer and I took his hand in mine. "Don't worry and follow my lead, okay?"

He blew out a nervous breath and stepped out with me. "Whatever you say, Snooky Poot."

Waving to the guards who I knew were watching through the security cameras, I pushed through the big mahogany doors into Mac's office. This time, however, I didn't worry about how dirty my shoes were. Once Mac saw what I had to give him and heard the idea I was about to spring on him, he'd give me a big promotion and one helluva raise.

Either that or he'd can my butt.

Mac swiveled around in his leather chair at the same moment the burly security guards rushed out of the elevator. I held up my hand and shouted for them to halt. They skidded to a stop with weapons pointed at my husband.

"Is this your husband?" Mac stood and came around his desk as if he had all the time in the world. Which, I guess, he did. "Your *demon* husband?"

I heard the click of weapons being readied, but I kept my attention on Mac. "Yes, it is." Nodding toward Mac, I started the introductions. "Mac, this is my husband, Blake Barrington. Blake, this is my wonderful and brilliant boss, Wilson MacNamara."

Blake put out his hand in greeting but only received a glare from Mac. "Cut the kissing up, Randall, and tell me why you breached security protocols to bring a demon inside this building. Have you lost your mind?" Nonetheless, he waved off the guards and let them shuffle back to their hidden posts.

"I've brought you a little present." Grinning more than I should have, I reached into my pocket and pulled out the Bracelet. The expression of delight on Mac's face was, as the commercial says, "priceless".

"It took you long enough. You were supposed to bring it in last night."

"Yeah, well, I figured it'd be safe enough at my house." I grinned at the guy. "Especially since you posted men outside my house all night."

Mac acknowledged the truth with a raised eyebrow, then wiped his hand on his pant leg before taking the Bracelet from me. "So this is the Bracelet of Invincibility, huh?" He studied it, reading the inscription inside and holding it up to the light. "Good job, Jennifer."

Good? Is he kidding me? All I get is a "good job"? "Uh, gee, thanks. But you should know. Blake used the Bracelet to vanquish Demogorgon." I really liked to use words like *vanquish.* It made me feel like Buffy the Vampire Slayer. "I suppose the backup crew told you about the cemetery?"

"Of course."

"Good. But you need to know. The Bracelet ran out of power and it doesn't seem to want to recharge." I expected him to blow his top.

Instead, he simply nodded and added, "We'll see what R&D can come up with."

Mac reached over to punch a button on the control panel sitting on top of his desk. Immediately, the guards returned. "Take at least twenty Protectors and get this to the main office. Do not lose it."

The guards exited with the Bracelet, leaving Blake, Mac and me alone again. "Blake helped me find the Bracelet."

"Oh, I see. And you thought you'd bring him into headquarters as a reward?" Mac snarled his words and leaned against his deck. "Or did you bring him in as a treat for me? I haven't eliminated a demon in a long time. Too much desk work, you know."

I took a deep breath, and refrained from kicking my boss in the shin. "No. Not quite. I brought Blake with me because I want you to make him a Protector." Glancing between Blake and Mac, I couldn't decide which one looked more stunned.

Blake continued to gape at me. "Me? A Protector? Holy shit, Jenn, talk about crazy ideas." He couldn't seem to keep his mouth closed.

"Make a demon a Protector?" Mac had the same problem with his mouth.

I couldn't help but feel a flash of a thrill since I'd managed to throw both of them off their game. "Yes, a Protector."

"No way. How in the world—"

"Come on, Jenn. Me? A Protector?"

"Stop repeating yourself, Blake. And yes, you can, Mac. After all, we have aliens working for us and quite a few other supernatural types, too. Why not a demon?"

Mac found his composure again by seeking comfort behind his desk. "Oh, I don't know. Maybe because we kill demons. We don't enlist them."

Blake appeared flummoxed by my suggestion. I reached up and gave him a peck on the cheek before placing both hands on Mac's desk. I leaned toward Mac and played my ace card. "Think about it, boss. Some demons, like Blake, would like nothing better than to forgo the evil Otherworld and return to living a decent life. Why not let them join in the fight against the Otherworld? Think of the knowledge, the information people like Blake can give us."

Mac glanced at my silent husband and back to me. "That's why we use some of them as informants. *Not* as agents."

"Let Blake be the guinea pig. He's proven himself already by taking out the High Demon Lord, Demogorgon. Give him a chance."

Blake finally found his voice again and came over to my way of thinking. "You can trust me. Give me a chance. Let me prove my worth."

Mac studied us, his gaze darting between us as if trying to decide whether to keep talking or throw us out. My heart jumped when I realized he was giving my proposal serious consideration. After several agonizing minutes, he reached for his phone.

"Yeah, this is MacNamara." He paused, as if reconsidering one last time. "I'm sending a new recruit down to you for processing. A very special new recruit."

He replaced the receiver and shook his head. "I ought to have my head examined. Or yours."

I squealed and ran around the desk to hug my boss. "You won't regret this, Mac."

He shrugged me off, pushing me away. "I'd better not, Randall. I'd better not."

Use Photo Shop to Remove Tattoos

"Chrissy, is it really you? Shit, girl, I haven't heard from you in such a long time. What've you been up to?"

The cheerful voice on the other end of the phone didn't sound like my college friend, Christina Taylor. Of course, I'm sure we'd both changed since the last time we'd connected over five years earlier. Now, out of the blue, she'd called me.

"You won't believe it, Jenn. I'm getting married."

Not having gone through the girly-girl stage where you utter a high-pitched scream of joy, I forced a bright-sounding tone into my voice and played my part. After all, I *was* truly happy for her. "Really? Oh, Chrissy, I'm very happy for you. Tell me all about him. What's his name? What's he like? Spill, girlfriend." Okay, sometimes I could get a little girly-girly without too much effort.

"He's wonderful, Jenn. I met him at a friend's birthday party. The party was at my friend's house on the lake and, since it was a full moon and the light was pretty on the water, I went outside to get some fresh air. All of a sudden, this thing jumped out at me from the bushes. I started to scream when, suddenly, this man leaps in between me and this creature."

Alarm zipped through me even though I knew she had to be all right since she was on the phone. Still, it didn't hurt to ask. "Are you okay? Were you injured?"

"No. I mean, I'm fine. But this man, my hero, caught this ugly animal by the throat and killed it. I didn't watch because I turned my head, but when I turned around, the animal was dead. He tossed it in the lake."

I relaxed. A little. "Chrissy, is there something else you're not telling me?" I could hear it in her tone and remembered from past experiences she always wanted a bit of coaxing.

"No. Well, okay, something else did happen. When I turned around, I thought I saw my hero change."

"Change? Change how?" Why did I have this tingle of dread inching up my back?

"Oh, I'm being silly. I must've hallucinated out of shock or something."

"Chrissy, tell me what you saw." If she didn't tell me soon, I'd find a way to reach through the phone and slap her upside her head.

"Well, I thought—and only for a second, mind you—the man looked like a...a..."

"A what?" I struggled to keep my voice under control.

"A dragon. Now isn't that the dumbest thing you've ever heard?"

My knees went weak and I reached out for the corner of the sofa to hold me up. "A dragon? Are you sure?"

"No, I'm not. I shouldn't have any said anything about this. I don't even know why I did. Let's talk about the fun things. Did I tell you he's wealthy? Not that that's why I love him or anything."

I had to take several seconds to regroup. Could the man she'd gotten involved with be a dragon?

"Jenn, are you there? Listen, I didn't realize the time when I called you, but I've got to run. I'll send you a photo and you can see for yourself what a hottie I've landed."

"Yes, do. Send me a pic on my phone."

"Will do. Bye-bye."

I held the phone to my ear long after she'd disconnected the call. "I have to sit down." Flopping on the couch, I kept my phone in my hand and waited for the photo.

Dragons are rare, but they're one of the easiest Otherworlders to identify. Most dragons have a birthmark that sets them apart from mortals. Younger dragons may have no discernible physical trait, but the longer they live, the more noticeable this physical trait becomes. At the base of the throat is a small marking much like a figure eight turned on its side.

At last the picture arrived and I flipped open my phone to

check it out.

"Oh, shit."

Chrissy stood next to a handsome man with strong cheekbones, a square jaw line, and piercing green eyes. At the base of his throat was the distinctive dragon marking.

About the Author

Beverly Rae's witty, sexy, action-packed romances leave readers experiencing a wide range of emotions. As a multi-published author, Beverly is always working on her next book, taking the "usual" and twisting it into the "unusual".

To learn more about Beverly, please visit www.beverlyrae.com. Send her an email at info@beverlyrae.com or join her Yahoo! Group to join in the fun with other readers as well as Beverly:

http://groups.yahoo.com/group/Beverly_Rae_Fantasies.

True love is better than infatuation.

To Fat and Back
© *2008 Beverly Rae*

Carrie Flannagan dreams of Michael the Magnificent, the office hunk. He can have his pick of women, and his pick isn't Carrie, the office chubby. He's only got eyes for her best friend, Shiloh of the slender, smokin' hot body.

When Carrie accidentally-on-purpose breaks Michael's arm, a self-professed sorceress with a secret agenda of her own gives him a pill to magically heal the bones. That little pill also has an accidental-on-purpose side effect—one that makes him balloon to over three hundred pounds. To Carrie's surprise and delight, he turns to her for emotional comfort. But those new layers of fat on his body reveal a side of him that wasn't part of her fantasy.

Billy Whitman will put up with almost anything to be near to Carrie, even if she sees him only as a blend-into-the-background, dependable friend. Even if it means putting up with her fantasies about Michael, and being the clean-up man as Michael's life falls apart.

For now, he's willing to bide his time, hoping she will someday see the light—the light of love in his eyes.

Warning: Side effects of this title include, but are not limited to, the following: Snorting milk through your nose, laughing until your ribs hurt, drooling over handsome heroes, fanning uncontrollably during hot scenes and subsequent severe cravings for more of Beverly Rae's books. Do not read while driving or operating heavy machinery. May be consumed visually with friends (especially that special friend) or alone.

Available now in ebook from Samhain Publishing.
Also available in the print anthology Magical Mayhem from Samhain Publishing.

Naked. Wet. Pointing a gun at your dream guy.
What a way to start the day…

Romancing the Stones
© *2008 Catherine Berlin*

Archaeologist Charlotte "Charlie" Blair arrives home from a dig in Peru to find a dead body in her house—and herself suspected of murder. Sorting out the truth, that a serial killer has been using her place to stash his kills, proves easier than shaking off the detective who's determined to protect her.

Detective Rob Vaiden's first sight of Charlie is naked, wet, and pointing a Glock at his chest. Oh yeah, this is going to be a hell of a case. Something about the bombshell has attracted the attention of Orion, a killer Vaiden's been pursuing since his days as a rookie cop. To catch Orion, he needs to be near Charlie. Trouble is, while she's easy on the eyes, the maddeningly independent woman is determined she doesn't need his help.

Vaiden gets on Charlie's last nerve, but she's got her own problems. The golden rod of Manco Copac, the greatest find in her career, has disappeared. In place of the gold phallus she finds a bag of mythical Ica stones. Stones for which Orion is willing to kill.

Charlie…the stones…Orion. What connects this deadly triangle? Vaiden and Charlie race to figure it out—before Orion chooses his next target.

Warning: This novel depicts a kickass heroine who enjoys steamy sex with a hunky detective, when not otherwise engaged in being chased, kidnapped, and mugged for a solid gold penis.

Available now in ebook and print from Samhain Publishing.

hot stuff

Discover Samhain!
THE HOTTEST NEW PUBLISHER ON THE PLANET

Romance, fantasy, mystery, thriller, mainstream and
more—Samhain has more selection, hotter authors, and
everything's available in both ebook and print.

Pick your favorite, sit back, and enjoy the ride!
Hot stuff indeed.

GREAT
cheap
fun

Discover eBooks!

THE FASTEST WAY TO GET THE HOTTEST NAMES

Get your favorite authors on your favorite reader, long before they're out in print! Ebooks from Samhain go wherever you go, and work with whatever you carry—Palm, PDF, Mobi, and more.

samhain
publishing
Ltd

LaVergne, TN USA
25 October 2009
161971LV00011B/1/P